M000237384

By the same author

NEITHER THE SEA NOR THE SAND

Dragon Under the Hill

by
Gordon Honeycombe

SIMON AND SCHUSTER · NEW YORK

Published by Simon and Schuster
Rockefeller Center, 630 Fifth Avenue
New York, New York 10020
First U.S. printing
SBN 671-21553-1
Library of Congress Catalog Card Number: 73-5253
Designed by Charles Mazarakes
Manufactured in the United States of America

1   2   3   4   5   6   7   8   9   10

To
A.D.
Doina
Marion
and
Sid

Contents

*Translation of a fragment of a Northern Chronicle
relating to events in the years 787–794 A.D.*

A king shall have a kingdom. Cities are to be seen from far-off times, the cunning work of giants which are on this earth: a skillful shaping of wall stones.
Wind is the swiftest thing under heaven.
Thunder is at times the loudest. The might of Christ is great. Fate is strongest . . .
The clouds go by. Good companions shall cheer the young prince in battle and the giving of rings. Courage shall be in the hero. The sword against the helmet shall make war. The hawk upon the glove shall remain a wild thing. The wolf in the forest shall be wretched, a recluse. The boar in the wood shall be strong in the might of his tusks. The good man in his country shall do glorious deeds. The spear in the hand shall be a weapon wrought with gold. The jewel on the ring shall sit high and broad. The tide with its waves shall stir up the ocean. The mast, the sail-yard, shall stand in the boat. The sword on the breast shall be lordly, of iron. The dragon under the hill shall be ancient, proud of his treasures . . .

Translation of part of an eleventh-century manuscript of Anglo-Saxon gnomic verses now in the British Museum.

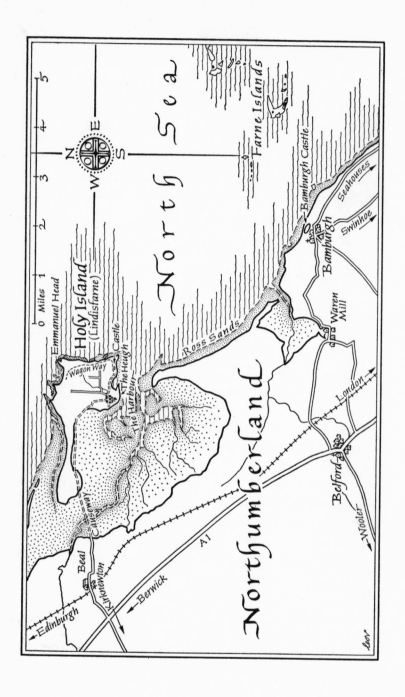

Wednesday

He dreamed. He lay like a rib of earth buried under centuries of waste and dissolution. Black night hung over him and filled every cranny of the spaces within him, and the silence seemed as final as death. But sometimes it was broken. Sometimes it was as if he had slept and now lay still with his eyes closed, listening to the roaring of the sea as it broke and boiled beyond him. He seemed to hear the sound of rain on grass and there were voices, of men and birds and beasts. But thunder was the loudest of all. At times he seemed to feel the hollow tread of animals, and the tiny tremors of the ground sent shivers through his bones, and the minute movements of insects and the feet of birds made echoes in his skull. He could not see. All he saw were pictures of the mind, images of burning, of a boat, and of his son. There was a fortress, and many men, and still his soul shuddered with despair when the hateful face of the one who killed him hung before him in the night. The sword that slew him entered him in ecstasy once more. His mind blazed with fear and shock as the iron edge tore through his throat. Robbed of its voice and soon its life, his furious being lodged in his eyes, which took in for a timeless moment the blood, his own, that cried for blood, the grinning boar on the killer's helm, the killer's hand all golden-haired, and the grinning, golden, triumphant face of the man who had gained the victory. His spirit cried out in despair again. A king must live. He should not die before he had done great deeds of glory, worthy of lasting praise and remembrance among men. But dead, he must be avenged. So he waited, locked in darkness, until the shameful agony of his soul might be purged, that he might join the feasting in Valhalla. A thousand years and more he waited. His weapons lay unused, untouched, about him. Nothing disturbed the eternal nightmare of his tomb. The only thing that stirred there was the snake upon his lap, the guardian of his treasures and the mark of his desire. So he dreamed, and waited. He dreamed of his death, and waited for the hour of his revenge.

Thursday

1

Ed awoke.

Where was he?

He peered at a ceiling and down a white wall and saw roses, red ones, winding upward and exactly similar rows of roses on either side. He was in a bed in Rose Cottage. It was really called Rose Cottage, and there were roses on the wallpaper in the bedroom.

Ed grinned to himself, and pummeled his cold and itchy nose and scratched his head. He became aware as he stretched himself of the animal warmth under the bedclothes of his naked body and the presence of his wife beside him. Turning his head, he squinted at the mass of her spreading hair on the pillow.

She had had a bath the night before—she had a bath every night—and a whiff of scented soap or shampoo reached out to him. Though the curtains were drawn, they were thin and let in the light, and some fine long wisps of her hair were silver-gilt in the gloom.

He looked at the window and saw that there were also roses on the curtains, and they were black against the dawn.

Was it dawn or midday?

He listened. There was silence. It must be early. Or maybe all the islanders slept late.

The islanders. . . . The Holy Islanders. . . . The islanders of Lindisfarne. This was the morning of their first day on Lindisfarne.

Wanting to communicate his pleasure at the thought, Ed moved himself so that he lay against the curled-up form beside him. He put his left arm over her middle and wondered again why she needed to wear a nightdress. The perfume of her body and hair enveloped him. She seemed to burn, and he buried his face in her tangled hair, and his hand slid over and down the silky heat of her stomach.

She muttered something in Norwegian and wriggled away, drawing the bedclothes after her, and flopped onto her front on the edge of the bed. His hand was left on her bottom. He made a face, gave her a slap and heaved about until he lay on his back beside her, with as much of the blankets over him as he could rescue. The quilt slid onto the floor.

Ed began to feel cold. He looked beyond his feet at the black bouquets of roses on the curtains.

Rose Cottage, he said to himself. Roses, roses everywhere, and not a corpse in sight.

He dragged his wristwatch into view and saw it was half-past seven. He also saw the date.

It's Thursday! he thought with excitement. Thursday morning on Lindisfarne. . . . Now it begins!

Beyond his head, in the other bedroom, the small boy lay at right angles to his father. Also on his back, with his fists holding the blankets about his neck, he stared at the ceiling without seeing it, trying to remember his dream.

The effort, and the ache in his forehead, made him frown. But the dream had gone—only the acid taste of fear remained. It made him think that as he felt so hot and head-achey he might be dying.

He knew he had not been well the day before. He hated traveling long distances by car, and had not wanted to go away from home. He had had a sore throat and a cough, and was sure at the time that he had a fever, though this was not supported by the thermometer—which had either, he believed, been misread or was out of order.

He stared at the ceiling and imagined his mother's grief when she found him all stiff and white in his bed—dead— when she came to wake him for breakfast.

He wondered what that breakfast would be like . . . if it would be eggs and cornflakes as in London—and orange juice, and toast and honey—or buttered fingers of bread to dip in the yolk of his egg.

Perhaps they'd had breakfast already and not told him!

He levered himself onto an elbow to look at his watch on the bedside table. It said—after he had frowned and thought about it—quarter past three.

Was it afternoon? What had he missed? Had they left him? Or had the watch stopped?

He picked it up, examined it, shook it, and wound it up. It started to go, but he didn't know where to put the hands. His father had given the watch to him as a birthday present that year, when he became seven. It was not nearly as big as his father's, and it had a habit of stopping when he forgot to wind it up. But it was *his* watch.

What time was it? He strapped the watch on his right wrist and sat up to listen.

There was no sound in the cottage. Outside somewhere a bird was chirruping.

He pushed the bedclothes back with his hands and feet and hopped onto the carpet. It was cold and brown. The furniture was big and dark. There were flowers on the walls. The windowsill was so low down that when he lifted a flap of the curtain, the garden seemed to run uphill away from him to a wall.

He saw with amazement that the sky was blue and that the left-hand side of some small trees and the building opposite were lit by the sun, which threw such shadows that it must be early, and not afternoon. The garden, he saw, was overgrown and enclosed by a wall that was high to his left and overtopped across some sheds by the roof of a large gray house. Opposite him, beyond the wall, was a long building lined with sunlight that rose in two steps to a thin tower with a pointed hat on it. On each step-end was a cross. It was a church.

He realized with a shiver that the rounded tops of stones he could see beyond the wall belonged to a graveyard. He had been sleeping with the dead!

Lindisfarne. . . . He knew this was Lindisfarne.

His eye caught a large white face in the garden. It was his own, reflected in the glass. To his surprise he saw that it was smiling.

Ed reawoke with a feeling of alarm. But everything was as it had been before he had dozed off. The light through the curtains was also the same. He could only have gone to sleep again for a few minutes. Yet something had aroused him. He noticed the tenseness of his muscles and the fact that he was breathing through his mouth in order to hear better.

Relax, you fool, he told himself, and did so, shifting slightly so that he faced the friendly form beside him.

That was different of course—she was sleeping on the right-hand side of the bed, and he was nearest the wall. Their reason for adopting these positions last night had been that the lamp and the bedside table on which he had to unload his money, wallet, pipe, matches and handkerchief were on his side, and that she wanted to be near the door in case she had to get up without disturbing him and see to the boy.

Ed was looking over her at the door, when he saw the doorknob move. He raised himself from the pillows as the door slowly opened. His gaze flicked down. In the gap stood Erik.

Their eyes met. The small boy frowned, biting his lower lip. His pajama trousers were hanging loose and slopped over his feet.

Ed raised his eyebrows and narrowed his eyes.

"What do you want?" he whispered.

With a jerk of his head Erik looked at his mother. Then as carefully as he had opened the door, he closed it after him.

Ed scratched his head and ran his fingers through his hair.

It was usual for Erik to look in on them when he got up in the morning. But he never knocked, and Ed disapproved of this. "Why should he knock?" asked Runa—"Is he a stranger?" Ed thought it might serve as a warning. "We might be blithely bending the springs," he said. "Oh, Ed!" said Runa, and laughed.

He looked down at her now with the pride and warmth of possession—at her small straight nose, her wide white forehead, the arching wing of an eyebrow darker than her hair, as was the delicate concave of her lashes. It was strange that these should be so dark when her hair that now flowed over her neck and onto the sheet should be so fair. He smiled. She was entirely his. Asleep, and without any makeup, she had no age. She was beautiful to him.

It was cold—his shoulders and bare back told him so.

A pause for decision, and a second later he slid quietly out of the bed and lit the gas fire with the matches on the table.

"Who was that?"

The voice from the bed was slow and dopey.

With his eyes on the blue-white pillars of flame in their cells, he squatted on one knee by the fire, warming the front of his body and his hands.

"Erik," he said.

She sighed. She struggled into a sitting position, and after a yawn began with her fingers to smooth the puffiness out of her eyes and then to arrange her hair behind her ears and off her neck. After blinking several times extravagantly, she beamed at Ed, who had been watching her over his shoulder.

"Hallo," she said. "Good morning, *min helt.*"

"*God morgen, kjerring,*" he said. "*Hvordan har du det?*"

He grinned at her and stood up with his back to the fire, and giving a mighty yawn, stretched his arms above his head and touched the ceiling. She watched his muscles mold and melt as they tightened and relaxed.

"It's not so cold," he said, and went to the window.

He pulled the curtains back, parted the lace curtains behind them and said, "Look, a blue sky!"

He stood there gazing out into the narrow street. Opposite was a high wall. Their cottage was one of two, he remembered—both were single-storied with slate roofs and television aerials. To the right he could just see a slice of the village square.

"My God—I forgot. There are also actually roses around the front door. Have you noticed the wallpaper and the curtains?"

What she noticed was the level of the windowsill—below his knees.

"Ed!" she squeaked. "Ed! Come from the window! People will *see* you."

"Happy people," he said. "I've got a handful and they'll get an eyeful. Ho-ho!"

"Virkelig!" she said and scrambled out of the bed.

"Never before in the history of this island," he declared, "was so much seen by so few."

"No, really," he protested as she fought with him for possession of the lace curtains, which opened and closed and lurched to left and right. "There's no one there. *Virkelig!* There's no one.

"Now then!" he said, gripping her wrists. "No grabbing below the belt."

He drew her arms slowly behind him despite her struggles. The curtains were still half open. He forced himself within her embrace until her nose made contact with his reddened neck and his breath divided her hair. They stood panting against each other. Suddenly he let her go and wrapped her in his arms.

"I win," he murmured. "I claim first prize."

He raised her head, and her eyes were closed. He kissed her gently.

"You win also," he said, being magnanimous. "You're second."

He turned to the window, meaning to close the curtains properly.

Outside in the street, not six feet away, a dark-faced man in a storm cape stood leering in at them, with one eye shut in a wink.

"Oh, my God," said Ed, and pulled the curtains together.

But in the shocking instant before he did so Runa saw that the strange dark man was not winking. He had only one eye.

The vision of the one-eyed man was still with her when, after putting on her dressing gown, she went in to see what Erik was doing. Her confusion found a direction in the vexatious sight of all the bits and pieces from his black tin box laid out on the carpet. Lumps of rock, stone and wood, together with marbles, coins, tin soldiers and the skull of a frog were spread about for the inspection of his golliwog, which was sitting on top of his special tablecloth on a chair. Furthermore the room was chilly, and Erik had nothing on but his pajamas. He lay sprawled on the carpet—which might not be clean—and was humming to himself.

She rebuked him as she lit the gas fire with matches she had in her dressing-gown pocket. Then she burrowed about in the chest of drawers for clean underwear and his track suit. Though she spoke to him in Norwegian, which she usually did when they were alone, he would never reply in Norwegian—not since going to Junior school, where none of his comrades knew the language. He had learnt it from her and on holidays at her parents' home in Tønsberg, so he understood what she was saying. But he now associated it with his baby years and would not use it himself.

She told him to get into his track suit and put *everything* back in the box, and brush his teeth before breakfast, which would be very soon.

In the doorway she turned to insure that the curtains were closed and remembered she had forgotten to inquire about his health. He stood with his golliwog clasped in front of him looking forlorn. With a swirl of her dressing gown she crossed to him and the blue and white toweling billowed out as she knelt.

"Hvordan står det til, lille gut?" she said.

"All right," he said, making faces.

He was so like her, everyone said—except that his eyes were bigger and bluer, his forehead wider, his hair more silver, his ears more round, his skin more soft than hers.

"No cough?" she said.

He screwed up his eyes, and staged a comic cough behind his hand.

"No cough," he said.

They smiled at each other. She stroked his hair, and gave him a quick kiss so as not to embarrass him, saying, "Good. This is holiday now. This morning we may find some more stones and there will be many things to explore."

With a reminder about his track suit, she went.

Erik pondered. There was no doubt about it—though his head still ached a bit, he felt better. But why had she looked at the window like that? He went there and turned the curtain aside.

The scene was the same, except it now included the top half of a man in the graveyard. He was moving from right to left. Without stopping, he looked at the house and gave a long wink, then vanished among the trees and higher tombstones.

Erik felt pleased. A sign had been given, a greeting made. The hint of secrecy and adventures made him want to squeal with excitement. He thumped and winked at his golliwog several times, and its mouth grinned broadly back at him. With a fierce "Din-din!" he gave it a last big thump and a huge wink and tiptoed back to his box.

2

"Isn't it warm?" said Runa as Ed locked the cottage door.

"Warm for October," he replied.

"Erik," she said. "If you get too hot, just take off your top —and don't lose it."

He was wearing his bright blue track suit with rubbers on his feet as he was careless about walking around puddles, preferring to splash a way through them.

"Will it rain, do you think?" she asked. "I mean—how far are we going?"

"Not far," Ed replied. "Not far from the village."

He was studying a map in the guidebook he had just bought in the general store while she had been buying provisions. They were now setting out to explore their surroundings.

"Let's go this way," he said. "We've been to the square, and down here there's St. Cuthbert's Isle."

"So," she said. "Come, Erik."

They set off together. But when they turned the corner of their little street, with Erik in front, he ran through a side gate into the churchyard, quite ignoring the track that went down to the beach. His mother followed. She called his name. His father continued doggedly down the track.

Erik's idea had been to scamper through the graveyard and hide. But as soon as he was among the tombstones, the thought of dead people under his feet made him go more slowly—especially as there was no path and no visible grave-mounds, just large assorted slabs of stone sticking up out of the grass. He made sure that his mother was near him. He saw she was reading the names of the dead. He pretended to read them as well, but was really looking for bones, or an open grave, and half expecting a shrouded thing to be crouched behind a stone.

He remembered the winking man. This cheered him, and he looked hopefully about. Perhaps the man lived here—in a hole in the ground, or under the church, or sat in the trees before lunch. He was sure the man lived *somewhere* near here. It couldn't be the vicar—the clothes and the hat were wrong. Perhaps he was a pirate and was hiding his gold in the graveyard!

"Erik!" His mother was calling. But she couldn't see him as a tombstone hid him from her.

He crouched beside it, with his hands up to his face, making himself as small as possible. His muscles twitched in anticipation of being caught.

"Erik! Where are you?" She paused. He shuddered.

"You're hiding," she sang.

He clenched his teeth. It was horrible not knowing where she was and when she would catch him. There was moss, he noticed, on the stone and it smelled rather strange. When she found him he would run.

On a wall nearby he saw a robin.

"Got you!"

He shrieked and ran.

Hiding was out. But he had to avoid being caught. She was following, chasing after him as he dodged among the gravestones.

"Mr. Stevenson!" she called. "Come back to your grave. I'm going to put you back in your grave, Mr. Stevenson."

He squealed with alarm. She was so much bigger. It was unfair—he was bound to be caught.

"Who's Mr. Stevenson?"

It was his father. The chase was over.

"Erik, of course. He was hiding behind the stone of a Mr. Stevenson."

"Oh. I don't know what the holy Holy Islanders will think. Hide and seek among their ancestors!"

"Did you find St. Cuthbert?"

"I found his island. It's just a low heap of rocks and grass with a commemorative cross on it—about fifty yards offshore. You can get to it when the tide's out. It's going out now.

The guidebook says St. Cuthbert used a little chapel there as a retreat."

The robin Erik was looking at flew over a wall. It was a low wall, and he was able to see into the garden beyond without much effort. With delight he saw there were now two robins—one on a bush.

"Look, look," he cried. "Mummy—come here. Two robins in the garden. Ssh."

His parents approached him.

"So there are," said his mother. "Ed. Isn't that *our* house?"

"Yes, it is. The robins are in our garden, Erik. That's your window. You'll be able to feed them in the morning."

The robins flew away.

"It's odd to see two together."

"Come along, Erik."

He went with them, wondering whether robins ate worms, or would prefer bacon fat, like tits—or buns, like bears and seagulls.

His parents were now reading the gravestones near the church. An old woman passed by him.

Erik moved on through a little avenue of oak and syca-more trees and found himself before some ruins, red and awful.

They were four stories high and had a square tower at one end. But there was no roof, and the doorways had no doors. No one would ever walk through them, for they led out of and onto the sky. Within were even higher walls and an arch that seemed to be highest of all—like a rainbow. The ruins were not those of a castle, though they might have been. He knew this must be the Priory. That meant a Church.

The gateway above him had two rows of teeth. This meant, he remembered, that it belonged to Norman. Inside, there was grass on the floor. A pillar was marked with zig-zags, like lightning, and the rainbow arch—it also had teeth—hung ready to fall and bite him.

This was the place, his father had said, where saints had lived, saying their prayers and singing hymns. It had been very famous. Then one day the Vikings came. They killed the monks, and stole their gold, and burned the House of God. Then they went away. But after that many more came back, and killed and plundered—and much worse—and tried to conquer the world. They also discovered America, his father had said, and they came from Norway, like his mother—and him.

This was where the winking man had vanished. He could be, must be, one of them—a Viking! He must never have left with the others, and have been here all that time!

"Where's Erik?" she said.

They looked about. Erik was nowhere in sight.

"Not again," Ed groaned, vexed at Runa's distraction. He had been telling her about the first Bishop of Lindisfarne, St. Aidan, who in 635 A.D. had come to the island from Iona to carry on the conversion of the Angles.

She walked away. "Erik!" she called.

"Oh, leave him be. He's probably in the church, robbing the poor box. He'll come back when he wants to be fed. And if he's hurt, he'll yell. He's not a baby."

"He's only seven, and needs to look after."

"He's seven and a half, and needs to *be looked after.*"

"Don't correct me!"

He was silent. They had had that kind of argument be-fore—she didn't like being put right even when she was wrong, and even after nine years in England didn't like to be reminded the language wasn't natural to her.

"You never care what happens to him," she said.

Another argument could develop out of that—but he kept silent again. He was preparing himself to say something neutral and disarming when she said, "There he is," and smiled.

Through the priory's west doorway Ed saw the silver head and blue track suit shape of his son in the transept crossing, below the rainbow arch. He was looking the other way, toward the altar, and his arms were raised above his head.

"He shouldn't be in there—we haven't paid." Ed's nostrils flared.

"Then let us pay," she said indifferently. "And look at the priory now."

"No. I said we'd do that this afternoon."

"You said 'later.'"

"Erik," commanded his father at the doorway. "Come back here."

"Erik," said Runa. "Come along with us. We are going to the church now."

He took no notice. Slowly, with his face to the sky, and his arms outstretched, he began to revolve.

"Erik," said his father. The boy ignored him.

"*Erik!*"

"Ed—there are people here," said Runa. "Let him alone."

"Stay here!" he ordered and crossed the threshold and strode over the velvet grass toward the revolving boy.

Erik was making the rainbow arch go around, to keep it from falling on his head.

He gasped as a pair of golden hands gripped his wrists.

The face of his enemy loomed over him.

"I told you!" it said. "Now do as you're told!"

A rage of frustration filled Erik. "No!" he cried.

He knew he was too small and weak, but he resisted as best he could. He pulled away, and jerked and wriggled, shouting "No! No! No!" In desperation he lashed out with his feet.

A colossal blow landed on Erik's ear.

Ed slapped his son on the side of the head. A scream went up, and he began to haul his howling offspring back along the nave.

Runa waited for their return with tears in her eyes. She could never take sides when her menfolk were fighting—she could not interfere. All she could do was comfort the vanquished and chide the victor—though they were always the same.

"Oh, Ed," she lamented, and knelt to receive the victim.

"I'm sorry," he said, and walked away, torn by the hateful noise of the sobbing child.

"I'll . . . get . . . you," Erik cried between his sobs.

"I'll . . . get . . . him," he assured his mother. "Some day."

In silence they returned to the gate through which Erik had bolted earlier. Runa held his hand as they walked down the track until he found a stick to play with. But he stayed near her, and as she had to match her pace with his, Ed led the way in advance of them. Occasionally he flung some comment back to her, which she acknowledged and passed on to Erik, who never spoke at all. In the long pauses each was able in his or her own fashion to view the sea and the island.

To the south of the church and the priory ruins they climbed up the western end of the Heugh, a miniature headland of some length edging that part of the island. Its grassy top sloped gradually down to the east.

As they ambled along it, they had more an eye for the church and the priory below them on their left than for the objects on the Heugh. These seemed to have little interest, and they slowly passed them by—a small square of ruined walls by the squat tower of the coastguard lookout, a lofty war memorial shaped like a cross, and a triangular wooden beacon on a pole. The view to their right, across the main channel, was even more eye-catching, though made a monochrome by the haze.

Two needlelike beacons marked the mainland half a mile away across the water, and a vista of the sands of Ross and the sea, punctuated by breakers, stretched south for miles, merging into the sands below Bamburgh Castle, which itself was only a far but magical outline upon the diminishing coastline.

Immediately below the Heugh on the seaward side, a set of boat houses hugged the cliff, and from them a path wound up to split the Heugh into two, before winding down to the harbor bay, where rowboats were at anchor or tethered to a jetty.

Four fishing boats nosing the ebbing tide were moored out in the main channel, which Ed discovered from the guidebook was called the Harbor. The small bay which looked like a harbor was called the Ouse.

They approached it by the path that cut across the Heugh.

No one else was about. Seagulls in shrieks and flurries were still picking at the morning's refuse from the jetty and the beach, but the fishermen had gone home.

Ed pointed out several hand-drawn two-wheeled barrows that, he said, were used to carry the morning's catch from the jetty to some black huts below the declining Heugh. There, among the litter of empty fish boxes, lobster traps, ropes and nets, they came across a stack of shallow crates, haphazardly piled on top of each other and packed with dehydrating crabs.

"They're still alive!" said Runa, hearing movement in the boxes.

Erik squawked as a projecting claw feebly waved at him.

"Careful," warned Ed. "Crabs have been known to jump six feet."

"Ho-ho," she said.

The three of them peered warily into the exposed parts of the boxes, out of which escaping claws and hairy white legs protruded.

Ed lifted up one of the top crates so that they could see the crabs beneath.

Russet shells and spiky limbs inside seemed inextricably crushed together. Very few crabs were stirring. It was the popping, gasping, rustling sound of their dying as they dried out that made them appear to be moving. Gingerly, Ed pulled out the largest crab by its rear for Runa's repelled inspection, and a smaller crab locked in its stiffened claws came with it.

"The one underneath is a female," remarked Ed. "You can tell by the broader flap below its body." He showed her. "Their position is known as the pincer movement—Kama Sutra, Number 10."

The legs of the larger crab stretched exhaustedly.

"Poor fellow," Ed sympathized. "Literally caught in the act."

He returned the doomed pair to their box.

The three of them drifted on past the black hulks of over-turned keelboats that cut in half now served as fishermen's sheds and lay along the beach like stranded whales. They came to a road that led about the Ouse.

To their right the outgoing tide had exposed a long ridge of sand for the inspection of seabirds. Far beyond, Bamburgh Castle was a misty cutout on the mainland. Near at hand, rotting posts, the remnants of a pier, stuck out of the water. Over all, the sun was a silver disk in the haze.

Before them now the rock of Beblowe thrust clumsily out

of the turf. A fort had once been raised on it and much later had been rebuilt out of ruin as Lindisfarne Castle.

"It's not open to visitors in October."

Ed was summarizing information in the guidebook.

"We can still go and look outside it. Yes?" asked Runa.

"Why not?"

She took off Erik's track suit top as he was looking rather flushed, and freed of her hands he padded after his father up the slope, while Runa dallied behind them with her eyes on the shimmering waters.

Ed walked on until he reached a grassy plateau, where outhouses of sectioned keelboats backed into the wind from the north. The castle wall now reared up sheer to his left and the track—now turned into a cobbled outer ramp—climbed up the southern face of the rock to a door high over the sea.

The plateau, though well below the chimneys of the castle, commanded a view of much of the island. A mile to the north the coast was shaded by indistinct masses of sand hills that wove a way westward for some miles to form a peninsula of nothing else off the northwest corner.

"What's that?"

Ed turned to see that Erik had materialized near him and was standing pointing regally to the north.

"There," said Erik, steadfastly not looking at his father.

Ed saw on the outermost northeast edge of the island what seemed to be a pyramid. It was large enough to be evident over a mile and more, and its white triangular shape engraved an alien figure on the coast.

"It must be a beacon," he said. "A sign for sailors—a landmark."

He was pleased that he and his son were talking again.

Then Erik turned to look at him, and his left eye was shut in a ghastly frozen parody of a wink.

"A sign," said Erik. "Like this?"

3

Professor MacDougall drove over to Holy Island from Bamburgh after lunch. At low water he traveled along the mile of causeway joining the mainland to the island. When he swung right on the other shore to the village, the tide had already taken its imperceptible breath between the ebb and flow and was arming itself against the land once more.

Twice a day the sea went out, leaving the island linked to the mainland by miles of sand and the causeway clear for traffic. Twice a day the sea returned, and then for about four hours the island was wholly itself.

He parked his grimy Volkswagen on the village's main square outside the Manor House Hotel. He got out and surveyed the Victorian, pseudo-Celtic cross in the center of the green with distaste and the small factory of the Lindisfarne Liqueur Company with disapproval. Then he locked the car. Two old women were gossiping outside the old Post Office, or general store as it now was, and a man was consulting the tide tables for October on a notice board. The chatter of sparrows in the ivy on the hotel and the scream of a seagull were the only sounds as he walked around a corner and down a lane toward the church and the priory ruins.

The object of his visit, the small museum, was by the main gate into the churchyard. It had originally been an outhouse of the hotel and its one room was not much bigger than a garage. He reluctantly paid his fivepence to the uniformed custodian and went in.

There it was—the Viking stone—in a petrified garden of fragments in the middle of the room, and by no means the biggest. On one side of the stone were two worshipers below a cross, above which were a sun, a moon, and two hands emerging from the sides as if in an embrace. On the other face were seven Viking raiders with swords and axes raised.

He nodded and scratched his beard. Professor Mac-Dougall had no doubt that the gravestone, of which only the rounded top remained, commemorated in part the sack of Lindisfarne in 793.

He knelt before the relic, wondering as he took out his glasses and put them on what its secrets were—whose death had given it life, and which of the figures on it was the king.

He touched the pale cold stone with superstitious care.

Suddenly there was a tramp of feet as people invaded the room.

Over his glasses he saw against the sky two Scandinavian giants. They parted, and between them stood a small heroic figure.

"My goodness gracious," said the professor. "For a moment I thought the Vikings were among us once again. 'All is lost,' I thought—'The end is nigh.'"

"You're not by any chance," he said, hoisting himself to his feet and putting his glasses away, "really Scandinavian?" He noticed now that the woman was a few inches taller than himself.

"Long ago, perhaps," said her partner. "But you're half right. My wife is Norwegian—or was, as she's very Anglicized now. Aren't you?"

"Oh, very," she said.

"And this," said the professor, "is your son?"

"Yes," said the man. "This is Erik."

"Eirik—the Eternal King," said the professor. "That's what it means, his name. Or did you know that?" The boy was contemplating the Viking stone.

"No," said the man. "But Runa's brothers are both called after gods, so it doesn't surprise me. We spell his name as a compromise—in the English way, but with a 'k' at the end."

"Erik," said the professor. "Did you say 'Rona' or 'Rune'?"

"Runa, with an 'a.' "

"Really? That's fantastically interesting," he said, wanting to know more but hesitating to probe. Runa, as far as he knew, was not a Norwegian name.

"Why?" said the man. "Are you a philologist?"

"Of sorts. Of sorts." He beamed at the handsome strangers, more interested in them now than in the ancient stones.

"Let me introduce myself," he said with a flourish of hands. "My name is MacDougall, Mervyn MacDougall, Professor of Celtic and Anglo-Saxon Studies at the University of Edinburgh! Formerly of Aberdeen! Commonly known as Fred!"

"Good heavens," said the man to his wife. "Another academic. You can't escape them. How do you do?" he went on, extending a large and powerful hand. "I'm Edmund Wardlaw, lecturer in Medieval History at King's College, London, formerly of Oxford, and commonly known as Ed. You know my wife and son."

"Splendid. An historian. Then you may know about this period," said the professor with a wave about the room.

"In part." Ed was glancing at the square plot of carved monuments. "My specialized knowledge dates from the Norman Conquest. Is this the famous stone?"

They crowded around Erik, who was standing beside the tombstone, his fingers tracing the weapons the raiders held. The stone was mounted on a pedestal and lower than him.

"Take your hands off it," Ed told his son, who did so and clasped his mother about her waist.

"A fearsome sight to the English," said the professor.

"To anyone in the Western world at that time, whether English, Irish, Turk—or Eskimo."

"True. Very true. Nonetheless, the first full terror of their

35

appearance was felt *here,* on this coast."

Ed looked at the professor with his eyebrows raised. Should he correct the little man, who *was* a professor of English, and must know the chronicles?

"Surely the first Viking raid on England was in Dorset— in Bertric's reign?"

"That's what the *southern* scribes claim. But they don't give a year to it. Do they? They say—excuse the rough translation—that in Bertric's reign—and he became King of Wessex in 786—that three ships came from Hordaland in Norway and slew the reeve of Dorchester, and that these were the first ships from the North to invade this country. They don't say when."

"It's a claim that hasn't been disputed."

"No. Not for a thousand years. But *I*"—he tilted his head and his eyes were slits—"I am ready to dispute it now."

"Why now?"

"I have evidence that the ships that came to Lindisfarne —and there were two, and they came from Westfold—*they* were the first. No. I'm not mad. I have the proof."

"I'd very much like to see it."

"You shall. You shall. But you've come to see the museum. Allow me to be your guide. There's not much, and some of it fearful rubbish, but the Viking stone is worth the pennies."

"Did you say they came from Westfold?" said Runa.

"They did. Near Oslo."

"I was born in Westfold," said Runa. "In Sandefjord."

"Where else!" exclaimed the professor. "I was sure you were the daughter of kings—and the wife and mother of heroes."

He looked at them all and lastly at Erik, who returned his gaze and grinned back at him.

"I am a hero," he cried.

He clapped his hands above his head and jigged away in a war dance round the room.

"I am the king!" he sang.

Ed and Runa were much taken with the professor. As they toured the priory ruins later, his comic manner, the exaggeration of speech and of his features, his fund of information, were an entertainment. This vivacity of his was evidently an assumed not an inbred display, for sometimes, when he happened to be alone with either Ed or Runa, he spoke with a proper professional seriousness and concern. But when he had an audience, or was talking to Erik, he put on a show, and his Aberdeen accent increased.

He was in his early sixties, they guessed, from his grizzled hair and beard, both of which were trim and thick, and from the lines that scored his forehead and edged his eyes. When he grinned, his eyes disappeared and his mouth stretched into his beard without showing his teeth. He looked like some whiskered rodent then—an impression added to by his thinness, by the tilts and jerks of his head and the almost continuous use of his hands to express himself. In repose he had a seafaring look. For his face and hands were weatherworn, and his small blue eyes farseeing. He was dressed that day in a baggy tweed suit, a check shirt, a plaid tie, a black jersey and brogues, and Ed never saw him in anything else on the other occasions they met.

They gathered he was living on his own in a flat in Bamburgh Castle.

"Didn't you know?" he said. "Half of it's turned into flats —and Lord Armstrong lives in the keep. Fortunately it's not open to the public in the winter—no, not now—but it's a fearful business in the summer, with cars and coachloads, and people staring in your windows and beating at your

37

door and expecting you either to be a guide or a ghost." He told them it wasn't his flat but belonged to an aging actor and his wife. "He's away filming some Roman epic in Spain, or a Western in Yugoslavia—I don't know. No doubts he's playing a senator in both." The professor said he had been at the castle a week since yesterday and that he had borrowed the flat to do a fortnight's peaceful work—"In appropriate surroundings."

Ed in turn told him that they had hired the cottage on Holy Island so that he could work during his Sabbatical term on a thesis about the Norman Conquest for his Ph.D., while his family had a change from London.

"But it's me that needs a holiday," he said. "They were away in Norway for a month while I was marking exam papers and spending a sunny September in the British Museum."

"With a sandwich lunch on the steps or a bite in the pub between," said Professor MacDougall. "Ah yes, I know how it is."

Ed turned his gaze from the rainbow arch to what had been the Chapter House.

"And this is where the Lindisfarne Gospels were written."

"Not *here*," said the professor. "On Lindisfarne, yes. But not here. They were written some five hundred years before the priory—all this—was built. Long before this. . . ."

He walked away from them, across the grass of the monks' ancient graveyard, and came to a halt facing the Ouse and the castle beyond. The Wardlaws followed him, led by Erik.

Between them and the meadow that sloped down to the Ouse was a low wall, topped with railings.

"They came down there, from the Ouse," said the professor.

"Who did?" asked Runa.

"The invaders."

"Who?"

"The raiders on the stone."

"The Vikings!" cried Erik.

"Really? What makes you think that?" asked Ed.

"No *reason*," replied the professor. "Just hypothesis. But why indeed should they do otherwise? They probably sailed boldly into the harbor in broad daylight and beached their ships. In the monastery, an attack was not expected, dreamed of, and the monks quite unprepared—apart from the omens. There had been a famine," he said to Runa. "And fearful weather—gales and storms, and fiery dragons were seen flying in the air." He grinned at Erik.

He's quoting from the chronicles now, thought Ed.

"How did they know about this place?" asked Runa.

The professor waved his hands. "The wealth of the Christian Church was well known even then. These men were adventurers, remember—after riches and fame. After gold. By the way, the Vikings *never* wore horned helmets. That's a fiction, as Ed will know. To continue. At that time the long sea kingdom of Northumbria, which stretched from Edinburgh to the Humber, was rich, embroiled in civil war—"

"How do you know that?" asked Ed.

"I know I'm not an historian," said the professor. "But *that* I know. . . . Are you listening, Erik? Good boy. It really happened, all this, you know. And it happened here."

Professor MacDougall paused before continuing.

"It was a summer's day in June. Two ships. About seventy men. They came up the slope from the Ouse, waving their swords and axes, uttering war cries to terrify their prey, also to encourage themselves, and make the murder a sport. And they miserably destroyed and plundered God's church on Lindisfarne and slew the servants of God."

Ed smiled—the professor was quoting again.

"Some of the brethren they carried off laden with chains —some they slew—many they drove out naked and shamed with insults—some they drowned in the sea. And so they came to Bamburgh."

"Bamburgh!" interrupted Ed. "That's not in the chronicles."

The professor grinned his toothless grin. "*You* come to Bamburgh tomorrow," he said, "and I'll prove it is."

"Go on," cried Erik. "What happened at Bamburgh?"

"Another time. I'll tell you another time. But *that*, I imagine, is roughly what happened here."

"You imagine well," said Runa, putting her arm through Ed's.

"Those slabs of stone by the railings are monks' graves. Imagine if the Viking stone once stood here—with its cross facing inward, toward us, and its pagan figures facing the sea."

They looked about them lost in imagining. The ruins seemed ghostly, the bay, the castle, unreal—reflections of the present on a glass that stood between them and the terror of past events.

Ed ran his fingers over the spikes of the railings.

"Do you know why *we* came here?" he asked.

"No," said the professor. "Why?"

"I was up in Edinburgh in January—being interviewed for a job . . ."

"Did you get it?"

"No," he said. "But coming back to London, on an early train, I saw the island against the dawn—very long, and low, and dark against the sunrise but still clear. It looked enchanted. And . . ." His voice trailed away.

"And?" demanded the professor.

Ed swung about and smiled.

"And so we came to Lindisfarne," he said.

The sun was setting, though he could not see it, when Professor MacDougall drove back toward the causeway. The air was mild and still. The arc of the western sky was a uniform mass of slate-colored cloud that lower down over the Cheviot Hills grew darker, almost purple where constricting yellow gaps let rays of gold escape for a second and search the sky. The tide had already covered the sand flats with a silky stippled sheet of water. High water, the professor remembered, was in three hours' time, at five to nine.

He had gone to Rose Cottage for tea with the Wardlaws after reviewing the priory ruins and the church. He had not unearthed many more facts about them, as the wife had been mostly engaged in keeping Erik occupied with chat and preventing noise and naughtiness, while the two men compared University methods of work and people.

Professor MacDougall noted with interest that Erik was left-handed—at tea he used that hand for lifting his cup and for spreading his toast with butter. When Erik was sent to his room after a row with his father—because he tried to insist on his rights to watch a children's television program about space—the professor discovered that no one else in either of the parents' families was or ever had been left-handed. Ed said there was a theory that a high proportion of left-handed people could be related to difficult childbirths. In Runa's case, he said, it had been like that, and now they had a sinister son.

"Very sinister," he said. "You should see his handwriting. It's not that it's bad or that he can't write. But it's backward. It goes from right to left, and every letter is reversed. Real mirror writing. It's one of the reasons he hates going to school. Even his drawings have the objects in them transposed. He's the original mixed-up kid."

The parents were far from mixed up. Professor MacDougall considered them to be most handsome representatives of their sex. Both were fair, but of different types. The man, who was six foot two or three, was long-faced, lean-nosed, and narrow-eyed. Strangely, his eyes were brown. The woman was pale beside him, with large blue eyes in a wide face and much less angular features than her husband. They had apparent faults of character—of self, of pride and possessiveness. But nothing seemed subconscious, all was known. His instinct had rightly called them hero and heroine. In another time, he mused, the tale of their love and lives would have enriched its hearers. What battles, adventures, deeds and doomed existence would have been theirs! They had no chance of greatness now, no fearful fated end.

Professor MacDougall smiled to himself at his romantic fancies as the car set out over the tallow ribbon of the causeway, beset with water. The last gold of the sunset had gone. Far inland a voluminous mountain of dark cloud lay over Yeavering Bell. Within it a silver whisker of light suddenly flashed.

He wastefully waited in the noise of the car for the sound of thunder, and heard none.

On the lookout for more lightning, he drove recklessly off the causeway up to Beal and toward the approaching storm.

4

Erik was busy at work on the floor of his bedroom. He was painting a picture of the monastery in flames against a dark-blue night, with round-headed monks in flight and bleeding on the green, and hairy helmeted Vikings making semaphore shapes with their arms and swords. The monks had faces like gingerbread men, but their destroyers had their backs to him or their faces turned away.

He showed the painting proudly to his mother when she entered his room to wrap his pajamas around a hot-water bottle and put them in his bed. She also draped his dressing gown over a chair by the gas fire.

"That's bright," she said. "*Akk!* All that blood! What an imagination you have. So. Put it away. It's bath time now— the water's running."

"All right," he said, tired by concentrating, his fantasy drained, his earlier animosity for his father a buried thing.

Runa returned to the sitting room.

After supper Ed had helped her with the washing up and made them both some coffee, and then while she briefly worked on a tapestry she was doing for a fire screen in their London flat, he had sorted out the notes and typescript of his thesis.

"You should see his painting," she said.

"It wouldn't be allowed." Ed was stacking his papers, files, and the typewriter on the table under the window.

She picked up the tapestry, and realized for the first time how well its picture fitted the cottage.

"Look," she said, and they laughed at the half-completed bowl of crimson roses.

Ed came toward her and put his hands on her waist.

"How are we?" he said.

"We are seeing to Erik's bath," she answered.

"I wish you would see to *me* sometimes," he said. "Scrub my back and dry me afterward, rubbing all over with a warm white towel."

"You are a big grown man—"

43

"You should know," he said.

"And he is a small boy. Though sometimes it is a problem which is which."

She backed away. "I must see to the bath," she said.

"All right," he said, then added, "Would you mind if I went out for a drink? I'd like to meet the locals."

"Go on," she said. "That's a good idea. And bring me back a Guinness."

She went into the bathroom, calling out, "Bath is ready now, Erik," while Ed thrust himself into his parka in the hall. He felt cheery and thought he should make some amends by saying goodnight to his son before he went out. At that moment Erik emerged from his bedroom in his dressing gown. He froze when he saw his father. The hubbub of running bathwater and the muffled roar of the heater filled the hall. A faint smoke escaped from the bathroom door. Ed smiled appeasingly at the pale-faced form in its slippers and long red gown.

"I'm going out for a little while," he said. "Look after your mother."

There was no response. He opened the front door making sure he had the key, his pipe and money.

"Goodnight," he said. "Be good. Sleep well."

"Goodnight!" said Erik. "And don't come back!" He shot into the bathroom and slammed the door.

Ed leaned on the turnstile into the meadow. His breath evaporated in steam in the glare of a street light high on a wall of the Crown and Anchor behind him.

Erik's parting words still rankled—the rejected parley irked him. There were times when understanding and sympathy were poor substitutes, he felt, for outright intolerance and rage.

44

Two distant shots that came from the southwest beyond the church distracted him, as did the approach of a man.

"What was that?" Ed inquired of the islander, for so he appeared to be.

"Duck shooting," said the young man, pausing at the entrance of the pub. "They should get a few tonight. The glass is falling. There'll likely be a storm."

"It seems all right." Ed wondered if the other fellow was also aware of their superficial likeness. Both had fair hair and both were wearing similar chunky off-white polo-neck sweaters.

"It seems," said the other. "But it will rain. Have you not seen the lightning over the Cheviots? Smell the air."

Ed sniffed. "It seems like best bitter to me."

The young man smiled. "Ay. And better in than out," he said. "Are you coming in for a drink, or are you waiting for the rain?"

"Are you coming out now?" said Runa, knocking on the bathroom door.

The noisy war games, involving Erik's submarine and the sponge and the face cloth, had subsided some minutes earlier—since when she had heard no battle sounds or splashing.

"I'm coming in," she said and opened the door.

To her horror she saw he was lying stretched out under the water, face down.

"Erik!" she shrieked.

He exploded out of the water into a sitting position, let go his nose and giggled.

"I was holding my breath," he said, fingering water out of his ears. "It's not very easy, and I only got to fifty."

"Oh, Erik," she said, on her knees by the bath.

45

She ran her hand over his dripping hair and down his cheek. She wanted to kiss him, hold him tight—but he was very wet and her blouse would get soaked.

"Oh, Erik, I thought—"

He saw the love and concern in her eyes. Somehow he had triumphed. He slapped the water with joy. "I'll get to a hundred and then I'll be a real skin diver and be able to live in the sea without any aqualungs, like a whale!" He put the sponge on his head to add to a comical face he made for her.

She laughed. "You funny man," she said. "Come now. Up. I'll make you dry."

She waited with the towel held ready while he retrieved his submarine that had sunk and pulled the bath plug. He climbed out and jumped up and down on the mat, with the submarine lodged in his fist like a dagger.

"Din-di-din-di-din-di-din!" he chanted.

"Keep still!" she ordered, capturing him in the folds of the towel and rubbing hard. He stood, crooning to himself and making circling movements with the toy as if it were flying.

"Turn around," she said.

She dried him thoroughly but carefully, as if she were polishing the limbs and torso of a statue of a young god.

He was over four feet tall, and the smooth solidity of his body was more that of a young man than that of a boy. There was a childish softness to his features, and the cream and white contours of his muscles were not as bold or defined as a man's, but his stomach was flat, his chest had form, and his legs and shoulders were strongly sculptured.

As a baby, as a growing child, he had been so well-proportioned—without a blemish apart from cuts and grazes—that it had been a delight for her to tend him. He was still the most beautiful child she had ever seen, and he was hers. She had made him. She had suffered in the making, in giving him birth. For forty-eight hours she had tried to force him out of her, until the sweat swam with the tears from her eyes, until the spasms possessed her, and became like the rhythmic heartbeat of the being in her womb, convulsing again and again. She had pleaded, she had screamed for help, to be rid of the torturing pangs, but more to be rid of the creature devouring her within.

They took a knife, and slit her stomach, and took away the pain.

She remembered all this, but with no bitterness. It seemed right to her that she should have suffered in producing a child so fine, so strong, so fair. She could not better her achievement, nor did she want to. Nor was she able to. For afterward, they had taken out her womb.

He was standing quite still now, his eyes half-closed. He lifted his feet obediently one by one for her to dry them. The hairs on his legs were the finest silk, and as fair as those on his arms, and as straight—not curly like Ed's, whose arms and legs had thickets of hair, a purer gold than the tousled tendrils on his forehead.

"Oh, look," said Erik fondly. "My little man is standing up!"

"So he is," she said with mock surprise. "Well, he will just have to lie down again, for it's time you all went to bed. So! I've finished. Put your pajamas on."

She puffed some powder between his toes and legs and helped him do up his buttons.

"Your throat is not sore?" she asked.

"It's O.K." he said.

"Good." She smiled at him. "Have you done your teeth?"

"Of course," he said.

With Ed's comb that was by the washbasin, she straightened Erik's hair. All the time he regarded her with grave attention.

"So! There you are—all ready for bed!"

Pleased with her handiwork, she stood up and gathered his clothes as he went into his bedroom. She found him at the window with his face hidden between the curtains. While she folded his clothes away and tidied the room his voice came to her from the window.

"There's no moon," he said. "No stars . . . I can only see my face. Do you know . . . ? There's a man outside," he said slowly. "In the garden."

For a moment she was incredulous. Then she dashed to the window and flung the curtains wide so that the bedroom light fell on the garden. There was no one there—and no one could have hidden away so quickly.

"Where?" she demanded. He grinned at her slyly.

"There's no one now," he said.

She hustled him into his bed, gave him his golliwog, and turned off the gas fire. It worried her he was seeing things in the garden. He still had the occasional nightmare, and such imaginings, together with the proximity of the church-yard and all the talk of Viking violence in the afternoon, might provoke another. And he had not had a very good day with his father. Yet he seemed unconcerned, even happy—for he hummed a tune as he traced the wallpaper pattern with a finger.

To reassure herself, and him, she sat near him on the bed.

"Do you remember what a happy time you had on the beach at Mandal, and all the things you found at Lindesnes?"

Yes—he remembered. He was always happy in Norway.

"Shall we go to the beach tomorrow?" she said. "In the morning? Let's do that. Let's see what we can find."

He thought of Norway and felt a yearning to return there and sail up Oslofjord again.

"Will we stay here very long?" he asked.

"It won't *seem* long," she said. "There will be lots to do. Think of that. And in the morning the beach. Just you and me."

He smiled. She stroked his hair. "Now we shall sleep," she said.

She blew him a kiss and was getting up when he sat up and reached out needfully for her. He flung his arms around her neck and he kissed her lips. He was very warm in her embrace. His heartbeats thudded through her in time with hers. His breathing gusted through the hair on her neck.

"I love you," he whispered. "You do love *me*?"

Later, when she had gone, he stood at the window again, peering out. It needed a lot of concentration, as it was very dark, but he was just able to see the rounded shoulders of tombstones beyond the garden wall. There had been no man in the garden itself, but a tombstone taller than the rest, with a vague blob like a head on top, had seemed like a man and could easily be imagined in the garden. He was not really afraid of the night, he told himself—or anything else —but before he went to sleep he wanted to check that all was well outside, and that no tombstones had advanced upon his room. None had, he was glad to see. They stood unmoving—waiting, he thought.

An image of the distant pyramid he had seen from the castle impinged on his vision—a pyramid that was also a beacon, a sign for sailors. He shivered, and as if in sympathy some bushes by the window whispered a reply. It was the wind that stirred them and made the dead leaves rustle on the grass. A thrill ran through him as he imagined the passage of the wind over all the grasses on the island, out to the pyramid on the headland.

Suddenly he heard a muted shot, and then another, like a

signal. He listened for some more, but there was none. He knew then that there would be a war, and saw the tombstones hunched before his room for what they were, the faithful followers of his army, asleep and awaiting his call.

Ed returned at half-past ten in time to see a television program about archeological discoveries in America that seemed to prove that Greenlanders had settled there about the year one thousand. Runa, who had had a bath, was curled up in her dressing gown in a chair by the sitting room fire, intent on sewing the tapestry, and gratefully received the bottle of Guinness he brought for her. He had also brought some beer for himself.

" 'Dumps' is the natives' name for them," he said. "They call them 'dumps.' Actually, they're bottles of light-brown ale."

In between lighting his pipe he said that she must come to the pub with him next time. It was a bit bare, he said, but the locals all seemed to be characters. They were very talkative if you wanted to talk to them and left you alone if you didn't. Their accents sounded Scottish, he said—some more than others, and some talked so strangely, either through loose dentures or drink, that he hardly understood them at all. In most cases their families had been islanders for hundreds of years, it appeared, and quite a few were related. The population of the island, he said—about 180—had declined a lot since the herring fleet and the limestone kilns had closed down. "There are only four lobster boats in operation now," he said. "And there are only eleven children in the school."

He went on to say that drinking hours seemed a bit fluid, rather depending on the landlord, the state of the tide, and whoever were his guests in the bar at the time. There were no policemen on the island to enforce the law, which was represented by a policeman who lived at Scremerston on the mainland—eleven miles away. Not that he was often required. The island community was apparently so well knit that any rift would mar the fabric of their interwoven lives.

"I met a man, a fisherman called Robbie," Ed continued. "You'd like him. He's like me. I might go out with him in the boats one morning if the weather's fair. But it means getting up very early—five or six. They come back to the harbor, to the Ouse, about nine or ten—which is why we never saw any of them this morning on the jetty."

She heard him out at intervals—during television commercials between programs, while she prepared a snack for him of crackers, cheese and pickled onions. He finished off one bottle of beer and then another. She contented herself with the one bottle of Guinness.

"We must buy some mead!" he said at one point. "I had a little in the Crown and Anchor—to taste it. It's not too bad —rather like a dry sherry. Not too sweet either, considering it's made of fermented honey. They make it here. It's almost the only industry, apart from fishing, fowling and farming."

"Didn't the Anglo-Saxons drink it?" she asked.

"We all drank it," he said. "Barrels and casks of it—Angles, Saxons, Swedes, Danes and Norwegians—from the North Cape to Normandy, and beyond. We must certainly buy some mead."

She watched him fondly as he rambled on—his diction overemphatic and his arms sweeping the air.

"Miss Ingram was there," he said. "In the pub. Boozing with her sisters two, in a corner. And knitting. I asked her if she would baby-sit for us. She said she would be glad to. So you've no excuse! We can both get tight as ticks every night!"

Runa was surprised to hear that Miss Ingram was in the

pub. They had only met her for the first time yesterday, on the evening of their arrival, and she had seemed a staid old lady. She was the owner of Rose Cottage. She owned the whole street, Ed had discovered. Runa had intended to thank Miss Ingram again for thoughtfully getting in basic provisions for them and lighting the fire, and to give her a little gift, but whenever they knocked on her door, there had been no answer.

A flaming coal fell out of the fire, and as Ed shoveled it back, she heard the bang of a window.

"It's the wind," she said.

"It's going to rain," he stated. "There's lightning over the mainland."

"Really?"

"There will be a storm they say in the Crown and Anchor."

"I thought there was something," she said. "The furniture was talking—creaking so much. A change of atmosphere, isn't it? I hope the roof is not leaking."

"Leaky," he said.

She went about the cottage checking that all the windows were secure. Erik was lying on his back and snoring slightly. She returned to the sitting room.

"I'm going to bed," she declared.

"It's early."

"Don't you want to join me?" she asked and left the room.

"I'm not a carpenter," he said. "But I'll join you."

He leapt to his feet and then crept into the bedroom where she was brushing her hair. He grasped her breasts from behind her, making her jump, and the brush collided with his head.

"Aowohh!" he groaned, and collapsed theatrically onto the carpet. "I die, I die, I die! Look how I die."

"Well," she said complacently. "It serves you right."

She stepped over him and grandly got into the bed on her

side and coolly arranged her hair over the sleeves of her nightdress.

"Go and do your teeth," she said. "Oh, and please put the fire screen over the fire. I forgot."

While he was in the bathroom, she wondered lazily why she had married this uncouth son of a Lincolnshire farmer. She was the only daughter of Doctor Eiriksen of Tønsberg, where they had conventional manners and social obligations and led decent ordered lives. All of which he scoffed at, though he observed their customs for her sake when he was there. She had been amazed, when she first met him at Oxford, at his rudeness and nonacceptance of accepted ideas, belief and behavior. He was also selfish, moody, and self-opinionated. But she had become used to these traits, and some of her own steadiness and passivity and her gaiety had rubbed off on him. She in turn had become more outspoken and aggressive. By now they were much nearer in character. Yet the obsessive passion that had brought them together had not changed. It ran more deep, more slow, more sure. She always delighted to be with him, to feed her love with looking at him—as she did when he returned to the room and undressed before her.

There was nothing overtly sexual in her gaze—the procedures of his dressing, undressing, eating, washing, getting up and going to sleep were so familiar that they aroused no feeling but reassurance.

Naked but for his socks, he gave his nose a blow, cleared his throat and knelt to turn off the gas fire. Then he took off his socks and, brightly lit by the bedside lamp, clambered onto the bed.

"Get off," she said, as he sat astride the blankets on top of her stomach.

"I'm just looking," he said. "My God, you're gorgeous tonight."

"The view is not so pretty from here," she said.

She pulled the sheet up over her head and tried to turn onto her side. He drummed on his chest and grinned, and ran his hands down his body and onto his thighs.

She lowered the sheet and playfully blinked at him over her shoulder.

Her action echoed in his mind for a moment, then was driven from it by the sudden enveloping sound of raindrops falling on the street outside and on the attic roof above them. The multiplying patter insisted they pause, and both gazed up at the ceiling. The sounds as suddenly ceased.

"Rain," she whispered.

"Rain," he said.

She stirred uncomfortably under him—as his hands burnished the hairs on his thighs and moved between them. She sighed, and as she did so, her stomach lifted under him. Her eyes were large, unblinking.

"Oh, look," he said, conversationally. "My old man has woken up."

A thunderclap shattered the night sky over the island and was answered at once by a barrage of cannon fire seemingly over the cottage.

As if a sign had been given, the sky loosed its burden, and torrents of rain struck everywhere on the island. It dinned on the tiles of the cottage and splattered in the street.

For an instant a flash of lightning suffused the bedroom. Runa winced. Ed shouted with glee and had tumbled under the bedclothes before the thunder pealed out about them again.

He held her closely, kissing her eyes, her nose, her lips, her neck. He worked his left arm up her nightdress, around her waist and roughly up her back until his hand emerged and seized her hair. He pressed himself upon her, holding a kiss until she could not breathe. Gasping she pushed him away and heard the rain above the pounding of her heart.

His left hand pulled away from her neck and worked the nightdress up her body until her breasts were bared. His mouth ranged over them, while his hand reshaped the satiny flesh of her warm, voluting form. His eyes and mouth followed his hand.

"You have the most beautiful body in all the world," he breathed.

The ghost of a lightning flash flickered through the room and made livid under his eye the long white seam across her belly. It speared his gaze and thought while he steeled himself for the thunder's baleful response. It lay like the shiny sloughed-off skin of a worm, and always when their bodies united it writhed between them. He hated the scar for what it had done, and its cause. Yet it was part of her, of her love for him, and he brushed his lips gently along it while overhead the thunder loudly resounded.

Erik woke from a dream in a flash of lightning. The night was alive with noises. Outside, the rain rapping against the window fused with its punishing swish on the garden and the pelting on the roof. Within, he was keenly alert to the presence of things unseen and to the sounds of his own existence when he moved. His excitement was intense. He seemed to be in a cave of sounds and was full of expectation that something vastly important might be said or be about to happen.

A crack of thunder exploded into a thousand fragments that rumbled and roared down over him, as if a mountainside had torn away and was plunging down to the sea.

He cried out in his ecstasy—and a faint cry came in answer.

It came again. It came from the wall—from the other room. He knew it was his mother.

He flung himself wildly out of his bed—he had to save her.

In seconds he burst into the other room, to see in a flash of lightning his father's great broad back and body heave and arch and beat down on his mother, while her neck was gripped by his hands and her head forced cruelly back.

"No! Stop it!" he screamed. "You're hurting her!"

He bounded onto the bed. He battered his father's head and shoulders with his fists.

"No! Don't kill my mother!" he cried—and was suddenly thrown on his back and overpowered, with his wrists squeezed tight and the sweating bulk of his father crushing his chest and legs. He twisted his head to see if she had been murdered. But although her breast looked beaten out of shape, she was alive and saying something. He stopped screaming to hear her words.

"Don't hurt him, Ed," she was saying.

"You monster!" said the red, distorted face above him, banging his handcuffed arms against the headboard.

Then she came to his rescue—she freed him—and he rolled into her arms. He was able to hold her and be held by her, not sure what he was saying, wanting as much to comfort her as be comforted himself.

But suddenly his father was laughing—showing his teeth and mocking him. The hideous sound engulfed him.

It stayed with him when she had carried him back to his bedroom, where he lay unmoving, face to the wall, hearing her tell him that they had only been playing, fighting together, but all in fun. She thanked him for his concern for her, and smoothed his hair, and left him on his own.

The rain poured down.

Alone in his grief Erik stared unseeing into the darkness. What was it they did that he could not? Why did she have secret ways of enjoying herself in which he could not share? Why did she spend so little time with him? She made the choice, and she didn't choose him. He was unwanted, not really loved. He was only a nuisance, did stupid things. He did not, could not, understand enough to make her his.

The tears slid silently onto the pillow.

He could never compete. He could never win. He had no knowledge or weapons. Even his father's gleaming Thing had been much bigger than his. It had meant to kill him, menaced him, like a shiny one-eyed snake.

His own eyes closed. He heard the assuaging sounds of the rain, soothing the pain of his living, making the nightmare a nothing.

It had been one-eyed, he remembered, like the man.

Friday

1

———————◆———————

Erik and Runa went to the north shore of the island in the morning. She had suggested to Ed that they do so, and he had thought it a good idea as he wanted to get on with some work. He was in a very good humor at breakfast, and when Erik would not eat with his father, preferring to keep to his room, Ed merrily loaded a breakfast tray for his son and took it in to him. Runa waited in the hall, expecting a scene. But although Ed's exhortations of "Cheer up, you might be dead," and "Don't worry, only the egg is poisoned," made her nervous, there was no rioting. Ed returned without a knife in his back, and Erik ate his breakfast—apart from the egg.

Ed gave her the guidebook, and she gave Erik a bar of chocolate, which he put in the pocket of his parka. They were both dressed in trousers and boots, wet-weather gear in case it rained again, and she had on a tan leather coat—no hat—she never wore one.

Erik was out into the street and off to the square as soon as the front door was opened. Ed stood in the doorway playing with a pen.

"Don't be late," he said. "I want my lunch at one." He waved to Runa and went inside.

It was a splendid day for walking, she thought. It had rained very heavily during the night, and all the buildings were streaked with rain, and puddles were everywhere. The day was bright, though there was no sunshine, and a fresh wind out of the north tugged clouds unwillingly after it.

They soon found there were only three proper roads out of the village. One led to the western beach, then along it and so to the causeway. Another had already taken them in the direction of the castle. The third road went straight from one end of the village to the banks of dunes along the northern shore. It was called Sandham Loaning, and once past a farm, it became a hummocky, rutted track, lined with bushes of thorn for most of the way. On either side were fields of sheep and flocks of lapwings.

Erik was looking for nests in the bushes, and rats, and in the changing prospects of the walk Runa forgot the tragicomic happenings of the night. It had worried her what Erik had seen, and worse, what he might have imagined. It shamed her that he had seen her so exposed, her body as well as her passion. Ed had assured her that her explanation to Erik had been the best one, and that anyway nothing sexually damaging could be thought by the boy, as at his age he had no sexual thoughts. She hoped Ed was right—he usually was. But she had been further disconcerted when Erik, who had been looking at her strangely while she made his bed, said he was glad she had not been squashed. She had not known what to say until she realized what he was looking at. "Your bosom," he said, and added—"It's blown up again." She then had to explain that it lost its shape when she was lying down. He wanted her to demonstrate, but she said there wasn't time.

It was funny of course. Yet she had remained uneasy.

He was not an ordinary child. He had grown out of the screaming fits and tantrums of his early years, but he still did and said the most unaccountable things, and his black moods and wild fantasies alarmed her. Yet he was immensely practical and athletic—he played alongside eleven-year-olds in the junior football team. But he did not appear to get on too well even with his contemporaries.

The track petered out in a sandy cove surmounted by the immobile wave tops of grassy dunes that seemed to toss their crests in all directions. There was no sight or sound of the sea. An incongruous stack of fire brooms made a mystic figure against the sky.

"Which way shall we go?" she said.

He was standing on a ridge in advance of her.

"This way," he said.

She saw why when she followed him. Veering to her right was a long valley between the dunes, with a windless floor like a filled-in crater. The matted carpet of soggy weed and bog grass was so flat as to seem unnatural and unsafe to her. But it was firm enough and, as Erik remarked, like a football field. He was hunting for finds. What he found straightaway were the tattered feathers and bones of a dead seagull. Farther on he found the pieces of another—and then another. They seemed quite clean, without grubs or ants, and must have been anatomized by the rain.

When they reached a ruined gateway of dunes at the other end they found themselves in a lofty amphitheater, which was littered with hundreds of tiny snail shells, most of them empty. The remnants of seabirds lay among them.

Erik started gathering snail shells, the yellowest ones he could find. To him the place was the hall of a palace strewn with treasures and surrounded by towering walls of sand and battlements of dune grass.

Suddenly she called out—"The sea, Erik! The sea!"

She stood in a high defile between the dunes, looking down onto a beach. He was soon beside her. The north wind blew in their faces.

"Zowie!" cried Erik, and went bounding down the damp dune-side and charged with a volley of battle cries onto the shore. Small flocks of feeding seabirds fled low along the water's edge, to settle farther around the eastward curve of the bay, to their right. They followed. Erik was intent on looking for crabs in the mounds of seaweed left by the tide along the high-water mark. Now and then he made detours in search of shells, or to inspect the debris of stones, planks, bits of wood, plastic bottles and salt-stained branches heaped higher up the shore.

Runa had her eyes on the ebbing tide and the seabirds.

The sight of the sea always made her meditative or sad. She had been born by the sea. Weekends and the holidays of her childhood had been spent by the sea and on the sea. The first time she had crossed the sea—going to Denmark didn't count—she sailed across the North Sea to England. That was when she was eighteen and going for a year to Oxford to better her English, as her father hoped, and see something of the world. She arrived there in October. By the end of the month she had met an attractively extrovert undergraduate from University College, called Edmund Wardlaw. He was twenty-one, and in his final year. They were introduced on a foggy day on the College Barge, one of the few that still remained then, and it was on the same barge on the river Isis that Erik was conceived in June the following year. She couldn't be sure, for they had been lovers for some months. But she had stayed away for ten days while he sat his Finals, and after the last exam she was waiting for him on the steps of Schools and stayed with him through the celebrations, until after dining out together, they went for a walk by the river where they had often walked before, and somehow he had a key to the barge, and a bottle of wine, and they stayed there all the night. It was the eighth of June. They married that September—principally at his suggestion, and for her parents' sake. They went on a cruise to the North Cape after, then returned to Oxford, where Ed worked for his Ph.D., and failing to get it, won instead a position in London. They had been in London, living at Fulham, for the last five years, and every year they had crossed the sea to Norway and taken Erik with them.

A rumor of all these events in her life ran through her thoughts as she wandered along the beach. She stopped to gaze across the sea—that way was home. Norway was still home to her. Living in a rented London flat was not an ideal existence, and she was most happy when Ed was with her in Norway, rude as he was about the "boorish bourgeoisie" there. According to him, all the Viking spirit had left Norway years ago, to enrich the blood of other races, leaving behind an anemic class of dull and listless tradesmen who had been there ever since. Yet to her the pleasing formalities of small-town life seemed more sweet than the vast indifference of the capital.

She had reached the arm of the bay where the sea was lapping a jumble of boulders and driftwood that fringed the low headland. She struggled up onto its grassy top and saw, about two hundred yards away, the white triangle that marked Emmanuel Head.

Erik was running toward it.

A gust of wind blew her hair across her eyes. She faced into the wind, and there in the water quite near her was what looked like a ship's bollard. It goggled at her, then sank out of sight.

It was a seal. Its head resurfaced, a dark prehistoric shape on the placid water.

Cautiously, so as not to disturb the beast, she sat on the turf to observe it.

Turning her head, she saw that Erik had reached the beacon and was standing by it. She hesitated to call out to him in case her voice would frighten the seal away, but at that moment he raised a stick he was carrying—to salute her.

A cough from the water distracted her. The seal had coughed. It looked at her and sighed and submerged again.

She waited for it to reappear.

As soon as Erik caught sight of the beacon after scrambling off the beach, he had started running toward it, rattling the snail shells in his pockets. When he reached it, panting a little, he saw it was at least three times as big as himself and could never be climbed. Nonetheless he claimed it, in proper mountaineering fashion, by raising his banner. As he did so, he noticed his mother's head some distance away— she glanced at him, then turned aside. He thought she must be sitting down and resting. With a sweeping gesture he stuck his stick in the ground. It snapped. He discarded the piece he was left with and walked once around the beacon.

Someone had recently whitewashed it—white spilled over its concrete base and onto the earth. He supposed the some- one had had a ladder, or a very long-handled brush, which in either case they would have had to carry, along with buckets of whitewash, all the way from the village. Or had they come from the sea?

He faced toward the sea and into the wind.

In a flash he felt tired and ready to sleep. He slumped at the base of the pyramid leaning his back against it. For a moment he shut his eyes.

When he opened them, the sea was very bright yet very

63

pale and like the sky, as if the rain had washed the color away. He could not see the waters clearly, although he could picture the boat upon them very well. It was a long boat with a square sail, and somehow very familiar. He blinked—and the boat vanished.

For a moment he did not know where he was. But the sea and the sky and the grass were normally colored again—the ground was hard—the beacon stood behind him—and there was definitely no boat heading toward him over the waters from the north.

To reaffirm his presence there, he hugged his knees and began to sing to himself. He sang in his head without moving his mouth, making the notes contend with the puffing of the wind in his ears. The song became quite loud, until he heard nothing else, concentrating as he was now on getting the song right, with its even rhythm and long ascending notes. He raised his eyes to the sky, repeating two notes like the sound of somebody's name.

He sang them a third time loudly, and everything went bright again and he froze.

He was not alone. He dared not move, but he knew someone was watching him, waiting for him to move. His singing had been heard.

Erik lowered his eyes very slowly in case they might creak in the white unnatural silence, and as he did so he became aware that nothing human was with him on the deserted headland. Nothing had been altered or been added to that he could sense or see.

Then it moved.

A reflex shudder shook him—he dared not gasp. His eyes looked at what they saw before they knew what it was. It was looking at him from the grass at the edge of the headland not six feet away—a snake.

The color came back to the scene. The sea and the wind

were heard once more. He was able to relax a little. He was not afraid of snakes as such, although he had never met one outside a zoo. He blinked, and the snake remained.

"Hallo, snake," he whispered.

As if in recognition of him and his presence, it raised its head, slavishly ducked it, and then streamed out of sight over the grassy rim.

After a pause to digest the unparalleled sight, he got up and approached the place where the snake had been. From where he stood he could see the foreshore below him—a disarray of heaped-up boulders, stones, and flotsam, which formed a barrier between the ebbing tide and the crumbling headland, which was no more than nine or ten feet above the sea. Immediately below him a segment of the bank had recently collapsed. Turf and sand had spewed out onto the stones, leaving a well-defined bite mark at his feet. Obviously, he realized, the collapse had been caused by last night's heavy rain. Or it might have been caused by a bolt of lightning. This idea pleased him better.

There was no sign of the snake from where he stood. So he cast about to find a way down. Nearby, the island edge was broken in ledges like steps. He made his way onto the boulders below with some caution, as the going was very uneven and he was wary of putting a foot on the serpent. But he was soon perched on the foothills of the landslide, which had been smoothed out by the rain and had shaped itself into a cone against the bank. Just above its apex was a small hole, surrounded by an area of much darker matter than the layered sand, with an arching outline like a mound. Some of the dark stuff—which was more like earth than sand—had also spilled out below. The hole could only mean one thing—that he had found the snake house.

Behind him the sea stirred over hidden reefs. He was nervous about arousing the secret snake, but he had to know what its house was like. Besides, it had disturbed *him*—and had to be unsettled in return.

After some deliberation he broke off a branch from the shipwrecked arm of a tree nearby to use as a probe. He stepped nearer the bank, extended his left arm and gingerly prodded under the hole.

There was a rush of sand and soil and shells. He jumped back—fearing the snake was attacking him—and almost fell, thinking he saw its twisting form in the scatter of dark earth. There was no snake. But the hole had widened and was now like a ragged scar across the bank.

Beneath it, he was surprised to see what looked like the horizontal rim of a bicycle wheel jutting out of the headland. Then something below glittered at him from the loosened earth on the slide.

He flicked at the dirt about it, and the object slowly slithered down the slope to his feet. He picked it up, dropping his stick.

The voice was calling his name.

"Erik," it said. "Erik!"

He heard the voice. He looked at the filthy thing in his hand. It was like a shriveled banana, though much flatter. He turned it over. A bright eye gleamed at him from the dirt, and it was red.

His name was called—louder now. He knew it was his mother.

Filled with the fear of being discovered, he thought of hiding—of fleeing around the headland, or forcing himself in the hole. It was too late. She stood above him commandingly.

"Erik!" she said accusingly. "I have been calling for you. Why don't you answer? It is time—long past time—when we should go home."

His hands went into his pockets—in his left hand was the

66

thing. He tilted his head to look up at her, making a face. She seemed like a figurehead above him, with her coat and hair blown back, her expression stern. She seemed to him magnificent, divine.

He smiled up at her like an equal. There was no need to apologize. No harm or hurt had been done. Nor could words describe for the moment the importance he now felt.

Without a word he returned to the headland. She watched him, puzzled. He came to her still smiling, and royally held out his right hand for her to take.

"Let's go home," he said.

2

They came to Bamburgh Castle later than Ed had wished. Erik had not wanted to go. What he wanted to do instead was not quite clear—he mentioned going to the beach at one point—but he was definite about not wanting to go to Bamburgh. It was not in his power to be adamant about it, and he was overcome by his father. His only riposte was "You'll be sorry," and sullen silence after.

Runa's part was to prevent her champions coming to blows and give Erik to understand that his submission was only to her pleasure—*she* wanted to go—and not to Ed's will.

They eventually crossed the causeway just before three and reached the village of Bamburgh after driving around the coast. No one spoke, as Ed, once aroused, needed some time to cool down, and Runa herself was on edge on account of the reckless speed of his driving and the difficulties of trying to decipher the map.

But the mile-away view of the castle that was theirs when they swung over the ridge between Waren Mill and Bamburgh dissipated some of Ed's and Runa's gloom—though it deepened Erik's in the back of the car, and he clutched the thing in his pocket tighter, as if in fear of losing it.

The castle lined the whinsill crag like the superstructure of a battleship stranded on the coast. It was imposingly large and unexpected, to be wondered at and admired. From the village it towered up flushed with medieval pride, a place for jousts and banquets, a castle for King Arthur and his knights.

Ed slowed down the car beyond the triangular village green of sycamore trees. "Isn't it magnificent?" he said. "You would almost think it was real—and not a late-Victorian reconstruction."

"All of it?" said Runa.

"Apart from the keep, and the foundations, and bits and pieces of walls. It was restored about 1900."

"I think I like it," she said.

"You would—it's got central heating."

"How do you know?" she said.

"MacDougall," he answered, changing gear as the car went up the curving road to the East Gate of the castle.

He parked the car on the esplanade outside, facing the twin pink towers of the gatehouse, beyond which bastions and battlements rose from a mantle of climbing shrubs. On all other sides the ground fell away—to the village on their left, to a dark wood and a wide sea of dunes behind, and on their right to mile upon mile of deserted sand and the Farne Islands flat on the sea like a school of whales.

"Why don't you drive in?" Runa asked.

Ed got out of the car without replying and surveyed everything about him as if he owned it. He heard the cawing of crows, and the wind brought a ceaseless whisper from the legions of dune grass below.

Runa got out on her side of the car.

"Oh, look at the beach," she said. "It's beautiful—all that sand!"

"It's low tide," he said.

"We can't *drive* in," he remarked when she joined him. "We should *ride* in, on a great white charger, with you side-saddle behind me. There should be trumpets, flags and flowers.

"This might in fact have been Malory's Joyous Gard," he continued. "The castle of Sir Lancelot—where he brought Guinevere when he saved her from the stake. Tristram and Isolde also stayed here as his guests. Here he was besieged by Arthur before the final battle. And here, says legend, Lancelot is buried. In Joyous Gard. . . . Here."

"It could not be a more fitting place for him," said Runa.

"Come on—we're late," he urged her, and strode toward the gateway, expecting her to follow him.

Ed knew that in reality Bamburgh had been the "capital" of early England. The Angles had taken it from the British after the Battle of Mount Badon—when the imagined age of Arthur had come to an actual end.

He breathed deeply, running his hands through his hair, and gazed about, trying to re-create a picture of that time.

Fifty years or so after the Battle of Mount Badon, a king of the Angles called Eoppa had landed near here with sixty shiploads of men and made or claimed or inherited a king-dom called Bernicia. The capital of that country entered his-tory itself when a former British settlement on a crag above the sea, then known as Din Guaroy, was refortified and named by the Angles after one of their queens. Her name was Bebba. "Bebba's burg" or fortress became "Bamburgh" in time.

Ed stood outside the capital of old England. It pleased him to think of it like that, though the thought was unaca-demic. Yet his instinct told him that here in truth it had all begun.

Where was Runa? He turned, to find her coming toward him with a blank expression that denoted disagreeable news.

"He doesn't want to go into the castle," she said. "He won't get out of the car."

Ed glared at the flaxen head visible in the back of the car as various courses of action flashed through his mind.

"Jesus-Christ-Almighty-God!" he exploded. "Who the hell does he think he is? *He* doesn't want! He won't—!"

"*You* go into the castle," she said, touching his arm. "See the professor, and then we'll all meet for tea in the village. I shall stay with Erik."

Ed looked at her, to see if she really minded.

"Is that the solution?" he asked, glad to think he need not share the castle with Erik.

She nodded. "It will be best. And I shall be as happy on the beach."

"He doesn't deserve it." Ed glowered at the car.

"Go," she said.

He caressed her cheek and smiled.

"In an hour," he said. "Back here then."

"All right," she said. "One hour." She returned to the car.

With mounting expectation Ed entered the castle. As he passed through the East Gate, feeling strangely proud, he glanced about him as if the stones were people, keeping a humble silence as he passed. Nothing and no one disturbed his progress. Yet there was a welcome in the sound of his feet on the road. Rebuilt and refashioned as it was, the castle was still an ancient friendly place to him. It was not as if he had been there before. It was as if he had just returned after the absence of a night.

The road curved up to the right and under a soaring tower. Further on the view opened out as the road turned in and forked to left and right of a massive four-square keep. The left road entered the Inner Ward, where a lawn, the highest level area of the crag, was surrounded by curtain walls and many-tiered castle buildings. The other road wound down to ranges of plainer buildings and passed through the archway of a small tower on the seaward side of the castle.

From Professor MacDougall's description, Ed knew this must be the Neville Tower, where the professor was staying.

A path cut down the slope toward the tower. But nearby was a line of battlements equipped with cannon that overlooked the sea.

Ed jumped down into the gun walk and, resisting the wind, paraded along to a bastion. From its parapet, the panorama enclosing the blue-gray ocean swept a full half circle. To the northwest lay the flattened mass of Holy Island. He identified the castle and the priory ruins and even thought he could see a speck of white, the beacon on Emmanuel Head.

"Mr. Wardlaw! Mr. Wardlaw!" said a voice.

Ed started back and saw on a level with him, but across the East Ward, the pixie bearded face of the professor poking out of an upper window in the Neville Tower.

"In here!" he cried. "Come on over! Where *have* you been?"

Ed strode quickly down the path to the archway under the tower.

"Not contemplating suicide, were you?" the professor called from above. "It wouldn't work there—no height at all —not for someone as tall as you."

"Where's the door?" asked Ed.

"Ach! I was forgetting you were calling on *me*. Under there." He pointed and vanished.

In the windy tunnel of the archway Ed glanced over the uncut grass of the West Ward, which was crowned by a high round tower like a windmill and ended in the ruins of another gatehouse.

"There you are!" said the professor at the open door. "But where are the others?"

He ushered his guest inside, as Ed awkwardly apologized

71

for the absence of Runa and Erik, his voice sounding strange to him in the bare stone passage. They descended a flight of steps.

"To tell the truth," he said, "we'll have more peace without him. And I doubt if he'd have much interest in your proof of the Vikings at Bamburgh."

"Oh, that! Ah, yes. But I thought he was very interested —enthralled even—by my woeful account of the Viking raid.

"In here," he said, opening a door and standing aside.

The room they entered was octagonal, and a bright coal fire accentuated the likeness to a cave. Above an ornate ormolu clock on the mantelpiece was an oil painting of Holy Island priory under a stormy sky. Dark watercolors of costumed figures and stage sets hung on the green flock walls, which were dominated by a large brass-rubbing of a knight with a lance. Heavy bookcases, a mahogany desk, an old-fashioned TV set, an Edwardian standard lamp which was lit, statuettes and Chinese plates crowded around the chairs and tables before the fireside rug. The room had an air of unreality, as if it had been designed for a scene in a film, as a set for a college study.

At one end was a mullioned window facing north. Under it was a wide table awash with papers and books. The jagged black shape of an ancient typewriter surfaced out of the turmoil and was guarded by a black anglepoise lamp. On the window ledge stood a silver candlestick, spiked with a new red candle.

The silence of the interior was increased by the muffled movements of the wind outside.

"You have a magnificent view." Ed leaned on the table, the better to see the spreading scene he had glimpsed from the archway. The window framed exactly the long line of Lindisfarne.

"I rearranged the furniture for that purpose," said the professor. "So that as I worked, the island would be before me. Sit down. Sit down."

They sat in chintz-covered armchairs on either side of the blazing fire.

"You prefer a fire?" Ed asked. The professor was peering at him over a bridge of interlocked fingers.

"Oh, I have the central heating on as well. I'm not *paying* for it, you know. But I like the metaphor of a fire—and I like to have a wee bit of movement in the room. None of this is mine," he added. "Except the mess by the window."

He went on to talk about the castle, about the occupants of the nine other flats, whom he characterized in a swift series of sketches. He admitted himself highly impressed by the castle's owners.

"Who would not envy them?" he said. "Having a castle of this magnitude as their home? Lord Armstrong lives here when he's not in London. Do you know him? He and his wife live in the keep, though not at the moment. Their son, I should imagine, must be Erik's age."

"How did they win the castle?"

"The first Lord Armstrong bought it. It was he who had it rebuilt. He was a great engineer and inventor by profession. Any machine that moved in those days he had made —bridges, boats and trains, but guns above all. The company became Vickers-Armstrong in time. It appeals to my mentality that the castle was rebuilt on the weapons of war."

"The family name's appropriate," commented Ed. "Armstrong."

"So it is. Strong by arms. This is truly Armstrong Castle. But so is *your* name—appropriate."

"My name?"

"Wardlaw. You know what it means? Old English, of course, in its origins, from 'weard-hlæw,' which signifies, as you know, 'guardian-hill.' A very apt title for this place as a protector of those within it and of the kingdom. You are Ed of the Guardian Hill, of Bamburgh."

The windy buffeting of the window distracted Ed for an instant.

"Do you study names as well as words?" he asked.

"The origin of language, semantics, is naturally part of my study," said the professor making arches of his fingers. "And a part of that is the root meaning of names. Ah yes. It's all the fault of my aged mother. You see, she christened me Mervyn—because there was a certain actor with that name she was daft about in those days. Oh, the disgrace! Fancy giving a Scot a Welsh first name! Naturally this made me very aware of names from the start. It wasn't until I was comparatively more mature that I came to know that under the skin 'Mervyn MacDougall' was originally neither Welsh nor Scottish as such but ancient British—that is, Celtic. Etymologically, Mervyn comes from *Myrrdin*, which is the true form of Merlin—he who was King Arthur's wizard. It means Sea-Hill. And Dougall derives from the Celtic for Black Stranger. Sea-Hill-son-of-the-Black-Stranger is my name."

"I suppose all names have a meaning," Ed murmured. "Names of people, and places."

"Indeed they have. Go deep enough—go farthest back— and you will find the origins of not just words. The past is not all past. The past is in the present."

"The Black Strangers were in fact *Northmen*," Ed remarked. "At least that's what the Irish called them."

"You're absolutely right." The professor feigned applause. "The words are Celtic in origin. But I may well be not."

Ed relaxed. He glanced at the six-foot brass rubbing, black on white, hanging opposite the fire.

"Sir John d'Abernon," explained the professor.

"Yes, I know," returned Ed. "I was wondering why the Northmen were 'black,' when most of them, one supposes, were fair-haired."

"The color of evil," said the professor. "The Welsh chroniclers usually threw in 'black' to describe the invaders. Remember, they were pagan. The writers were Christian, and Christ of course is white. The emissaries of the devil are therefore black.

"In the sagas," he went on, poking the fire, "the spirits that haunt the grave mounds—the undead that walk about at night—they are described as being black, with black faces. Like a golliwog," he said, and chortled.

Ed thought of Erik's golliwog, which Runa's brother Arnulf had given to him.

"They're always very noisy," said the professor, banging a block of coal with the poker. "They thump about and beat on doors and on roofs. You have to fight them—kill them again—to get some peace."

A window blew open behind the professor and the papers on the table fluttered and came alive. Some flew up and fell on the carpet. The tall brass rubbing of the knight swayed against the wall, and a cloud of smoke billowed out of the chimney.

"Damnation!" said the professor and slammed the window shut. "The catch is loose. I really must get it wedged."

He darted about the floor snatching up sheets of paper. Then he opened the door to let out the smoke that had filled the room with an acrid smell of burning.

"This is the windiest place in Middle Earth," he said. "You wouldn't believe it. And always from the north. However, fortuitously it reminds me of the purpose of your visit. I'll sort out these pieces later. Come here. . . . Let me show you my secret."

As Ed rose from his chair, the professor closed the door.

"Prepare to be confounded!" he exclaimed. "Prepare to feast your eyes on what no man save myself has seen and understood for a thousand years. Behold!"

He whisked away a sheet of tissue. Side by side on the table were two pages of brown parchment, blocked in with unbroken lines of hieroglyphics.

An historian's joy in manuscripts flowered in Ed's mind. With a praticed eye he soon surmised that the antique letters, though stained and faded here and there, were Anglo-Saxon, penned on what must have been originally a single sheet of vellum before being torn in two. This was evident from the alignment of halves of stitching holes. He also saw that the edges of both pages were scorched and that the right-hand page had a horizontal tear low down on the left-hand side.

"Well?" The professor waited, tensed for a verdict, with a fixed grin on his face.

"Two pages. . . . Written on both sides?"

The professor jerked out a nod.

"Is it an original?—Forget that. Clearly it is."

Then Ed saw there were dates in Roman figures on the leaves—788 and 792.

He smiled at the professor. "An Anglo-Saxon chronicle," he said.

Professor MacDougall sighed. "Yes," he said. "So it is. But not like any you've ever read about or seen."

"I didn't think the British Museum or the Bodleian ever allowed their manuscripts out on parade."

"They don't. But this is unique. This one, for the moment, is mine."

"Yours?" Surely, Ed thought, it hadn't been stolen. Or wasn't it genuine after all?

The professor delicately turned over the page on the left. "Regard this page," he said. "How does it begin?"

Ed stooped to decipher the writing. A magnifying glass was nearby, but he scorned to use it. The letters were faint at the top of the page and the vellum was marked with creases. Yet the man who had made the characters had inked them in with care.

The first word must be *"æt"* he thought. The second was much longer. Even when he had deciphered it, he doubted its truth. For the chance of reading it there was so remote as to be unbelievable. His shoulder muscles prickled with shock. But his voice was toneless when he spoke.

"Æt Bebbanburge . . ." he said.

"At Bamburgh!" translated the professor. "Now you realize why I came here. The manuscript starts *'at Bamburgh'* and this indeed is where its meaning will be unearthed— where else?—despite the ravages of time and fire. You notice the latter? It was evidently saved from being burned by its position as the innermost leaf in a quire. Unhappily this page has also been badly torn, as you can see. Several words have been lost forever. But the tear affects the other side more importantly—when the Vikings are at Bamburgh. Oh, yes! They came *here* after the sack of Lindisfarne!"

The professor gently turned over the right-hand page.

"See! It says *'ond pa geswor he beot pæt he wolde—'* 'And then he swore a vow that he would—.' Then it tears. . . . The nature of the vow will never be known. When it continues—here—it deals with the tragic, heroic death of Sicga. Then it ends, burned away—at the start of a new sentence."

Ed looked and saw the last three words.

" *'Ond his sunu,'* " he read. " 'And his son. . . .' "

The horseman came silently on toward them, galloping out of the north over the sands and along the edge of the sea. The fortress was to their left, and the wind blew strongly against them, making them narrow their eyes and, as it seemed to Runa, bearing the horse and its rider with it, like a dead leaf bowling along to its grave.

They were poised by an old sand castle, much erased already by the wind. Erik stood with a foot in the moat before the tumbling gateway of two towers. He was watching the rider's approach with an eagerness fit for the coming of vital news. He was softly repeating something that was unintelligible to Runa, but matched the rhythm of the scudding hooves on the sand.

The horse was black. Together they saw that the rider about to sweep by them was a woman. Her flying dark hair redoubled the streaming mane. She looked at them as she passed, at Erik, and flew with the wind to the south along the shore.

Runa walked over the leveled banks of sand to the sea, whose terraced waves were rolling in on the beach again, soon to efface the tracks of the running horse. She pushed the windswept meshes of her hair off her face, recalling Erik's refusal to go any further under the shadow of the castle. She had not argued. She had felt too proud, and the nearness of the sea had awakened heartening thoughts of home.

The tracks of the horse made ugly slurs on the shore, which would have been unblemished but for them.

A shrill cry came from the land.

She turned to see Erik trampling on the sand castle, crushing it with his feet.

"*Sla! Sla!*" she heard him say. "*Sla! Sla! Sla!*"

She did not understand the cry. But the grim destruction of the castle harrowed her—as would an act of unrelenting revenge.

3

They stood before the manuscript like worshipers before the relics of a saint, gazing at it as if its sight were a promise of salvation. Sunshine coursed over the West Ward outside the mullioned window. It went unnoticed, though an added brightness in the room seemed to come from the manuscript on the table.

"I leave it here—just to look at it," said the professor. "I sit here imagining its history and the history it relates. Its mystery entrances me. And for the time being it is in my keeping. Temporarily, it is mine."

Ed was oddly affected by the professor's ardor, by the visionary light in his eyes. He looked like Merlin now, thought Ed—a wizard weaving a spell with his hands. All he needs is a pointed hat.

"How did you come by it?" Ed asked.

"Ah, yes," said the professor. "Indeed. Let me explain. Have you heard of Norris Aylmer? Of course you have. One of the great authorities on Scottish life and literature. Did you know he died last year? Drowned, poor man. A fishing accident while he was on holiday in Sutherland. So be it. He was at Edinburgh University like me. In his will Professor Aylmer left me part of the contents of his library. Most of his personal collection of manuscripts and rare books he bequeathed to the National Library of Scotland. A great bequest. Among the volumes that came to me was a sixteenth-century edition by Walter Chepman of Dunbar's poems. Well, the edition of his poems was falling to bits, the spine had split, the binding was exposed. And in the binding, acting as stuffing for the hard cover of the book, were two folded pieces of parchment. One was an inventory of a household. The other was *this*! Oh, it makes you grieve to think what other fragments of chronicles, sagas, poems, might be hidden in the bindings of ancient tomes in the British Museum. Entombed they are—till fate reveals their presence!"

He paused. The brightness went from the room as clouds passed over the sun.

"You believe in fate?" asked Ed. The professor smiled.

"I'm a foolish, fond old man," he said. "Is that what you're thinking? Remember, I'm no historian like you. And I'm only an academic in my *work*. Not here in my heart. I deal in fictions most of the time, not in facts. Fictions that are heavy in fate. . . . When we say something is 'weird' we mean it's uncanny, incomprehensible. Is there not *much* that passes understanding?—that is '*wyrd*'—which used to mean 'fate'? 'Wyrd is strongest,' said the poet. Have you never felt fated? I have. Yet your fate can never be fully known until the hour of your death—truly the 'weirdest' moment of your life. . . . But enough of this rabbiting. Let us sit down. Sit down."

They sat again in the armchairs by the fire.

Ed gathered that the professor, without informing anyone else as he should have done, had brought the manuscript to Bamburgh with the intention of working on it himself, of editing, translating, and preparing his find for publication before proclaiming its existence to the world. His actions and his motives were, he admitted, selfish and unethical— the appropriation of such a priceless fragment would not be approved of by the National Library or his colleagues. But the professor did not care. The discovery had been his. He would share it when it was time.

The manuscript, he revealed to Ed, could have been written about a century after the events it described, events between the years 787 and 794. If it had been written in 894 it would be one of the earliest of seven extant chronicles, though only a fragment. More important than this, the manuscript was evidently part of a lost northern chronicle —written at York or Ripon—which was known to have existed. It had details similar to the other chronicles covering the period, but had many additional details of great historical interest. But what excited the professor most was the fact that the manuscript gave the names of the Viking leader and his son who had plundered Lindisfarne.

"What were their names?" asked Ed.

"It's not complete," said Professor MacDougall obliquely, and was saved from further evasion by the chiming of the clock on the mantelpiece.

"My goodness gracious," he exclaimed. "It's four o'clock. Time for tea! But before we go, I would like you to meet my familiar. Just a minute."

Surely it can't be a black cat, thought Ed. That would be too much. He got to his feet and took advantage of the professor's absence by making a closer perusal of the manuscript.

The scorched and torn page that dealt with the raid on Lindisfarne drew his attention. Near the bottom of the page was an ill-defined date—794. Under the tear was a word which must be *"Sicga."* It was a name he thought he knew. Then he saw he was looking at letters that formed a word much like Lindisfarne. The word he deciphered was *"Lindisfarena"* followed by *"ee,"* which he did not understand. But two lines down a row of short words transfixed his eye and understanding. Slowly he read—*"ond lægde man hine on bate ond bærnde hine on sæ."* My God, he thought as he pieced the meaning together, it says "and he was laid in a boat and burned at sea."

Was it possible the chronicle actually mentioned a boat-burning, a Viking funeral? What a find the manuscript was! But who was Sicga?

His speculations were ended by the professor's return with a black tin box, which had a series of holes in the lid.

"I see," he said. "Having another peep, were you? Have a look at this instead."

He rested the box on some books. Ed could see it had a glass front. He thought for a panicky moment that it must contain a reptile—a snake—as the professor unhooked the lid and rummaged about inside.

"Come on now, sleepyhead," Professor MacDougall said.

A chirring noise came from the box. "Rise and shine," he continued. "I'd like you to meet a new friend of mine. Come along."

His hand emerged from the box, and on his palm was a querulous golden hamster. Its fur was ruffled, its eyes half shut. It sniffed about and sneezed.

Ed burst out laughing. The professor showed all his teeth in a smile.

"Mr. Wardlaw," he said. "I'd like you to meet a very good friend of mine. Mr. Wardlaw—Mr. Longbottom."

"He's got a hamster called Longbottom, and MacDougall's real name is Merlin. After midnight he changes into an owl."

Ed whispered the information to Runa as Erik and the professor got out of the car in the village. She had no time to express surprise, for the professor opened the car door for her, and soon they were all walking toward the Victoria Hotel.

The compact village was set in rising ground below the castle, which was obscured from them by the three-sided grove of wind-swayed sycamores in the village center. The ordered houses nearby were Victorian in appearance. Ed thought the hotel where they were to have tea was like an Edinburgh manse. "The proprietress is Scottish," Professor MacDougall remarked. Runa noticed that a lane beside the hotel was called Ingram Road. "Our landlady is Miss Ingram," she said. "Perhaps she comes from here."

"Her first name isn't Bebba, is it?" asked Ed.

"No, it's Maud," said Runa.

"Splendid old name," said the professor. "Means Mighty Battle-maid."

Erik giggled. He was carefully leaping from square to square on the pavement, avoiding the cracks. If he trod on one it would mean bad luck. But he didn't and safely entered the hotel, still clutching the thing in his pocket.

In the lounge he became momentarily fretful about losing his parka—which he had to take off. But he was allowed to leave it over the back of a deep settee on which he found himself with his mother.

Tea itself was more interesting to start with than the conversation about the county, the castle and the village. There were different sorts of sandwiches to taste and consider—scones as well—and much thought was required about the merits of the cakes. There were also other people in the lounge to be inspected, and pictures on the walls. He was quiet, as he wasn't supposed to talk when his mouth was full —which it was for the first ten minutes. He was also, after the shocks of the night, still in awe of his father.

"More tea?" asked Runa with a smile at the professor.

"Mm-yes. Thank you," he said, pausing in his praises of Northumberland to watch as she refilled his cup.

"What is this 'relic' you and Ed were talking about?"

"What? What relic?" The professor feigned stupidity.

"She means the manuscript," Ed explained peacefully, smiling at Runa. He thought she was looking especially enchanting—with the colors of her hair and eyes and cheeks brightened by the wind. He gazed at her admiringly, relishing each movement as she poured the tea and returned the cup to the professor.

"*Vaer så god*," she said.

"Thank you. Ah, yes. The manuscript."

"The greatest discovery in the field of Anglo-Saxon studies since Sutton Hoo," Ed proclaimed.

"I hope so," said the professor. "Forgive me if I am coy," he said to Runa. "But no one knows about the manuscript. Apart from Ed. You see, I have the primitive superstition of not saying a word about anything I am engaged in until it is quite finished. If I begin to blether about it, I feel that its worth will be diminished, or that it will turn to dust and ashes."

"Make up your mind, Erik," Runa said. "Which of the cakes do you want?"

"Have an eclair," said the professor and winked at him.

Erik smiled. He took hold of the eclair cautiously, as if it might bite, and began to attend to what the hairy-faced man was saying.

"Where was I? Ah, yes," said the professor. "But pride of possession and vanity overcome formless fears. You have to *boast* about your prize, so that its glory will be acknowledged—and so reflected on *you*. Well, my work is nearly completed. What harm is there, I thought, in showing the fragment to a friendly historian? And having shown it, I can't just *stop* there. All must be revealed. But not a word to anyone else. No one else must know."

"I swear," vowed Ed with a hand on his heart.

"So do I," said Runa.

"Do you swear?" Professor MacDougall asked Erik—he was licking his fingers.

"Yes," he said.

"Are you sure?"

"Cross my heart and hope to die," said Erik.

The professor then told Runa about the finding of the manuscript, its condition, the period it covered and its possible origins. He began to expand on the subject. His tea grew cold. Ed interposed some comments, while Runa made sure that everyone was fed. Erik became impatient. His appetite being largely satisfied, he now felt a need to have his presence acknowledged and to be entertained.

Thinking to acquire some favor and attention, he offered the professor a cake. "Will you tell me about the Vikings?" he said. "Please."

"Thank you," said the professor, taking a macaroon.

"Det var pent gjort," said Runa approvingly.

"What we really want to know is what is new in the fragment. Don't we?" Ed appealed to Runa, taking a boat-shaped cake that Erik had fancied.

"Oh, yes," she said. "If you are able to tell us. Some more tea—Ed? Erik?"

Ed gave her his cup. *"Ja, takk,"* he said.

"It starts at Bamburgh," he went on. "Literally. With those words. It ends with someone swearing a vow. And there is someone called Sicga, and a boat-burning. Isn't that right?"

"Yes, it is," said Professor MacDougall. "But no, no, no. Now is not the time. I'll tell you about the Vikings," he said to Erik.

Runa wanted to please the professor and avoid a clash between him and Ed. She also wanted to hear such a story as he had told them in the priory. Moreover, she felt that Erik, who had been so good at the tea table, deserved a reward.

"Yes, that would be very nice," she said. *"Bry deg ikke om det,* Ed. What would you like to hear about, Erik? It's your turn now."

"Ragnar," he said. "In the snake pit."

"He means the legendary Ragnar Hairy-Breeches," explained Ed.

"Do you know that there was a real Ragnar?" said the professor to Erik, who shook his head. "He was a Viking king."

Ed listened to the professor's tale more for errors of fact than for education or entertainment. Surprisingly, the professor appeared to know the period well, though he oversimplified events and gave them too much color.

"Go on," said Erik, when the story of Ragnar's adventures in France had been concluded.

"Should I? Shall I?" asked the professor.

"Why not?" said Runa, with a soothing glance at Ed.

"Well, yes. There's not much more. . . ."

"Go on," said Erik.

"Some years later," continued Professor MacDougall, "Ragnar went to Northumbria. Why, we do not know. He came here with sixty men to see the king, Aella. Unfortunately Aella was not a gentleman. He had just been made king—the proper one, Osbert, having been turfed out—and was no doubt full of swagger and mead. Most likely there was nothing on telly worth watching."

"They *didn't* have telly!" cried Erik.

"Quite right. They had only the court poet and he only knew epics like *Beowulf*—nothing jolly or new. So for a bit of amusement Aella had poor old Ragnar thrown into a pit of poisonous snakes! But Ragnar wouldn't play ball. He jumped on the snakes and strangled a few, and all he said before he died—with no yells or curses at all—was, 'The piglings would grunt if they knew of the plight of the boar!' Then he died. Everyone loved puns and riddles then, and they spent a year trying to work that one out. When they found out what it *did* mean they didn't like it one bit. The piglings were Ragnar's sons. There were three of them, and they came to avenge their father. They landed with a great army in England and came thundering up to Northumbria and captured the city of York. Aella joined forces with Osbert and besieged them in the city. There was a most tremendous battle all over the town and terrible slaughter. In the end the Vikings won, and both of the kings were killed. So Ragnar was avenged."

"*How* were they killed?" asked Erik.

"They were cut to pieces while they were still alive."

"How horrid!" said Runa. "*Akk!*"

"*Sla! Sla! Sla!*" exclaimed Erik.

Runa and Professor MacDougall looked at him but said nothing.

Ed spoke as if to himself. "That was in 867—the end of the kingdom of Deira, and the beginning of the Danish occupation. In the end, in 1066, the fate of England and of Europe was decided by three men of Viking blood—Harold of England, Harald of Norway, and William of Normandy. The Norman won."

"It was Ragnar's sons who killed your namesake, Edmund," mused the professor.

"What?" said Erik. "What did they do?"

"They killed the king of East Anglia, who had the same name as your father."

"How?" demanded Erik.

"They shot him with arrows."

Professor MacDougall looked at the manuscript on the table. He felt he had somehow erred—but in what he did not know. From his tower window he saw the red-gold edge of Holy Island that flared like a spear in the light from the dying sun. They would be crossing the causeway now, he thought. Behind him the fire glowed, giving no flames, and there was silence in the room, for the wind was also dying with the sun.

Where had he gone amiss? he wondered. What had he done that was wrong?

He had wanted to please. Perhaps he had overdone it. He had chattered as much as he had so that they would then have no time to observe him, or think him boring. Nonetheless they had each become quiet at some time or another—the boy to start with, then Ed during tea, then the wife when they walked around Bamburgh parish church after tea.

Before going Ed had invited him to dinner on Sunday—not lunch, as the tides were wrong for that.

Ed had said as they shook hands, "Bring Mr. Longbottom with you."

Thus reminded, Professor MacDougall took the hamster out of its box, in which it had guarded the manuscript while he was out. Mr. Longbottom was his watchdog as well as companion and confidant.

"We're going to dinner on Sunday," he said.

The hamster trembled and dithered about as he slid it from hand to hand.

"Which reminds me, you've not had your tea."

He carried his flatmate up to the kitchen and gave him a biscuit to store in his cheeks. The professor watched this performance with pleasure, then returned Mr. Longbottom to his box to eat his snack—he would never eat anywhere else.

The sun had set. The northern sky was already dark with clouds. Professor MacDougall rearranged his papers for an evening's work. He liked to have the hamster by him in its box as he worked. In fact the box was only moved from the table when there were visitors in the room, which was rare. Now it took up its usual position.

He looked at the candle—he would light it later. Its light in the window would answer the pinpoints of light on the island. He had meant to ask Ed if it could be seen from the island—a light in the tower—but he had forgotten.

The hamster was thoughtfully gnawing the biscuit. What would he have himself for supper? Some crab, he thought— cold, with a dressing of cream, gherkins, capers and the usual. Also some tinned asparagus with the lettuce, and a consommé to start with. The thought of the wine, *pouilly blanc fumé*, and the fruit and brandy to follow, made him beam in the darkening room.

Below him, under its covering of tissue, the manuscript lay like a face under water.

An idea came to him—he would take them a copy, a carbon copy of his translation, which he should finish by Sunday. There was not much left to do. He uncovered the parchment, removing the books that weighted the tissue's sides. Using the magnifying glass in place of his glasses to see where his labors had reached, he peered at the script. He switched on the lamp to see better.

The ancient characters loomed in the lens—*"micel wæl geslagen"*—"there was great slaughter." Three of the letters swelled under his eye. That's odd, he thought. He was looking at *"sla."* The boy Erik had said that very word, as if he had known what it meant. But how could he know the imperative of an Old Norse verb—which meant—*"kill"*?

4

Erik was cleaning the find that had come to him that morning. He had locked himself in the bathroom. His parents were out of the way—his father in the sitting room, and his mother in the kitchen, where she was preparing their evening meal. He had told her where he was going, though not what he meant to do, and then in order to deceive her had ostentatiously thumped the kitchen table with a rolled-up comic in his hand. This provoked the expected response— "Now don't stay in there reading all the night." Supper, she said, would be ready in half an hour.

At that point an awful thing happened. The object, which he had lodged like a dagger in the waistband of his track suit trousers, slid inside them and down his leg. It was only prevented from falling onto the floor by the elastic around his ankle. That was also loose. Pink with alarm, he managed to swivel on one foot and ease himself out of the kitchen like a soldier with a wooden leg.

Runa smiled after him, wondering what game he was playing.

Safely locked in the bathroom, he perched on the edge of the bath, giggling to himself, while he retrieved the awkward object from his trouser leg.

"Cripes," he said. "That was close."

Most of the dirt on his find had now rubbed off. It lay heavily in his hand. Clearly it was made of some metal. Bits of it gleamed at him. One side seemed to be patterned—the other was rougher. The red eye on the side with lines on it flashed encouragement. Action was called for.

Washing it in the basin made little improvement. It needed to be scrubbed. He tried scratching it with his nails without much effect. The teeth of a comb were far too big. He needed a brush.

Inspired with a feeling of devilry, he seized his father's toothbrush and set to work.

Runa was making a kedgeree with an abstraction that was uncharacteristic of her. Images of the beach below Bamburgh Castle, of the horsewoman coming toward her as if in slow motion, swam through her mind. The sand castle was destroyed again to shrill outlandish cries.

Her eyes ached. She stood back from the gas fire for a moment, trying to concentrate on her cooking.

She was utilizing the leftover haddock from their lunch. Fish on Fridays was a culinary habit she had acquired in England—it narrowed the choice of menus—and as they were now by the sea, she had felt more sure that the fish would be fresh.

It occurred to her that lobster might make a good meal for the professor when he visited them on Sunday. She thought she would see if there was any practicable recipe in her cookbook.

The rice was boiling, the eggs had boiled. She was stirring the flakes of haddock into the melted butter when she realized that there was no curry powder in the cottage. She sighed and scolded herself for being so stupid. Instead she would have to use red and black peppers. It would do—but it would not be right.

From the bathroom came the sound of the toilet being flushed. Erik reappeared in the kitchen door without his comic.

"Can I have a pin?" he asked.

"*Hva sa du?*" she said. "What have you done?"

"I'm . . ." He stopped, ostensibly watching her actions. "I need it for my painting," he said. "To pin my painting."

"Supper is almost ready," she said. "Oh, all right."

After checking that everything on the stove was safe, she dashed into the bedroom, found a pin in her workbasket and gave it to Erik.

"Just put it in the paper," she said. "Nowhere else. And not in your mouth." He took the pin without looking at her.

"Thank you," he said as he walked away. His bedroom door closed behind him.

Left to herself Runa stopped working and gazed about her in the harsh white light at the kitchen cupboards, containers and utensils as if she were a prisoner doing an inventory of her cell. She liked cooking, but to do so three times a day seemed for a desolate moment to be no part of her duty, nor any expression of her love. What would she give to be free as a child—to ride with the wind!

She shook the mane of her hair, and it fell back dully onto her shoulders. Conscientiously she returned to her task.

Ed removed the unlit pipe from his mouth, tapped it on the ashtray though it contained no tobacco, and unconsciously played with it as his thoughts meandered away from his papers and notes. He gazed at the inverted half moon of the oil lamp that Runa had set on the table. She had found the lamp in the kitchen when they returned from Bamburgh and had put it on the table in the window, as an ornament, and a cheerful sight when lit to people passing by. Ed recalled the man who had winked at them—when? Was it yesterday? Time had flown.

He stared at the lamp. Abstractedly he raised and lowered the wick, so that the light grew brighter or dimmed and cast a corresponding change on his face. The typescript of his thesis lay unattended before him.

He had been—until that night—determined to get his Ph.D. He had always considered it necessary for the advancement of his career. It had not been enough to get a B.A. (Second class) and then after seven years to buy his M.A. A Doctorate, the letters Ph.D. after his name, would give him the true status of an academic and the recognition of others. He had worked hard for this, as study and erudite scholarship had not come naturally to him at school. But the

History Master, the Headmaster of the Lincoln School, and his Uncle Sid had thought the advancement of Farmer Wardlaw's boy worth promoting, and when a higher social order and standing were opened to him by his capacity for work, his vanity had not allowed people's expectations of him to be unfulfilled. His ebullience, his self-possession and air of dependability, combined with his athletic achievements and heroic appearance, had taken him to the top of the school. On the way his industry acquired for him the qualifications for university entrance, and the citadels of learning, Oxford and Cambridge, stood ready to be stormed.

Cambridge turned him down—his G.C.E. results were not exceptional, and the papers he wrote for his entrance examination were neither astute nor original. The peasant within him had been daunted by the impossibility of the attempt. But when he tried at Oxford, he was by that time Captain of School—more engrossed in the present and less concerned about his future. It was a great moment for him when he learned he had been accepted. Many years later he was told by his affable tutor that although his scholastic record had been good, and his entrance papers commendable, it had been his apparent sterling character and cricketing ability—he had played for Lincolnshire—that decided the Board.

Ed grimaced to himself. He was not sure, having been to Oxford, that he approved of some of its teachers or teaching. It had nonetheless taught him much beyond his studies —introduced him to people, ways of life and manners and thought, outside anything he had known before. The presumption of his presence there at times amazed him—which made him the more determined to be accepted, to master this learned world, to teach where he had been taught.

He had not intended to marry so soon. Erik had been a mistake. Yet marriage seemed part of his new maturity. A wedding had also a formal grace, a pageantry, that appealed to him. But much as he cherished and loved his wife, he never fully appreciated her absolute love for him until later. In his three postgraduate years at Oxford, while he labored for more academic honors, there were occasional rows, clashes of will, mostly arising from domestic demands—mostly caused, as it seemed to him, by the baby. He had hated Erik for the pain the birth had caused her, for the promise of life which his birth had destroyed in her womb. Each estrangement he blamed on the child, and in particular his failed first attempt at a Ph.D.

"If it had not been for Erik" was a phrase that had found a recurring place in his thoughts and words. It came to him as he switched his gaze from the lamp to the typescript below.

But Erik would not prevent him from getting his Ph.D. this time. He had worked on his thesis all that summer while Runa and Erik were in Norway. He had typed it out just before they all came north, and not much seemed wrong with it now. Was it really as uninteresting as he found it that evening?

Whether it was or it wasn't, he suddenly didn't care. It was as if he felt he was wasting his time.

The night retreated before the advancing headlights of the car, showing the sand-strewn road being chewed up and the pallid shore gliding by them. To their left the squidlike stain of the sea encroached on the road. The tide had not yet reached its highest mark that day. No other cars went past them.

"There should be a road on the right."

"I am looking," said Runa.

"It's marked on the map. It goes to a place called Snook House." Ed reduced the speed of the car.

"I never saw any road here in the day."

"It's there. But it's probably only a track."

They drove on.

"Is that it?" said Runa. A break in the shoreline of sand hills, which fell back from the road at that point, seemed to offer an entry.

Ed swung the car off the road so that the headlights could light up the scene. He stopped the car with the engine running on a wide bay of stones and sand. There was no other road. "It's deceiving, isn't it?" he said.

"Do you know I saw a seal this morning?" she announced, having just remembered to tell him. "It was when Erik and I were out on the other side of the island."

"A seal?"

She nodded. "It was floating about very near, and diving down, and looking at me. It was so strange to see it."

"There are quite a few on the Farne Islands." Ed revved the car. "Gray seals. They're protected." He put it into gear. "So should you be. You've got so many admirers. All coming to have a look. Dirty old men are bad enough. But dirty old seals!"

He let the clutch out—the wheels spun and the car stayed where it was.

"Blast it!" he said.

The engine revved seven more times before Ed angrily conceded that the car was stuck in the sand. They got out to find that both rear wheels had sunk in a depression misleadingly leveled with drifting sand. The car would not move without Runa in it nor when she tried to push it from behind. He tried reversing while she pushed from the front. They tried rocking it. Ed went red in the face trying to lift

95

it. When he had calmed, they began tearing dune grass up by the roots to stuff in front of the wheels. It was all no use. His weight in the car defeated what pushing she could do. He switched off the engine.

Ed stood with his hands on his hips, his hair and back prickly with sweat. Runa's shoulders ached—her skirt was covered with sand, and her hands were sore with rending the tough grass. She unbuttoned her coat.

"It's no use," he said coming over to her. "We'll have to get help."

"Why don't we leave the car here, and walk?" said Runa, with her back to him and the bright swath of the headlights.

"No, we'll wait," he said. "Wait a minute!" he added, his voice hardening. "What's the time?"

He found his booklet of tide tables in the car.

"Hell!" he said. "It's high tide *now*! The causeway's impassable for over two hours. No one will come this way."

"But, Ed, that will be after twelve o'clock! I told Miss Ingram we would be back at eleven."

"All right!" he said. "We will."

As she waited for his irritation to cool, for some decisive action, the utter silence of the night swelled in the blackness beyond the headlights, making her self-conscious of any sound or move she made.

Ed swore and kicked a stone across the road and into the liquid darkness. There was a plop and silence again.

"It's not going to stop us. We'll go there all the same."

He plunged back into the car without hearing her question—"Do we have time?"—and switched off the headlights.

The enveloping darkness was like a blow. Runa closed her eyes. She heard him lock the car doors and test the handles. When she opened her eyes she was still blind. Frightened to move, she called his name.

"Ed?"

"It's all right," his voice said. "I was seeing if we could get by without using the torch. There should be a moon. But the sky's overcast. No stars."

Light from the torch made an island at her feet. In its reflected glow Ed smiled at her.

"Come on," he said. "The north shore can't be far from here. On the other side of these dunes."

"But do we have time?"

"It'll take us as long walking back by the north side as by the road. Come on."

He gave her a hand up the bank, then, preceded by the roaming light, he led her through the maze of hillocks, defiles and deep grass. The night closed in about them, isolating them on their trek, which took them away from the known road and the car. Runa wanted to hold Ed's other hand, but could not, as she needed both hands to balance herself, to keep herself from falling into the darkness beside her. Ed strode on stealthily, his instincts at work to find the easiest route, his senses straining to catch imagined dangers in the night. The only sounds were the variable rustle of their passage and their fitful breathing.

"There's the beach," whispered Ed, flashing the torch before him.

They tumbled down onto the level sands. Ed walked on in advance of her to the edge of the sea. He stood there shining the torch out over the gray waters until its beam was lost in the night.

"You can't see far," she heard him say. Then he disappeared.

He had switched out the light. She was blind again.

She waited, unaware if she was blinking or not until the image of torchlight faded.

"That's Berwick," said his voice.

Far away to her left a row of planetlike dots made a line for her horizon. Nothing else was definable, though the faintest luminosity hovered over the land. She had no being herself and was filled with dread at the formless, threatening beach. An ancient terror of darkness flowed into her mind, to be given shape by a blackness moving toward her.

It could only be Ed. But seeing him again when the light went on made her smile with relief.

"I didn't know if it was you," she said.

"Perhaps it isn't. Out there," he said, "I may have been taken over by an alien."

"Oh, really," she said reproachfully.

"Actually—no, *really*—I thought I heard something in the water."

"Don't say things like that. It makes me nervous."

"Ah, poor Runa," he said consolingly. "Were you lost and lonely then?"

"Oh, *you!*" she said, backing away from him as his hands reached out for her, and trying not to laugh.

"Come here," he said.

"No."

"Come here," he repeated patiently.

"No."

She had reached the dunes—their ramparts were behind her—and faced him, ready to resist an assault. But he stopped a short distance away and flashed the torch in her face. It transfixed her like a butterfly on a pin. She stared back at him through the light, feeling naked as the languorous beam left her face to dwell on her breasts and body.

He moved slowly toward her, seeing the beam contract and brighten on her, until its lunar circle below her stomach was eclipsed by the head of the torch.

Before it touched her, he extinguished the torch and let it fall. His arms wrapped around her inside her coat, pulling her body against him, so that all his length was pressed upon her. With a shift of his hands he lifted her, sank on one knee, and lowered her to the ground.

The thought of her crumpled coat and the sand in her hair was forced from her by the weight of his body, by his mouth on hers and his arms enfolding her head. Automatically her arms tightened about his sweatered back, to mount his shoulder blades and clasp his neck. She shut her eyes.

Raising himself, he roughly rubbed the flat of his hand over her breasts, then down to her skirt. He began to undo it.

"Not now," she whispered, and opened her eyes.

Again she was blind, but alive to the menacing darkness of the beach. Her hearing caught a sigh from the sea and a shivering slither of sand in the dunes. She thought of snakes, of someone watching—though who could see when she saw so little herself? Yet she was not as alarmed as she might have been. She felt displaced, detached from what was happening, though a ghost of absurdity tickled her mind at the thought of her boots with their soles bared to the sea.

"No," she whispered, as her flesh was smoothed and fingered, and caressed by the cold night air.

Her hands fell weakly back on the sand, with her chill palms upward. She felt bound with invisible fetters, incapable of resistance, of feeling, of protest, though people out of the sea were watching, and seemed to be wherever her eyes saw unseeing into the night.

A violence was being done to her, and no one could prevent it. But cold and hard were the long-dead eyes of the watchers on the shore, as cold and hard as the earth below her, in which she was being forced.

She closed her eyes and her mind to his unrelenting assault until she was overwhelmed, and abandoned.

Surfacing into consciousness, she heard quite clearly from far away a call like a trumpet call. Two notes in an unfulfilled sad cadence died away.

In disbelief she shook her head, becoming aware of where she was, of his heavily beating heart upon her. Protectively she put her arms around him and listened.

"Hallo," he whispered. "It's me. What happened to you?"

"Did you hear . . . ?"

"What?"

"I heard. . . . Oh . . . nothing."

In his bedroom Erik knelt in his pajamas before his black tin box. Its lid was open—the padlock on the carpet—and all his treasures reposed in order within, lit from above by the bedside lamp.

He heard faint voices from the television set in the sitting room—where Miss Ingram was hunched by the fire, he imagined, playing with a toad and drinking gin.

In his box among the stones, tin soldiers, bits of wood, marbles, coins, and the frog's skull were the small yellow orbs of the snail shells collected that morning. His golliwog, flat on its back on the bed, had been banned from the display. In its place, on his special tablecloth, was the thing he had found in the sand.

He would return to the headland in the morning—whatever they said—to unearth and redeem what had been buried there. It was his. He was only afraid that someone would claim it before him. That was unthinkable, therefore impossible. Yet he fretted to uncover the rest, which, if it looked like his first find, was a treasure out of this world.

His rapture at the object he gazed on was so unbearable he could hardly keep from singing.

It was made of gold—it had to be gold. With brush and pin he had scraped the dirt and blackened skin off every surface and out of each cranny, until it shone in all its former glory. The pattern, on one side only, was clearly defined, though what it defined had been for a long time a puzzle. But at last he decided. The thing was a beast—with a ruby-red jewel as its eye. Its mouth was agape with triangular teeth, and its tail, curving in under it, was forked and finny. Its back was scored with shapes like flames, which might be wings.

On his tablecloth, snug in his box, lay an ancient, golden dragon.

Saturday

1

This time Erik was better equipped—he carried a bucket
and spade. He skipped along a track beside the sea, rejoic-
ing in the summery sunshine and in the exciting fact that
he was returning to where he had found his dragon. Off the
track that once had joined the quarries on the north side of
the island to the lime kilns by the castle white-faced sheep
paused in their chewing to eye his progress with blank
alarm. He scorned them, refraining from shouting at them
or chasing them—as he might have done on another day.
Today he was a collector of gold, a treasure seeker, and
single-minded about his quest. But it was no time for singing—and when he thought about it, no time for skipping. So
he stopped and plodded on purposefully along the trail, eyeing the seashore to his right and the view ahead with the
keen gaze of an explorer in Antarctica or Africa. The view
to his left was impeded by a stone wall that hedged the fields
of the interior.

His squaw or captive ambled behind him. But she really had no place in his adventure and was not to know about it, though he was still bothered as to how he could avoid her when they got there.

He had done his best to provide her with a diversion, after much concentrated frowning and thumping of his golly. The idea that came to him was to persuade her to do some drawing—she had sometimes done some sketching when they had been together in Norway. So when his father had set off after breakfast to get help to bring back the car—which had made him laugh so much at breakfast when he heard of it being stuck in the sand that he couldn't look at his father without giggling and had to leave the room—he and his mother had gone for a walk.

She carried the sketchbook in a string bag, along with Erik's box of crayons, some apples, and tissues, which she usually took with her in case Erik got dirty. He was going much faster than usual, with no diversions or questions, and the pace had made her quite hot—despite the fact that she had dressed in her lightest trousers and wore no coat. But she would not be hurried, made indolent by the glorious morning, and wanting to relax after the chills and alarms and exertions of the night before and Ed's moroseness at breakfast.

They had been very late returning to the cottage—it had been midnight. Miss Ingram was still ensconced by the fire watching television—or rather, the set was still on, and Miss Ingram was "thinking things over," as she said, and doing some knitting. "I like the sound for company, *and* the pictures," she said. "But I don't always see what's there, nor hear it. You dream when you're my age."

Runa was so tired that, after looking in on Erik, who was strangely without his golliwog, and going to bed herself, she fell asleep before Ed got in beside her, and in the morning the night's events seemed as unreal as a dream.

Her memory of the night was aroused by a pond like a water hole lying to their left as she and Erik walked north along the Wagon Way. The pond was a dreary shallow of water surounded by mud, by marshy grasses, and the thin white arms of petrified trees which had clearly been dead for some time. It should be the scene for some haunting, she thought, and quickened her pace after Erik, who was now some distance ahead.

He waited impatiently for her at a fence. Once through it, they approached the wilderness of dunes that guarded the north shore. There was the path, by which they had returned from the headland the morning before.

Was it only the morning before? thought Runa. It seemed so long since they had been there—since they had come to the island. Yet this was only Saturday morning. Time was slowing down or stretching itself to include much more. Or was the island, she wondered, itself enchanted?

The snow-white apex of the beacon beckoned in front of them. The sight of it gladdened her. She walked on faster, feeling increasingly lighthearted, almost childish.

All at once she was running through the dunes, and so was Erik, and they raced to the beacon together.

"I won," he said.

"You won," she replied.

He thought she was looking very dishy—like strawberries and cream—as she smiled down at him, leaning on the southern sunny side of the pyramid. But pretty or not she had to be got rid of. It was awful being so near the dragon's lair without being able to visit it.

"Come on," he said with resolution. "You don't want to draw here, do you? Let's go over there."

He set off toward the bay by which they had approached the headland yesterday morning. When they came in sight of it, near where Runa had watched the seal, he halted.

"That's a good view," he said.

"Do you think so?" She saw no sign of the seal.

"Don't you?"

"Well," she said. "There's not much life in it."

"There are some *birds*. And you can always *invent* things to put in it."

His anxiety was too strong to be masked. Why he was so concerned that she should make a drawing of the beach was a mystery to her. But she wanted to please him, and the chance of seeing the seal again was reason enough for staying there.

"All right," she said, searching for the place on the bank where she had sat before. "But what will you do?"

He was so pleased, he felt a wild urge to tell her everything, to share his secret, and when they got home to show her the treasure that lay in his padlocked box. He bit his lip in the fight to compose himself. He knew he could say nothing until he possessed all that the snake house held.

"Just digging," he blurted, and hung his head in self-accusation in case he had said too much.

"Where?"

He indicated the area of the pyramid without looking at her.

"Go on then," she said. "You know where I am."

He gave her a ravishing smile and scampered away.

Runa surveyed the bay, where the tide was full in under the dunes, and wondered what she would draw.

The sea was alarmingly near the jumble of flotsam that fringed the headland. From the pyramid it looked as if the still waters might have washed away the sand slide and be right under the bluff. But when Erik rediscovered his steps down onto the stones, he saw that the shallow sea was lapping the shore some four yards away from the slide, which itself was as high above the sea. Nothing had changed.

He stood once more in front of the sinister gash in the face of the bank. Wary of the snake—though he did not expect to see it again—he poked his spade inside the hole. It went in as far as his hand without meeting any obstruction. When he pushed it along to his left, it soon hit something hard, like a stone. When he prodded about in the other direction, the object his spade encountered made quite a different sound, such as a spoon might make on a kettle.

Clearly there was more than the dragon and the bit like a bicycle rim to be discovered.

Erik made a face at his red plastic bucket. It was sure to prove too small for whatever the sand concealed.

The sun was hot upon him. He sensed he was about to do wrong, and knew his mother would not like it. Perhaps he should just go away. What if he gave her the dragon and left the rest? No, he could not give her the dragon. That belonged to him. He pictured it, and its glorious golden image lay again on the sand, provoking in him a lust to find the hoard of which it must be a piece.

He probed the fallen sand with the metal head of his spade. Something might have been buried *under* the fall. He would have to sift through it all to make sure nothing escaped. Not only that, he would have to search every spadeful of sand he dug from the bank—that is, if he was going to do the job properly. What a task it promised to be! *Could* he do it? *Should* he do it?

His lack of years and size and wisdom oppressed him. He stood in a pink flush of uncertainty, overcome with impossibilities and the heat of the sun.

A soft splash from the sea shocked him out of his trance. He turned his head to see what had made the splash. But the waters were like oil silk, like the limpid calm of a lake, unmarked but for wide-apart lines of little unbroken waves. As he looked, a fleeting vision of the strange long boat with the striped sail swam on the clear blue sea. It was a fine and cheering sight. Then it vanished.

When he faced his task again he felt braver and more capable. He knew he was not alone—that behind him on the empty sea was the high-prowed boat, and in it were silent sorrowing men with their eyes on the shore.

Runa looked up from her drawing with a sudden awareness that had nothing to do with her previous concentration on the scene. She felt the warmth of the sun like a hand on the side of her head. Putting down the sketchbook and crayons, she ran both her hands through her hair, lifting it off her neck and then spreading its load about her. As she did so, she saw that a haze was misting the further reaches of the bay, making impressionistic what had already been ill-defined. Yet that change was not all that had spoiled her absorption. She looked to her right, out to sea, with a faint alarm that was an echo of the night. Nothing was different that she could see. Nothing was out of place.

She returned to her drawing. How dead it looked, like a beach at the end of the world! What it needed was something living, a figure to give it meaning. She would have to imagine one, for the shore was quite deserted. The birds had flown away. Choosing a crayon, Runa began to outline a man on the beach.

Erik unearthed an arrowhead. Corroded as it was, there was no mistaking its shape. The shaft was missing, but the socket in which it would have fitted, once cleared of sand, readily accommodated a twig he snapped from a dead branch nearby.

He twisted the dull red arrowhead in the sun, wondering if he could make a bow for it, and decided he first must provide it with a workable shaft.

This discovery was not as exciting as it might have been, as his painstaking sifting through the fallen sand had previously produced several flattish objects like narrow beads, which despite their surface filth were plainly made of gold. He had only to scratch them to see that. Moreover, each of them—they were all the same—was embellished with a red jewel. The arrowhead was just as plainly made of rusty iron, and though a weapon of war, had commonplace associations with cowboys and Indians and was in a very bad condition. One of its flanges had already broken off in his hands.

He persevered, and when he removed a great lump of turf, it revealed a nest of four more arrowheads underneath. They looked so evil, like vipers' tongues, that he hesitated to pick them up in case they might sting him. But soon they had joined the other arrow and the thin flat beads, of which there were five, in his plastic bucket.

Nothing else came to light, though he cleared away all the debris.

At last it was time to remove the projecting arc of metal from the bluff and explore the hole from which the dragon had fallen.

Before he did so, he needed to stretch himself—also to check that he was still safe from interruption. He wiped his hands on his trousers, rubbed his eyes with his knuckles, and parked his bucket and spade against the bluff. With a quick greedy glance at his new possessions, he scrambled up onto the headland.

His wider horizons confused him. For a few seconds everything was inexact and out of focus. Then the scenery readjusted itself into remembered expanses—the sea was empty of any boat—and he was able to pick out some distance away his mother's immobile head.

He ran along a path toward her—then crept up behind her, bent on giving her a fright.

"Oh," she cried with a jump when he covered her eyes with his hands. The sketchbook fell on the grass. Her head leaned back against his stomach. He felt very strong and strange.

"Who's that?" she said in a playful voice.

He had to answer, but delayed while he struggled within himself to disguise his childish treble.

"I know who it is," she went on. "It must be Erik!"

He took a deep breath, lowered his chin, pretended he was a big grown man—a warrior, a king.

"Erik," said the woman, as the hands pressed hard on her eyes. "Is that you?"

He opened his mouth.

"Nay," said a man with a deep hoarse voice.

Erik and Runa both froze with surprise. How had he managed to do it? She loosened his grip and turned to look up at him.

"It *is* you!" She began to laugh. "I thought it was someone else."

"Of course it was me." He giggled. "I bet it scared you though."

"Oh, it did. But where have you been? Have you had enough?"

"I came to see how *you* were. Have you finished?"

"Very nearly. Look what I have drawn."

She passed the sketchbook up to him, for he was still standing beside her, on her left.

The drawing was far too wishy-washy for his liking—all

pale and fuzzy—though he allowed a certain resemblance to the bay. What fixed his attention was the dark figure of a man on the edge of the pale blue tide.

Erik looked at the real bay. No one was there.

"Why did you—? Who is *he*?"

The man in the drawing was leaning on a stick, so it seemed, with his back to them, and was wearing a cape.

Runa retrieved the sketchbook. "I don't know," she said. "I thought it would have more—significance, if someone was there."

She had made him much too dark, she thought—out of keeping with the landscape.

At that moment, unconsciously, she glanced to her right. Out of the sea without a sound rose the disconnected head of a seal—*her* seal.

"Oh, look," she whispered, delighted. "Look. He's come to see us again."

Before they returned to the village Erik had time to conceal the hole in the bank with castaway branches of trees and spars, and wedge them in place with stones. The objects in his bucket he hid from view with a piece of seaweed.

"What do you want with that?" asked his mother. "You can't bring it into the cottage."

Under the seaweed were his haul of arrowheads—he now had nine—the fingerlike beads of which there were twelve, four small half orbs, and *another* dragon.

The weight of the bucket seemed little in his haste to get home, though he regretted having had to leave behind several pieces of rusty metal and the whole of the bicycle rim, which had snapped into three bits when he dragged it out. He was perplexed by the scrap-iron objects—especially by the broken circle, which if it really was a bicycle wheel should have had some spokes. The tire, he realized, would have perished long ago. It was clear to him that the treasure —he was quite positive now he had found a treasure trove— had been buried years before. He was only disappointed he had found no bones, nor a treasure chest. There should have been a skeleton guarding the gold, and a terrible curse to go with it.

His mind ablaze with imaginings, with eagerness to clean and examine the spoils of the morning and return to dig out the rest, he walked lopsidedly after his mother, the sun in his eyes.

Arrows! he thought. Arrows and dragons and things!

They reached a rise in the dunes. A mile before them was the sudden dark mound of the castle, stark against the noon-day sky.

Erik paused for breath, while he exchanged the loaded bucket with the spade—from his left hand to his right. That done, he turned for a farewell glance at the headland.

The pyramid was brilliant white in the sun.

He saw a man standing near it, on top of his treasure. The man, outlined against the sky, was motionless and in shadow—which was odd as the sun was full upon him. He seemed to have a stick in his hand, like the man in the drawing, and to be wearing a cloak. But the stick was raised in the air, in salutation or blessing.

Erik felt no dismay—no danger threatened. He was glad to see the treasure had a guardian. It pleased him also to think that his mother had seen the man, though she had pretended otherwise. He suspected she was hiding something from him, that she also had a secret. They were both conspirators now.

It was not until they were halfway along the Wagon Way that he suddenly understood, with dreadful delight, why the man had been so dark, and what he held in his hand.

He had seemed in shadow because he was black—all over.

A specter of the night had stood triumphing in the sunshine, and in its hand had held aloft a black and sunless sword.

2

"Who's this?" Ed examined the drawing with exaggerated concern.

"He wasn't there," said Runa. "I made him up. It's Art."

"It's artful," he said. "Assignations with other men and seals! Anyone would think you were deprived. Most likely, just depraved. From now on, you don't go out alone."

"I was with Erik." She took the sketchbook from him and put it on the mantelpiece. Ed finished his glass of beer.

"The only person that Erik looks after is himself," he said. "What's for lunch?"

He followed her into the kitchen, noting in passing that Erik's bedroom door was closed. At least he's out of the way, thought Ed, and wondered what Erik was doing.

"That will be useful for Sunday," said Runa.

"What will?"

"The mead."

The bottle of mead he had brought back with him was on the table, beside the fudge—for her and Erik—and several "dumps."

"Why Sunday?"

"When the professor comes for dinner," she explained, cracking the eggs for their omelettes, which were going to be savory, though she was short of herbs.

She wished he would go away and stop prowling about the kitchen while she made her wrist ache beating the eggs with a fork—there wasn't a whisk. He happily watched her do this without offering to help.

"You have a lovely action," he said.

"Thank you," she said, wondering how many beers he had had with his fishermen helpers after rescuing the car.

"He's a funny old sod, is MacDougall." Ed took the fork away to wash it.

"Leave it. Leave it," she said. "I must beat the eggs again in a minute."

"Oh," he said. "A funny old sod is MacDougall . . . With a nose like a trumpet or bugle. . . ."

"Oh, Ed," she laughed.

"Do you know," he said, after a pause, "I think he fancies me."

"That makes two of you."

"He kept on looking at my hands."

She glanced at them. In the sunshine that came in through the kitchen window, the short fine hairs on the back of his hands reaching from his shirt cuffs almost to his knuckles were as glossy as the gold ring he wore on his right hand. His fingers were long and graceful.

He appraised them himself. "Perhaps they remind him of his hamster."

"Go and do some work," said Runa. She lifted the first omelette out of the pan and put it in the oven.

"I don't feel like it," he said. "It's much too glorious a day to be indoors. Anyway, it's Saturday. Now that we've got the car back, why don't we go for a run this afternoon?"

"That would be nice," she said.

"Where would you like to go?"

"You know best. You choose."

"I thought we might go to Alnwick."

"That would be lovely," she said abstractedly.

Ed realized it was a waste of time pursuing the matter until lunch was made and served. He had, however, already started to plan the trip on his way back to the cottage from the Crown and Anchor, where he had been buying drinks for Robbie and his brother Roger, who had helped him free the car. The publican had suggested to Ed that "Robbie might give you a hand," and told Ed where to find his cottage. Roger was also living there. He was another fisherman, smaller and darker than his brother, and quicker in word and movement. They had both been out in their lobster boat that morning and had just finished a very late breakfast when Ed arrived. Robbie had an amazingly pretty, dark-haired wife and two small sons who were younger than Erik. He and his brother, without fuss or flannel, as soon as they had the details of Ed's dilemma, had loaded a van with ropes and some boards and driven him to the scene of the night's mishap. The tackle had not been used, for with Ed at the wheel their combined strength was enough to push the car out of its trap. After that, they had driven in convoy back to the village to celebrate their feat with several rounds of beer in the Crown and Anchor.

Ed had spoken briefly about his morning's adventures to Runa when he returned from the headland, but with none of the warmth they in fact had awakened in him.

Working, talking, and drinking with the brothers had struck a complex chord of nostalgia for the simpler outdoor life that had been his on his father's farm—when away from school and on vacation. Ed doubted that Robbie envied him, but he knew that for a time he had envied Robbie.

None of this could he explain to Runa. But the memory of the sweat and satisfaction of working with his hands in the open air, the pleasure of shared labors, of earthy jokes, of earnest and honest exchanges in the fields, and afterwards over a pint and a game of darts or dominoes—a memory of this stirred in his heart, making him restless and disinclined to revise his thesis that day.

This restlessness had provoked the idea of leaving the

island, and so he had planned an outing with his family. "We'll go to Alnwick," he said. "Have a look at the castle and the church, and come back via Dunstanburgh and Bamburgh—a tour of the castles." Then he left the kitchen.

He was back in five minutes, having directed his unexpressed high spirits into the creation of a limerick to amuse her.

He burst into the kitchen just as she set the salad on the table, and he put a saucepan on his head. Having got her attention, he struck a theatrical pose, and declaimed: "There was an old man called MacDougall, whose pleasures were fearfully frugal. The worst of his vices was waltzing with mices—while Longbottom played Bach on a bugle!"

The afternoon started badly for Erik. He did not want to go to Alnwick or anywhere. He wanted to stay on the island, and if possible return to his secret place, or if not, spend the time cleaning and sorting his treasures. But after lunch he was told they were going for a run in the car and that he was coming too. He thought of running away, of locking himself in the bathroom, of sabotaging the car somehow, but any such action was likely to make them really angry and might prevent any future outings to the headland. Nonetheless he signified his unwillingness to go by refusing to finish his lunch, although the pudding was strawberry yogurt, which he loved—by slamming doors, by threats of self-destruction, and just by saying loudly that he didn't want to go. His father for once was surprisingly tolerant, though he mocked him by shouting back and saying he didn't want to go either. It was his mother who subdued him this time by coming into his bedroom, where he had curled himself up on the bed in a tight demonstration of grief, and by telling him very firmly that his behavior was naughty, childish, selfish, silly, and a waste of time, as they were definitely *all* going to Alnwick.

Before they left, he wrapped his finds in his tablecloth, laid his golliwog on top, and locked them all in his black tin box.

Finding Alnwick Castle closed to the public cheered him up. So did seeing a large stone lion on the bridge below the castle and another one over the gatehouse. There were also mysterious figures of men on the castle walls and towers. His father said they were statues, representing defenders repelling an attack. But they seemed very real to Erik, and threatening. So he sheltered beside his mother and was on his guard for spears being flung from above. He wished he had not left his dragon behind.

The Duke of Northumberland lived there, said his father, though Erik didn't believe him—especially when his father said the Duke was a Percy. That was really funny. *He* knew in fact that the most important man in Northumberland lived in Bamburgh—though he couldn't remember his name.

They then drove on to Alnwick's parish church, which was large and spacious and saved for him from being dull by an unexpected wealth of flowers, fruit and vegetables inside.

The church was being adorned for a Harvest Festival on Sunday. The pungent smell of chrysanthemums in the air overlaid the subtler scents of dahlias and roses. Masses of autumn flowers spread gaudy heads from vases raised up all around the church, with heaps of every sort of vegetable beneath and along the walls, and apples, plums and pears arranged in bowls on window ledges. Sunlight fell from stained-glass windows in shades that failed to compete with the richer beauty of the blooms, and women went about like devotees, attending to the images of nature.

Erik gleefully capered around the aisles, sniffing and touching—and even felt like dancing in front of the altar. He contented himself with tracking his parents along the stalls and hiding behind pillars when the women arranging flowers came near.

From one of his hiding places he saw a monstrous box that looked like a great big coffin. He approached it carefully, alert for possible danger, and as he did so, he saw to his delight that on its sides were carvings, and among them several dragons.

He was glad he had come to Alnwick. It was clearly all part of a plan. Where it would lead him he did not know. But he knew he was going in the right direction when he came across certain signs—such as the one his dragon at home had sent him now.

"Who is it?" said Runa, shrinking from the nearly naked man with arrowheads stuck in his body.

Ed consulted the duplicated sheet of information they had picked up on entering the church.

"It's believed to be St. Maurice," he said. "Like St. Sebastian he was martyred by being shot through with arrows. As was St. Edmund," he added.

The statue's eyes were closed, as if in blind acceptance. Its hands and feet were bound. The arrowheads protruding from it were large and out of proportion with the small and stylized figure of the saint.

"St. Maurice was a Northumbrian saint, it says. He was martyred by the Danes. Like St. Edmund again."

Runa's eyes roamed over the cold gray body.

She took Ed's arm defensively. He patted her hand. They were waiting by the entrance door of the church for Erik to come and join them—when he had finished his examination of the interior.

Their own tour of the church had finally brought them to the Baptistry and the font, which in itself was not remarkable. But near it stood the statue of the saint, among a collection of grave covers. It had drawn their attention more than anything else in the church, though they had never stopped admiring the flowers on display.

"Isn't it marvelous?" Ed exclaimed. "Marvelous how these pagan festivals survive! *This* has a meaning," he said. "Not crosses and bleeding hearts."

"Isn't it rather late in the year to celebrate harvest?" Runa asked—and went unanswered, as Ed was still glorying in the odorous, colorful offerings filling the church. She was suddenly struck by the thought that nothing was growing, that everything had been plucked and rooted up, and soon would be dead.

"What a horrible way to die," she said, with a closer look at the statue. Ed turned his attention toward it.

"Really, no," he said. "I doubt if you would feel much pain. Great blows upon your body as the arrows thudded through—but so long as they didn't hit your face or private parts, it couldn't have been too awful. Rather slow a-dying though, if they didn't get your heart. *He* seems very peaceful, old St. Maurice. He had it easy.

"He could have been done to death," Ed continued, "as Aella was at York. You remember MacDougall mentioned him at tea at Bamburgh. Well, in fact the Danes carved a blood-eagle upon Aella's back—that is, they cut away the ribs from his spine and pulled out his lungs to lie like wings on his back. The Danes could be quite nasty when they wanted."

She looked away at a vase of scarlet peonies hoping to blot out the horrid image. But finding no comfort there her eyes came back to the strange serenity of the saint.

"I didn't think arrows were a very Danish weapon," she said.

Ed looked up from a close inspection of gigantic carrots below the font.

"It amazes me how ignorant you Norwegians are about your past," he said. "You know less about the ancient gods and heroes of the North than I do. Scandinavian legend is full of the skills of bowmen. Arrows are a very ancient weapon. The Egyptians were the first to make the most of them. If you think about it, the pyramids are built like arrowheads."

"That's just coincidence," she protested.

"Who knows?" He touched the statue's chest. "Coincidence, or design? It depends on how you look at it, and to what degree you yourself are affected. It's easier to see patterns looking back. For instance, it's just coincidence that we met—and yet it doesn't seem so in retrospect. It wasn't someone else I met on the College Barge—it was you."

"I nearly never went to Oxford," Runa recalled.

"The same with me. I also nearly never went to the barge that day. But I did. And so did you. And so we met. Doesn't it seem inevitable now?"

"Yes, it does." She smiled at him. "Isn't that fate?" she said.

He paced away from the statue. She followed, and picked up a rose from the floor.

"MacDougall would say it was fate. Or weird. Yet everyone *wants* to find a pattern and a purpose to their lives."

He smiled at her to show that he was not being serious. But Runa pursued the matter, sagely regarding the rose.

"Some people *do* find a pattern—by looking," she said. "If you look, you always find something. Which means it is there—it must be—in the first place."

"Not so," he said, returning to the statue. "Imagination will play you tricks—your mind will even betray you. You find what you want to find, what you *need* to find. You see what is not there."

"I don't think so," she said.

"Can you tell me what has brought us here today?" he asked. "It's just by chance that we are here, discussing this by St. Edmund."

"St. Maurice," she corrected.

"I beg his pardon. *Mea culpa.*"

"It could be fate," said Runa. "We can't be sure."

"No, we can't. Not today. Nor tomorrow. And if there is a significant pattern in our lives, we would probably be the last to see it, and come to know it too late."

At that moment Erik appeared between them.

"Oo—look!" he cried, and pointed to the statue. "It's Daddy—Daddy dead!"

"You'd think there was a war on," remarked Ed, looking at what they could see of the marketplace from their corner of the café. They had come there for a cup of tea after leaving the church—also for a rest, as Ed and Runa were feeling weary and more depressed than they liked to admit by Erik's apparent joy at the imagined death of his father. Their low spirits had been added to by the difficulty of parking the car, by the shambling crush of market people, and by the squalid condition of the café which they had entered for want of finding anything better. Outside, the market was coming to an untidy close.

"Look at those people," continued Ed. "You'd think by the way they dress that this was an occupied country. Look at their shabby clothes and sallow faces! And this is farming country. Alnwick is a *country* town, not a smoky industrialized city. You'd think they just got through a very hard winter—not had the fine old English summer that there's been."

Runa sighed. The strain of keeping Erik under control in the streets and keeping him quiet in the café had tired her, which was unusual. She had even been irked into slapping Erik's hand when he persisted in beating a tattoo on the table with his spoon. He had gone very white, and glared. But since then he had been silent while they were talking— though when they were silent themselves he had softly hummed a few notes of an unrecognizable tune.

"It is not too clean in here," she said, contemplating the tea-stained table, the cluttered ashtray, the littered floor. "The tea is not so good either."

"The tea is foul."

He turned his gaze from the marketplace to the few teen-age occupants of the other tables.

"It makes you despair. Look at that lot. The only thing that's modern about them is the length of their hair. And that's a mess. Look at the girls. Don't they *care* about their appearance? You'd think the working class would have learned to make itself look middle class by now. The young ones at least. But people in the mass—the generality— haven't changed. The outer garb is different—there are new ways of spending money, new ways of earning it—less be- lief, more machines, but no new human beings. Just *more*. Those over there, and those outside, are basically the same as those who've come to Alnwick market since it began. Be- fore that they were at markets in Jerusalem and Rome, and at Gizeh when the pyramids were built."

"*Everyone* is not the same," said Runa, wondering how to raise his spirits when she felt so low herself.

"Not the same, but similar. We are only more *aware*."

Ed leaned back in his chair and swallowed a swift mouth- ful of the muddy tea. Having lightened the weight on his spirit with an outpouring of words, he felt less down. It was his way to turn a conversation into a lecture when he was depressed or had drunk too much, and conversely to turn a college lecture into a conversation when he was calm and confident. He reasoned with himself that Erik's horrible pleasure in the church in visualizing his death had only been a fantasy and not real. Their eyes met.

Ed saw the angelic cast of Erik's face, the air of thoughtful innocence, and as usual could not consider his son dispassionately. Erik did not look like *his* son—did not look as he had looked at that age—did not belong to him. The faint antagonism that Erik produced in Ed—which had grown as Erik grew older and bigger—would have been more reasonable and manageable if the child had been in some way flawed. But physically and mentally the boy could not be faulted—only his emotions were at error.

His eyes were oddly blank now as he stared unmoving at Ed. The humming noise he made was machinelike in its abstraction. He sat in his chair like an effigy, within which was a dynamo singing a secret song.

All at once the humming stopped. He blinked, and his eyes were watchful and expectant.

"Why are there so many dragons?" said Runa.

Ed's speech had thrown her into a daydream, in which his mention of pyramids had somehow reminded her of a peculiar feature of Alnwick's monuments.

"How do you mean?" Ed switched his gaze from a short-skirted girl at the counter.

"Well, on the road below the church there was a dragon on the wall and another one on the fountain over there." She indicated the street beyond them.

"There was also a man killing them in both cases," observed Ed, fiddling with a teaspoon. "He's St. Michael. The parish church is the church of St. Michael."

Runa raised her eyebrows. "I thought it was St. George who killed the dragon."

"I don't know my saints," he confessed. "St. Michael must have encountered one as well."

"There was also a carving of dragons on the old chest in the church," she mused, looking for tea leaves in her cup and finding none.

"There never was such a thing as a dragon, was there?" she asked. Outside the market sank in shadow as a cloud passed over the sun.

"I imagine not," he said, with a final hasty swallow of his tea. "Ugh!" He stretched his arms.

"It's a symbol of the powers of evil," he said. "The soldiers of Christ took over the killing of dragons from the heroes of legend. No hero was a hero unless he had killed a dragon. It was the ultimate test."

Runa remembered the storybooks of her childhood.

"They guard treasures," she said. "Inside graves. Under—" She described what she meant by shaping a hill with her hand.

"Barrows," he said. "Grave mounds, howes." He filched a lump of sugar from the bowl.

"Why is that?" she asked, removing the bowl from his reach.

"Probably because dragons are associated with snakes and worms. All are phallic symbols as well. A dragon is just a monstrous serpent. It's ever-watchful—like a snake, I suppose—which has no eyelids and sleeps with its eyes open. And worms are of course to be found in graves.

"When was the thunderstorm?" he asked, crunching the sugar.

"Thursday night," she said. "You must remember that."

"Oh, yes—that!" he said. "Well, if you'd had time or been able, and looked out of the window, you would have seen some dragons—flying dragons—like the ones the chronicle of 793 records."

"Explain," she said, pushing her cup away.

"Lightning," he said. "It was their way of describing

lightning—scarifying flashes of light snaking through the air."

"Is that all?" She looked across at Erik, who had been so quiet, he might have gone to sleep. But he was wide-eyed, obviously intent on what she and Ed were saying.

She picked up her coat. "No real dragons? Not even then?"

She made a sad face at Erik. "What a shame. Shall we go now?"

From Alnwick they drove to Rennington and on and under the railway line to Embleton, after which the road ran roughly northward a mile inland.

Runa did not mind where they were going. The drive was its own justification—such was the splendor of the late afternoon, with the sun spreading low across the moorland-like fields, and a freshness in the air. She lowered the window, for the sun was hot on the left side of her face, and her hair blew onto Erik's arm—where he leaned on the back of her seat.

"Oh, great!" Ed exclaimed, and chortled. He stopped the car.

They had reached the crossroads at Swinhoe, and by the road were enclosures containing pigs.

Ed had a passion for pigs. His father had kept none of the animals on his farm, although a neighbor had had a set of Saddlebacks that Ed as a boy had worshiped from afar. He himself ascribed his obsession to the tales of Beatrix Potter which his mother had read to him. "It's all the fault of Pigling Bland," he said. "It was my favorite story until the age of eight. I identified with him."

He leaned over a stone wall and tried to scratch the sows. They were Landrace sows, blotched with mud and bearded with age. Ed's flirtatious calls and whistles they regarded with disdain.

Runa watched this performance with amusement. Erik turned away in disgust. The pigs were dirty, large and dangerous looking to him. He began kicking pebbles along the road.

In a pen by himself was a lean but massive Large White boar, with ears like inverted leaves flopping over his tiny eyes.

"God! Isn't he magnificent?" Ed murmured, lost in admiration at the animal's great length and the globulous testes on display.

As if he had heard, the boar swung his bristling bulk about to face the challenger, his portly head acknowledging Ed's presence with a series of searching grunts.

Ed grunted in reply as best he could.

"What a lovely scene!" said Runa. "Such perfect understanding."

"Quiet." Ed frowned. "This is serious." He grunted twice.

The boar replied with a final explosive snort and suddenly sank to his knees. With a great sigh he rolled heavily onto his side and seemed to expire.

"The king is dead! Long live the king!" Ed saluted and turned away.

They drove on past another farm and fields dotted with black-faced sheep. In looking out for the course of a disused railway, they missed a right turning to the coast.

"Not to worry, there'll be another," he said and sent the car speeding along the narrow road. But very soon he slowed it down, as a thrilling vista was revealed on their left.

A field of many acres was filled with the tented shapes of a camp in shadow against the sun. Between were many creatures running about as if on army business.

"Good God," breathed Ed. "Will you look at that? Would

you believe it?" He stopped the car and sprang out.

The field was divided into fenced-off sectors, each containing three or four lean-to shelters of planks and corrugated iron, and in each sector were several sows attended by tribes of piglets. There were shelters and pigs in receding perspective for acres and acres. In all, there were, he reckoned, over three hundred sows, and nearly three thousand piglets.

"My people!" cried Ed, addressing the pig encampment. "I have returned!"

Several piglets nearby pointed their noses toward him. A young sow raised her head. He rattled the boundary wire to encourage them, and offered his hand to them in lieu of food.

"You do not recognize me," he said. "But I am he who will lead you against the foe!"

"I never knew you had so many relatives," said Runa, who had joined him after failing to get Erik to leave the car.

"Doesn't it make you proud?" he said. "Come, piggies! Acknowledge your lord."

Two groups of piglets in the sector by the fence came scampering over to him, squealing and pushing to reach his hand. But when they found it held no food—when he tried to touch them—they scooted away in search of other sensations.

"Alas, they know me not," he said, and felt disappointed, until a sow ambled over and let him scratch her back.

"Sexy beast," he said.

"I hope you'll be very happy together," said Runa.

"You're jealous," he said. "But really—isn't she beautiful? Aren't they *all* beautiful?" He nodded toward the nearest piglets, who were romping along the fence. "So full of beans, bright-eyed and on their toes."

"Trotters," said Runa. "Pig's trotters. Very nice for soup."

"I shall never eat bacon again," he vowed as the sow departed toward her children.

He would have stayed longer, admiring the games the fatherless families played, had not Runa taken his arm and said she was feeling cold.

"What I *should* do is set them free," Ed reasoned, pausing by the car. "Then with an army of pigs I could march on Bamburgh—expel the usurper—and reclaim the castle as my own. Imagine—over three thousand pigs, with me at their head, riding on a great white boar! Invincible. Triumphant. Wouldn't it be superb?"

His fantasy made her sad. But she smiled.

"Yes, it would," she said.

"As it is," he said, turning into the sun. "I shall have to do it alone."

She said, "Yes, you will," and smiled again.

At Bamburgh, on the landward side of the castle, a football game was being played on the sports field beneath the castle walls.

"Stop! Stop!" cried Erik. "Football!"

"Shall we have a look?" asked Ed.

"Oh, yes," said Runa. "Let's stop and watch."

They joined the small scattering of spectators on the touchline—others watched from the road that ran by the field. Above, the overgrown crag was almost sheer to the towering walls and heights of the castle, whose whole breadth was rust-red in the light of the sinking sun.

Ed wondered which of the two teams—both were in striped shirts—was playing for Bamburgh. He decided to support the team in the amber and black defending the sunny half of the field below the castle.

Five minutes later the whistle blew. The game was over.

On their way back to the car, Erik boldly approached a man who was carrying a stick.

"Excuse me," he said, frowning with the effort of being both adult and polite. "Do you know—? Please. Who won?"

"Bamburgh," said the man. "Nine—five."

"Oh," said Erik, feeling sure that his team in the black and white had lost.

"Which are they?" asked Ed.

"Them in the amber and black," said the man, pointing at some home-going players led by a tall blond youth, who caught Ed's eye and seemed to smile.

Ed felt pleased at having identified himself with the winning side and with Bamburgh. He looked down at Erik and put a hand on his shoulder, which was at once displaced.

"Who were the *losing* team?" asked Ed with a grin at Erik.

"Seahouses," was the answer. "It was a hard game—always is when these teams meet. You're not from hereabouts, are you?"

"From Lincolnshire," replied Ed.

"Passing through?"

"On holiday. On Holy Island. Though we've been to Bamburgh once before," Ed hastened to add.

"It's a grand evening. I'll wish you goodbye," said the man and hobbled away.

In the car, Erik's gloom at his side not winning grew less as they drove by Waren Mill. The prospect of going home to Holy Island to watch television and have supper was not, however, as enlivening—which it once would have been— as the thought of the finds in his box still needing to be cleaned and the prospect of digging out more of the buried treasure.

When they drove down the slope of the hill from Belford, the sandy strip of the island appeared far away on their right—now no island, for the tide was out and mud flats joined the island to the shore.

Erik sat with his nose on the window, imagining where the cottage was, and the priory—he could make out the castle—and the headland where he was sure the man was waiting. His resolve to return to the headland that night was fixed. He did not know how it might be managed, but he promised himself it would be.

The car's shadow preceded them over the causeway through the miles of mud, where birds in their hundreds were feeding on thousands of worms. Erik's eyes remained on the shadow supernaturally leading them on.

3

Back at the cottage, Runa retired to the kitchen, while Ed sat down to watch the television news. She wondered, as she prepared a meal, at Erik's behavior. Without a complaint about missing the soccer results or his favorite Saturday evening program, he had gone to his bedroom and busied himself there, or in the bathroom.

With the meal prepared—it was cold meat and salad, with soup to start—she joined Ed in the sitting room, and he gave her a glass of mead as an aperitif. She lit the lamp in the window, and they watched television together until he said he was going out for a brief walk before supper.

When he went out, she took the opportunity of invading Erik's room, on the pretense of giving him back his sketchbook. He had said he had something to show her.

It was dark in the room, though enough light still came from the window for her to see that he was on his knees by his box, with his back to her.

Hearing her enter, he hastily slammed the lid—accidentally trapping a finger. He twisted about, fierce with accusation and pain.

"You didn't knock!" he cried. "It's very rude. You're supposed to knock!"

She switched on the light. "I'm sorry," she said, and returned to the door and knocked on it.

While her back was turned, he removed the cut and bleeding finger he had caught in the lid and hid his hurt right hand behind him, trying not to wince.

"Will that do?" she asked. "I came to see how you were. Here's your sketchbook. Thank you for lending it to me."

She held it out—her drawing uppermost—and he stood up and took hold of it with his left hand.

"Oh, Erik," she said reproachfully, and he blanched, fearing she knew what he had been doing—which she sometimes did—though how, he had no idea.

"You should have asked me to light the fire. It's cold in here. And how can you see in the dark?"

"It doesn't matter," he said.

But she went to the kitchen to fetch some matches, and after lighting the fire, drew the curtains across his view of the church, rosy in the sunset's afterglow. As she moved briskly about, he had to shift his feet to face her.

"How are you?" she said, standing before him. She thought he was embarrassed for some reason by her presence.

He shrugged his shoulders.

"Is there something you wanted to show me?" she prompted.

He shook his head.

"I thought you had something to show me," she said.

He looked at the carpet.

"Not now?" she asked.

She thought he whispered, "Tomorrow."

"All right," she said. "I'll go. But if you change your mind, you know you can trust me. Supper in half an hour."

Alone again he sighed with relief and examined his painfully throbbing finger. It was the index one, and he gave vent to all the grimaces he had controlled while his mother was in the room. The cut was deep and near the nail—the blood was ready to run.

He put the sketchbook on the bedside table, and in doing so, a drop of blood ran off his nail and onto his mother's drawing.

An image of the man on the headland with sword upraised stuck in his mind. He had forgotten that his mother had also seen the man. But she had drawn him leaning upon his sword, whose point was now about to be stained by a circular pool of blood.

This, he thought, was exactly what the drawing needed. After a battle, a warrior would rest on his sword, and the blade would drip with blood, making a stream of it at his feet.

Carefully poising his finger, Erik let it drip again on the paper. Then using the little finger of his left hand he smeared the double stain into a spreading stream and reddened the blade as far as the hilt, until a river of blood ran down it over the sand.

Proud of his work, he paused to view its effect.

The hissing of the gas fire was loud in his ears for a moment, and then it faded away. He knew his eyes were fixed on the drawing, and yet it was dissolving under his gaze, while a darkness grew over the edges of his vision until, as if at the end of a tunnel, the dark figure was all there was on the paper.

He saw it move, and he wanted to blink but he could not. And suddenly it was *him* that was moving, over a beach of blinding sand. He was looking down at his feet, which were large and strangely clad and stained as red as the gory tip of the sword which swung into view as he strode along. A muted mingling of cries invaded his ears, and a muffled metallic clangor rang out and matched his movements. Then he saw that he halted. He heard the sea. He stared at the sand. He slowly began to write his name on the beach with the sword.

His left hand moved, and it made a line with the blood-stained pin on the paper.

On the high Heugh, Ed watched the tide in crescents coming up the Harbor channel towards St. Cuthbert's Isle. The sun had set in fiery clouds and the earth was dark. But a shark-blue light was in the sky and mirrored on the moving tide, which also caught the southern moon's reflection, making it into silver slices on the sea. Eider ducks clucked to each other, and there was a lapping of water. Ed turned his eyes from the waxing moon to the clouded furnace of the west above the Cheviot Hills. Hesitantly he walked that way, not seeing where his footsteps fell on the turf.

He swore at himself for not bringing the torch. He would have to hurry before it became any darker.

A plop and a splash came from the water below on his left. A sleepy duck, he thought—or a seal. He glanced down, but the advancing tide showed no unusual ripples.

He reached the western edge of the Heugh, where the track broke up in rocky ledges. Here the slope caught the last dull light of the sunset. Ed paused, with his eyes on the cross on St. Cuthbert's Isle below him, silhouetted against the lambent water.

A bird on the darkened shore piped two warning notes. Suddenly he had the feeling that somebody was behind him, that someone was standing looking at him, from the same place where he had been only minutes before. A dark shape grew out of the ground behind him, darker than the eastern sky already beset by night. His jaws tensed, his muscles tautened. He told himself his fears were foolish and turned around.

There was nothing—and yet there was.

Across the bay, blacker than the night, was the distant dome of the castle rock.

So that was it, he thought. How strange it should impress itself on him when his back was turned. He realized that subconsciously he must have noted it earlier and had had to make it accountable to his consciousness.

Ed looked again at St. Cuthbert's Isle.

Were his ears at fault as well as his eyes? He thought he heard a subterranean grunting.

"You were afraid," said Runa.

"I may have been slightly scared. I was not afraid."

She took a sip of her vodka and orange. "I believe you."

"You're never afraid of anything, are you?" Ed smiled. "That's why I married you."

"No," she said. "That's why I married *you*."

Ed drew on his pipe and leaned back so as not to blow the smoke in her face. He had sat her down near the door of the bar, so that people coming into the Crown and Anchor could not miss seeing her. He was feeling very proud of her. She had washed her hair before coming out, and in her russet woolen dress with its gold belt she looked like Perdita or some princess in disguise.

"Do you remember the one-eyed man?" she said.

"He wasn't one-eyed—he was winking. Dirty old sod."

"I'm not going to argue," she said. "But if you ask your

133

Mr. Allison I am sure he will bear me out. He must know everyone on the island."

Earlier, Ed had explained that the Crown and Anchor and some nearby cottages were owned by four brothers and sisters called Allison—all of them over fifty. Selby Allison, who was host behind the bar, had been Ed's chief source of information about the island. His family had lived there for hundreds of years, and he was the last of the line.

Ed looked at her. "All right," he said exhaling. "I will."

Runa occupied his absence by a consideration of nearby pictures of grounded ships and photos of fishermen wearing caps. They were less faded by time and the bright central light in the room than a portrait of the Queen wearing the sash of the Garter which was over the fireplace. By the fire was a fruit machine.

"Wrong," exclaimed Ed, parking himself beside her again and taking a swig of his pint. "No one-eyed man on the island. Some with four eyes, Selby says, and a few with eyes in the back of their heads. No one-eyed man."

How strange, she thought, gazing around at the other people in the room as if her eyes were playing her false again. In a corner sat two elderly women—Miss Ingram's sisters, Ed had said. With them was a woman in a trouser suit. At the bar stood three men, not together, but sharing a conversation. All three were middle-aged. One was a farmer, according to Ed. Another was evidently a fisherman from his garb of dark suit, black polo-neck jersey and cap. "He's one of the domino-playing tribe," Ed had explained. "And observe his great hooked nose—there are several like that about." The third man had a curious nickname. "They nearly all have nicknames," Ed declared. "It gets confusing. Selby is Sparrow. And there's Crow, Booner, Maggie, Wonker, Tinko, Clinker, Goff, Step, Farmer (who's a fisherman), Bash, Shy, Bobo, Terick, Schneider, and more."

"How do you know?" she asked.

"Robbie told me about them," he said. "No one is quite what they seem."

Two other elderly men and a younger man were sitting by the door, engaged in animated chat that was incomprehensible to Runa. A TV set was lodged in the wall angle above them. She was, she thought, the youngest person there, and she and Ed were the only strangers.

They had not felt like strangers when they arrived. People had nodded and smiled at them, and Ed had exchanged a "Good evening," here and there. It was not like a bar at all. It was more as if the room they were in, off the hall, was a front room in a private home set aside for drinking, and the people in it who had come for a drink were more like guests for the evening—a gathering of neighbors.

"No one-eyed man," she repeated, and refrained from saying she didn't believe him and was sure that she was right, as that was not proof to him.

Then she remembered the trumpet call she had heard on the beach the night before. Had *her* ears also deceived her? An echo of the call sounded again in her mind. She frowned. No trumpet had made that call. It had been a horn.

"Well, we all make mistakes," she said. "Even you."

Ed was puffing contentedly at his pipe.

"That's true," he said. "Actually, I did think I was hearing things when I heard the grunting. . . . I also thought I was being followed. I had that feeling."

"Were you?" she asked.

He had told her about hearing but not seeing some pigs in an enclosure below the Heugh—between it and the church. But the other fact was news to her, and an intriguing admission, coming from him.

"No," he said.

Ed gazed at the wisps of smoke ascending from his pipe.

"I used to be afraid of the dark," he said. "When I was small."

This was something she had not heard from him for many years—not since those nights long ago in Oxford when they had made a habit, on Ed's insistence, of seeing horror films.

"We went on holiday to Cornwall once—stayed in an old hotel, an inn, at Callington, for a night. I was ten or eleven. Had a room on my own. I woke up, and there was a dark figure standing at the bottom of my bed. I was petrified—couldn't move. It took me hours to inch my hand to the lamp to turn on the light. Nothing there of course. It was all the fault of a book of ghost stories I'd been reading."

He had never told her that story before. He smiled at her bashfully, as if he were ten again.

"I was a very sensitive child," he said. "No, really! Easily hurt, easily fooled, very trusting and susceptible. Until I went to school, as a boarder. That's when I became aggressive. You had to—to survive."

She believed him. She knew his extrovert, outspoken character had been in part assumed, as a defense originally, but also because of the individuality and attention it gave him. He was forthright now in his words and actions because he believed it was hypocritical and insincere to be otherwise.

"Everyone is afraid of the dark, at some time," said Runa, thinking of the north beach the night before.

"It's a primitive fear," observed Ed. "A fear of the unknown, of unseen presences. In some places it's much stronger than others, and if you were in a certain frame of mind—a receiver switched on to a certain frequency—you could, I imagine, pick up ancient terrors, *embody* them even."

"They're not necessarily evil."

"No," he said. "But happiness and contentment aren't such strong forces as terror, hate and fear, which are therefore more likely to be transmitted and arouse similar emotions by the fact that they *are* unknown, unplaced and un-accountable.

"Drink up," he said, nearing the end of his pint. "Then I'll buy us another.

"I've told you," he went on, "about *my* only adventure with a ghost."

"Go on," she said, having forgotten the details.

"Not that I *saw* anything. Can't have been switched on for viewing. But I *heard* him." Ed contemplated his pipe.

"It was a game, and I don't know how we learned to play it. But we sat at the piano in the music room, on the first floor—it was an old-fashioned vicarage—and I would sing. . . ." He was looking at Runa, but seeing the scene his memory presented. "I didn't really like the other little boy, by the way. He was younger and smaller than me—and vindictive. But I would sing—anything—la, la la. And we would hear these footsteps coming up the stairs—creak, creak. The stairs weren't carpeted. They would come up the stairs, and along the passage. And the music room door, which was closed, would slowly open." He paused, remembering.

"What happened then?"

"We ran away—out the other door. That was all. It doesn't seem possible, but I remember it happening."

Like the horn and the one-eyed man, thought Runa.

"I must have been seven or eight," mused Ed. "About as old as Erik."

Runa finished her drink.

"Ed, will you excuse me? I think I should go and see that he is all right." She stood up.

"Oh, as you like. All right. I'll get you another drink."

"Can I have the key?"

He gave it to her and said, "Don't be long."

As there was no one else about and because it was cold, Runa ran across the moonlit village square and back to the cottage. She had felt guilty about leaving Erik on his own, although he had expressed great scorn at the idea of her staying in just for him and had reminded her that he wasn't a baby.

He wanted her to go out, he said. Yes, he knew where the inn was. He understood where they would be. Yes, he would be quite all right, and no, he didn't mind. He was tired and ready for bed. Yes, his finger wasn't hurting now— he had owned up to having cut it earlier and she had bandaged it. He hoped she would have a nice time, and said she needn't hurry back. She told him she would look in on him in half an hour or so.

Runa tried to open the front door quietly and went inside. She had left the hall light on. After tiptoeing the few paces up the hall, she listened outside his door. Carefully she opened it. In the light from the hall she could see that he was sleeping peacefully on his back.

She noticed that his sketchbook had been propped up against the bedside table and thought of removing it in case he knocked it over. She decided not to bother, as her movements might wake him up.

Less carefully Runa closed the door, left the cottage, shut the front door, and then ran happily back to the pub.

Erik waited for a minute before sitting up and turning on the lamp. He was wearing his track suit top. He looked at his bandaged finger and then at the propped-up sketchbook. His mother had come back sooner than he had expected, but she had not caught him out. His watch said half-past nine. He hoped they would not be too late, as he was already feeling sleepy. He wanted to keep awake—he had to—so that he could embark on his expedition as soon as they returned and went to sleep. Assembled in readiness under his bed were his track suit trousers, a jersey, socks and shoes, the big yellow plastic bucket from the kitchen, his spade, his own red bucket, and the car torch, which he had found in the sitting room. In the meantime, there was still some cleaning to do. Cautiously he folded back the counterpane, revealing on top of a towel on the blankets his cleaning equipment of brasso—which he had found in the kitchen—dusters, paper hankies, pins, a nail, a pan scourer, his penknife and a scouring pad. The towel and its burden were spread over his lap. On his left side were the objects he had already cleaned, among them his very first dragon. On his right were those—mostly arrowheads—that still needed his attention. He picked up the second dragon, which, he had decided, was not suitable to give to his mother, and resumed his private task.

Selby Allison produced a small cardboard box and emptied the contents into his hand. Runa had found Ed talking to him when she returned and had been introduced. In her absence, Ed had let their seats be taken by a mixed group of young people, whose belligerently colorful casual clothes and loud voices marked them out as "visitors." They had been identified by the farmer at the bar as weekend ornithologists.

"These are St. Cuthbert's beads," said Mr. Allison spilling some onto the bar top.

Runa thought he had eyes like a sorcerer, dark and secret, which were emphasized by black eyebrows slanting above them.

"Ah, I've read about the beads," Ed remarked. "So that's what they look like."

"What are they?" Runa asked.

The objects were like tiny cogs, or faceted beads of different shapes. The largest was about half an inch across.

"They are fossils," said their owner with somber reverence. "Millions of years old. Fossils of an *animal* like a plant, with a stem and five branches. These are pieces of it."

"It's called a crinoid," Ed added.

"That's it. A crinoid. They used to live in the sea. You still can find them washed up on the shore. Some people make them into necklaces and bracelets. They're called St. Cuthbert's beads."

"Gosh," said Runa. "Aren't they interesting? We must look for some."

Mr. Allison began putting his treasures back in their box.

"There's many an odd thing still to be found along these shores," he said. "Especially after a storm."

He looked at Runa. "What made you want to know about a one-eyed man?"

His curiosity abashed her. "I thought I saw such a person," she said.

"There's no one of that appearance on the island," he said firmly. "Not to my knowledge. Unless it was a visitor."

"She was mistaken," Ed remarked, shifting himself and rearranging his elbow on the bar. It was getting hot where he was by the fire.

"Maybe not," responded Mr. Allison, closing the lid of his box.

He put it away and busied himself with serving the Ingram sisters. Ed saw they were drinking whisky and water.

"Robbie's not here yet," he said to Mr. Allison, who replied, "He'll be along."

At that moment Robbie came into the room. Ed hailed him, bought him a drink, and introduced him to Runa.

She noticed a superficial likeness between them, but the islander was an inch or so shorter, probably younger, with a gaunter face, pale-blue eyes, and dissimilar in detail. She liked him straightaway.

They exchanged pleasantries about the island, the weather, and her impressions of Northumberland, but Robbie was more at ease talking to Ed. He was reserved with her, constrained into being respectful and well-spoken, though she saw he noted her figure well.

When his brother Roger arrived soon after, she withdrew from the conversation, which was about cars, and the cost of living on the island, and the economics of land—and later, when Miss Ingram appeared with her knitting, Runa was invited to join the three sisters in the corner and give an account of herself and Norway and how she had met Ed.

In the meantime, more people came than went, and a guitar-playing group from Newcastle occupied the overflow bar next to the main room, adding their music to the background noise. Runa could not recognize their songs, and was prevented from listening to them by the demanding chatter of the other women.

All of the sisters volunteered to act as babysitters for Erik, when she explained how guilty she had felt in leaving him alone that night.

She managed to use the fact to excuse herself and rejoin Ed, intending to remind him she ought to return to the cottage. But another round of beers had just been bought—including another vodka for her—and Ed wanted her to meet a fair-haired man who was now with the group.

"You won't believe this," Ed exclaimed. "But guess who we have here."

Runa looked curiously at the newcomer, who smiled engagingly back at her and shyly tucked in his chin. He was broad-shouldered, about her age, and almost as tall. But he was not dressed like an islander—he was wearing an open-necked shirt. What struck her most about him was a real resemblance to Ed—apart from the smoky blue of his eyes.

"This is Danny," Ed announced. "Danny—my wife, Runa."

They exchanged cautious "Hallo's" and looked at Ed, waiting for him to continue.

"Danny," he said to Runa, "is married to Selby's niece, Ann, and related somehow through her to Robbie and Roger. But best of all, he comes from Swinhoe!"

"Swinhoe?" she repeated.

"He owns the Large White boar!"

She smiled, remembering.

"I've a few *other* guffies as well," protested Danny.

"Guffies?" she said.

"Articles!" said Robbie and Roger together.

"Articles?"

The men laughed at her bewilderment.

"It's a superstition," Ed explained. "You cannot call a P-I-G a P-I-G on the island. It brings bad luck. They call them articles."

"If you spoke the other word here," said Danny, "they'd all touch metal—just in case. Selby there would clutch the beer-pump handle, and these two"—he nodded at Robbie and Roger—"would seize the coins in their pockets."

"If we had any," said Robbie morosely. "We're not all in the farming business and kings of the bleeding earth."

"Go on," said Danny. "You must be making a fortune. Fifteen hundred pounds a year at least."

"Away, man!" derided Roger. "You're talking through a hole in your head! No fisherman makes that kind of money. It's impossible."

"Is it?" Ed inquired.

"Aye. It is," said Robbie. "Half the time you cannot put to sea. You don't make a penny then."

"As soon as they have a day off work they go on the dole," said Danny.

"You bugger! What's wrong with that?" demanded Roger.

"Nothing," said Danny merrily. "It's a lot more pleasant than work."

Their belligerence, which Runa had taken for real, she now saw was assumed. Everyone laughed. Ed turned to her.

"I'm going out with the lobster boats, with Robbie and Roger and Farmer and Tam in theirs, on Monday morning," he said.

"If the weather's fair," said Robbie.

"Any excuse for a day in bed," Danny suggested.

"Why not?" said Robbie, rubbing his nose. "If the wife's willing."

Runa looked at the laughing men. She sipped her vodka and smiled.

"But," said Ed, "you mustn't come and see me off. That's bad luck as well."

Robbie explained, gazing more boldly at her. "I've just been telling your man here that if a fisherman on his way to the boats sees a woman—"

"Or a priest," interrupted Roger.

"*Or* a priest on his way to the boats, or a nun, he won't put out."

"Any excuse," said Danny to Ed.

"Oh, away and play with your articles!" Roger exclaimed.

Ed laughed. "What an ignominious name for a pig!"

"Don't *say* that, man!" Roger said in mock alarm.

"We'll never put to sea," said Robbie. "For someone will be drowned, and that's a fact!"

"*Pigs!*" laughed Ed. His merriment was infectious and Danny from Swinhoe started to laugh as well. "*Pigs!*"

"Oh, what a beautiful night!" said Runa, when she and Ed staggered out of the Crown and Anchor soon after eleven.

The cold and silence were shocking after the warmth and noise of the room full of people, who had shown no signs of leaving. Before them was the priory meadow, and the silver moon in the south hung high above the ruins.

Ed stretched his arms.

"It's almost high tide," he said.

"Is it?"

"It is. If we could see it. And the moon is almost full."

They looked toward the Ouse, but despite the moon it was too far and too dark to see the water.

He put his arm around her.

"Shall we go for a sail?" he said.

"Not now," she said, leaning against him. "Later."

A shout of laughter came from the inn.

"They were like your knights," said Runa.

Ed knew she meant Robbie and Roger and Danny.

"And you were Guinevere," he said.

"No," she said. "I'm Gudrun. Always Gudrun."

They moved toward the cottage.

Someone was singing in the night. A guitar was being played. One of the men from the Newcastle group in the overflow bar was singing a song she knew.

"Listen," she said.

As they strolled away from the muffled clamor of the inn toward the square, the voice became clearer, the melody stronger. Runa hummed the verse, her body taking the rhythm.

Ed waited for the slow and lilting chorus before he gathered her gently about the waist and waltzed her slowly, lovingly, homeward over the square.

"Speed, bonny boat, like a bird on the wing," he sang. "Onward, the sailors cry. Carry the lad that's born to be king, over the sea to Skye."

144

Sunday

1

They were late getting up on Sunday morning. Runa had woken first, but as the light from the curtained window was so dim, she thought it was earlier than it was and fell asleep again. She woke again to find the bedroom as dark as it had been before. Her watch had stopped. Ed's watch was too far away to see without disturbing him, so she clambered out of the bed to look at it and saw it was ten past nine.

When she opened the curtains she found the reason for the bedroom's gloom. Outside, the street was obscured by a heavy mist.

Breakfast was a scrappy affair in the kitchen. Ed complained of a headache, and Erik dourly munched his cornflakes in between the occasional yawn. Runa herself was feeling lethargic and indecisive.

"What shall we do today?" Ed asked, stretching his arms and tilting back on the kitchen chair.

"Do?" asked Runa. She was reading through lobster recipes.

"Well, we've seen the sights of the island, and the beaches won't be any fun in the fog."

"Shouldn't you be getting on with some of your work?" she asked.

"It's Sunday." He banged on the wall. "I don't want to work. And anyway we might as well make the most of our time here, don't you think?"

"I have enough to do today," she said, recalling there was washing to be done.

"What are you planning for dinner?" he asked, leaning his elbows on the table. "No. Don't tell me. Make it a surprise."

If it was to be a surprise, she thought, she would have to collect the lobsters herself from the cottage next door. Miss Ingram had happily promised to boil them for her—which relieved her from the harrowing process of jamming a live lobster into a pot of boiling water until it was cooked and red.

Ed looked at Erik. "What would *you* like to do?" he asked.

Erik stopped scrunching his toast and honey and stared at his father.

What is he thinking? wondered Ed, reading a conflict of some sort in Erik's eyes.

"Can I go to the beach?" said Erik.

"Do you want to go with me?" asked Ed.

"No," said Erik.

"Then you've had it, I imagine. Your mother won't have time to take you. Will you?" he said to Runa.

Lobster thermidor, she thought, seemed to be within range of the materials she had available. "No," she said, and added—"Would you buy a bottle of dry sherry, Ed, when you go out for the papers?"

He assented, and on an impulse left the kitchen to fetch the tide tables and maps from the car.

While he was out of the room, Erik asked if he could go to the beach by himself. It transpired he had the headland in mind. Runa said she could not allow it and did not want him out in the fog alone.

Ed returned to the kitchen—the fire had not been lit yet in the sitting room—and, after consulting the tide tables, said that as it was high tide just after twelve, they were too late to drive to the mainland that morning, and wouldn't be able to cross over until three. He suggested that they go for a run to Kirknewton in the afternoon. The fog was probably only coastal, he said, though they needn't decide until after lunch, when the weather might improve. Runa protested that she didn't have the time to go out for a drive. But Ed said he would help her tidy the cottage and volunteered to make the lunch.

Erik watched them, awaiting their verdict on how the day was to be spent. But the only decisions that were reached were that Runa would do her washing after the breakfast things had been cleared away, and that Ed, after doing the washing-up, would go and visit the pigs.

"Why don't you go with your father?" said Runa.

Erik frowned and wriggled in his chair.

"All right," he said.

"I'm honored," Ed remarked.

Runa told Erik to get changed into his parka and jeans, and he vanished into his bedroom.

It was half-past ten when Erik and Ed left the cottage. But before Runa set about gathering up their socks, shirts and underclothes that needed washing, she made the beds.

She did Erik's second. In the process she noticed the pillow was marked with smudges. So she removed it, puzzling how he had managed to get it dirty when he always had a bath before going to bed. There was also some sand between the sheets and pieces of grit on the blankets. She made a face, expressing her displeasure. What had he been up to now? She couldn't imagine how he could have got sand *inside* the bed. And what were those bits of dirt? They weren't from his collection of stones—they were more like flakes of rust. She would have to question him when he returned.

When the bed was made she discovered traces of sand on the carpet and sand in the socks he had been wearing yesterday afternoon. She could not understand it, but decided that Erik's room would have to be cleaned before she did the washing.

She armed herself with a brush and pan and knelt on all fours on the carpet. In doing so, she glimpsed the yellow plastic bucket that should have been in the kitchen. It was under the bed, beside the black tin box.

Inside the bucket she found Erik's red bucket, and Ed's car torch—all of them covered with sand.

Runa sat back on her heels. What on earth was Erik doing with all these objects? And where was his spade?

Her questioning eyes fell upon the sketchbook, which was still on the bedside table. Its appearance faintly disturbed her.

She picked it up and examined it, as if its contents held some clue to the mysteries of the bedroom, and Erik's vivid imaginings of storms, shipwrecks, wars and fiery sunsets unfolded before her.

The last page with a drawing on it was hers. To her dismay she saw it had now been grossly disfigured. The scene was blotched with dried blood, dark as rust on the soft sands she had so carefully drawn.

She shuddered to think of the care with which Erik must have transferred the blood from his cut finger—Had he cut it on purpose?—to the paper. But what perturbed her most was the dawning revelation that where she had drawn a man with his back to her leaning on a stick, there now stood a man looking at her, with a sword in his left hand.

He was waiting. He had the air of someone who had turned about on hearing his name being called. She thought he must have been waiting for a long time, as such a pool of blood had spread from his sword over the sand. But that was not all. Where the dark stain ebbed away, it extended itself into a series of scratches—like the tracks of birds, or tiny semaphore figures gone mad.

She knew what they were though her disbelief at finding them there for a moment blinded her reason.

On the beach were written six runes—six letters of the Old Norse alphabet. But what they stood for she did not know, nor the word they formed on the sand.

The mist seemed to hover more thickly over the priory ruins than in the churchyard, wreathing their crumbled tops with a white smoke, as if the fires of their destruction still smoldered.

Ed had delayed to chat with the guardian of the priory when the man hailed him from inside the museum. It was surprising to find the museum open on a Sunday morning. But he took the opportunity to reexamine the Viking stone.

Erik meanwhile wandered off into the churchyard under the trees, and Ed had to go after him to forestall any unlawful forays into the ruins.

The distant bass of a foghorn ghosted through the mist, and as they passed around the east end of the church, a man's voice could be heard loudly singing a hymn.

The morning service must have begun at half-past ten, Ed surmised. There could not be many people in the church, he thought, for the vicar's voice was the only one to be heard above the organ. It seemed that the islanders had abandoned even the form of worship and reverted to pagan ways, only coming together for seasonal festivals and to solemnize the ceremonies of birth, marriage and death.

He stopped to listen to the vicar. The hymn was one he recognized from hours of tedium spent in Lincoln Cathedral when, as a boarder at school, he had had to attend as many as three services every Sunday. He had always enjoyed the more martial and dramatic hymns—such as the one that now infiltrated the damp and misty air.

"Lord God Almighty," sang the vicar, ending a verse. He began another. "See round thine ark the hungry billows curling. See how thy foes their banners—"

"Come on," Ed said to Erik, and set off about the church toward the side gate.

"Lord, o'er thy rock nor death nor hell prevaileth," sang the vicar, his voice fading.

Ed joined in singing "Grant us thy peace, Lord," and began to hum the last verse.

"Don't *do* that," said Erik.

"Why not?" demanded Ed.

Erik pouted and made no reply.

"Are you the only one who's allowed to sing? I'll have you know I have sung in Lincoln Cathedral and on cricket tours. Can you better that? Few could. Is it the singer or the song that pains you?"

Again Erik kept silent—out of policy, Ed thought.

When they emerged from the side gate onto the road and Ed turned left toward the Heugh, Erik halted.

"I don't want to see the pigs," he said, toeing the ground.

Ed regarded him coldly. "You can do what you want," he said. *"I'm* going this way. Well?"

Erik spoke without looking at his father. "I'm going home."

"Go on!" Ed exclaimed, disgustedly. "Do what you want. Push off. It's a waste of time me trying, isn't it? Go on. Vanish!"

Erik turned about and stiffly walked away. His exasperated father watched him go, until Erik turned right and disappeared into the street that went past the cottage.

Ed swore to himself, and pounded down the lane, venting his aggravation on the stones beneath his feet and breathing curses into the mist.

In the right foreground the rising tide was a flattened silk of ashen water that had almost disconnected St. Cuthbert's Isle from the island. Oyster catchers piped to each other on what was left of the beach.

He paused to get his bearings.

Off the lane, beside him, was a farm gate in a high stone wall. The lower half of the gate had been covered with a sheet of corrugated iron. It was not until he looked over it into a small sunken field, backed by the Heugh, that he saw the pigs.

There were three sows and about thirty piglets, and a young fellow in Wellington boots and an off-white sweater was scattering cobs on the ground for the articles to feed on.

Ed leaned on the gate. The other man turned and looked at him.

"Good morning," he said. "It's not so fine today."

"Good morning," Ed replied, startled by the familiarity of the smile and the face. It was not just the other man's occupation that reminded him of Danny of Swinhoe. He wondered if they were related.

The two of them, he thought, and me—the three of us could be brothers.

Erik danced along the track, swinging his spade as he went. Like a sea monster, the voice of the foghorn lengthily marked his steps. Great clouds of mist sluggishly swirled across his path from the invisible sea. It was so like steam from extinguished fires that he sniffed the air to see if he could smell burning. But all he could sense was the damp yet slightly acrid air, like an essence of mushrooms. He imagined that he was at the end of the world, surrounded by sunken continents, and all that was left was the piece of earth he trod on.

It was very warm, so he stopped skipping, undid his parka and settled into a fast walk. His mind was alive with his cleverness in having escaped from his parents, each of whom would think he was with the other—and if he was lucky, would not notice his absence for some time. It was a pity he had not managed to bring his bucket, but anything he had to carry back could go in his parka's pockets, or in its bulging front, or down the leg of his jeans, where his spade had been until, after creeping on hands and knees under the windows of the cottage—so as not to be seen by his mother—he had been able to run triumphantly out of the village with the spade in his hand.

He had left the village by the same route he had taken the night before, after escaping from the cottage fully equipped with buckets, torch and spade. His parents had gone to bed soon after their return, which had been luckily noisy enough to wake him up—though this had been a bad moment, finding he had not only fallen asleep but left his light on. However, when his mother looked in on him, the light was out, and he was only pretending to be asleep. Later, when there was silence in their room, he had dressed in the dark and crept out of the window. Then, by way of a mound of heaped-up garden refuse, he had struggled over the wall into the churchyard and set out on the moonlit trek to the headland. It had taken him half an hour to get there, and the strangeness of his journey and the time of night—he had never been up and out so late before—had made it seem like a dream the following morning when he was awakened by his mother. But under his bed were the discarded toys of his childhood, which he remembered having emptied out of his box in order that his latest treasures could have a home, and *in* the box, lumped on top of his other acquisitions, were the awkward pieces of rusted iron, and the four stupendous new finds he had labored to bring back with him. He gazed at them rapturously, before gathering up the paltry stones, soldiers, marbles and other ordinary playthings and tossing them into his tablecloth, which was in turn banished to a bottom drawer. He could not quite renounce his golliwog. It was removed to the top of the chest of drawers. Then he returned to feast his eyes on his hoard. He could not admire it for long for fear of interruption, nor could he start as yet to restore his newest finds. And as the afternoon was apparently booked for a drive, he resolved to return to the headland that morning, to unearth what more was there and carry back what he could.

He followed the same route he had taken the night before, feeling at home now on the Wagon Way, which by daylight seemed less alarming. It was like a grassy parade above the shore—and it *was* the best way to the grave.

He was certain it was a grave where the treasure was, though it still puzzled him why he had not found any bones.

Erik grinned to himself. Not only had he been clever that morning, the success of his nighttime endeavors had shown him how well his plans were working. He could not fail— more than that, he was winning. And when he had unearthed all the objects in the grave, restored their glories and stowed them safely in his box, his next course of action would become clear. Everything, he felt sure, was directed toward a final victory over his father, who was the enemy. Erik had often thought of him as this before but had never been able to give his feelings any force or definite resolution. Now he had an ally. Now he was not alone. Aided by the man without a face, with no shadow, he was going to bring about his father's destruction.

"Revenge!" he said, lifting the spade left-handed over his head—as the man had done on the headland.

The foghorn blared, and he burst into fits of giggles.

The feeling she had was indefinable. Wherever Runa went in the cottage that morning, she kept on glancing about to see if anything was out of the ordinary and would pause in what she was doing to listen, thinking she heard something unusual.

It started after she had tidied Erik's room. As soon as she closed the bedroom door she thought she heard something fall inside. She opened the door—but nothing had changed, everything was in order.

Then when she took the carpet sweeper into the front bedroom, stopping for a moment to look out of the window, she felt that someone was watching her from the open door. But no one was there, and no one was in the hall. She closed the door and got on with her housework. Yet under the noise that her actions made there were sometimes other sounds, out of place, that ceased when she stopped to listen. Once she thought she heard singing. She explained that to herself by attributing it to a distant radio or someone in the village.

But while she swept and dusted the hall and the sitting room—where she also laid the fire—and got on with the washing in the bathroom, there were moments when from the corner of her eye she thought she saw some movement, or thought she heard someone speak, and whenever she left a door open behind her or went out into the hall, she had the feeling she was not alone.

Runa was not afraid—more baffled than anything else—and told herself she was tired and imagining things. Yet when she had hung the washing to dry on a clotheshorse in the bath and gone into the kitchen for a drink, she felt a surge of relief at the sight of Ed in the churchyard.

She wanted to knock on the kitchen window and wave. But he was engaged in talking to a red-haired man and might misinterpret her action as a call for assistance. It was enough that she saw him. Erik she could not see, though she imagined he was somewhere about, hidden by the garden wall and the gravestones.

With the kettle on the boil for some coffee—and the kitchen door closed—she sat down to consider her next step.

The paté and syllabub could wait until early evening. The lobsters need not be collected from Miss Ingram until after lunch—that is, if they were going for a drive. Suddenly the thought of leaving the island was cheering and welcome. Ed was right. It *was* a Sunday, and they should make the most of their time in Northumberland. When he raised the subject again, she would agree to their going.

Over coffee she gaily assembled the materials for the professor's dinner. Lunch was not her problem today. Ed had volunteered to cook it, and so he would—she would remind him.

Some minutes later, having forgotten her earlier sense of not being alone, she started when the kitchen door banged open behind her.

It was Ed. "Hallo," he said. "Is it coffee time?"

"I didn't hear you come in," she said, going to him and kissing him.

"Mmm. That was nice," he said. "But I'd rather have some coffee at the moment."

"All right," she said, lighting the gas under the kettle. "Where have you been? You've been away a long time."

Erik must have gone to his bedroom, she thought.

"Talking to the articles." Ed sat down. "Also to the man who keeps the articles. Actually, he calls them pigs. His name's Jimmy Patterson. . . . Then I met an ornithologist in the churchyard. We found a collared dove in one of the trees. It was all in. He said it had flown over from Scandinavia. They're all doing that now. The island is a stopping point for birds going south for the winter. . . . Did you hear the foghorn?"

"No," she said, thinking that Erik might also like some coffee.

"It's stopped now. The fog must be fairly local."

Runa went to Erik's bedroom to ask him if he wanted anything to drink. The room was empty.

"Ed," she called.

"What?" he said, getting up and going to the kitchen door.

"Where's Erik?"

Ed looked at her and into the bedroom.

"Isn't he with you?"

"No," she said. "I thought he was with *you*."

"He was—for about five minutes. Then he said he didn't want to see the pigs and came back here. Well, he went in this direction. Obviously, he's pushed off on his own."

"But that was over an hour ago. Where has he gone?"

"I don't know and I shouldn't worry." Ed took her hand. "He'll be back in time for lunch. Or perhaps the news that I'm making it has driven him away. He'll be back."

"Do you know—?" she began, about to mention the sand in the bed and the bucket and torch beneath it.

"What?"

If she told him, he would be annoyed. She turned away

from him to change the subject, and caught sight of the sketchbook.

"What?" he repeated.

She picked the sketchbook up and found her drawing to show to him. "What do you think of that?" she said.

"Isn't it the drawing you did yesterday?" he asked, then realized what was grimly different about it.

"Hey! Is that blood?"

"You remember Erik cut his finger last night? Well . . ."

"My God. The little beast."

"That doesn't matter," she said. "Look here."

She pointed. Her head was close to his. "There is writing. They are *runes.*"

He tilted the drawing toward the light from the window, for the room had become appreciably more gloomy.

"So they are," mused Ed.

"Do you know what they say?"

"No," he said. "But MacDougall will know." Ed looked at her.

"How can Erik know how to write them? Runes?"

For an instant the drawing flared with a strange white light.

Ed and Runa faced each other. The room now seemed even darker.

"Lightning," he said.

"It's not raining, is it?" she whispered. "What about Erik?"

"You don't get fog *and* rain," he answered. "Listen!"

From far away came a brief dull rumble of thunder.

On the misty headland stood Erik, with a sword held high in his hand.

2

"The rain has cleared away most of the mist," said Runa.

She was looking across the sand flats. The far shore and the hills beyond rode parallel with the car.

"Let's hope it's clearer inland," Ed remarked and glanced toward the mainland. But the hilltops were beset with cloud. He might not be able to climb Yeavering Bell.

In the back of the car, Erik ran his fingers, one by one, through a golden ring in his pocket.

It was the only one of his latest finds he had been able to clean after lunch, while his mother was in the kitchen preparing the evening meal and his father planning their journey. They had asked surprisingly few questions about his morning disappearance. He told them he had been looking for shells on the beach and forgotten the time. They had both been friendly and followed him into his bedroom. His mother said there had been some rain and thunder and lightning—none of which he had noticed, though she seemed not to believe him when he said so. His father showed him the drawing with the man on the beach, and asked him what he had written on it. The writing had been pointed out to him—all he saw were little scratchy lines—and again he was not believed when he said he had written nothing. The lines weren't writing, he said, and asked what was meant by "runes." To this there was no reply.

When they set out for Kirknewton, he was still in a mood of self-congratulation at having returned to the cottage with his booty unnoticed. He had merely come in quietly by the front door—which was not locked—put his three new prizes in the box, gone out the front door, closing it after him, pressed the bell and come in again. He was not even late for lunch. He had thought about not eating it, as it was made by his father. But there was tomato soup and poached eggs on toast with buttered carrots and a lot of biscuits and cheese and he was very hungry. Nothing would be gained by not eating, and when he said afterward, "That was good," he felt by his father's expression he had somehow gained a victory.

Erik wriggled with satisfaction on the back seat of the car. He clutched the ring and thought of the iron sword, which had been so large—it was half his height—that he could not bring it back with him unconcealed. Instead, he had reburied it in its grave. He could not use it yet, though a time for its use would come.

After driving halfway along the causeway, they came to a halt. Two sections of the road were still covered by running water, with waiting cars at either end of the flood. This did not discourage Ed, for after a brief appraisal of the scene he drove slowly into the swiftly flowing shallows—to his own delight, to Erik's excitement, and to Runa's apprehension. The churned-up water fanned noisily from their wheels.

"Wee-hee!" cried Ed. "We're all at sea! A life on the ocean wave!"

"Oh, Ed," said Runa, "is it safe?" She raised her feet in case the water came in.

"Why? Do you want me to stop and go back?" He put his hand on the gears.

"No, no," she said. "Go on. It's too late now."

"We'll all be drowned!" shrilled Erik, bouncing about in the back.

"Not while I'm at the wheel!" declared Ed, and tooted the horn.

When they reached the other side unscathed—the first car across—he accelerated exultantly up the slope toward Beal.

"Wasn't that great?" he demanded. Runa smiled. He looked in the driving mirror at Erik.

"Hey, you in the back—adventurer! Wasn't that great?"

Erik considered his father's eyes. He was unwilling to admit any merit in the crossing. But his own recent achievements were so large that he felt inclined to be generous—and in a flash of insight, he realized one's enemy had to be worthy of oneself.

He wrinkled his nose. "Not bad," he said.

Ed laughed. "Gosh, thanks," he said and smiled at Runa. Then he addressed the driving mirror again.

"Is it a truce today? I say 'pax.' "

Erik fingered the serpentine ring in his pocket, and thought of his other treasures in the box and the one he had had to leave in the headland. He was supremely powerful now, a keeper of gold and of secrets. His mission could wait.

"All right," he said, reclining grandly on his seat with his feet off the floor. "Pax."

"Ed!" cried Runa. "What are you doing?"

They all jerked forward as he braked the car.

A cock pheasant flew off the road with a whirr of wings and over a hedge.

"Blast," Ed murmured. "Missed."

The temptation of running the pheasant down had been too much. He had often chased after pheasants in the fields when he was young, though he never caught them. He had also tried to knock them out with a well-thrown stone—again without success. Once when he was fifteen he had used a cricket ball and succeeded. But the bird had not been stunned or killed—its wing was broken. He had caught it easily, despite its desperate attempts to escape, and then had not known how to kill it. He had not been able to destroy the beautifully feathered, living, pleading creature in his hands. It had squawked and flapped its one good wing in protest, and he had been shamed into letting it go. Then, conscience-stricken at its plight and seared with grief at what he must do, he had flung himself upon it, pinned it down with his jacket and arms, and squeezed its glossy green-black neck with all the force of his hands—his eyes tight shut. Voiceless now, the pheasant fluttered and twitched until, at last, it died. When he was able to stand, he looked down without emotion or feeling at his prize. He could not take it home for dinner, nor leave it as evidence of his crime. He hurled its body into a copse before going home.

Some of its long tail feathers he had kept for several years as a trophy, using them later as the basis of an anecdote on his cricketing prowess concerning the day he bowled a pheasant for a duck.

"After you go through Lowick, go straight on," said Runa. "Don't turn right."

She was concentrating on reading the map, trying to find the quickest way among the maze of brown and yellow "B" roads to Kirknewton, being apprehensive about returning to Holy Island by seven o'clock. The professor was expected at half-past seven.

After steering Ed through the complex of junctions beyond Lowick, she took them onto a yellow road across Bar Moor.

"It doesn't look yellow to me," declared Ed.

"You have no imagination," she retorted.

"There are a lot of earthworks about," she continued, having the chance now to study the map the right way up.

"It's a feature of hill country," Ed observed. "The ancient Britons couldn't cope with the marshes and forests of the low ground. They were for the most part a hill people, living on whatever pieces of high ground they could grow crops on. It was also safer there, and they made the earth-works to protect themselves and their cattle from wolves and bears and enemies. It was the brave new world of the New Stone Age, not long after Britain became an island."

He changed gear. "Even in those days the British were way behind the times. They didn't get farming from Meso-potamia for over five thousand years, and they didn't put the stone into Stonehenge for four thousand years after the pyramids. What do I do here?" he demanded.

The road forked ahead of them.

"Oh, wait!" she cried, trying to find the place on the map. He drove the car down the left-hand road.

"Why didn't you wait?" she asked.

"It's what is known as progress," he replied.

"Well, in fact it doesn't matter," she said. "We can go down here to Fenton and then turn—"

"Pheasants!" he yelled. The field on his right was full of them. "Look at them! Christ! If I only had a gun—"

"Pheasants!" cried Erik, seeing several in a field on his left. "Bang! Bang!"

In the road ahead a cock pheasant was strolling along by the hedge.

"The cheeky bastard!" muttered Ed and trod hard on the accelerator. "Charge!"

The car sped straight at the startled bird and the roadside bank, missing both by inches as the pheasant flew up over the hedge into a small plantation. Ed stamped on the brakes.

He tumbled out and hurled himself over the hedge after the bird. At the same time Erik leaped out and ran madly after another cock pheasant, which flew off into a plowed field to avoid him.

Runa got slowly out of the car and waited, while flocks of chattering pheasants launched themselves into the misty air on both sides of the road, in flight from their pursuers.

Some minutes later Ed emerged from the plantation and Erik reappeared out of the field. Both were laughing and undamaged, though somewhat dirtier. Neither had made any captures. Runa was glad to see them united in such a merry mood.

As Ed went around the car to the driver's door, Erik seized her hand.

"I *do* have something for you," he whispered. "It's not what I promised—not so big—but *better*—for *you.*"

Before they set off again, Ed consulted the map, while Erik sang softly to himself in the back of the car. Runa pointed out where they were, leaning against him as he explained the symbols on the map for her instruction.

"You're right about the earthworks, camps and enclosures," he said. "It's a very ancient area this. . . . Do you see how near we are to Scotland? And there's Flodden! I'd forgotten it was in Northumberland. 'Flodden Field, 1513.' I'd like to go there."

He looked out of the window, wishing he had realized this sooner. But the die was cast for Kirknewton and Yeavering Bell.

Fifteen minutes later they were driving westward up the valley of the River Glen, which ran unseen below them to their right, while the high ground to their left rose up to be lost in cloud.

These hills were the northern bulwarks of the Cheviots, and one of them was Yeavering Bell. With his eyes on the road ahead, Ed could not be sure which base of heather and fern was the one he wanted to climb.

Runa said they had passed a mansion in some trees to their right which was marked as "Yeavering" on the map. Further on they came across a memorial by the roadside— a high alcove of stone with a plaque at its center.

Ed stopped the car. He got out to read the inscription.

In the windless silence on the valley floor enclosed by the green hill slopes and a ceiling of gray cloud there was an apt solemnity to his reading of the words. He felt like a mourner at a cenotaph.

The plaque said: *At this place was Gefrin, royal township of the seventh-century Anglo-Saxon kings of Northumbria. Here the missionary Paulinus in* A.D. *627 instructed the people in Christianity for thirty-six days and baptized them in the River Glen close by.*

He turned about and saw at once that the hill facing the memorial must be Yeavering Bell. For from where he stood its wide and appropriately bell-like silhouette was most exact, despite the fact that clouds concealed its crest. He could not climb it today.

Ed moved out of the alcove in order to get a better view of the meadows where Gefrin once had stood—a royal palace by the river.

His gaze roamed up the valley. Many travelers and traders would have come this way, he thought, from Edinburgh and Carlisle, stopping here for food and rest before going down to Bamburgh on the coast.

"Gefrin," said Runa, mispronouncing the name. She moved over to where Ed stood by the fence.

"The 'G' is soft," corrected Ed. "Pronounced as 'Y.' And 'F' is 'V.' It would have been pronounced 'Yevrin.' That's what we almost call it now—Yeavering."

"What was here?" she asked.

He told her his imaginings from the facts, concluding that Edwin, king of all Northumbria, had built Gefrin.

"Edwin was a heroic king in the poetic tradition, and also the first great Christian king of England, of all the English. I wonder how he reconciled his might with his humility. For he was a mighty conqueror before he became baptized. In ten years he enlarged the realm until his authority extended from sea to sea—from Edinburgh to the Isle of Wight, from East Anglia to Anglesey."

Ed looked at the empty meadows, edged on one side by a wood, and tried to picture the timber buildings that had stood there.

"Gefrin must have flourished in Edwin's reign," he said. "I see it as a summer palace, a royal retreat from winters spent at Bamburgh and York. In fact I doubt if Edwin ever stayed at Bamburgh, for Bebba was still there and kept the fortress right through Edwin's reign, waiting for her exiled stepsons to return. Edwin wasn't one of Eoppa's line, you see—not one of *us*."

"Us?" said Runa. But Ed was deep in thought.

"Do you know—?" He hit his head. "I've just remembered. Eoppa, who in the beginning came to Bamburgh, came—not from over the sea—but up the coast from Lindsey. From Lincolnshire. The Angles there were slowly expanding their territory, and a pirate band of them, led by Eoppa and his son, sailed up the coast, and took over Lindisfarne, and later Bamburgh. *They* were the voyagers from Lindsey who gave the island its English name—Lindisfarne—'*Lindisfarena ee'*—which means, according to MacDougall, 'the island of the travelers from Lindsey.' I have a double claim to Bamburgh now, and therefore to Gefrin. They came from Lindsey—and so do I!"

"Shall we go on?" asked Runa, and again Ed did not hear her.

"After Eoppa, there was Ida," he recited. "Then his three sons—Adda, Athelric and Theodoric. Then Athelfrith. Then Edwin, who was killed in battle by Penda, king of Mercia. Edwin was forty-eight and six years a Christian. Penda was fifty-six, and every year a pagan. After Edwin's death, the kingdom fell apart. It was overrun by Penda and his British allies from Wales. Gefrin was burnt to the ground. Everyone that Penda caught was cruelly slaughtered. Then Oswald, son of Athelfrith, took the throne. He came south from Scotland where he had been in exile, and in the early winter defeated Penda's allies. Oswald became a famous king, a saint. He ruled for eight years. He began to rebuild Gefrin. It was almost finished when he was killed in a battle fought at Oswestry. Penda was the one who killed him. And once again he came north and burnt Gefrin and ravaged everywhere, though Bamburgh survived. Oswy, Oswald's brother, was then king in this country. He ventured south to Oswestry, for his brother's head and arm were still displayed there—though his body was buried in Lindsey. Oswy gave his brother's head to the church of Lindisfarne and the arm he gave to Bebba, who was very old. In Bamburgh she built a chapel for the holy relic, and then she died. Oswy, from the age of thirty, ruled for nearly thirty years. He restored Gefrin. Many people conspired against him, even his son and nephew. But he died in bed. He it was who avenged his family's blood by killing Penda, so becoming overlord of England. . . ."

He stopped and closed his eyes. His hands gripped the wire of the fence.

Runa looked at him with sad amazement. The intensity of his long recital had been extraordinary—as had been his knowledge of the valley's past. He was clearly affected by it. His face was pale and drawn. She wanted to touch him, comfort him, but could not, as he was not real to her, not the man she knew.

Ed rubbed his face with his hands and took a handkerchief out of his pocket to blow his nose.

"They all came here," he said. "Athelfrith, Edwin, Oswald, Oswy, Penda. They saw the same hills, the same sky. And at night in time of peace you could have heard men singing in the mead hall—songs about the old gods and the deeds of heroes. . . ."

Veils of mist began to sweep over the hills across the valley, making the meadows darker. A thin rain fell about them.

Runa laid her hand on his, but he did not seem to notice. He stared straight ahead and his voice was low when he spoke.

"The summer after Oswy's death there was a plague at Gefrin. All who remained here died. No one returned. No one dared—they thought it would bring bad luck. The buildings rotted and were blown down in the gales. People spoke of walking dead among the ruins. Slowly Gefrin sank into the ground. It was the end of the golden age of Northumbria. The great kings had gone, and Gefrin with them. All gone. . . ."

Ed turned and looked at her with a haunting sadness in his eyes that she had never seen before.

"Shall we go?" he said. "It's getting cold."

He was still cheerless and remote from her when they left Kirknewton after looking over the church. By this time the rain had stopped. For want of anything else to do or other idea they then continued driving westward, toward Scotland and away from the coast; and as they did so, the mist and cloud receded, and for a moment there was sunshine in the valley of the Bowmont Water. But Ed remained like a man shadowed by mourning.

Then they were in Scotland, and came to Yetholm, where a contest of clay-pigeon shooting was taking place in a field. They watched this for awhile, then searched for somewhere to have tea. But this was Sunday—everything was closed.

"We'll have to go back," said Runa.

"Go back," echoed Erik.

"The time is getting on," she said.

"All right," Ed answered.

So they returned, driving slowly back the way they had come. The three of them were silent, watching the road ahead.

Once more they passed the stone memorial to Gefrin.

"How do you know so much about the place?" asked Runa.

"I don't know," Ed answered. "I must have read about it somewhere."

"It's not your period, is it?" she persisted. "You don't go back that far. Do you?"

"No. Not usually. . . . But I will have read about it sometime."

"You should write a book about Gefrin," she said.

"He can't!" cried Erik from the back.

"Why not?"

"Because—" Erik paused to think. "Because there isn't time."

As they traveled eastward by a different route back to the coast and Lindisfarne, the mist grew thicker in the air and the clouds descended lower. Soon they could not tell which was which, and rode along in a weird world, without shape, direction or substance.

3

"What a fearful fog," said Professor MacDougall, as Ed showed him into the sitting room. "Fearful. Much worse here than it is at Bamburgh. Colder too. Ah, a fire," he said, rubbing his hands before it, then taking note of the oil lamp in the window, the neat pile of books and papers below it, and the small dinner table set with three places opposite the fireplace.

Ed apologized for Runa's temporary absence, saying she was giving Erik his supper in the kitchen and would join them shortly. He offered the professor either a whisky or a sherry, and the latter was accepted.

"Did you hear the thunder?" asked Ed as he poured out two sherries.

"What thunder?"

"Just before lunchtime. Some rumbles and flashes of lightning."

"No, I can't say I did," admitted the professor. "But then, when I'm working, I'm deaf to the world. The trumpets of doom wouldn't disturb me. Oh, thank you," he said, taking his drink.

"Your good health." Ed raised his glass.

"*Slainte!*" said the professor. "Cheers. And lang may your lum reek. . . . Mine isn't. It's out of commission."

"Oh, yes?" Ed expressed interest with his eyebrows, without knowing what the professor was talking about.

They sat down on either side of the fire. Professor Mac-Dougall cast a quick glance about the room.

"Longbottom's up the lum," he said, and explained—"up the chimney."

"He's escaped," suggested Ed.

"Good heavens, no! He's just gone for a walk."

"Up the chimney?"

"Well, he's nowhere in the sitting room," said the professor. "I've searched high and low. I let him out for a run in the room this afternoon. For some exercise, you see. Usually, I go out for a walk and take him with me in my pocket and let him have a wee run in a field or a flat place where I can see him. But I was working on the fragment this afternoon —as I would be out in the evening—and for the same reason hadn't lit the fire. When I looked for him he had vanished! And the only place he could have gone is—"

"Up the lum."

"Precisely. Oh, he's climbed up *curtains* before. He's a very adventurous chap. But he falls off when he gets above six feet. No head for heights. In this case I think he must have found himself a ledge. I had a look, but couldn't see him."

"You're not too worried then."

"No, no. He'll be back. I put some toasted cheese on a lettuce leaf in the fireplace. He'll come down when he's hungry."

The professor neglected to say that he had also put two cushions in the fireplace to soften any fall Longbottom might have. Such information, he thought, might arouse the wrong kind of amusement.

Ed smiled. "Well—here's to absent friends."

They raised their glasses and drank.

Professor MacDougall noted the alterations that Ed had made to his appearance in honor of his guest—his curling hair had been combed and given a parting, and he was wearing a fresh white shirt and a tie—no jacket. Nor was a vest apparent beneath the thin material of Ed's shirt, which also revealed that the solidity of his frame had not been belied by his bulky sweaters. The professor, who was wearing jacket, jersey, shirt and vest, was undecided whether the mere covering of a shirt showed hot-blooded good health and hardiness or a daft disregard for the climate.

The professor relaxed in his armchair. He had been looking forward to his evening out and hoped that Ed's slight abstraction was not evidence of some domestic difficulty. Professor MacDougall wanted to be, and feel, welcome, and to end the evening without getting too drunk or talking too much and with his presence being genuinely missed when he left. At the latest, that would have to be at eleven o'clock —because of the incoming tide.

Ed removed a slip of paper from the mantelpiece.

"Something for your expert eye," he said, giving the paper to the professor. "What do you make of that?"

Professor MacDougall groped for his glasses and put them on.

"They're runes of course," he said.

"What do they say?" asked Ed.

The professor pursed his lips and angled his eyebrows. "As they are . . ." he began. "The symbols read . . . *d, r, o, w, u, n*. Have I got it right?"

"I don't know," Ed replied. "Does it make sense?"

"Not as it stands. '*Drowun*' is no word that I am aware of—though it could be an anagram of the Old English word '*wundor*,' which as you know means 'a wonder,' 'a marvel,' and in a poetic context, as in *Beowulf*, can mean 'a monster,' 'an apparition.' That's if it is an anagram, and if you have it right. The first letter could be an '*m*.' Runes aren't easily copied, for all their simple strokes. A missed stroke, a dash or a dot, could alter everything, and even if the symbols are right, they may have a special significance not at once apparent. Where did you find them?"

"Erik drew them." Ed laughed.

"Erik drew these runes?" The professor waved the paper.

"Not *those*. I copied them from his original—which has since vanished—probably up the chimney." Ed looked at the fire. "Like Longbottom. I just wondered if they had any accidental meaning."

The door opened and Runa came in, leading Erik, who was in his pajamas, by the hand.

As the two men rose to their feet, Ed removed the paper from the professor's grasp and put it on the mantelpiece.

"We meet again!" said the professor, removing his glasses. "Hallo! How are we all?"

His pleasure was sincere and unconcealed. Runa was

looking ravishing, he thought, and Erik bright as an angel. He shook hands with them both, making the most of being able to look down at Erik.

With the lavish exchange of greetings over, Professor MacDougall was about to reorganize the seating when Runa said that Erik wasn't staying. Erik said he was. Runa said the fire was on in his bedroom so he could play in there until it was time to go to sleep.

"Why can't I stay?" said Erik plaintively. "I want to talk to MacDougall."

"Professor MacDougall," said Runa.

"Please, Professor MacDougall, can I talk to you?" pleaded Erik, detaching himself from Runa and slipping his left hand trustingly into the professor's right.

Ed stiffened. "Erik," he said sharply.

The professor was abashed by the boy's soft hand in his and by the thought of the family conflict that might ensue. With a tilt of his head he appealed to Runa under his eyebrows, firmly gripping Erik's hand as he did so to reassure them both.

"Why not?" he said. "If your mother doesn't mind."

"Well . . ." she began and looked at Ed, who made a dismissive gesture and sat down.

"It's your affair," he said.

"All right," she said to Erik. "Half an hour." Whereupon he relinquished the professor's hand and returned to her.

Runa and Erik sat on two chairs removed from the dinner table in spite of the professor's persuasive efforts to get her to take his armchair—while Ed busied himself with pouring a sherry for Runa.

"What did you want to talk about?" inquired the professor, leaning toward Erik, who was perched on a chair beside him. Erik wriggled and frowned.

"Runes," he said, swinging his legs.

"But you know about them already," remarked the professor, glancing at Ed.

"No, I don't," Erik insisted. "What are they?"

Professor MacDougall tried to explain.

"You're wasting your time," interrupted Ed, giving Runa her sherry.

"Can I have one too?" asked Erik.

"No," said Runa. "And keep still."

Ed sat down and spoke to Runa. "We were mistaken in thinking the runes on your drawing had any significance—unless Erik was making an anagram of an Anglo-Saxon word, which isn't likely."

"Why?" said Erik.

Ed looked at him, said "Shut up," mildly and went on with what he was saying.

"It must have been an accidental half memory of something he's seen—possibly in the museum down the road."

"Interesting, though," interposed the professor, who had been admiring Runa's upright composure on the chair with her hands in her lap. Apart from the attraction of her person and her dress—she was wearing a low-necked white silk blouse and a dark blue velvet skirt with a matching band around her neck adorned with a small jeweled brooch—he had been most drawn by the rings on her left hand.

"I *do* know runes!" said Erik.

"You said you didn't," Ed accused him.

"I do. I do," cried Erik. "I do."

Runa hushed him. "Not so much noise."

"You don't," Ed retorted. "How could you?"

Erik was silent. Professor MacDougall, wishing to restore the balance, said, "The letters you showed me *were* runic characters."

"I do," said Erik softly.

In aggravation Ed stood up to grab a pen and the folded

173

foolscap on the mantelpiece. He gave them to Erik.

"Prove it," he challenged.

Erik looked at the paper, then at the fire. Professor Mac-Dougall observed how oddly worried Runa appeared to be now—she was twisting one of her rings. Ed's tense attitude also seemed out of keeping with the absurdity of his demand.

They all waited for some reaction from Erik, whose face was now flushed with concentration on his problem.

Suddenly he got up, dropped the pen, crushed the paper and tossed it into the fire.

"I won't," he said. "I'm going to play in my room."

Ignoring the adults, he made a dignified exit from the sitting room with an air of self-possession that aroused the professor's sense of theater—he felt inclined to applaud.

Ed and Runa glanced at each other. Both visibly relaxed. Ed seized the poker to scatter the flaming remnants of the paper. Runa retrieved the pen. Professor MacDougall, uncertain of his part in the next scene, waited for a prompt.

"That's got rid of him," Ed said, replacing the poker.

Runa sighed. "You never know what will happen next with Erik," she said to the professor. "So. I shall go in and see him later, and when I have put his light out, we shall eat. How's that?"

"That sounds like a very good plan," replied Ed.

"Splendid," said the professor, and drained his glass.

"Another sherry." Ed stood up. "Come on. I'll have one too."

Runa refused and asked the professor how his work was proceeding. He replied that he would probably finish his analysis of the fragment by Wednesday. He went on to tell her about his labors that day and about the disappearance of Longbottom. Then he asked what they had been doing and heard of their afternoon excursion to Kirknewton—

where he had never been, though he knew about Gefrin.

"You must go there," Ed urged. "It's a most evocative place."

"It certainly is," said Runa. "From the way Ed was talking about its past you would think it had once belonged to him."

"What did he say?" inquired the professor, making a steeple of his hands.

"So much history!" she exclaimed. "So many kings. I never knew there were so many before King Alfred. All fighting, killing and burning. How many times is Gefrin burned?"—Ed shrugged her question away—"And in the end there is a plague and nobody returns."

Professor MacDougall turned to Ed. "What made you say that?"

"What?"

"About a plague at Gefrin. There's no account of that in any chronicle or history of the time—as far as I know. And no archeological evidence either. Not much is actually known about Gefrin, apart from rough dates and positions of buildings and that it was burned down twice and finally abandoned. Where did you get your details?"

"I don't recall offhand." Ed examined his fingers. "But I wasn't making it up."

There was a pause as Ed's manner appeared to discourage any further discussion on the subject. But Runa was not to be put off.

"You said no one would go back there because of the bad luck."

"Did I?" Ed seemed surprised. "I don't remember that."

He stood up. "Would you excuse me for a moment?" he said to the professor. "I arranged to go out with one of the fishing boats tomorrow morning. With all this fog about I think I had better check that it's still on. I won't be long," he said to Runa. "But I think I should get it sorted out before we have our meal."

"Oh, as you wish," she said.

He left the room. In a minute he reappeared, pulling on his sweater.

"I'll get some more mead while I'm at it," he said. "Anything else? No. Right. Be seeing you." He closed the door and a moment later the front door slammed behind him.

"Mead!" exclaimed the professor. "The local brew no less."

"You don't mind?" asked Runa.

"No, no. It will be most appropriate to the place and the occasion. An excellent idea." So he said, though he would have preferred a dry white wine—depending on what they were having to eat. What went with mead? he wondered.

"Can you tell me—?" began Runa.

"If I can, I will," said the professor, sinking lower in his armchair, slightly ill at ease at being left alone with her.

"What does Lindisfarne mean?"

"Ah," he said. "It's disputed of course. But there's only one real meaning, and that is, 'the island of the travelers from Lindsey.'"

"And where do the kings of Northumbria come from?"

"That's not certain, though a recent theory says they came from Lincolnshire—from Lindsey, which is its northern part. Their earliest kings, Eoppa and Ida, may have been responsible for the renaming of the island. Before that, the British called it Metcaut."

Runa smiled. "That's what Ed was saying. He said they came from Lindsey, like him."

"Where did his family come from in fact?"

"He says they've farmed in Lincolnshire for many years," said Runa. "Although there *is* a tradition that the Wardlaws originally came from Yorkshire."

176

"Which was for hundreds of years part of Northumbria," said the professor. "The wheel has come full circle. He is here. The traveler from Lindsey has returned."

They both fell silent in contemplation of this fantasy. MacDougall rested his eyes on Runa, while she gazed at the puttering fire. His attention was drawn again to the rings she was wearing.

"Those are very fine rings you have," he remarked.

She started. "What? Oh, yes," she said, holding her hands before her and spreading her fingers. "You mean on my *left* hand. This on the right hand is my engagement ring. In Norway, we have no wedding ring. We exchange rings on the day of our engagement—it's called 'Forlovelses-ring'—and are wearing them at the wedding. The man also. On the *right* hand. There is no giving of rings in the church."

"Where did you get the other two? If I may ask."

She removed them from her left hand.

"They are both family rings," she said. "For special occasions only. This one my grandmother gave me." Runa passed it over to the professor. "Diamonds and sapphires," she said. "The same as the brooch at my neck. They are a set."

He examined the delicate dazzling workmanship through his glasses. She gave him the other ring, which was quite different, being thicker and made entirely of gold. It was very finely engraved, with an odd pattern of intertwining lines.

"This one my father left to me," she said, her Norwegian accent becoming more pronounced. "It has been in my family for many years and is always worn by the first boy whose name begins with a 'G.' If you look very carefully, you will see a 'G' in the middle. My father's name was Gunder, and my eldest brother was Geir. But he died. So he never had the ring, and when my father died, it came to me."

Professor MacDougall stared at the "G" on the ring and then over his glasses at Runa, his mind for some moments refusing to recognize the connection, obvious as it now was.

She smiled at him. "My name is really Gudrun. Ed never liked it, and always called me Runa instead. But really I am Gudrun . . . Ed thinks it is a terrible name."

She laughed.

4

During the dinner it seemed she never stopped laughing. The professor had a fund of comical anecdotes about his early days in Aberdeenshire that were amusing in themselves but enormously added to by his zest in telling them. Most of his stories centered around the characters in a village called Strichen, whose misadventures he recreated with an expressiveness of face and voice that was a delight to his listeners—as was the rapturous laughter with which he greeted his own narration, with his head flung back and his eyes like slits while he quivered and hooted with glee.

Ed was as entertained as Runa. But when he tried to interpose some Lincolnshire anecdotes of his own, which Runa had heard before, the general merriment lapsed. There was no alternative but to let Professor MacDougall hold the stage—which he did without any prompting.

When Runa brought in the coffee, they retired to their chairs around the fire, which was now a fiery glow of embers in the grate. Ed lit his pipe, and Professor MacDougall produced a cheroot. The men's actions had slowed, becoming more expansive and considered.

Before sitting down, Ed had looked out of the window, and reported that the fog seemed even thicker. This had led the professor to consult his watch, be amazed at the time, and then to congratulate Ed on having postponed his fishing boat trip. In its place, Professor MacDougall proposed a visit by boat to the Farne Islands on Wednesday, by which time he should have completed his work.

The tide tables had then to be examined to make certain the tides were favorable. Low tide was at 9:17, and high tide at 15:12—which meant that the Wardlaws would have to leave Holy Island in the morning, and after lunching in Bamburgh, could see the Farnes in the afternoon.

"Splendid, splendid!" said the professor. "Wednesday it is . . . There's a full moon that night if I remember. It will light you home."

Runa felt the fierce dying heat of the fire too hot upon her and sat herself on the arm of Ed's chair. Involuntarily she moved the damp curls off his shiny forehead and rested her hand on his shoulder.

Professor MacDougall gazed at them through a cloud of smoke.

"Gudrun," he declaimed.

"A dreadful name," commented Ed—all earlier strangeness forgotten, aware only of Runa's presence and touch, the savor of his pipe, and the words of the professor.

"Not at all, not at all," Professor MacDougall scolded. "A name of glorious womanhood, of invincible female courage and resolve. The name of Osvif's daughter in the Laxdale Saga—above all the name of the wife of Siegfried and Eonakir and Attila the Hun."

"All three?" queried Ed.

"According to legend. But Siegfried was the finest of her husbands. . . . It's all in a superb poem—'Gudrun's Lament.' At the end of it she says, 'Do you remember, Siegfried, what we two swore, when in bed we lay together?—that you would come even from death, proud hero, to visit

179

me, and I you from the world.' Then she says, '*Hlathit er, iarlar, eikikostinn!*' 'Build high, my lords, the pyre of oakwood! Make it under heaven rise highest of all!' "

"And then?" asked Runa when the professor stopped talking, sunk in his imaginings of the scene.

"She dies in the flames."

"Faithful lady," murmured Ed.

"Did these things ever happen?" wondered Runa.

"Of course!" replied the professor, sipping his coffee. "These things *have* happened. A woman—sometime, somewhere—*has* done these things. Not the same woman, nor at the same time. But even the most fantastic fiction has its basis in truth—especially when its roots are human nature, which has not altered much these last few thousand years."

Ed relit his pipe. "I'll go along with that," he said.

The professor exhaled. "I would even say it has not altered at all." He sat back, cast up his eyes, and raised both hands as if in prayer.

"Take away the gloss of modern living and you still have the natural man of instinct and emotion. These things still rule the mind in any struggle for existence—as in a time of war. Kill, or be killed. An eye for an eye. Are we so civilized we are no longer frightened of the dark? We *are*—afraid. Given the occasion, we lose our minds to primitive emotions, deeds of instinct. Given the circumstances that led Gudrun to do what she did, you might do the same," he said to Runa. "You are Gudrun. Perhaps in more than name."

"Then you are Siegfried," she said to her husband. "My hero! *Min helt!*"

"Get away," he mumbled.

"But who is the professor?" she continued. "Which character in legend is he? Which are you?" she asked.

"He *is* legend," answered Ed.

"Very good," said the professor. "In truth, I am the

Wizard of Id. And I have a thing for you."

He threw the butt of his cheroot into the fire and archly grinning at them drew out some papers from his inside pocket.

"A thing?" repeated Ed.

"A small token of my great esteem. A little gift in thanks for such a pleasurable evening."

Runa stood up to take the folded missive from him and passed it on to Ed, who was knocking out his pipe. "What is it?" she asked.

"Don't look at it yet—until I've gone," warned the professor. "Otherwise I shall be here all night, explaining." He rose to his feet. "I'm afraid it's time I was off. Or else be cut off. Time and tide, etcetera."

Ed stood up and put his pipe on the mantelpiece.

"You can't leave until you tell us what this is. Is it a secret code? We might be compromised in taking it. Become involved in espionage, or worse."

Professor MacDougall looked up at them and felt the same alarm and admiration that his first sight of them in the museum had aroused. He had gone there, he remembered, to renew his acquaintance with the Viking stone. He had not known the Wardlaws then, though now it seemed as if he had always known them.

He touched the papers held by Ed. "The sack of Lindisfarne is here," he said. "And matters no one knows about but me."

"The fragment!" Ed exclaimed.

"A copy of my translation of it. For *you*."

"That's very generous. Many thanks." Ed smiled at Runa. "Isn't that great?"

Professor MacDougall felt an indefinable pang, as if of guilt. Somehow he had erred. He looked up at the handsome, happy pair with sudden foreboding.

"It's not for publication of course," he said. "Just for your personal interest. I felt you had a claim to it—being here, and being an historian. But no one else must know. Keep it, but keep it to yourselves. Let it be a secret between us three. No one else must know who came to Lindisfarne. And who it was that died."

Erik was cold. He had not noticed before how chilly his bedroom had become, how hard the floor, how stiff and painful his limbs in his dank pajamas. But now that he had finished, he knelt on the floor by his bed feeling not at all well and very tired. His head and eyes were hot and heavy, his shoulders ached. The fingers of his left hand were sore and smelly with all the scraping, polishing, cleaning and repairing he had done. But he *had* finished—his obligation to tidy up the treasure as best he could had been performed. His solemn task for Sunday night was done.

Despite his aches and tiredness, he wiped his fingers on a cloth with a dull triumphant sense of satisfaction, added to by the fact that no one had found him out.

Sometimes the sound of adult laughter from the sitting room had startled him. He had tensed when his mother burst into the hall. But these alarms had only made him work the harder. He did not have much time.

With a noisy sigh Erik gathered up all his cleaning gear and stuffed it into his bucket—the kitchen ·bucket and the torch he had managed to return unnoticed after lunch to where he had found them.

Then he dragged his black tin box from under the bed. Within it all the objects of his great discovery had lovingly been laid, after he had made them bright and clean again. He had not been able to do much for the rusted bits of iron, but he now knew what they had formed.

The bicycle wheel had been the rim of a circular shield—
with the gold beads part of its border and the other iron
pieces the center and rear. It must have been a wooden
shield, whose face had been adorned with dragons and fit-
tings of gold. He could picture it so well that he had to be
right.

But these earlier finds of his, including the arrowheads,
had paled beside the more thrilling and recognizable objects
acquired on his last two expeditions.

Erik raised the lid of his box, exposing the riches within
to the yellow glow of the lamp that was outshone—it seemed
to him—by the golden, glittering brilliance of his treasure.
There were the broken ugly iron pieces of the shield, the
twelve gold mounts, the gold half orbs, the jubilant flying
dragons, one of which had been his signpost to the grave.
There was the jagged clutch of arrowheads—for which he
must make some shafts. There was the buckle of bronze
and gold and two large golden brooches, engraved with
whirling swastikas, with a red jewel at their hub. There was
the golden ring, shaped like a biting serpent—this he would
give to his mother. There was the great gold collar, twice as
wide as his fist—a mass of interlocked chains, nine rows of
them in all. There was the glorious golden horn, its vaunt-
ing arc embossed with vivid dancing figures of men and
beasts. There in the midst and on top of the rest was the
iron frame of the helmet—its panels long-since disintegrated,
though the guards for nose and ears and neck were still intact, still joined to the cage of the crown. On its crest was a
golden dragon, with folded wings, and a tail of flame, and
great red eyes, and gilded claws as sharp as the teeth in its
wide and ravening jaws.

Erik's eyes shone with pride at the ancient treasure within
his keeping. He exulted in the possession of such gold, such
kingly arms. Now they were his, to guard and hold as if he

were the dead king's son. And hidden in the headland was the sword.

Frowning fiercely, biting his lip, he raised the iron helmet from its golden lair. He dared not put it on his head—much as he wanted to. This honor had not been earned yet. Slowly he turned it about, so that it and its dragon crest faced him.

"Guthorm," he breathed, and his breath was visible in the cold air of the room.

"Guthorm," he sighed, and softly blew the mist of his breath into the darkness between the iron frame, surrounding the dragon with smoke, as if it were alive.

5

Ed retired into the sitting room to read the translation of the fragment as soon as Professor MacDougall had left. He loosened his tie and flopped into his armchair. Runa had cleared the dinner table before they sat down to coffee, so having collected the coffee cups from the sitting room she took them into the kitchen to be included in the washing up. "I'll dry," he said. But when at last he followed her into the kitchen she had not only done the washing up but also the drying, and was putting the pans and cutlery away.

"Hey, you've finished!" he said with much surprise.

"All done," she said.

"You should have given me a call. I'm sorry."

"What does the fragment say?" she asked, taking off her apron.

"Amazing things. Fascinating! It's a find of great significance. Come into the other room and I'll tell you."

Before she joined him she looked in on Erik. He was

sleeping peacefully—lying on his back again. Usually he lay curled up on his side.

Ed wanted to give her some mead or whisky, or MacDougall's mixture of both, but she had already had a glass of water in the kitchen and did not want to aggravate the slight ache in her head. Ed poured himself a measure of whisky, while she sat with a sigh where the professor had been sitting and briefly closed her eyes.

"Listen to this!" Ed ordered. "I'll read it to you. It begins halfway through 787.

"At Bamburgh," he said. "That's how it begins, at the top of a page. You ought to see the manuscript. It's written on both sides. Two pages or leaves—four sides in all. Beautifully written—about 900 A.D.

"At Bamburgh." He read on—*"That was 100 years after St. Cuthbert died. . . ."*

She found she was not paying too much attention to what he was saying. But rapt as he was in the revelations of the past, he would not notice. As he read, she listened to his voice more than his words and looked at him more than she listened, letting her eyes dwell on his face and form.

She saw how his hair was fairest at his temples, how short his eyebrows were, how long the bridge of his nose, how soft the indent of his chin, how firm the bony line of his jaw leading strongly back and up to hook on to his ear, itself how subtly formed, and now, how rosy. She saw how shadowed his eyes were—and that he needed a haircut.

He looked in her direction, not at her. She started, for his eyes revealed his preoccupation with other matters, not with her, and she had not been attending to his words.

"They must have been misbehaving themselves in Northumbria," Ed was saying. "Not being as godly as Pope Adrian would like. And that bit about them being urged not to slay any king, and being warned that *it was plain how swiftly* *they depart from this world who have become the slayer of a king, and how wretchedly they forego all rights both heavenly and earthly—*the writer has put that in not only because of what's happened before but also because of what happens later. You don't often get such a display of personal concern in the chronicles—or such a sense of the dramatic. For the next year, 788, begins: *In this year aldorman Sicga betrayed Alfwald king of Northumbria and shamefully slew him at Scythlescester near the wall*—Hadrian's wall—*and a heavenly light was frequently seen where he was slain and he was buried at Hexham within the church of the Holy Apostle Andrew. And Osred, son of Alcred, succeeded to the kingdom after him, who was his nephew*—that is, Alfwald's nephew."

"Why is he called an aldorman?" asked Runa, seizing on an unexplained curiosity to show how attentive she was being.

"Who? Sicga?"

"Yes."

"It's a rank, rather than a title. It means 'older man' or 'counselor'—possibly a kinsman of the king."

He went on reading.

When his eyes were averted from her, she realized how much less meaningful he became, though no less dear, and how her own existence was the less without his gaze on her. Her love was sustained and cherished by his looking more than his looks. When his eyes were shut in sleep, she felt alone and unimportant. Without his gaze, she died.

"That's what MacDougall meant." Ed looked up.

"What?"

"When he said the Viking raid on Lindisfarne was the first raid on English shores. It says *correctly calculated, seven years after Bertric came to the throne*—of Wessex, that is— in 793. Are you listening?"

"Yes," she said.

"And King Osred's servants fought a great battle in the streets of York—it was the capital of Northumbria then—*and killed the citizens.* Shades of Verona. *And in that summer there was an unusually severe plague in the kingdom so that a great quantity of cattle died and the wretched people starved. 790 . . ."*

Strange, she thought. How unlike Erik he was. The only similarity was that they were both fair-haired, though even in that they were at odds. For Ed's hair was the color of harvested wheat and tended to curl—whereas Erik's was straight and pale as flax. She wished they were better friends, or that she had been able to have another child to redress the balance, a child for Ed.

Ed looked up at her. She felt guilty, sure that he knew she'd been inattentive.

"He was Bishop of Lindisfarne at the time," Ed explained.

"Who was?" She told herself to concentrate on his narration.

"Higbald." Ed continued. *"And Sicga*—the one who murdered Alfwald—*seized all the kingdom to the north of the River Tyne as far as Edinburgh.* He must have had his HQ at Bamburgh if that was so . . . Sicga—his name runs through this like a theme."

Ed smiled at her. "This is true, all this," he said. "The history of my ancestors. The early history of England."

He looked down at the carbon typescript. "We're into 791 now."

She pictured him being very English, playing cricket for his college—with his sleeves rolled up, his shirt awry, his white flannels stained where he polished the ball—purposefully bounding down upon the wicket, where his legs scissored wide as he hurled the red ball like a javelin at the defending batsman. No other man she had ever met had been as forceful—or as gentle. None in Norway, where she had always supposed, like her parents, that she would marry and settle down. But this Englishman, this foreigner, had changed all that. He had said—"Would you like to marry me?" And she had looked at him, and known there was only one answer.

She looked at him now and heard what he was saying.

"And in the same year Athelred the king caused Alf and Alfwine, the sons of Alfwald, to be seized from within the church of St. Peter in York—where they would have taken sanctuary—*and then to be most evilly drowned.* Athelred was making sure of his position by exterminating other candidates for the throne. *And in the winter, aldorman Athelhard*—he drove out Osred you remember. Perhaps he was Athelred's brother. Anyway—*aldorman Athelhard led his forces to the River Tyne and fought against aldorman Sicga. But there was a snowstorm, and neither had the victory.* Athelhard must have tried a surprise attack in winter to regain the lands seized by Sicga. Can you imagine the two armies fighting in the snow?"

In the snow, she repeated to herself, seeing again the falling snow outside the window of his digs in Oxford, that January nearly nine years ago. They had met under the entrance arch of his college by the Porter's Lodge—it was just before term officially began—and then after a warming lunch in a pub, they had walked around the frozen Meadows, comparing Christmas holidays and seeking to fill the gaps in their letters. They had gone back to his digs for tea and crumpets, and afterward in the darkening room their conversation had waned, constrained by unexpressed desires. He grasped her hand, and would not let go until she let herself be taken to his bed. Convulsively she held him, more to stop herself trembling than out of passion, and was powerless to stop him doing what he desired, wanting his body to move upon and within her. It did not hurt as much as she'd expected. There was pleasure. Then it was over. Heavy upon her he seemed to die. Outside she saw that snow was falling. Such delight that was—it was like a blessing, a touch of home, of Tønsberg, which she had left all white with snow three days before. No one would reproach her for this, or could, if she made of the inevitable, irrevocable act an everlasting gift. He had been her first love. He would be her last.

Runa found herself smiling at Ed and twisting the golden ring on her finger. When he looked up he smiled at her, thinking she shared his amusement at what he had been describing.

"You see why Athelred was nervous—he had no sons of his own to succeed him. *God's curse was on him,* cries our writer, and you can hear the scratchy disapproval of his pen as he writes that Athelred *was frequently with concubines.*"

Ed finished his whisky. "Not much more," he said.

"There's an awful lot for a fragment!" Runa murmured.

"Attend," commanded Ed. "This is a tale of our vanished past, brought to light, and life. No one else has heard it told since this was written. . . . It's about to deal with events that affect us closely—with this island, Lindisfarne. Attend.

"And in this year—792—when Athelred was journeying in Mercia, the king's hall and all the city of York were treacherously set on fire, except the minister, and that was spared. And it was only thirty years after the city was rebuilt. Then Osred came secretly to the kingdom, and Sicga was unable to go to him because he was sorely wounded. And Herewulf—another of Athelred's nobles—*marched against Osred, and Osred's army deserted him, and he was captured later at Aynburg. And then Athelred ordered Osred to be cruelly killed*—the blood eagle perhaps. *And two*

weeks later—his throne saved—*King Athelred married Al-fled, Offa's daughter, at Catterick.* Thus securing an alliance with Mercia and perhaps some sons to succeed him. And so we come to 793. The famous passage follows."

She was fully attentive now, caught by the spell of past events.

"*In this year, there were terrible portents over Northumbria and they sorely distressed the people. These were exceptional windstorms and bolts of lightning, and there were seen fiery dragons flying in the air. Upon these omens swiftly followed a severe famine, and shortly after this, on the eighth of June, there came two ships of Northmen out of Westfold, and they were the first ships of the Northmen to arrive in this land. And they miserably destroyed and plundered God's church on Lindisfarne, and slew the servants of God. Some of the brethren they carried off laden with chains; some they murdered; many they drove out naked and shamed by insults; some they drowned in the sea. And so they came to Bamburgh. And Sicga rushed out of the fortress with sixty men, and they fought in the water against the heathen men, and there was great slaughter on both sides. And although they could not prevail against them, nevertheless, one of the heathen ships was burnt, and Guthorm, king of the Northmen, was killed. Then Guthrod, Guthorm's son, desired to avenge his father. And he burnt the village and harried in every direction, and slew the wretched people wherever he could find them. And then he swore an oath that he would. . . .*"

Runa waited for him to continue.

"Go on. What happens next? What does he say?"

"The manuscript is torn there," Ed replied. "Several words have been lost. It continues in 794. Just listen to this!

"*And in this year aldorman Sicga died by his own hand, and his body was carried to Lindisfarne.*"

Ed paused. . . . "One wonders why he killed himself. Because of the pain of his wounds? Some disease? Remorse at his ungodly murder of Alfwald? He must have died at Bamburgh, the capital of the ancient kingdom and of the one he had claimed as his own. They take his body to Lindisfarne. . . . *But Bishop Higbald would not allow him to be buried there, and he was put in a boat and burned at sea.* As his pagan ancestors had been. Imagine it! A Viking funeral! A boat-burning at sea!"

Ed glanced down at the typescript. *"And his son—"*

"Yes?"

He gathered the pages together.

"That's all there is," he said.

She gazed about the room as if looking for a clue as to how the story continued. Ed's eyes were on the white-ash embers of the fire, in whose midst a volcanic glow still lingered. He was sunk in a dream of the past, with his head on one side. The oil lamp on the dinner table was smoking— a weird black line was issuing from the globe.

Runa went to put it out. She lowered the wick. Then she sat on the arm of Ed's chair and took his left hand in her right. He went on talking, more to himself than to her.

"Sicga would have been the one who killed the old king Guthorm . . . Sicga had suffered that year, with the failure of his hopes of uniting the kingdom, with the crops ruined by the weather and a famine in the land. When his watchmen saw Lindisfarne on fire, when the invaders' longboats boldly came to land below the fortress, he took desperate action. With his men he left the stronghold and recklessly and revengefully attacked the Northmen in the water. He killed the Northmen's leader, sticking his sword through Guthorm's throat. And Guthrod made his vow. . . . He would have sworn some kind of revenge. He would have shouted his defiance at the defenders in the fortress, standing where his father had been killed, standing out of range of spears and arrows, with the smoke from his burned-out ship answered by the flames of the burning village. His words would have sounded strange to the defenders, but understandable—for they both spoke versions of the same language. Guthrod, Guthorm's son, would have addressed himself to Sicga—and his son."

"Who was his son?"

"It doesn't say. I don't know."

"Nothing more is known about Guthorm, or Sicga, or their sons?"

"Not that I know."

Runa examined the rings on her left hand.

"I wonder what happened next," Ed mused. "Did Guthrod ever keep his vow? Did he ever return to avenge himself on Sicga's son? Who knows?"

Professor MacDougall descended the steps to his sitting room in a fuzz of thoughtless movement, with one hand on the cold stone wall to steady his downward progress. The concentration of driving back to the castle had drained away, leaving him weary and only half conscious of his actions. Breathing heavily through his nose, he entered the room, and, in the light from the stairs, propelled himself over to his worktable under the window. He dimly saw that the manuscript, his papers and books were all in order. He also saw that the candle on the window ledge was unlit.

With matches from his pocket he managed to light it and was pleased with its reflection on the paneled glass. Then he tossed his head in self-rebuke. How could anyone see the candle's light in the fog! He needed a foghorn now.

At once one answered, lowly bellowing like a beast fathoms deep.

The Longstone lighthouse out on the Farnes, he thought, and pondered why he had not noticed it when he left his car. With his eyes on the transparent root of the flame, his ears caught the mournful submarine sound again—and something subtler.

A green-edged ghost of the candle flame flickered around the room as he looked about.

Still with its shadow stuck on his vision, he picked up the candle and ventured toward the dark of the room.

There it was—in the fireplace—something alive. And there was Mr. Longbottom, black as soot all over, eating a piece of toasted cheese.

Ed suddenly awoke. His throat and lips were dry, his head burned, the pounding of his heart vibrated in his face. Every muscle of his body was tensed as if for action, and his right hand, flung behind him on the pillow—he was lying on his back—seemed to weigh a ton. It was nerveless and immobile. He awkwardly levered it off the pillow with his left hand, and painfully, movement and sensation returned. The fingers, locked into his palm, uncurled. He made himself relax and wondered what the time was. To ease the rapid beating of his heart, he took a deep and noisy breath.

Runa stirred beside him. She sighed plaintively in her sleep—such a soft submissive sound it aroused a hard aggressive feeling in him. A reminiscence of her smooth voluptuous form beneath him determined him to gratify his pent-up sexuality. He would take her as she slept.

She was sleeping on her right side, with a childlike curled-up abandonment of limbs. He brushed his hand along her outer thigh so that it carried back a section of her nightdress as far as her hip. There he pressed his hand down heavily on her until she turned with a querulous murmur onto her back. In the dark his hand sent sensual signals to his mind as he forcefully pulled her nightdress from about her legs up to her waist. Her cool left hand accidentally rested on his thigh and moved upon him as he moved. He pushed her knees apart and laid himself full length luxuriously upon her, feeling her breasts and body yield to his weight. She murmured more agreeably as he kissed her face, glorying in her comfortable pliant passivity and his body's complete possession of her. Her hands came up to rest upon his buttocks, as he lifted himself and lowered himself, and entered at his leisure.

Far away a dog was barking, and the phrases of an unknown tune were dimly reechoing in his brain—a tune that Erik had been humming in the car.

In the dark of the bed, her body suddenly, dreadfully, shook in a violent spasm, making him rock above her. Her fingers dug into his back, her arms clasped tight about him. She seemed to have stopped breathing, and he knew that her eyes were open, staring into the night above and behind him.

"Ed," she whispered fearfully.

"*Ed!*" she screamed.

A sound like something enormously heavy being dragged under the roof came from the attic over their heads—to be followed by a long and echoing exhalation.

Ed wrenched himself about to look upward, his body now as tensed as Runa's, his scalp crawling. She buried her face in his shoulder.

He knew that nothing other than a trapped bird or a rat could be in that black triangle formed by the roof and the ceiling—nothing of the size suggested by the sounds they had heard.

A faint tapping came from the ceiling above the window

—a tentative, irregular sound, that blindly tapped its way to above their bed, and paused. Then something shifted, gratingly, and settled on the ceiling over the door.

Runa whimpered in the suspenseful silence. Tremors of her shuddering ran through him as he peered into the darkness, petrified as she was, and prevented from any thought or action by a terror of the unknown.

The uncanny tapping repeated itself, sounding like a giant beak tapping within a monstrous egg, trying to break out of the shell. It ceased, and again great lungs exhaled a slow tormented breath and expired in silence.

Ed's heartbeats sounded loudly in his throat. He swallowed noisily, wondering whether he was dreaming. It *must* be a dream.

A jarring thud on the ceiling seemed to course down the walls and shake the floor and was followed at once by a series of rending, splintering crashes that were magnified under the roof and reverberated shockingly in the room. For a moment there was a lull. Then they heard the sound of something sniffing.

Runa clung in anguish to Ed, who still stared upward, expecting the ceiling to crack, and a nightmare foot or a hand or a face to emerge.

"What is it? What is it?" she moaned. Neither of them could move.

As if from miles away came a muted sequence of scattered blows. And then they blasted through the bedroom in appalling explosions of sound. It seemed as if the whole ceiling must collapse under the grim, concussive onslaught repeated insanely as the thundering blows redoubled, quadrupled, until it seemed that a maddened beast was under the roof, plunging and rearing, tearing at the attic floor. They heard a baleful hissing, as of its breath, a furious clashing, as of great teeth, a frenzied scraping like that of giant claws, and all the time a demented pounding, like the lashing of a scaly, huge, and unwieldy tail.

Suddenly Runa found she was thinking of Erik, alone in the other room. She had to reach him, protect him from the raging terror above them.

Ed tried to restrain her as she struggled from the bed. But his fear had weakened and unnerved him. She flung him off. She fled from the room, as the shattering barrage of sounds increased to a stupefying intensity.

As she opened Erik's door there was such a sudden bewildering silence, which left her senses spinning in a vacuum, that she had to lean against the doorpost. She hardly had the strength to switch on the light.

Then she saw.

Erik was fast asleep on his back, with a fixed and hideous grin on his face and his golliwog torn to pieces on the floor.

Monday

1

———————◆———————

Ed stood in the street, looking up at the roof, while a cold wind scattered the last of the morning mist. The blue-gray slates had a hard metallic sweated surface seen against the sky, which seemed to have sucked up all the amorphous qualities of the mist and was itself an indefinite ashen mono-chrome, given distance by the occasional silhouettes of sea-gulls passing over the churchyard. The slates told him noth-ing—they were undisturbed, as were the rigid arms of the television aerial. The roof was quite intact.

He looked about the street and down to the square, with no real expectation of seeing anything untoward. No one was about—the only movement was that of a cat padding along by a wall and the perturbation of a small tree losing its leaves to the wind.

It began to rain.

Ed went inside the cottage, stepping over some fallen

petals of the roses by the door. Their edges were brown, he noticed. Few of the buds in the coming frosts would ever open now.

"It's started to rain," he said to Runa in the kitchen. She was washing up the breakfast dishes.

"Oh, is it?" she said abstractedly, looking out of the window.

He touched her waist. "I'll lay the fire," he said.

She made no reply, in keeping with her uncommunicativeness since getting up. He had tried to discuss the terror of the night with her when they awoke, heavy-lidded and later than usual. But she appeared to accept the conclusion that they had shared the same nightmare, which had ended —had it not?—when she got out of bed, awake, to find that Erik was fast asleep next door. How could he have slept through all that noise if it had been real? Did any of the villagers come running last night to find out what was happening? Had Miss Ingram been around to talk about it this morning? For she must have heard it as well. But no one had called. No one else had heard anything, only the two of them. So, it must have been a nightmare.

This explanation left Ed unsatisfied. But when he pursued the matter, inquiring how two people could have the same nightmare, she said, Why not? They were in the same bed, weren't they? And married. So, why not? He said this was irrational. She said it was the lobster, and got out of bed. Erik ate no lobster, she reminded him, and hoped the professor had not suffered as they had.

Ed was prepared to concede that shellfish dinners *could* produce curious dreams, but not *that* extraordinary, and not shared by two people. It was very unlikely, he said. Whereupon she asked him, "What is *more* likely?" and said she wanted to forget it, as she wasn't feeling too well.

Later, she told him Erik wasn't feeling very well either,

and, though Ed objected, gave him his breakfast in his bedroom. Over their own breakfast Ed tried to read the unread Sunday papers, but he found himself staring at the print as he had stared at the ceiling, while echoes of the night confounded his reason.

To reassure himself he returned to the bedroom, which looked no different from any other morning with the bed still unmade. Feeling foolish, he inspected the carpet and bedclothes for signs of dust or flakes from the ceiling and found none. Gingerly he reached up and touched the uneven off-white surface of the ceiling with his fingers, gently prodding as if it might be made of paper. Although it was peeling here and there, and shadowed by the heat of the gas fire, it was unremarkable and quite undamaged. He hit it with his knuckles in vexation and several flakes of paintlike confetti fell to the floor. But it was the sound his hand had made that fixed him like a statue with his fist upraised. It was just a dull rap, like none of the seemingly magnified sounds of the night, not even the tapping.

He then went outside to look at the roof, and returned to the kitchen no nearer to an explanation of what they had heard. There *had* to be an explanation for those sounds— and he had to find it. Yet as he raked the ashes from the sitting-room fireplace into a shovel, his memory of the violent night took on the quality of a dream—he found it hard to recall exactly what had happened, and in what order— and Runa's explanation began to make more sense. But still he doubted.

He dumped the ashes wrapped in paper in the kitchen trash can. Runa was mopping up the sink with a cloth.

"What are you doing this morning?" he asked.

"The same as every morning," she answered. "Housework."

"Yes—well," he said. "I think I shall do some homework

myself. Perhaps we should stay in today."

He looked outside at the weather, feeling unaccountably dejected.

"We could always go out tonight," he continued.

"Again?"

"You've only been out once," he said. "And if we're going to be in all day, it seems like a good idea. You had a good time on Saturday."

"That was Saturday. Today is different."

"Yes," he said, becoming irritated at her obtuseness. "It is. But we don't have to stop enjoying ourselves. Nobody's dead."

She looked at him dispassionately. "I thought you were doing the fire," she said.

The way she could sometimes cut herself off from him—renege all association with him—angered and alarmed him. When she was like this, words were useless—nothing had any meaning. She returned his glare with apparently total indifference. Controlling himself, he gripped the shovel.

"We'll speak about this later," he said, and left the kitchen.

He was back in a minute, having forgotten to take the kindling and newspaper with him, which when he returned were lying on the kitchen table by the door, waiting for him to collect them.

When the fire was laid to his satisfaction, he sat back on his haunches to admire it. He refrained from lighting it, as Runa had also to acknowledge his achievement—which would be greater, he realized, if he made a thorough job of it and refilled the now depleted coal scuttle.

He grabbed it and trudged back to the kitchen, where Runa, he observed without looking, had set up the ironing board. He mentioned in passing that he was going out to get some more coal. There was no response to this magnanimous gesture, which was further dampened outside the kitchen door by the forgotten and cold fact that it was raining. A drop from the gutter fell on his head.

At the end of the dingy garden stood Erik, hidden inside a long black plastic mac and sou'wester hat—his attitude stiffly expressive of hostility. He had a spade in his hand and seemed to have been doing some digging.

Ed shoveled coal from the bin into the scuttle, wondering what Erik was up to now. How had he slept through the rumpus of the night as Runa had claimed? Unless he had somehow been the cause. . . .

Ed stopped shoveling to think, and the lightly falling rain impinged on his hearing as it struck the slates, the stones, the grass, the garden and the churchyard, and splattered on the glistening lumps of coal. Thought evaded him, and he swung his head about to see that Erik had not budged, but grew like a bush out of the refuse by the wall.

He filled the scuttle and went back into the kitchen where Runa was ironing one of his shirts.

"What's Erik up to in the garden?" Ed asked.

He had to wait for an answer.

Without looking up she eventually said, "He's burying his golliwog."

"His *what?*"

"His golliwog."

This defeated Ed. He expressed stupefaction with his face, and said, "My God! What next!"

He continued on his way to the sitting room, not wanting to know any more about Erik's aberrant behavior, as knowledge of it would make it more not less insoluble. Burying his golliwog? What grim tricks he got up to! What endearing little games!

After parking the coal scuttle by the fireplace, he returned to the kitchen. "It's ready," he said. "Come and light the fire."

"I'm ironing," she replied.

"Oh, go on. I've got the matches." He had them in his hand.

"Oh, Ed!" she said in exasperation. "I'm not playing games. Don't be a baby. Go and light it yourself."

His face went stiff. Without a word he stalked out of the room.

Runa felt a guilty pang at having rejected him—and it would not have put her out at all to have gone into the sitting room, admired his handiwork and lit the fire. But really, she told herself, his demands on her were sometimes so ridiculous, so childish, that it was insulting to both her and him to accede to them. And she was busy ironing.

She was in fact in a peculiarly apathetic mood, well-matched by the dull thud and rhythmic glide of her actions.

She finished smoothing out the cuffs of his shirt, then draped it on a hanger to air.

Out in the garden she could see Erik, intent on his self-imposed task—he had a stone in his hand. Why was he taking so long? she wondered. Should she call him in out of the rain? She should of course not have allowed him to go out in the first place, as he had all the symptoms of a fever—without however a temperature. But any denial of his wish to bury the golliwog would have clearly resulted in such tantrums—which this morning she could not cope with—that she had given way, only insisting that he was warmly dressed and thoroughly protected from the rain.

Runa had not told Ed about finding the golliwog dismembered on the floor of Erik's room. When she returned to the room in the morning it was still disturbingly there. It had seemed so much part of the nightmare that she fully expected it to have vanished in the daylight. But there it was, literally torn to pieces. She had put the remains on the chest of drawers before waking Erik, who was so flushed and fretful she had become quite worried. He complained of a terrible headache and a sore throat—which had bothered him, she remembered, on the day of their arrival on Holy Island. She hoped he was not sickening from anything, and insisted on taking his temperature, which turned out to be subnormal. Nonetheless she gave him an aspirin, told him to rest, and made him a special light breakfast. When she brought it to him, he was fast asleep again.

It was while he was eating his toast that she asked him about his golly—Why had he done it? she asked.

"Done what?" he demanded.

"Why did you break up your golly? I thought you were very fond of him."

"I am," he said.

"Then why—?" She gestured toward the chest of drawers. He followed her gaze, and looked back at her with a stubborn incomprehension that provoked her into fetching the golliwog's remnants and dumping them on the bed.

"Well, if you didn't do this, who did?"

His gasp, his look of pathetic consternation, made her at once regret her bluntness, and his eyes communicated such genuine grief that she realized he had been not only innocent of his toy's destruction, but ignorant of it until then.

"Oh! Look!" he wailed. "My golly! Who *did* this? Who did it? Why?"

He became hysterical with questions and accusations mostly directed against his father, trying at the same time to put the pieces together and hold back his tears.

"Stop it! Stop that now!" Runa commanded, removing the breakfast tray to safety.

She had not known what to say in consolation, and was forced in her defense of Ed into saying that Erik must have done the deed himself in his sleep. This he vehemently denied.

"I would *never!*" he shouted. "*Never* do this to my golly! Never!"

She knew he had to be wrong.

But in retrospect his denials were sufficiently confusing—as much as the senseless act itself—that in not knowing how to explain it to Ed, she had decided to say nothing.

Runa saw that out in the garden Erik was not building a cairn as she'd thought but arranging his stones about the golliwog's grave.

For the sake of peace and to please him, she had not been able to refuse his solemn request to go outside for the burial. He had come into the kitchen, fully dressed, looking well again and composed, and when she agreed, having checked his health and stipulated that he wore his plastic mac and rain hat, he soon reappeared, properly attired, struggling with a large bundle made up of his tablecloth, with obviously more than his golliwog inside. However she asked no questions. She only opened the kitchen door for him with suitable gravity and said, "Don't be too long."

This had been while Ed was out in the street and before she had finished washing up.

Before Runa continued with her ironing—while Erik was out of the way—she thought she should make his bed and tidy his room.

In doing the former, her foot collided with the tin box under the bed. The sound this produced was not what the box would have made, and did make, when it had Erik's collection of marbles, tin soldiers and stones in it. The sound was a harsh metallic reverberation, a searing echo of the night. And the box had not moved an inch. What was in it that weighed it down so much?

She glanced out of the window. Erik was bending over the golliwog's grave.

Swiftly she crossed to the chest of drawers, where yesterday, in a bottom drawer, she had accidentally discovered the complete contents of his box, all his childish possessions, wrapped in the tablecloth. She did not expect to see the latter when she knelt and opened the drawer—but all the objects it had contained had vanished. He had buried them all in the garden.

What was in his box?

What she could see of it under the bed took on an air of menace. Yet its twinkling blackness in the shadows drew her like a magnet. She crawled toward it—and saw it was not padlocked.

What was in it? What had he collected? She had to know —and she had the right. She was his mother.

Her hands seized it, to drag it out. Her ears caught the hiss of the gas fire—and something else.

Runa twisted about. At the window was a hooded figure, peering in at her. It was wearing a frighteningly familiar cape and hat. Was it winking? No.

She realized it was Erik.

He stood against the glass, dark against the light, watching what she was doing.

She scrambled to her feet, and escaped from the room, her heart pounding. After a moment's uncertainty in the hall, she entered the sitting room.

Ed was hunched in an armchair in the chilly gloom. He was reading the copy of the chronicle—and the fire had not been lit.

"Oh, Ed," she exclaimed, switching on the light. "Sitting in the dark. Oh, really!"

"It *is* dark, isn't it?" he said, looking thoughtfully outside where the street was dismal in the rain. "It's because we're facing north."

"You might have lit the fire. It's cold in here."

"I forgot," he said, and smiled.

She knew what he expected her to do.

"Come on, then. Give me the matches."

He unfolded himself and got to his feet, still holding the professor's typescript of the chronicle.

"You'll have to get them," he said. "I can't."

"Where are they then?"

"In the back pocket." He turned about.

She felt in the rear pocket of his trousers and dug out a book of matches.

"There you are," he said. "Clever girl."

"And how clever you are to make such a fire," she replied, kneeling on the hearthrug.

"Isn't it good? That's how a fire *should* be laid. Go on."

She hesitated. There was a feeling of something uncompleted, something missing, something perhaps she had forgotten to say.

She struck the match, and shuddered at its flaring.

Inevitably, she lit the fire.

"It *could* be explained by a poltergeist," Ed declared.

"What could?"

"Last night. Erik could be the cause of it all—although he's so young."

"How?" Still on her knees, she watched the smoke snake up from tiny flames.

"By unconsciously giving a physical manifestation to a disturbed state of mind. It could be very interesting if it continues."

"I don't believe it," she said.

"There's nothing to be alarmed about. A poltergeist is a mischievous ghost, if noisy—and inclined to throw things around."

Instinctively, she knew this explanation of the terrors of the night was wrong.

Under her eyes the flames spread. She felt afraid, and reached up for his hand.

2

It stopped raining after tea, and Runa took Erik out for a walk about the village. Devoid of people, there was a desolation about it that, with the still-running gutters, the wet roofs, the discolored walls and pools of water, gave the village the appearance of having just emerged from the sea. A cold north wind blew through the streets and the sky was overcast.

They returned to the warmth of the cottage, where, in Erik's room, they happily played cards on his bed until it was time for Runa to prepare supper. They played in the bedroom, as Ed was supposed to be working on his thesis in the sitting room, though when Runa visited him later, he was sitting inertly before the window in the semi-darkness, and the room was full of smoke from his pipe. She switched on the light.

"How is it going?" she asked.

"Oh. . . . Not well. What have you been doing?"

She told him she had been playing Snap with Erik, and asked him what he would like for supper.

"Food," he said.

Food, she thought, and became at once depressed.

"What time is Miss Ingram coming round?" he asked.

"Eight," she replied.

He caught the wan inflection of her voice, and gave her a wry smile.

"Are you under the weather too?" he said. "Poor old girl. Come here, and I'll give you a kiss."

But she just looked at him sadly and remained where she was.

Ed left his chair and went to her. He rested his arms on her shoulders and his forehead on her downcast head.

"What's the matter, love?" he murmured.

She made no response. He lifted her face with his hand, and her eyes, avoiding his, closed. Gently he nuzzled her nose with his and smoothed the hair off her temples. He kissed her shuttered eyes and, fiercely protective all of a sudden, wrapped her in a comforting, strong embrace.

"Not to worry," he said. "We'll have a good time tonight. We'll go and plunder the bars of all their 'dumps' and pickled onions and paint the village red. Give them a night to remember."

She withdew from his arms. "You smell of smoke," she protested. "Your sweater niffs of tobacco. Haven't you done any work at all this afternoon?"

"Frankly, no."

"What, then?"

"Thinking about the chronicle," he answered, moving away from her. "Wondering what it was like then. Reading between the lines. I think I know it quite well now—almost what Athelred the king and the others were like. Especially Sicga—and Bebba's fortress."

He told her some of his imaginings over supper, which they had in the kitchen. Erik seemed to listen with great interest, for as his father talked he regarded him attentively—though his wide-eyed watchful gaze gave none of his thoughts away.

Ed conjured up that summer in Northumbria when Sicga and the remnants of his men not killed by the plague sat in the wooden halls of his fortress, the capital of his ancestors' kingdom, waiting for the war band from the south, from York, where King Athelred had his court, to come and wrest his possessions from him. He had reestablished the kingdom of Bernicia. But for whom? For the last of Alfwald's direct heirs had been killed by Athelred—and only Sicga, himself a cousin, a kinsman of Alfwald, survived, together with his son, the last of Eoppa's line. The expected assault from the south did not arrive. Athelred the king was engrossed with containing his quarreling thanes and satisfying his bride. The assault came from the sea, betokened by the smoke from Lindisfarne. Who were they, who had done this thing? the watchers wondered. Soon they knew, when two ships came presumptuously to Bamburgh, two strange longships with fearsome prows and garish sails. "I am Guthorm, king of Westfold over the sea," said their leader, holding high his sword. "I am Guthrod, Guthorm's son," said the other boatmaster. "And I am Sicga, Selward's son," cried the defender in his despair. Then they fought.

At that point Ed's narrative was ended by Erik. Dropping his spoon, he seized his bread-and-butter knife and began to battle with an unseen enemy, uttering savage cries, his eyes alight with bloodlust.

"Erik! Stop it!" Runa said. "Behave yourself."

"Lay off!" ordered Ed with his mouth full of apple crumble—for the knife was flashing uneasily close to him. But Erik continued.

"Sla! Sla!" he cried, parrying, thrusting and slashing with the knife as if he were berserk.

"Hold opp med det der!" Runa exclaimed. *"Sitt pent!"*

On a furious impulse Ed clamped his left hand around Erik's wrist—still holding his spoon in his right—compelling him to stop his sword play. The knife blade in Erik's fist trembled to attention and stood erect between them.

Ed vengefully increased the pressure of his grip.

A grimace distorted Erik's features.

Then his eyes, which had shown his malevolent outrage for a moment, suddenly defocused and went blank. Ed's pressure was returned. He found his hand being dragged forcefully down onto its back on the table—both their elbows were resting on it—and such was his surprise at Erik's extraordinary challenge, and strength, that the back of his hand was about to touch the table before he met the challenge and resisted. The advantage was naturally with Ed, whose fist swallowed up half of Erik's forearm and had a better leverage—even though he was using his left hand.

Runa sighed and looked away, waiting for the usual, inevitable outcome. She spooned up more of the dessert.

Having checked the downward pull, Ed gave a bragging glance at Erik, who was not as he expected in a fret of impending subjugation, but gazing back at him with a scorching intensity, and baring his teeth like a beast.

Erik's demonic expression unnerved Ed for a second. At once an enormous pressure began to drag his hand backward onto the table. Remorselessly, inexorably, it dragged him down. Though he resisted with all his might, a greater force, exerted as it seemed from below, made his resistance as puny as that of a child—as if another hand, as large as his own compared with Erik's, enveloped his powerless fist in a vise and brought it down and crushed it on the table.

For a moment his hand, still grasping Erik's wrist, lay helpless on its back. It was not until he gave up all resistance, subconsciously admitting his defeat—acknowledging the impossible—that he was able to loosen his grip on Erik and let go.

His hand was limp and white—it ached abominably.

Exhausted, Erik still held the knife, and stared at it insensibly with his mouth open, panting like a dog.

Not having seen the outcome, Runa looked from one to the other with puzzled concern.

Erik's heavy breathing turned into breathy giggles. He struggled to his feet.

"I *won!*" he shouted.

He waved the knife in an arc overarm and plunged its point in the kitchen table.

"I won! And I'll win on *Wednesday!*"

Erik lay curled up under the bedclothes. His face still flamed from the blow his father had given him, from the things his mother had said—though it was well over an hour since the confrontation in the kitchen. His head burned with a slow fuse of anger at his treatment, at the indignity and injustice of being treated like a child.

After being banished to his bedroom, he had been allowed into the bathroom, but not for a bath, as his mother had with reason suspected that in retaliation he plotted some mischief there—like locking himself in, refusing to come out, or accidentally flooding the room. She had even had the galling cunning to remove the key from the door. Thus humiliated and frustrated he had sunk into a sullen brooding silence and did not answer when she knocked at his door to wish him goodnight. He would not look at her and lay in the bed with his face to the wall while she tried to talk to him. He made no reply. He would not even say goodnight. This ultimate naughtiness of his pained him terribly when he heard her hesitate and then say sadly, "Well, goodnight all the same, *lille gut*. I hope you will be all right in the morning. Sleep well." He had wanted so much to be forgiven—so that he in turn could say he was sorry, be comforted, and loved. But his stubborn sulkiness had evidently been so convincing, admitting of no repentance, that she had made no motions of conciliation. So she went without kissing him or tucking him up, and his grief at being unloved and unforgiven had been great.

It had been replaced by a dull rage as he heard his parents making preparations to go out. But such was the turmoil of his mind, he could not concentrate his sparking fantasies of revenge into one explosive idea, and nursed his left hand between his legs, for it still hurt and was strangely cold.

He heard the old woman who further demeaned him by being his babysitter arrive. Soon the front door closed. Then there was silence, apart from a faint hum of television voices from the sitting room.

In the dark he began to picture consolatory scenes of his incredible triumph over his father. What power had been his! What strength! The expression of astounded alarm on his father's face as he yielded had been more rewarding in its way than the finding of the treasure. Again, it was another sign of *his* importance—another step toward the final victory.

He knew he was saying things, and doing things, which did not quite make sense—but they were such adult things, they made him proud. And they gave him power.

The thought of Wednesday excited him. He wriggled ecstatically and stuffed his hands in his mouth to stop himself squealing. His hand felt better, more his own. He wanted to see it, check that it really was better. He rolled over and switched on his bedside lamp.

Under its light his left hand looked thin and white, obviously incapable of competing against his father. Yet it had done so. He could not fathom this out. But what had happened before might happen again—to more effect. His eyes shone with a wicked light at the thought. And then dimmed as he recalled with a pouting grimace his failure with the arrows.

He had tried to make a workable bow for them with a bamboo stick and a piece of string. But easy as this should have been, it had proved the reverse. The arrows had nose-dived onto the floor, their shafts, also of bamboo, had come unstuck as well as their feathers, and bits of their iron heads had broken off. When he stretched the bow too far in rash exasperation, the stick snapped—and that was the end of that.

But perhaps there was *something* he could do with the arrows.

He slipped out of the bed, groped under it in the blackness and dragged the weighty box into the light, giggling to himself at the memory of his mother's fright at seeing him at the window. It was just as well he had remembered leaving it unlocked. *That* had been silly. Silly boy, he said to himself. The box would always be locked now when he was out of the room, and for safety the key was now hung on a piece of string around his neck. He removed the circlet swiftly and pierced the lock with the key.

A shiver of pleasure brightened his eyes as he gazed in reflected glory on the golden hoard. It was still unbelievably his, and his joy in it increased with each reviewing. With a tender smile he stroked the dragon crest of the helmet and fondly touched the horn, the collar, and every piece he owned. The ring as usual was disappointingly too big for his fingers, even his thumb. It would have to go to his mother. He realized, incuriously, that it was not unlike the one—his grandfather's—which she had worn the night before.

Erik remembered his golliwog. He would get his father for that, for killing it so cruelly as he slept, giving it the blood eagle and tearing off its limbs. How *could* his mother have thought that *he* would do such a thing! Even though he had gone off his golly after finding the gold, he would *never* be so beastly. Only his father was like that—cruel and brutal. How else would an enemy behave? Still, he had given the golly a proper burial, with all the special possessions that had belonged to him in life, and marked the grave with an oval shape of stones. As a sacrifice, poor though it was, he had skewered several worms with paper clips and pins and squashed them under the stones. But his golly would not rest until it had been avenged.

How? he wondered grimly, looking at the wasted arrows with their useless shafts which had formed themselves into an X in his left hand.

An X—that was somehow familiar—not only the crossed diagonal of the arrows, but the way he held them, arrowheads uppermost. It had a meaning, and was a sign for . . .

He jerked his gaze away and let it be trapped by the two red eyes of the dragon on the helmet.

From somewhere music entered his head—a hollow beat of drum and woodwind, insistent, slow and muted, as if it came from underground. It came, he thought—it had to come—from the sitting room, from some television program. But it was no music he knew.

He listened, and then began with a creepy thrill to recognize the rhythm. His childish treble echoed it. His body swayed, his shoulders dipped as he piped a solemn descant to the dance of war and death.

The barroom of the Iron Rails was like a smugglers' haunt, with its rows of flagons, tankards, mugs, ancient bottles, glass floats, and a gigantic lobster claw suspended from the rafters. Brass candlesticks, arrays of shells, and pictorial charts of British birds adorned the walls. The room was smaller, darker, than its Crown and Anchor counterpart, though the fire was bigger, the central ceiling light more dazzling on the bar end, which was high enough for a group of men to rest their elbows on and gossip round its edge. The only similarity was the portrait of the Queen.

Ed and Runa had gone to the Iron Rails after finding a dearth of people and conversation at the Crown and Anchor. This was partly their own fault, for although Selby Allison had been disposed to be sociable, they had been preoccupied with their own thoughts. After half an hour, a restlessness drove them out. "We can't just wander around," said Runa. "Miss Ingram must know where we are." Ed asked what other pubs there were. "The Northumberland Arms, the Castle Hotel, and the Rails," said Selby. "The Rails?" "The Iron Rails."

Struck by its name they went there, after asking Selby to tell Miss Ingram if she came looking for them.

On seats of imitation red leather they sat against the windowed wall opposite the bar, below which was a long seat occupied by a dozy Doberman bitch. By the blazing fire was a large-bellied man with white whiskers, like a genial English buddha. At the bar end stood four islanders leaning on the bar top and looking like a conspiracy of wreckers.

Ed had been amusing himself and Runa, who was the only woman present, by trying to match island nicknames to the faces about them. But the attempt was artificial—his mood was far from lighthearted, and his mind buzzed uneasily from supposition to surmise, trying to find an explanation for Erik's bewildering powers.

The poltergeist idea had taken root in his mind, strengthened by the extraordinary contest at the kitchen table. Unwilling as Ed was to admit it, this had to be the hypothetical reason for what had occurred. Physically, Erik could not have overpowered him on his own—there was no doubt of that. But he had, and therefore must have been aided by some unknown agency, a force similar perhaps to the manifestation known as a poltergeist—though such a force had never been known to trouble a child of Erik's age. But whose then was the tormented spirit that Erik had awakened? *What* had possessed him?

This kind of thinking was so foreign to Ed that, having at last allowed himself to venture on a quest for possible light in such improbable darkness, the enterprise had its own peculiar excitement. It had the elements of a dangerous journey—at the end of which, so sure was he of his reasoning and reason, the ghost would be laid.

He must question Miss Ingram when they returned to the cottage about any deaths therein or odd occurrences. Before they had gone out he had asked her whether her sleep had been disturbed by any noises the previous night and had been told that she had noticed nothing unusual, light sleeper that she was. This had thrown him slightly, as she *must* have heard something. But perhaps she in fact slept heavier than she liked to admit—being the seasoned whisky drinker that she seemed to be.

Ed looked at Runa—she was drinking her half glass of lager with a stiffly self-conscious angle to her elbow and a surreptitious swallow. She was wearing her father's ring, he observed, and wondered why, as she usually only wore it on special occasions. There was an abstracted apprehensiveness in her manner—as if she were afraid of being caught out of bounds. He was about to ask her what was the matter when she said, without looking at him, "I want to go home."

"Why?" he demanded. "What's wrong?"

"I don't know," she said unhappily.

Wide-eyed, Erik trod an uncertain war dance in slow motion around his box. It was slow because he was unsure of the steps, and because if he went any faster or leaped about, the iron boss of the shield which was on his head might fall to the floor. It was acting as his helmet. Around his neck was the key on its string, and around his waist was a belt—his pajama-trousers' cord which he had removed and threaded through the ring. Otherwise, he was naked. In his left hand was the X of arrows, in his other an arrow on its own, pointing downward. Thus equipped he circled the golden hoard, lit by his bedside lamp. Facing inward, he took three steps, with his knees bent, as if he were a hunter after his prey. On the fourth step he knelt, counting three beats as he did so, and facing outward, raised his arms and bared his teeth. Then he continued as before, until he had circled the box three times. His concentration on the rhythm was such that he hardly heard the words of the chant—only the muffled drumbeat in his head . . . Up, two three. Down, two three. Facing in. Facing out. It would be shame everlasting if he made a mistake. But his helmet gave him strength, and his grip on the arrows sustained him.

When it ended, there was a pause as he stood where he had started and he felt the weight of the golden ring press upon his navel. Then he repeated the dance—but in the reverse direction and faster, fiercer, and so returned to his place. There was no pause this time. At once the drum notes deepened, quickened, sounding louder in the room. This was the start of the last two circles, the seventh and eighth. He flung himself in a growing ecstasy about his open box, doing everything in threes, and faster, faster—skipping, bending, reaching, twirling—first one way and then the other, trying to do what was expected of him as best he could. Then it was the ninth time, the magic round, and he whirled about where he was like a mad thing, deafened by the pounding in his ears, his eyes spinning from light to darkness until neither had distinction and ran into redness shot with hypnotic flashes of light, like the ruby-red eyes of the dragon. The horns blared. For a second he stood, his arms, his weapons upraised in exaltation. Then he fell to the floor.

Though his eyes were closed, his body prone, still his senses reeled through the steps of the dance, and the sacred grove again revolved around him, its hallowed trees hung with the bodies of nine of every different creature that was male. And their heads—of man and beast and bird—flamed on the sacrificial pyre.

Around it, in the torchlit night, he and the other young heroes once more did their ritual dance of dedication and worship, displaying their weapons, skill and strength, asking that these be trebly enhanced, so that the praise, the power and the glory of the god might be the greater—the god of battles and death, whose awesome, golden image loomed above them, while men with horrific animal masks grunted, barked and howled his names—Mimir's Friend! Fenrir's Foe! Gallows-Lord! Evil-Worker! Terror-Maker! Father-of-Victory! Father-of-All! *Odin!*

3

Ed and his five companions stood about the bar end in the Iron Rails. All of them were his age or younger, and all of them were fishermen, except for Jimmy, whose pigs below the Heugh had excited Ed's attention. Robbie was late that night.

They had listened while Ed tried to describe the object of his thesis, and losing interest in it himself, had recreated for them the sack of Lindisfarne and its aftermath at Bamburgh, as revealed in Professor MacDougall's fragment. He had felt it was their right to know the story, and clearly it had impressed them.

"You ought to write a history of the island," said Malcolm earnestly. "It's not been done—apart from the guidebook. And would be worth the doing. There's many interesting things have happened here." Malcolm was the youngest brother of Jimmy and Farmer.

Roger made a derisive mouth at his pint. "There's a lot

that's just as interesting *now*," he informed Ed. "You've no idea the goings-on there are—just as odd as what you have in London. You should write a book on *that*. You'd make a fortune."

"The islanders wouldn't like that," remarked Ed.

"They'd not object, if you gave them a percentage."

There was a general laugh at this from the other five. Charlie always gave good value when he spoke.

Runa looked up with a smile from her seat below the bar, peering past Ed, who was kneeling on the imitation leather beside her, an elbow on the bar—an accepted member of the group of islanders. She looked up at the laughing faces, harshly lit from above, and they seemed like grinning masks, cadaverous and alien. She felt remote and doleful, and as tired as the other female in the room, the slumbering Doberman bitch at the end of the seat.

At first, she had stood with the men at the bar, whom Ed joined when Roger came in. Evidently they were not in the habit of sitting down for a drink. The older men had moved aside or moved on as the younger men arrived. No one had bothered with introductions, as the islanders already seemed to know who she and Ed were. If Ed was unsure of someone's name, he asked Roger, and then told Runa. So she had identified the four she did not know as Jimmy, Malcolm, Hector and Charlie, though none of them actually spoke to her. She was taller than most of them, and clearly put them in some restraint by her presence. The group had seemed in fact in danger of breaking up until she sat down and became unobtrusive beside Ed. Then they flourished and quickly emptied their pints and halves—Ed was the only one drinking "dumps." She noted how they seemed to defer to him, as if he were their leader; and as she listened to their voices, to what she could understand of the dry humor and dogmatic views being aired above her, she studied the older grizzled men who were sitting near the fire. What *they* were saying, in island accents much stronger than those of Ed's companions, she could not understand. But their characters and clothes and gestures were enough for her to read. Meanwhile, Ed was enjoying himself, all earlier tension forgotten for the time.

"The same again, Bash," said Jimmy.

"Are *you* Bash?" asked Ed of the short and round-faced landlord.

"Bash by name and nature," commented Roger.

"Far from it," returned the landlord, cheerily pulling pints. "My name is over the door—Moody, George Moody."

"Don't you believe it," said Malcolm. "It's Bash, for 'bashful.' "

"No, it's never," said Charlie, cradling his half pint. "He's got four kids. It's Bash because he's always bashing away. Ask his wife."

Mr. Moody tried to remain impervious to the laughter. He addressed himself to Ed. "Truthfully, when I was small, I could never say basket. It came out 'bashket.' That's the real reason. It's natural for people in a small community to have nicknames. Like a school. It means you belong."

"Away," said Roger. "I got no nickname. Nor"—he looked about—"nor has anyone here."

"You're just about the only ones on the island then. Strangers in our midst."

"There aren't no strangers here," protested Roger. "Cheers," he said to Jimmy, raising his glass.

"Cheers," repeated Ed, and Jimmy flashed him a smile as bright as his brown eyes. "Cheers!"

In the meantime Bash had moved away to work out Jimmy's change, and finding this too complicated, said, "I'll take you up on your offer, James, and have a beer. That'll take care of the change."

"What do you think of Holy Island?" Malcolm asked Ed, who paused before he answered.

"I like it very much," he said, not knowing how to explain his feelings.

"There's not much to do," prompted Hector.

"No—but there's time to be yourself. And space. And company when you want it. You're part of the mainland, but it's not part of you. Half the time you're free of it, of all its machines and people."

"Aye," said Jimmy. "That's the best of it. When the tide comes in, the visitors go."

"We're not supposed to be very friendly," Hector said. "To visitors."

Ed smiled. "I wouldn't say so. I suppose it depends on why people come here."

Runa felt Ed's hand rest lightly on her shoulder.

"Well, nobody comes here for the beer," said Roger. "Bash—what do you make it from? Tea leaves?"

"Next time you pull a pint," said Charlie, "make sure you flush it first!"

Ed's hand on Runa's shoulder shook as he joined in the laughter that drowned Bash's denials.

She looked away from the fire and up at the men, at Jimmy, who was leaning on the bar in the full glare of the light with his hands clasped to one side of his neck. His forearms, bared by his pulled-up sleeves, were golden-haired and even broader than Ed's. She thought he could have been Ed's younger brother, or even as Ed might have been himself if he had lived all his life on the island.

"Why do you have an interest in articles?" asked Jimmy.

"I'm not sure," Ed answered. "Maybe they're my ancestors. Do you know Danny of Swinhoe?"

"Of course," said Jimmy, and smiled. "I know all the farmers hereabouts that have guffies. Pigs to you."

The fishermen made mock-indignant protests. Jimmy went on smiling, and his smile was echoed by Ed.

"I'm glad someone else is bold enough to call a pig a pig!"

"Mr. Wardlaw," said a voice behind Roger. It was Miss Ingram. Ed turned about, revealing her to Runa, who stood up as soon as she saw their babysitter.

"Oh, Mrs. Wardlaw," said Miss Ingram. "I didn't see you."

"What is it? What's happened?"

"Your little boy is not in his room."

Ed and Runa left the Iron Rails with Miss Ingram straightaway. Ed departed in some annoyance at having to abandon the fellowship of the bar, assuring them that nothing was the matter, that he'd return as soon as he could, and if he didn't, he'd see them soon enough. "I'll see you tomorrow morning," he said to Roger. "You'll come for me at five?" "Aye," said Roger. "If the weather's fine. We'll not forget."

Runa was much more disturbed than Ed at Miss Ingram's appearance and news. All the dormant unease of the evening crystallized into a splinter of fear in her heart.

The three of them hurried through the windy night, past houses astir with the sway of street lights, the shift of shadows and the rustle of autumn leaves. The wind made sea drift of Runa's hair, and Miss Ingram's pale and furrowed face was beset with a white corona despite her hairpins. She explained how she had thought to look in on Erik, to see if he was all right—for no other reason than that there happened to be a change of program on the television at the time and she had just cast off in her knitting—and had found him *gone*, the bed empty, and his pajamas on the floor.

When they reached Rose Cottage, it was as she had described, loath as Runa had been to believe her, and visions of abduction by one-eyed men deranged her thinking. The bedroom window—its curtains pulled apart—was ajar at the bottom. The missing pajama cord of his trousers must, she thought, have been used to tie Erik up. She felt sick at imagining what had happened.

It was Ed who pointed out the orderly state of the room and the bed, with the bedclothes tidily turned back. He asked Runa to check if anything was missing. She saw at once that the clothes she had laid out for Erik to wear the next day were absent, as were his shoes, and his parka.

"He's dressed himself and gone out—by the window." Ed glowered and clenched his hands.

"Is it serious?" asked Miss Ingram.

"No, not at all," Ed replied. "And it's not your fault."

"Just a minute," he said, going into the hall, while Runa folded the pajamas before putting them under the pillow and pulling up the bedclothes.

"Where's my torch?" he demanded, returning to the bedroom.

"It was on the hall table," said Miss Ingram. "I noticed it there."

"I bet he's taken it with him." Ed crossed to the window.

"Why do you need it?" asked Runa. "Are you going after him?"

"*Where* do I go? Where has he gone? Do *you* know?"

"No."

"I wanted it to see if . . ." Ed raised the window, and leaned out. The curtains flapped and a cold breeze flowed through the room.

"It's all right," they heard him say. "Yes." He swung himself back, and frowned in the light. "The earth is still damp. There are footprints—his—going away from the window, away, and no one else's. He's just gone off for a walk and taken my torch."

"What shall we do?" asked Runa.

"Wait," said Ed.

He reassured Runa and absolved Miss Ingram, telling her that Erik was up to one of his tricks and that she need not stay. Runa thanked her for her promptness in calling them and finding in the first place that Erik had left the cottage.

Miss Ingram stood in the doorway, the wind catching at her hair and her knitting. "He'll be safe on the island," she prophesied. "And there'll be no more rain tonight. So he'll come to no harm, so long as he minds his going."

In the sitting room, Ed held Runa's hands.

"Do you want me to go and look for him?" he asked.

She pondered, and answered, "No." She was on edge still, and unwilling to be left alone.

"Let's have some coffee," he said, and kissed her hands. "If he's not back in an hour, I'll get some help."

Erik stood with his back to the impalpable wind and the dark north and the sea, which he heard champing over the boulders behind him, as the north wind spurred the tide toward the shore. Before him was the headland, bleached by the cold white light of the torch and blackly shadowed, whereon the flotsam, the fallen turves, the branches, boulders, grasses, stones, and sand made mystic animal shapes and heads that crouched and leaned as the torch beam swung from left to right, along the horizontal fissure in the wall, which was, he thought, like the silhouette of his very first dragon, though longer.

He remembered he had thought of it in the beginning as a snake house. Now he had returned, for the very last time, to unearth its final secret.

A conviction that he had to return had come to him in his prostration after the dance. So he had dressed, carefully locked his box before pushing it under the bed, and left by the window, with the ring on the pajama cord around his neck. It was very risky, but he did not care. He was not afraid of anything, or anyone. Once he had recovered from his dancing—and it hadn't really tired him—his strength and courage seemed enormous. He felt bold and invincible, and not seven years old at all.

Erik braced himself against the cold north wind and flashed the torch about. He had the feeling he was going to discover something he had forgotten. What he *had* forgotten was how long and gaping the scar in the headland was, and how much sand and earth and stones he had had to shift—mainly stones, as the treasure house had turned out to be a more or less hollow, cavelike rift, choked here and there where the roof had fallen in and where its encircling wall of stones had collapsed. The stones, very large ones, had caused him much toil and trouble—he had had to remove most of them on the seaward side—until he realized that they were in fact the walls of the house and gave it an outline, rather like an oval diamond. This had given him the idea of marking his golliwog's grave in a similar fashion.

But was this really a grave? It didn't seem to be important enough, and there were no bits of a skeleton, none at all, and no rotting coffin, or funeral writing. Anyway, who would want to be buried out here?

Was it not a tomb after all, but a sort of cellar?—A secret place which someone had made in which to hide his treasure?

He remembered how the first dragon had revealed itself. The sandslide had turned out to be at the left-hand end of the stone-lined burial chamber, where the shield had been, and the arrowheads. Working laboriously to his right and inward, he had then uncovered the helmet, the collar, the brooches, the buckle, the horn, the ring, and the sword, which he had reburied there. But he had not quite reached the other end, where there had been a cave-in. He had forgotten about that.

The spreading beam of the torch picked out the glinting details of the interior. How snug it seemed—how bright and warm.

Blown forward by the wind, and lured on by the light of the torch, Erik approached the tomb. The light constricted, compressing itself against the opposing wall, drawing him in irresistibly after it, until the beam became a round and white-hot eye of light, and the torch, his hand, his arm and all of himself were swallowed up and extinguished.

He lay on his stomach in utter darkness, with the snuffed-out torch beneath him, and below him the buried sword.

As if in a dream the darkness paled and he saw from high up, though his eyes were closed, that it was daylight, and because of the shadows, and the sun low in the west, that it was evening. The sea was a dark, deep blue now, and the sky to the north—he was facing north—was clouded along the horizon. There, just off the headland, was the longship, its dragon prow toward him, much nearer than it had been before, though the edge of the headland was now much further away. There was more of the island between him and the sea; there was grass, and windswept bushes, and below him three stunted trees of thorn. The ship, he saw, had been grounded on a shelf of rock, with its sail still spread— there was little wind—ready to leave if the heroes' task was disturbed. They had not much time. The tide was coming in, but would soon be on the turn. As he watched, tethered as it were like a kite far above the ness, men left the ship by a gangplank leading onto the rocks. Among them was a woman. Then a heavy burden was passed to them, and a horn blew a lone lament. He knew what and who was in that burden, wrapped in an ancient tapestry. But he felt nothing, nothing at all, and watched to see what they did.

The nine heroes made a procession and walked unevenly, like their shadows, over the rocks toward the shore. The horn sounded again. At their head was their new king, helmeted and armed with a sword, and garbed in a make-shift ritual robe that fell to his feet. Behind him, six war-riors, armed but shieldless, bore on their shoulders the body and weapons and trophies of the old king, enveloped in the ornate tapestry that had always lain on his bed. Another warrior bore on his back the sacrificial beast, a piglet, bound to a pole, and carried sacks of food and flagons of ale and mead. Then came the dark-haired woman. She was a cap-tive, soon to die, hardly able to walk, being drunk with the ale forced down her, and racked by the men who had used her on the ship in honor of her master—all twenty-three of the war band who had survived. She was prodded along by the last hero, who carried the king's tall spear and the king's shield, which hung behind him on his shoulders.

The nine were weary with drink and wounds and battle the watcher knew, but their purpose gave them strength. A king must have the burial that was his due, even though it was on foreign soil and could not be rightly performed.

As they approached, his viewpoint sank—until he was on a level with the thorn trees as the heroes came over the bluff. Finally, he was among them, and remained so, floating softly six feet over the grass—over the place where the young king began to mark out a grave with his sword.

This done, he stood by his father's body, mouthing the words of the god, while three of his companions cut off the top layer of turf with long knives, laid it aside, and then dug out the grave with axes. As they did so, the fifth man made the captive drink more strong ale until she was sick and raving, and the other four fetched suitable stones from the shore. When the grave was dug, in the shape of a boat, with its prow to the east, they rested under a tree, passing around a beaker of mead—though not to the king—before they continued as best they could with the rites.

Two of them untied the piglet and held it upside down. A third hero held a bowl for the blood when the king cut the animal's throat. This he did, and went once about the grave, starting from its eastern end, through the south, and west, and north—each of which he marked with his sword dipped in the blood of the pig. So also he marked the forehead of the captive, who was making so much noise that she had to be gagged with a belt. She should have been saying a chant in praise of her master. Instead, she kicked and clawed so much that they had to tie her hands and feet, and they also blindfolded her, as the rites decreed. They must not hit or harm her, but her keeper flung her roughly on the grass.

The king stood at the head of the grave—in the east—and said the words which he as a king should know; and cutting off the pig's head, stuck it on the pole, which he set in the prow. Then the eight warriors began to line the walls of the grave with stones, going left and right—four to each side—going south and north, until they met in the west. As they advanced, the king stood in the grave itself, going from side to side, marking each stone with blood and saying the runes. When he reached the stone at the stern of the grave they crushed the pig's body beneath it. The king did likewise with the pig's head in the prow—burying it under the bow stone, which he set up himself. Then the ship was ready for the voyage to Valhalla.

As the king withdrew and talked on his knees with the god above, his companions prepared the dead king for his final journey, though one of them was so fuddled he hindered more than he helped. The tapestry they laid on the floor of the grave and on it the dead king in his cleanest, richest clothes, with his royal mantle about him, his helmet on his head, the great gold collar around his neck hiding his death wound, his horn at his right hand, his sword at his left. Above him, in the prow, they placed his shield and arrows, and by him his bow and spear. Bowls of food and beakers of mead they set around his body. At his feet they cast the only piece of gold they had found in the church.

After an argument, the last hero to leave the grave tied a long piece of twine to the dead king's belt, leading it as straight as he could from there out onto the grass, where he lashed the other end of the cord about the largest stone that they had brought there.

Then the warriors, four on each side of the funeral boat, knelt with their backs to it and bowed their sweaty faces. The young king, when he had finished his prayers, stood up and went to the foot of the grave, where he removed his helmet and the robe and everything he wore. Naked, he entered the boat.

He followed the path of the twine with his feet until he stood before the body of the king, and with his arms out-stretched, first to heaven, he made of himself a mast. Then he knelt, crying his father's name, and embraced his father's knees, and in grief and joy at life and death, laid his face in his father's lap. So he made his vows, and having ended, reached out above him for his father's hands, and drew them down to rest upon his head.

He lay there thus until the shadows of the thorn trees had advanced the width of a finger—until the woman began to moan—until two of the kneelers had fallen asleep and snored. He shouted the name of the god to wake them up and then unsteadily rose to his feet, with his eyes closed, and backed away, until he had reached the stern of the boat where the eight heroes had gathered. They lifted him with difficulty out of the grave, four on each side, pulling him out until he lay on his back on the grass. Then they raised him to his feet. They poured some ale over his head and gave him some to drink.

All this time the watcher over the grave, although so near, was remote, untouched and uninvolved by the actions of the creatures under his gaze. He heard nothing, though he knew by their expressions and gestures what thoughts and feelings were represented, and their purpose.

His eye now turned on the woman, whom he knew the dead king had entered the night before, after the victory feast. She had been the youngest, shapeliest, of the women they had captured in the huts of the shaven priests. He had had the first choice at the feasting, as was right, and when someone had been needed to go with him on his journey—there being none willing among the male and female captives taken as slaves—she it was who was chosen by his son. She had seemed most fitting and not unwilling to begin with to undertake the ceremonies on the ship. Now her final part in the burial would be performed.

They untied her first, and stood her on her feet. Then they supported her to the foot of the grave, where they removed the blindfold so that she could see the glories of the ship. There was no time to describe the history of each weapon, but they were named and praised in brief. Then they turned her about and led her to the king. He spoke to her of paradise and everlasting life, and when he made them take off her gag, she did not reply as she should have done, but wailed and reviled them. It did not matter, for they did not understand what she said. The passion of her words was good enough.

When she began to repeat herself, and sob, they laid her on her back on the grass. The king withdrew once more. Two of the heroes knelt on her hands, and two on her feet, and drew her into an X. Her skirt was pulled up over her head to muffle her cries, and make her unable to see her champions, in case one failed in serving her and their king, her master. Then each of the eight entered her in turn and fought in her service as well as they could, giving a part of themselves to her in honor of the king. The others turned their faces outward, making a noise with their voices and hands and calling the name of the god. When this was done, two of the warriors placed a cord about her neck, with an end at each side which they held. The king now approached and lay on her as his men had done, thrusting himself within her. As he exerted himself with all the strength of his manhood, he grasped the hands that held the cord while the warriors chanted the song of life. And when it was time for her to go to the god bearing the gift of the king, he cried his father's name, clutching their hands—and they pulled, and choked her with the cord until she died.

The young king wept as they raised him to his feet.

Then the heroes lifted her body up and placed it in the boat at the feet of her master.

The watcher knew the end was near. For the new king now walked backward to the foot of the grave, to the stern of the boat. His left hand was between his buttocks, to guard against evil entering there, and in the other he held a fistful of earth, which he threw without looking behind him into the boat.

An echoing shiver of fear ran through the watcher, which grew as the warriors hastily filled in the grave, heaping earth upon their dead lord and on all he needed for the next and eternal life, until every piece of gleaming gold had sunk out of sight. They replaced the turf on the low mound, which should have been as big as those at Borre. But they dared not make it too conspicuous, and for this reason had buried the stones with the body. Then they knelt before the new king, who had arrayed himself once more in his robes and helmet, and kissed his sword, and he thanked them. Then, as the sun began to set, he led them, saying the runes, three times about the grave, while the heroes swung their swords and axes and shouted the name of the god. The watcher felt the beginnings of despair.

At the foot of the grave, at the stern of the boat, where lay the stone from which the cord led under the earth, the new king gave a beaker of mead to all the heroes to drink. He drank himself and then smashed the beaker into pieces on the stone, on which he had already carved the name of the king, his father. He stretched out his arms, facing the east and the approach of night, and made his final vows. Then he took his sword and held it high. Then he swung it once and severed the cord that tied the ship to the land.

A shadow like a smoky glass closed over the watcher's vision—he hardly saw the final valediction, the blessing and the thanks, being performed by the kneeling heroes and the king. But as his eyes dimmed, his hearing grew, and he seemed to hear their gruffly spoken chant above the waves.

The sun set, and a darkness more deep than the coming night began to invade his mind. He had never felt such sharp despair, such loneliness and fear. Suddenly he became aware that the nine were walking away from the grave among the thorn trees—leaving him, returning to the ship. Hopelessly he called to them and tried to follow. But he had no voice and could not move. They disappeared over the bluff. With a superhuman effort of will, he made himself ascend once more, struggling upward into the sunlit air, as if he were drowning, weighed down by his weapons, his shield and helmet. All at once he was masthead high, shot through by the rays of the setting sun, which pained him so much that he lost what sight he had. But he heard the sea—and the horn.

Then he saw, and he knew that the tide had turned. For the oars were out in the longship, keeping it from going out with the tide. The nine were stumbling over the rocks toward the gangplank. He saw that they reached it; went on board. The dragon head of the longship began to yield to the sea.

The sun set a second time. He felt as heavy as death and began to sink to the shadowed earth, abandoned and abandoning all he had known, all warmth and light and color and movement and life. Down he sank to endless night, unredeemed except by dreams of dead emotions, men and deeds long dead—sole solace of the nightmare sleep of death. As he sank toward the mound, irrevocably down to the boatlike pit, his yearning made him see, or think he saw for just a heartbeat, the image of the longship on the waters—turning broadside to the land—then out at sea, diminishing, a distant dusky shape, slowly heading north and homeward, leaving him behind.

Then the grave consumed him wholly, towing him down to the mound of grass, whose matted blades and mesh of roots he saw for an instant before they covered the sky, and him. And then he was swallowed by such a silence that blotted out his soul.

Yet out of this annihilation, after a time, atoms of his consciousness returned and clung together, making the insensate sensible, the darkness visible, the silence audible, and giving life to death. He became aware that his body lay stretched out before him, pressed upon by crushing depths of earth. He seemed to hear the thousand soft but strident sounds of movement as the soil resettled, and the sudden tiny random cracks as objects around about him fractionally yielded to the pressure from above. Not all the sounds were outside him—some came from within, as cell and tissue, bone and muscle, contracted and congealed. The grim unpiecing of the case that housed him had begun. His body's majesty, which once had moved, felt, fought, loved, lived and been a god to him, would meet its fated end.

But the treasures of his tomb would survive—and an immortal longing for revenge.

He heard the forces of his dissolution stirring in the soil, unknown and sightless organisms creeping to the feast.

He cried out at the terrors of his dying. He seemed to cry in terror at his fate, to try to force himself out of the grave, to fight his way through night and silence into the air.

He dreamed.

Erik awoke with a terrified shock in utter darkness, covered in sweat and earth, conscious he had been struggling to escape. He could hardly breathe, being curled in a ball, with his clothes twisted and his fists before his face. His heels had been wildly kicking at the walls of the tomb.

A different darkness came from a gash beside him. Convulsively he launched himself toward it—and tumbled out of the grave.

For a long time all he heard was the pounding of his heart. Then he became aware of the sounds of the sea. The friendly wind revived him. But he still felt very weak and cold.

Crawling up to the grave, he recovered the torch. In its light the barren tomb seemed ghostly, like a chrysalis dried and empty.

Then he remembered what it was he had forgotten.

Tuesday

1

―――――◆―――――

Runa awoke from a restless sleep to find Erik standing beside the bed, regarding her with grave, unblinking eyes. She felt a moment's embarrassment at have been observed while she slept—then a feeling of guilt and some alarm. Her drowsy mind was confused by a needling memory of his hysterics last night when he returned, and by the remembered nightmare sounds of another time.

Why didn't he speak? she wondered. What did he want?

His waxen face was almost as white as his pajamas. He looked frail and insubstantial, and he stood there like a ghost of himself, silent and stock still.

She realized he was waiting for some sign from her, as Ed would do on the rare occasions when his need to be loved was so great that it became incapable of expression. He could not, as a man, ask her to take him in her arms and cherish him like a child. She had to sense this from his extreme passivity at such moments. So it was with Erik now.

Runa raised herself off the pillows, and languidly, with a little yawn, tucked her hair behind her ears.

"What's the time?"

He continued to gaze at her for some seconds before replying. "Half-past seven," he mumbled.

She wondered where Ed and the fishing boat were and what he was doing at that moment. He had said he would not return until about ten o'clock.

With a slow smile at Erik she said, "Would you like to come in beside me?"

Again he paused before replying—his eyes were large with longing. This time he only nodded.

"Go around to the other side," she said. Automatically he obeyed. She turned the bedclothes back from where Ed had lain and, reclining on her left side, held out her arm to enfold Erik as he crawled clumsily onto the bed. Without looking her in the eye, he slid within her embrace, bumping against her as she pulled up the bedclothes about them.

"Oh, you're so cold," she whispered, holding his passive body close to her to make him warm. "Poor baby."

While the sunrise made the curtains paler and the roses on them darker, she caressed and comforted him, murmuring in Norwegian words of assurance and love.

Slowly he came to life in her arms, beginning in spasms to wiggle and jerk and talk to her, saying how nice she smelt, how soft and warm, how much he liked being with her—until all at once he flung his arms about her neck, and with passionately uncoordinated kisses, breathed incoherent vows of love and eternal service.

She was deeply affected by his innocent declarations and the almost adult desperation of his need. He wanted her, and only her, so much—more than she could give—and the tragic imbalance set tears in her eyes.

What could she do? What could she give? For him, and for Ed.

The metallic sound of someone's footsteps in the street approached the cottage. Erik stiffened, and sat up violently with wild conjecture in his eyes.

"It's all right," she whispered in Norwegian. "It isn't your father. Lie down. He won't be back till later."

The footsteps passed. She smiled at him.

"Your father's gone to sea in a boat."

As the amber sun rose out of the ocean, ever revealing more of its molten mass through a skein of mist, the fishing boat called *Cocoon* slowly lurched toward a marker buoy. Endless wastes of striving sea, into which the dark-blue night had sunk, made and unmade unceasingly, mountains and valleys whose peaks and slopes extended in instant destruction and creation of the horizon.

Ed stood beside the wheelhouse, holding on to the doorpost and bracing his feet on the deck. At first there had been an exhilaration in being on the boat. But having seen twice how the fishermen performed their tasks, he had now less to distract him, and the physical discomfort of the boat ride was wearing him down. Waves came crashing over the bow and sometimes over the sides. The fishermen, who were dressed in voluminous yellow oilskins, with black rubber waders up to their thighs and woolly hats with pompons on their heads, had given him an oilskin to wear. But though it gave him some protection against the wet, it gave no warmth. His body inside it was clenched against the cold, and the skin of his face and hands, exposed to the wind and the keen sea air, was tightly pale, seeming to have atrophied like his muscles. The chill gnawed at his bones.

Above him, the masthead light drew crazy graphs against

a somber sky. He had looked at it only once. Its wild career-ing had made him feel weak and unbalanced, though he had not so far felt sick.

The fishing boat reached the marker buoy, whose little black pennant, reeling above the waves, indicated the south-ern end of the third line of lobster pots that were to be raised.

Each line was called a fleet, as Ed had gathered, and each ran roughly north and south. There were six of them in all. Fathoms down under the heaving surface, they flowed with the tide above the seabed, held by the weighted pots that hung along their lengths. At each end, anchored by chains, a rope rose up to the marker buoys above.

The boat began to churn her way along the path of the undersea fleet, seeming to pull herself along by the winched-up line, whose yards of rope and lobster pots, both streaming with seawater, accumulated on her deck. Roger worked the winch in the bow. Farmer dragged on board the dripping pots—two-compartment cages made of bamboo sticks with covers of netted mesh—and swiftly undoing one of the sides, plucked the catch from the trap. If crab, it was flung in a box. If undersized crab or lobster, starfish, sea urchin, soft crab, or anything else, it went over the side. As much was thrown back into the sea as remained on board. Farmer swore when the pots were empty and the bait inside them gone—also when the refractory creatures caught at him with their claws and especially when red jellyfish pieces stung his hands. The larger lobsters were left in their cages for Robbie to remove and sling into a box behind him. He then rebaited the pots from a box of plaice and whiting, and after nimbly replacing the mesh of the sides, carefully stacked the pots in the order in which they would leave the boat again. Half in and out of the wheelhouse, his face a subtle cast of green from the starboard light above him, Tam kept as steady a course as he could toward the marker buoy at the northern end.

Already the deck was littered with dozens of starfish of all sizes and colors. The odd escaped crab sought refuge in the scuppers, and assorted whelks rolled about before righting themselves and gluing themselves to the deck. Astern, black-backed gulls waited on the waves for discarded morsels of bait.

This time there was a bigger haul. Ed counted more than thirty crabs—sometimes more than one in a pot—as they clattered irately into a box near Farmer. And eighteen agitated lobsters were gnashing their claws and snapping their useless tails in their box by the time the end of the fleet had been dredged from the sea.

By then the sun had pulled itself out of the ocean and hung, a misty orange ball of light, above the chaos of waves. It was like a primeval dawn, a vision of creation, and on the deck, the creatures from the sea enforced the fantasy.

Something about their scaly backs, their rending claws and inflexible fury, struck an unpleasant chord in Ed, which was heightened by the sounds they made. And their frenzy was not unlike Erik's the night before.

Was it really last night that all *that* had happened?

He remembered that in his growing impatience in the cottage he had gone to lie in wait for Erik in Erik's bedroom. "Keep out of the way," he said to Runa. "Nobody will get hurt. I would just like to give Master Erik a little surprise." But standing guard by the window—through which he was sure his errant son would return—was a tedious business, and as seizing the wanderer when he entered might unduly frighten him, Ed lay down on Erik's bed, with his hand near the switch of the bedside lamp. Nonetheless, when Erik at last returned through the window, shortly before eleven o'clock, by which time Ed had begun gloomily to think in terms of search parties, tragic finds and funerals, Erik's reaction to his father sitting up on the bed, switching the light on, and saying, "Good morning. Had a nice walk?" was to have hysterics.

Runa found it difficult to believe that this was all Ed had said and done when she burst into the room and saw Erik curled up on the floor, with his fists in his mouth, writhing and kicking, and screaming. Ed's protestations—"I never touched him!"—were useless, and he was banished from the bedroom. He retired to the sitting room, refusing to be harrowed by the racket, and riled by what he thought of as Erik's dissembling. He poured himself a whisky, cursing the state of fatherhood and Erik's damnable cleverness at turning on a tantrum to avoid being rebuked or questioned. Where had the boy been? In the instant of the light being switched on Ed had himself been startled by Erik's ghastly appearance, his face like chalk, his eyes red and staring, and all of him besmeared with dirt. What had he been doing? The missing torch he had dropped on the floor before following suit himself.

There were several questions Ed wanted to ask—but when Runa came into the sitting room it was to tell him, in her sternest manner, that Erik had fallen asleep, completely exhausted, and was to be left alone. Ed followed her back to the bedroom, where she undressed Erik, washed and wiped his face and hands, and all without waking him. There was no doubt about it—Erik was dead to the world.

Ed retrieved the torch, telling Runa that there would have to be some explanations in the morning. She told him to go to bed.

Later, when Runa joined him, he said, "I'm sure tonight's little tantrum connects with last night's rumpus. And the connection is Erik. He's being a bit excessive—even for him."

"Do you think he needs a doctor?" Runa asked.

"A witch doctor, more likely. Or an exorcist."

"What do you mean?"

"Nothing much," he answered. "There's something going on that has its source in Erik. Nothing serious," he assured her, "though unusual."

"I'm worried," she whispered, and turned to look at him in the dark. "Nothing else will happen tonight, will it?"

"No. I doubt it," he said.

Ed did not sleep much. Neither did Runa. Both were shocked awake by a knocking on the window.

A fearful moment passed before Ed realized it was Robbie. He knocked on the window again.

Ed switched on the bedside lamp as a sign that he was awake. His watch said ten past five. He dressed as quickly as he could and, taking his torch to light the way, stumbled out of the cottage into the night, and down to the jetty, where the four crews of fishermen had gathered in the dark.

Cocoon swung around across the icy wind and into the path of the risen sun. Already the mist of daybreak was resolving into clouds, which would soon completely cover the sky and the sun itself. But the last fleet, rebaited, had still to be dropped further out to sea—as they had done with all the others. It would be left below the waves until the next day's dawn, to entrap another haul of carnivorous crustaceans.

Their prehistoric presence was heavy on the boat. Four boxes full of scrabbling crabs and two of clacking lobsters stood on the hatch, and the latest captives still contorted themselves in epileptic fits. To Ed's tired and straining sight, their spiky limbs and feverish feelers, their palpitating jaws and eyes on stalks, seemed to suggest such grisly threats, such rabid rage at being caught, that he half expected them to advance and attack their captors. The crab that he had shown to Runa, although unpleasant to handle, had been dying, helpless. Here the creatures vastly outnumbered the men and were very much alive, with the menace of inconceivable dark places still dripping from their shells. How many there must be, he thought, in the unknown depths off Holy Island, if the four boats that put out to sea in six months of the year came back with a thousand such sea denizens every day! How many more were seething below them now?—Armies of crawling, scuttling, fighting crabs and lobsters flying like demons from hell in the night sky of the sea.

While Ed held grimly onto the wheelhouse roof, the others relaxed, and lit cigarettes—except for Robbie, who now set about his task of binding the lobsters' claws. The crabs were packed upon each other, with legs and claws embroiled, and crushed by the base of another box pressing down on them from above. But the lobsters, fewer in number, were capable in their paroxysms of clawing each other to pieces. This had to be prevented, as they were to be delivered alive and whole to a warehouse of seawater tanks in Eyemouth, before being sent abroad. The crabs were cooked and canned on the mainland.

Robbie picked the blue-black lobsters out of their box one by one, and crouching on the casing where Ed had sat, jammed a claw between his knees and wedged the body between his thighs and an arm. With both hands he forced a rubber band over each of the creatures' claws in turn. Then he laid them neatly back in their box. Ed watched his expertise with some approval but more repugance. He found the long scarlet antennae flailing the man's hands especially repellent.

He turned away, feeling weary and alone. For although Robbie was working only a few feet from him, Ed might not have been there. None of the fishermen had spoken much to each other since leaving the harbor, and none, not even Robbie, had made much conversation with Ed, though they answered his remarks and questions. It saddened him to realize what a gulf lay between him and the fishermen—not only in what they were, but also in what they did. He realized that even if he had had a simpler life, closer to nature, he would not have been content—not even as a farmer or keeper of pigs. He needed to extend himself, to satisfy a lust for strife and daring, for achievement and adventure, which he got at second-hand from the substance and study of history. But the root of his quest, of his most private, impossible dream, had been to make a mark in the world somehow—to make history himself.

Ed smiled wanly at Tam, whose face and eyes were puckered against the light as he concentrated on the boat's eastward progress out to sea.

"I would never make a fisherman," Ed confessed.

"Thousands wouldn't," said Tam. He was slight and dark, the same age as Ed, with a fast and pithy way of talking that belied the reserve and doubt of his features in repose.

"Why are you a fisherman?" asked Ed.

"Oh . . ." said Tam, and sighed. "I don't know. I don't know anything else. Do I?"

Ed looked at the changing sea, and sensed some of its incommunicable spell. It could also be one's opponent, he thought—though not one that *he* would fancy fighting.

Tam said, gazing up at him, "Why are you what *you* are?"

"I don't know either," Ed admitted. "At least, not yet."

He turned his back on the rising sun and looked astern.

The boat was now some two miles out to sea, off the northeast edge of the island. It was far away and eclipsed with a golden haze, bright against the lowering mass of clouds. Soon he would be returning there—to Runa. Soon he would be himself again, and safe.

Something winked at him across the waters out of the misted coast. He recognized it as the white beacon marking Emmanuel Head.

She stood motionless, observing in front of her the length of her uncertain shadow stretching westward over the headland. It lay strangely still upon the quivering grasses, though the hair on its head blew wildly about and an edge of its coat made signals. The shadow of the pyramid threw an elongated facsimile from behind her on her left. How long would it be before she could turn around? How long before Erik revealed his surprise?

He had brought her to the headland because, as he said, he loved her, and because she had the right. "Where did you go last night?" she had asked him in the bedroom. He had gazed at her for fully a minute before replying. "I'll show you," he said at last. "If you promise not to tell."

She had promised, and he had told her to get dressed. "Now?" she queried. "Now," he said, and she thought there would be time to do what Erik wanted before Ed returned.

"Now!" said a voice behind her.

She turned into the wind and thought for a moment there was something on the sea. Then her hair flew over her eyes as she faced the east.

He was standing near the pyramid's base and directly against the sun. She could not see him clearly, but saw with a shock that his shadowed stance and what he held were the same as those of the man she had drawn on the beach.

In his hands he grasped the hilt of a sword, with its bloodless point on the ground.

"Come here!" he said in Norwegian.

She approached him, hearing the wind in her ears and the song of the incoming tide.

The sword was very old and dark.

"Kneel!" he said, his voice loud and imperious, competing with the sounds that rang in her head.

Amazedly she obeyed, wondering where he had found the sword.

Then he made a speech. But the strangeness of his accent, and the harshness of his voice, made what he said difficult to follow—and all the time the wind and the sea contended for her hearing.

"What?" she said. "What?" But he went on speaking.

She thought he mentioned Westfold, and said something about a king. "The king is dead," she thought she heard—though he then seemed to deny this. Once he distinctly used the phrase "his daughter."

From where she knelt, he seemed in shadow against the sun to be bigger than he was. But that was only some trick of light.

He stopped speaking. He approached her with heavy deliberation, like a robot, and enveloping her with his shadow, gave her the sword to hold. His eyes were fixed and alarmingly unseeing, like glass, and when he kissed her forehead, his lips were ice. So were his hands as he roughly pushed a ring onto the third finger of her left hand—a golden ring—something else he had found!

What was he saying? Where had he got these things? What crazy game was this?

There was now no doubt that he was the king and that she was his daughter. There was also no doubt that when he reclaimed the sword, and held it out horizontally, he wanted her to grasp its blade. She did so.

"Swear!" said a voice, sounding within her.

"Swear!" reechoed the wind, and the sea, and the nine men standing beyond him.

"Swear!"

2

"Where have you been?" Ed demanded, coming out into the hall from the kitchen as soon as Runa and Erik returned.

"Oh . . . out for a walk," she said abstractedly, beginning to take off her coat. Erik pushed past Ed and disappeared into his bedroom.

"That's marvelous!" Ed exclaimed. "I come back here at ten-fifteen to find the place deserted—the fire unlit—and not a welcoming breakfast or wife in sight! Literally not a sausage! I thought you'd been abducted—or run off with the pigman! You *knew* I'd be back round about ten. Couldn't you have waited?"

"I'll get your breakfast now," she said, pushing past him as Erik had done—nor looking at him either.

"Forget it. I'm not hungry. I've made some coffee. Do you want some?"

"Oh, yes, please," she said, sitting down on a chair, and playing with the ring on her right hand. She had still not looked directly at him, and her demeanor was vague and distant. She also seemed very pale.

He wondered what was wrong. Then his grievances crumpled up under his pleasure at seeing her again and in trying to puzzle out her mood.

"Where did you go?" he asked.

She hesitated. "Nowhere," she said.

"You must have gone *somewhere!*"

"Well—we went to the north, to the north coast of the island. That's why we're a bit late. I'm sorry."

246

"But why go out, when you knew I'd be rushing up here as soon as I landed? Here's your coffee."

"We were longer than I'd thought. Oh, thank you."

"Was Erik being bloody-minded?"

Ed had the suspicion that Erik had caused the delay. Runa would never let him down. It must have been Erik's fault.

"No," she answered. "It just took longer. Anyway, we can't have been more than ten minutes late."

"I suppose not. But I missed you."

She looked at him, and smiled. "I'm here now," she said.

"You weren't when I needed you," he complained.

"What can I do for you?" she said, getting up. "Don't you want breakfast? How was your sea trip anyway?"

"Cold as hell," he said. "I'll never make a fisherman. It's too tiring, wet and alarming. And most of it is in the middle of the night. Give me the land. And in fact, give me a bed. I think I'll have a lie-down. I'm shattered."

"You do look tired," she murmured.

"You're not so bright yourself. Why don't we *both* go back to bed and sleep it off?"

"Why not?" she said. "All right. I'll join you in a moment. But first I'll have to see to Erik."

"Damn Erik."

Ed left the kitchen, and Runa preoccupied herself with laying out some breakfast food for Erik.

When she entered Erik's bedroom—after knocking on the door—she found him standing at the window, gazing out on the windswept, sunless garden.

"What are you doing?" she asked.

"Thinking. . . ."

She knelt to light the gas fire and then switched on the bedside lamp. While she quickly remade the bed, Erik remained at the window.

"I'm going back to bed now, to have a little rest. So is your father. I've put some breakfast for you on the kitchen table, and we'll all have a very big lunch later. How's that?"

He shrugged his shoulders, as if it was a matter of indifference. Yet something about his solitary stance at the window with his back to her seemed to indicate that his indifference was a part of a deeper sense of isolation. Runa wondered what he was thinking about—or if he was in fact secretly watching someone outside.

When she joined him at the window, she saw that no one was in the garden or in the churchyard, and that although he might have been viewing his golliwog's grave, his face and eyes denoted a mood of introspection. Perhaps, she thought, she could question him now about the morning's happenings on the headland.

"This morning . . ." she began. "What was it you wanted me to swear?"

"You *haven't* forgotten!" Erik said, with a sharp look of rebuke.

"No," she said. "But some of it I didn't understand."

"I *told* you. You promised not to tell! About the sword and everything else. You promised. You won't *break* your promise, will you?"

"No."

"You can't. If you did, you would die. It was that kind of promise."

"Where did you find the sword?" she asked—casually.

"Oh, really! Bloody heck!" he said. "I've told you! Why don't you listen? It's very important. I couldn't *show* you where I found it, but I did tell you. I can't tell you where I've put the rest, so don't ask!"

The rest? What did he mean by "the rest"? She had seen the sword and sworn on it, and she had the ring—it was in her coat pocket. But that was all. She supposed the sword was hidden near where they had been on the headland,

248

though she had not been allowed to see from where he got it, nor where he hid it again.

"You've got the ring?" he asked anxiously.

"Yes," she said.

"You mustn't lose it." He was very emphatic. "It belongs to you. I wanted you to have it. But don't show it to anyone else. You promised you wouldn't."

"Yes," she assured him, though not remembering any such thing.

"I think you ought to wear it tomorrow," he murmured.

Tomorrow? What part of his plan or game was this? she wondered. "What for?" she asked.

He chewed his upper lip. "Because . . ."

"What?"

A sulky frown creased his forehead. Either he would not answer, or had no reasons of his own. His confusion mystified her and added to her own perplexity—as had something else.

"Why did you call me your daughter?" she asked.

He regarded her for a moment with tolerating scorn.

"I didn't," he said.

"You *did!*" she vowed.

"I didn't!"

"But—"

"You're my mother, aren't you?"

His question, intended to be dismissive, raised such extraordinary echoes in her mind that she was speechless.

Runa walked away from the window, in hazes of uncertainty, as if her mind were in her eyes and dazzled by the rising sun. She stopped herself at the door, almost forcing herself into her usual role.

"Your breakfast . . . is on the table. Don't make too much noise now. And . . . don't go out of the house. Promise. No wandering off this morning. Promise me that."

"All right," he mumbled nonchalantly. "I promise."

When she had gone he opened the window, and leaning over the windowsill, retrieved the latest and last of his finds from the grave. It was lying on the earth against the wall, and he almost overbalanced in the onslaught of the wind outside and in his excited recollection of what had happened the night before.

He had returned with his prize openly held in his hand. His dream had led him to it, though not a bone or buckle or brooch had he found of the woman. What he *had* found was much more likely to prove a real weapon than the useless arrows and as yet unusable sword. Leaving it on the windowsill as he clambered into the bedroom had been a bit of luck. For in his struggle to get in he had knocked it off and so had not been caught with it when the light was switched on. That had been a terrible shock—to see a dark figure rise from the bed and then to realize it was his father!

Erik hoisted himself back into the room and closed the window. He took his prize to be examined under the bedside lamp. It needed a cleaning, of course, but seemed to be in a much better condition than the arrowheads. There were circles on it, he saw, and runes. He pondered, and decided that if it was provided with a shaft, then the foot-long spearhead in his hand could be put to its proper use.

In the darkened room Runa lay between the blankets and the counterpane. She had not wished to arouse Ed from his slumbers. So after lighting the gas fire and removing her skirt and jersey, she had carefully composed herself on the blankets beside him and pulled the counterpane over them both. She had refrained from touching him, much as she wanted to—for she needed him to look at her and hold her, to drive away encroaching fantasies by the positive warmth of his love. But she let him sleep, remaining aware of his presence beside her, of his curling hand quiescent on the pillow, and his nakedness under the sheet. She could not sleep herself. For a time her eyes roamed over the furniture in the room, taking in Ed's clothes and her own possessions, while she listened to Erik's movements in the kitchen and hall. Then the climbing lines of roses took her gaze to the ceiling. But in looking at it, such thoughts of irrational terror grew in her mind that she closed her eyes and tried to think of pleasanter fancies.

At once a woman riding a horse as black as her flying hair galloped over a white and stony beach toward her, provoking in Runa a wonder that the horse could gallop on stones —so smoothly, and so silently. The image of rider and horse then seemed to split and redivide again and again, so that two women, then four, then eight, then more and more, redoubling all the time, came thundering over the stones toward her. She saw that the beach was not made of stones, but of countless paper-white skulls and the scattered bones of vanquished armies. Dumbly she watched their advance, knowing that nothing would stop them. But after a time she realized that something held them back, that they drew no nearer. Then they parted, sweeping away to left and right, vanishing like mist. And there in the distance stood a man, drawing lines on a golden, sandy beach with a stick. She knew it was Ed. She was riding now herself toward him, eagerly, rapturously, gliding over the silken sand, which was now awash with the streaming tide, which burst into fountains of spray as she charged across it, making a gleaming corridor as she approached. She was almost upon him and distraught that he took no notice. Then he turned—and the stick was a sword, and the man unknown, and he only had one eye.

3

Squalls of rain swept over the island, preventing the Wardlaws from going out after lunch and making them grateful for the shelter of the cottage and the comfort of the fire. Once the coffee cups had been cleared away, Ed and Runa settled down in the sitting room—he to study his thesis and she to work on her tapestry for the fire screen—and Erik sat in his bedroom drawing. They were all very quiet, absorbed in what they were doing, having banished for the moment all uneasy speculations, fantasies and dreams.

As far as Runa was concerned, worry about where Erik had got the sword and ring—she had dismissed the thought that he had stolen them from the museum—was a waste of time. She had tried to question him again, without success, and decided to let the matter rest until his resolve relaxed and he volunteered information, which he was sure to do, as he could never keep a secret for long. She wished she could have told Ed, but having been sworn to secrecy, she was loath to do so until it was absolutely necessary. What she *had* sworn was still something of a mystery, but she had undoubtedly promised not to tell.

Runa wove the varying scarlet strands of the roses into her tapestry, remembering adventures of her childhood involving her brothers in Norway. And she thought of her father, whose daughter she really was.

Ed's mind was on his manuscript, to which he had returned with an eagerness he had not felt for some time. The problems of Erik's behavior, his seeming possession by paranormal influences—which had not been proved and remained just a possibility—disappeared in the reading of his thesis, the lucidity and ordered prose of which were a saving reminder of sanity and good sense. Sometimes he would absentmindedly observe what Runa was doing, and when she looked up, they would smile at each other, and then continue with their silent occupations.

By teatime, Runa had completed the last red petal of the roses, though she still had to sew the vase and background. She was putting away her multicolored threads in a bag when Ed announced that he had written a masterpiece.

"I've been insensible to its excellence," he said. "As it turns out, there's not much I can do to improve it. You're married to a genius. Let's have tea."

At this point Erik entered the room to show his drawing to Runa. Ed was also allowed to see it, and both commended it highly. The drawing showed a pale man on a pale horse against a jet-black background. The details had been drawn in with a black pen. The man was helmeted, holding a round shield, and in the act of spearing a serpent whose heavy coils looped along the base of the picture and up the sides.

"It's St. Michael and the Dragon!" Runa exclaimed. "Isn't it good? But why has the horse got eight legs?"

Erik looked at the picture and shrugged.

"What's this on his shoulder?"

Erik frowned. "A bird."

"And there's another flying overhead—and a dog following behind."

"A strange-looking dog," remarked Ed, impressed despite himself by the strong and simple lines of the picture and its iconographic power. It seemed familiar. He wondered if it also held a clue to Erik's conduct.

The drawing was put on the mantelpiece, and then Runa prepared tea and biscuits, which they had in the sitting room, cozily seated around the fire.

That afternoon was the pleasantest they had spent together for some days. There had never been such harmony between them since their arrival on Lindisfarne. Mostly, they talked about the islanders and Ed's outing on the fishing boat. He had a strong imagination and a way with words that made his hearers share the pictures of his mind. Erik's basic questions and his forceful observations, combined with Runa's mild though sometimes ironic comments, made the occasion an interweaving happy exchange of information and entertainment. The time passed quickly, and their domestic accord continued with a game of cards after the tea things were cleared away. They played "Damnation," and although neither Ed nor Erik tended to treat such diversions lightly—both being eager to win and hating to lose—this time honor was satisfied, as they ended up with the same score, and Runa won.

By six o'clock, the weather had cleared. So after watching the television news, they went out for a walk and some fresh air—sauntering through the village square past the Crown and Anchor, across the Sanctuary meadow east of the priory ruins, and down to the Ouse and the ebbing tide—by which time the sun had set.

The wind had abated but still blew in gusts, as if a great door in the cold dark north banged open now and again, letting blasts of frozen air sweep southward. The sea was still a pitchy turmoil beyond the bar and the heavens a darkening mass of formless cloud. By the jetty they climbed up onto the lowest end of the Heugh, and then wandered back along its rising length, from east to west, toward a colorless sunset over the mainland.

There was no one else about. Ed led the way, dreaming that he was king of the castle, wondering how he would fortify and protect the Heugh from attack. Runa followed, anxious to return home before darkness, yet finding time to gather the small wild flowers along the path, while Erik plunged among the thick long grasses of the center, off the path, chasing little insects of the twilight.

"What's that?" said Runa, hearing a far continuous roaring, like a breaking wave along an endless beach.

Ed listened, looking northward, inclining his head.

"It's a train on the mainland. Look. Over there."

Distantly, on the shadowed land, a dotted line of lights spasmodically moved south, preceded by a warning rumor of its coming.

"It's like a luminous worm," he said. "You know what I was thinking? I was wondering why the priory was built where it is. Why *there?* It doesn't seem right."

They looked down on the ruins, glimmering in the dusk.

"Why not?" asked Runa. "Wasn't it built on the site of Aidan's monastery?"

"Not necessarily. No sign of that was ever found apart from graves and gravestones. All that's known is that the priory church was built—in 1093—on new foundations. By a monk called Edward. The parish church was put up fifty years later. You have to remember that Lindisfarne was abandoned by the original monks in 875 for nearly two hundred years. During this time the wooden buildings must have disappeared, vanished into the grass. Did people forget where Aidan had his church? When they returned, to find only stones and crosses, did they think that *those* marked the site of Aidan's settlement?"

"It's getting dark," said Runa.

They ventured off the western end of the Heugh and with no more delay returned to the cottage.

Later, after supper, when Erik had gone to bed, Ed and Runa watched television. She sat at his feet, with an arm draped over his knees. He held her hand. Now and then his fingers smoothed her hair. Now and then she laid her head against his thigh. All the time they savored each other's presence, the quiet bliss of being together and in love.

When her position on the floor became uncomfortable, she sat upon his lap. "You're heavy," he said. She replied, "Not as heavy as you."

With their arms about each other, with his face close to hers, the attraction of the monochrome small screen grew less, and gently and slowly his mouth closed over hers and rested there, so that he gave her breath and life—as she did to him.

So they stayed, until a change of program aroused them to the time. "It's coffee time!" cried Ed. And when the coffee had been drunk, and the TV set switched off, they lay together on the carpet, lit only by the fire, scarcely moving, softly talking.

"Do you remember—?" said Runa.

"Do you recall—?" asked Ed.

In loving reminiscence they retraced their early days in Oxford, wondering how it had all begun—what they were like, had seemed to be like, in those days—never dreaming that it would ever end.

At last it was time to go to bed.

While Runa was in the bathroom having a bath, Ed went out for a late-night stroll. It was nearly midnight.

He amused himself under the light in the square by making vaporous clouds of his breath which were blotted out by the wind. He thought of seeing if Robbie, Roger or their companions were still in the Crown and Anchor or the Rails, but decided he did not want to break the spell of his night with Runa. Tomorrow would be time enough to see them, to thank them again for taking him with them to sea. Once around the graveyard, he thought, and then home.

Ed turned into the small dark lane that led to the churchyard from the square. He paused before the gate, with the museum on his left, to accustom his eyesight to the blackness between the gravestones. Somewhere, very faintly, he heard a clock toll the hours of midnight, and counted them as they chimed, while high in the southern sky over the Heugh, the moon, now nearly full, emerged from the clouds.

His throat contracted in the cold and he coughed.

Out of the darkness a fearsome object flew toward him. Before he had time to move, it rushed past him—so near that he felt its breath and heard the swish of its flight. It thudded against the museum door and stuck there, parallel to the ground.

Ed's shock was changed to incredulity. Impaled in the door was a spear.

Who had thrown it? He looked back along the direction of the shaft, and under the gloom of the churchyard trees saw a flicker of something pale. Fearful again, he retreated against the wall and grasped the spear with both hands, prepared to defend himself. In pulling it out he wrenched the shaft from the spearhead, which had transfixed the door. Thus armed, he waited.

Nothing happened. Nothing moved but the wind in the graveyard trees. But the stones below them hid so much menace he had to stir—to flee from the terror that lay there. One step, and another, and then he was running out of the dark lane into the square, and back to the cottage.

He burst inside the hall as Runa came out of the bathroom in her dressing gown.

"Ssh!" she said at the noise he made, and then seeing his expression and what he held, said, "What's the matter?"

"Someone just threw this at me!" he blurted out. "Someone *threw* it at me! A spear!"

Runa passed around him to close the front door. "But—" she said, seeing only a wooden pole. "It isn't a spear. Where did you get it? It's the handle of the floor mop. From the kitchen."

Ed gazed at the weapon in his hands with stupefaction.

She was tempted to laugh. "It's only a floor mop, though it's lost its head."

He turned his baffled glare on her and without a word charged out of the cottage.

Runa went to the open door and looked out, in time to see him disappear into the churchyard lane. The wind was cold and plucked at the hem of her gown. Petals from dead roses blew into the hall.

Remembering that Erik's sleep might have been disturbed, she withdrew, closing the door after her. But a careful, quiet inspection of his bedroom showed him to be safely asleep.

With a crash, Ed returned, slamming the front door behind him.

"Ssh," she said again and closed Erik's door. "Ssh! You'll waken Erik."

"Look!" he hissed. "A spearhead. I had to fight to get it out. *This* is the rest of the spear. *This* is what nearly killed me."

A chill shiver ran through her. She saw at once that it was old and dark and made of rusted iron.

"Its socket fits on top of the pole," Ed declared. "Like this. See. A spear!"

Its venomous blade was at least a foot in length, its edge serrated.

"But who—?" she began.

Ed removed the evil-looking spearhead and noticed now that the shaft had been carefully shaped to enter the socket —and that the carving was new.

"Did you say—?" he began, and saw that the pole *was* what she said it had been, that it must have come from the kitchen, from where it had been removed and made into a spear-shaft. And flung at him. At *him*. From the churchyard. He remembered the flash of something white. He remembered Erik.

"Erik," he whispered, knowing his enemy.

"Erik!" he roared.

Ed jammed the spearhead onto the shaft and plunged into Erik's bedroom. Thrusting the bedclothes aside, he seized his resisting son by the arm and hauled him forcibly out of the room and into the light of the hall.

"Let me go! Let me go!" cried Erik.

"Ed! What are you doing?" protested Runa.

"He tried to kill me! Didn't you?" Ed demanded. "I saw him in the churchyard. In his pajamas. I *saw* you," he stormed at Erik, gripping his prisoner's left arm with all his unrestrained might and buffeting Erik against the bathroom door, although he had stopped resisting.

"Ed!" cried Runa.

"Don't you interfere! He won't get away with it this time."

Ed released his hold, and grasping the spear with both hands, held it at an angle before him, barring Erik's escape. The basilisk fury of Erik's eyes excited a similar fire in him, an impulse to destroy.

"Now!" he began, with the spear point skimming Erik's neck—"What were you doing in the churchyard? Five minutes ago? With this! Hey?"

"Ed—are you sure?" asked Runa from behind him, a hand to her face.

"I saw him? Who *else* could it be? Where does this come from?" he asked her, shaking the shaft. "From the kitchen."

He glared at Erik, who had lowered his head and hidden his eyes, as if in guilt and shame.

"I didn't throw it," they heard him say.

259

Runa laid a hand on Ed's arm. "He didn't throw it," she said.

"He's a bloody liar," retorted Ed. "A scheming, evil, cold-blooded, unnatural beast! Don't you try to excuse him. He's *always* hated me—and now he's out to get rid of me! Aren't you?" he demanded, threatening with the swinging spear. "Aren't you? You little monster!"

Softly, Erik began to sing.

His parents stared at him, shaken out of their other emotions by the abnormal sound.

With his eyes still lowered, he sang a fast and moaning scale of notes, undulating up and down, and getting louder.

Runa clutched Ed's arm. He tightened his grip on the spear.

"Erik . . . ?" Runa called his name.

"He's mad," Ed murmured, aghast.

Then Erik slowly raised his head and they saw that his eyes were white—the pupils had disappeared under his eyelids.

"Oh, my God," Ed whispered—and still the demented song went on, issuing out of the boy's mouth, rounded like his eyes.

"Listen," said Runa, hearing something else, something outside approaching the cottage.

Ed's scalp began to crawl, his shoulders twitched. Runa sighed in anguish beside him. They half turned, and listened.

The tread of something enormously heavy moved up the street toward them—something so huge and unused to the earth, its steps were labored and painful. It sighed as it moved, and a sound of iron screamed out with each step as it neared the door. The building shuddered, but within the hall, Ed and Runa were like blocks of stone.

A vastness settled outside the door, and they heard its searing breath.

The singing stopped, and at once a blow of unimaginable force reverberated against the door, seeming to make it bend. It came again. The walls shook. Echoes of the terrifying onslaught on their bedroom ceiling dinned through the hall, as the banging on the door assumed insensate, colossal proportions.

It seemed that the door swelled with each blow like the beating of a heart. It seemed it must burst like a bubble before such pressure and deliver them to the night. The noise drowned them in waves of sound, crashing, swirling, breaking and booming off the walls.

Then Runa, made mindless by fear, yet knowing what she must do, walked like a dreamer toward the door.

She opened it. The wind rushed in, blowing leaves and petals about, filling the hall with movement.

There was nothing outside.

Ed leaned, exhausted, against a wall. Erik collapsed on the floor.

Runa returned, having shut the door. She looked at Ed and did not see him. She looked at Erik, her son, her king, and without any effort picked him up in her arms. Without a word, she took him into her bedroom and closed the door.

In the empty hall, the expression of Ed's weakness, grief, and abject fear could no longer be withheld.

He turned his face to the wall, and so began to cry.

Woden's Day

1

Ed dreamed—and his dreams were fraught with images of burning, of a boat, and of his son. Tongues of flame swept over the beach below Bamburgh Castle, streaming inland from the sea. Then the moving beach was a mounting tempest of waves and he was on a foundering, wide-bottomed boat, empty of sail and crew, in imminent danger of being swamped, of being overturned by giant lobsters jutting out of the foam. But he was not alone. From his perilous perch in the rudderless stern he saw a malignant face in the prow—Erik, and he was smiling. In his hand was something like a sword—but the sword in his own hand was bigger. So was he, and growing larger all the time, until the boat was rowboat size, and growing smaller, further away, and Erik in it. He realized he was now high up, looking down on a ship—two ships, drawn up on a beach below, and out of them were issuing what first he had thought of as tongues of fire, but now saw were fiery worms or serpents speeding across the sand toward the fortress. He felt sick with fear—he would never survive. It was his fate to die. But a much-loved woman behind him laid a hand upon his arm, and a small boy brought him his helmet. Such pride was in the boy's brown eyes that they gave him boldness as well. He took the helmet, seeing the bristling boar on its crest, the royal emblem of his ancestors. He would join them if he failed. But he could not, would not fail. In his dream he knew he would win. Yet suspecting a trick, he still doubted. Then suddenly another helmet loomed before him, with a red-eyed dragon upon it—alive, and spitting flame. The uneven odds, his body's vulnerability, his own despair, made him feel like weeping. And in the grim, relentless battle that followed, his anger was mixed with anguish. And although he knew he would win, he was still afraid.

Ed awoke, and slept again, and still the battle raged. His adversary was faceless. Blackness dwelt where a face should be, and a revengeful shape armed with a sword was his remorseless foe.

When he reawoke, fatigued and aching, such a figure stood at the foot of his bed, motionless, but of such malevolence that he was powerless to move, and sweated out his blind fear though he *knew* the nightmare shape was Erik's dressing gown hanging behind the door. Yet knowing he was awake increased his horror, and waking or sleeping, fear possessed him and filled his mind through the long dark night he spent in Erik's room—in Erik's bed.

At daybreak, a kind of victory had been won, with the dismemberment and dissolution of his foe, though nothing was there, and nothing could be vanquished. Then he slept indeed, as if dead himself, and awoke for the last time, full of foreboding, to find himself strangely alone.

He saw by his watch it was half-past nine. Divesting himself of the weight of bedclothes, he jerked himself into a sitting position and swung his feet onto the floor, where they trod on the spear.

His weary brain registered the fact while it propelled him toward the window, whose curtains he had to open to let in the light. When he did so, the prospect was a melancholy one—a pale gray sky containing the dusky outlines of the church, the graveyard, and garden, still infested by the presence of the wind.

The spearhead, he thought to himself—he would have to take it to Bamburgh. The professor might know more about its origin. Evidently it was very old, as he had noticed the night before when he studied it distractedly on Erik's bed. But where had Erik got it from? More importantly, what was to be done with him? Hard as it was to believe—in answer to Erik's singing something had come banging on the door, a thing possessed, summoned by a child possessed. Or was he the possessor?

Ed knew he would have no peace of mind until Erik's warring senses were pacified or defeated. The holiday was over.

The thought depressed him further. Heavy-headed he wandered from the room, looking for his heart's ease and support in Runa, stupidly oblivious to the whereabouts of his son.

Naked as he was, he opened their bedroom door, and was stunned to see who lay in her arms.

They faced toward him. She was asleep. But Erik opened an eye to view the intruder.

Ed, now dressed, sat in the kitchen playing with a knife. Reminded by it of a battle of wills and hands, he put it down, joylessly recalling the associated demoniacal banging on the ceiling and the door, whose echoes lingered still and dulled his reasoning. No obvious lines of thought presented themselves to guide him. No light of his own experience could show him a way through the gloom. Yet somehow it had to be dispelled.

Looking for something else to lay his hands on, he removed the spearhead from the floor mop pole and examined it with baffled care. The narrow blade was a foot in length. Its edge and surface were darkly corroded. But visible on it were sets of engraved and inlaid little circles, like targets, and on one side were some scratches that must be runes.

Ed placed the spearhead on the table before him, where it lay like the severed iron tongue of a gigantic snake. He remembered how it had flown at him out of the night, how it had pierced the door—at head-height, parallel to the ground.

He started when Runa came into the kitchen, tying up her dressing gown.

"Where's Erik?" she demanded.

"Where's Erik?" he slowly repeated, and added, without looking at her, with his eyes on the spearhead—"It's not Erik I'm looking for.

"The angle," he mused. "The force with which it was thrown. . . . Perhaps he could have managed the force. But not the angle. No. Erik never threw the spear, although he was there. It must have been thrown by someone else, as tall or taller than me . . ."

"I don't know what you are talking about," she said, going to the window and looking out. "But Erik is not in the house."

"Cottage," he said.

"Cottage!" she cried. "That's all you care! To play with words—when your small boy is losing himself. Don't correct me! He's run away. To where?" She put a hand to her face and covered her eyes. "And why?"

Ed looked at her dispassionately. "It's happened before," he said. "You know he'll be back by lunchtime. Why all the fuss? He's probably keeping out of the way—of going to Bamburgh. Or to avoid being questioned. That's more like it. After last night."

He added, "I hope you slept well—both of you. I slept very badly. He's not going to take my place again—ever again. I'll see to it."

She turned to the window. "He's not well," she said.

"What do you mean—he's not well?"

"In his mind."

Ed was silent. Encouraged, Runa continued.

"He dreams. He dreams when he is asleep, of course, but also when he is waking. He has a nightmare in his mind— and he is awake."

"So are we. So do we," Ed answered. "It's in our minds as well."

"But are we sick?" she asked him, and added, "He needs to see a doctor."

"Perhaps. But what exactly do you think is wrong?"

She moved about the kitchen, her arms tightly folded.

"I don't know," she said. "I can't explain it. But it is not a dream—what happened last night. It *did* happen?" She looked at him anxiously for confirmation and hopefully for denial.

"What do you think?" he asked her patiently.

She sighed. "Yes. It happened. And you are right—it has happened before. And other things. Ever since we came here, to this island."

She gazed out of the window. "I had such dreams myself when I went to sleep at last," she murmured wistfully. "Happy dreams of home, though it wasn't home. And I don't remember what they were."

"Was I in them?"

"No. But there was everyone I knew. I knew everyone there. . . . It was a feast!" she recalled. "A feast, and I was very welcome. Everyone greeted me, and took me to a man who— No! I don't remember."

"Was Erik there?"

"Erik? No. . . . But where *is* he?" she demanded, re-awakening to his disappearance. "We must find him, Ed, and take him to a specialist." She sat in a chair on the other side of the table.

"Do you want some coffee?" asked Ed.

"*Nei!*" She dismissed the matter, and addressed him very seriously. The spearhead lay between them.

"He was talking in his sleep," she said. "For a long time."

"What about?"

"About a dragon."

He gazed at her intently, as if what she was saying was a matter of life and death.

"He seemed to be reciting something—like a list," she went on. "I can't remember very much because that was in the night and after everything, and this is morning—when all that seems . . . unreal. Also, he was speaking very bad Norwegian. I think it was Norwegian. Something Scandinavian. But very strange. And with a voice so *old*. At first I didn't think it could be him—he was not moving, and not as if he were dreaming. But it *was* him, and he said something about animals and birds, about a wolf, and a horse—an eagle, a raven, and a boar. And then about a dragon."

"*What* about them?"

"I don't know. But the dragon was under a hill, and the wolf was in the forest. And he said something about thunder and glory and swords. And about a king. 'A king must live,' he said, quite loudly, and—'Fate is strongest.' Then more about a king."

"He said all that?"

"More than that, but I didn't understand what he was saying." She paused—he waited. Then she said, "I think he was also saying the name 'Odin.' "

"Odin?"

"Yes. Like a chant—'Odin-Odin-Odin-Odin-Odin . . .' "

"Stop it!" ordered Ed, inordinately irritated by the sound. "I won't have you saying the name of one of your pagan gods on Holy Island," he said, meaning to be humorous. "Even if this *is* Odin's day—Woden's day."

Runa bowed her head, and her falling hair swung off her shoulders and veiled her face.

Her seeming contrition moved him. He reached out a hand across the spearhead to touch her arm, her left arm, and saw that she was wearing her ring on her *left* hand, not her right. He wondered why—and then saw that there *was* a ring on her right hand. She was wearing two rings.

"Where did you get—*that?*"

She looked up at him, followed his gaze, and appeared to be astounded at what she saw.

"Where did you get it?" he demanded.

Still she was speechless, staring at both her hands, palms down, with the fingers spread on the table.

"I never gave you that," he said accusingly. "Who did?"

She held her left hand up, like a fan, before her face.

"I didn't put it on," she whispered. "I never put it on. It was in my coat."

"You're wearing it now."

She looked at him through her fingers, her eyes wide with incomprehension. "Yes," she said, "I am."

"Where did you get it?" he repeated. She looked away and was silent.

"I'm asking you," he said. "I'd like to know."

"I'm sorry—I can't tell you."

"Why not? What's so special about it?"

268

Runa shook her head, as if to deny and deflect his questions.

"Be reasonable," he persevered. "I just want to know where you got it. That's all. Why can't you tell me?"

"I can't."

"Why? You've never hidden anything from me before. What makes the ring so different? I *want* to know!"

"Don't ask!" she cried. "I promised not to tell."

Ed's eyes grew colder, as his face and thinking flamed at her willful denial of him.

"Erik," he said through his teeth. "It was Erik."

Ed hated evasion and secrecy, especially when applied to him, and when it cut him off from someone he trusted. It made him feel betrayed and miserable and heightened his aggression.

"Let me have a look," he ordered, extending his hand.

"No," she replied, covering her left hand with her right.

"Give it to me," he said.

"No."

His hand shot out and seized her wrist and forcefully dragged it toward him. At the same time his left hand fastened on her, bent on tearing the ring off her finger.

"I told you to give it to me!" he said.

"Ed! You're hurting!" she cried, as her arm in a vise was twisted backward and her fingers mangled.

The table pitched and banged in the struggle. The spearhead jerked and spun about, until it was pointing at Ed.

She gasped as the ring was pulled from her finger.

"Give it back to me," she pleaded, nursing her hand, yet much more hurt by the violence of his manner.

"No chance," he said, getting up. "Not until I find out where you got it from. Are you talking?—No. Then I'll keep it."

Ed examined the ring at the window. "Gold, I do believe.

Could be valuable. And evidently rather old. That boy will have a lot of explaining to do when he returns. Now what about some breakfast?" He put the ring in a trouser pocket.

She was silent, in apparent contemplation of the ring on her right hand.

"I see. I'm in the doghouse, am I? It doesn't occur to you it was *your* attitude that provoked me. You know I can't stand secrets—not between you and me."

"You should have shown respect."

"As much as you have shown in keeping things hidden from me? There's more—isn't there?—that you haven't told. I bet there is. *More* you haven't told me. And I've got a right to know. Who are you married to anyway—me, or him?"

"I promised not to tell."

"What?" he exclaimed, exasperated. "What, for God's sake? All right. *Don't* tell me. Just tell me this—whose side are you on?"

"I'm not on anyone's side. Please stop it, Ed."

"Oh, yes, you are! At this moment. Since last night in fact! You're in this with him, aren't you? Well, despite you both, I'm going to get to the bottom of this."

He seized the spearhead, waved it about, and stopped.

"It wasn't *you* that threw this?" he demanded.

"How can you *think* such a thing!" she cried, springing to her feet. "What a terrible question to ask!"

"Well, answer it."

"No!"

They faced each other, shaken by such antagonism, by feelings and thoughts they had never felt or said before, that they were afraid to speak. Neither saw the person that they knew, only a kind of enemy, the more dangerous for being so near and unknown.

Ed edged toward the door, holding the spearhead before him.

"I'm going to Bamburgh," he said, expressionlessly. "Now. We're expected there. A trip to the Farnes, if you remember. Are you coming?"

Runa crossed to the other side of the kitchen.

"You go to Bamburgh," she said, controlling her despair. "You go, and leave us here. Leave me alone to look for Erik. We don't need you here. What do you care what happens to him? He's ill! Sick! He needs a doctor—help—and *you* go to Bamburgh. Go on then. Go! I'll find help. I'll look after him. He's my baby, my son."

Ed turned at the door. "Oh, for God's sake, don't talk such bloody crap! There's nothing wrong with him that can't be put right by *us*! By me. All I need is some advice. And help from you. Especially some help from you. If I knew everything—"

"Why do you stand there talking?" Runa cried, advancing on him wildly. "Go on! You are going? Then go! Go!"

2

Once again the castle was displayed on the skyline above the village, as the road swooped down and straight toward the coast. Ed tore along the road in the car as if there were an emergency. For the third time he entered Bamburgh, passed through the village and then drove on up to the castle. This time he came with no romantic notions of its past and boldly drove straight in, as if he were its owner with urgent matters at hand.

But when he had parked the car below the keep, the panorama of sea and sand, the battlements and bastions about him, the towers and massive walls of stone, lifted his heart and cleared his mind. The wind was strong and gusting out of the north, but its power was small against the might of the castle.

Ed felt protected and more in control of his fate as he strode down the slanting path to the Neville Tower. This time there was no one on the lookout for him and he had to wait, after ringing the bell, in the wind tunnel of the archway before he was admitted. In his hand was the spearhead wrapped in newspaper. In his trouser pocket was the ring.

Professor MacDougall was clearly disappointed by the absence of Runa and Erik.

"Well, well, well," he said, descending the stairs to the sitting room with Ed. "Oh, dear. Oh, is that so? Erik not feeling well. . . . Poor lad. I'm sorry to hear it. But *you* at least are here. I'm glad you came. It was good of you to bother in the circumstances."

They entered the sitting room. "Welcome to Bamburgh Castle, once again!" said the professor.

The room was very warm and darker than Ed had remembered. The central heating must be on full, he thought —in addition to the fire, which was burning brightly. There also seemed to be more order in the room. The professor must have tidied it up, especially for Runa. On a table Ed noticed a sherry decanter and three glasses, together with a larger glass and a bottle of orange squash—presumably for Erik. But what drew his attention most was the table on which the precious manuscript lay. Here also was evidence of orderliness in the neat piles of books and papers—the typewriter was in its case and the anglepoise lamp on sentry duty at one side. On the central edge of the table below the window was the hamster's black tin box, and before the box was the sheet of tissue paper, its corners held down by books. There was a symmetry to the arrangement not unlike an altarpiece, and the arches of the mullioned window behind added to the illusion.

"It looks as if your work has been completed," Ed remarked, laying his newspaper package on the table.

"Very nearly," said the professor. "In fact I may return to Edinburgh tomorrow."

"Tomorrow!" Ed was disconcerted. "So soon? Well, you mustn't go away without saying goodbye. Come and see us before you go."

"That I will. I won't just up and disappear."

Ed was reminded by this of the hamster. "Did Longbottom come down the chimney eventually?"

"He did!" Professor MacDougall chortled. "He was sitting, black as a rat, in the fireplace when I got home. He's in there now, in his box, having a sleep. He's my watchdog at night, you see—guarding the fragment."

"Very necessary," commented Ed, with his eyes on the masking tissue.

"Oh! One thing I'm always forgetting to ask you—"

"Yes?"

"Have you ever observed the light from my candle in the window? From afar—from Holy Island?"

Ed considered the tall red candle in its candlestick on the window ledge and looked beyond it to the island.

"I light it in the evening," explained the professor. "A beacon was here in Roman times, and probably later. It's just an imbecile fancy, but it makes a wee link with the past, and I've wondered if it was visible out at sea—or on the island."

"I haven't noticed it."

"Look out for it tonight. I'm curious to know. Look in this direction and see if you can see this spark in the night."

One of the windows banged and rattled for a moment as a gust of wind exploded against the tower walls and went whistling through every cranny.

"I will," Ed promised.

"I sometimes feel like a lighthouse keeper here. Maybe I should have been one. In my bedroom at the top of the tower I have a pair of binoculars, with which I scan the sea for ships in distress." He smiled conspiratorially at Ed, then changed his tone. "Talking of lighthouses, I'm reminded that our outing to the Farnes is regrettably out of the question. Would you like a sherry?"

"Oh, yes—please—thank you. Why's that?"

"It's medium dry. Is that all right?"

"Fine."

The professor filled up two of the glasses and went on talking.

"I telephoned the place in Seahouses down the coast that organizes these things, and they tell me the season's over. Imagine! Daily trips have ended. If you want to go out to the Farnes, they say, you'll have to make a special booking and hire a complete boat! But that's out too. It appears that in any event they won't put out in such a wind." He gave Ed a glass of sherry.

"It's not a gale. Oh, thank you."

"No—but it's now coming from the northeast, and that's bad."

"What's wrong with the northeast?"

"Heaven knows! But that's the way it is. They'll not put out to sea today." He raised his glass. "A thousand blessings!"

"Cheers."

Ed thought of Robbie and everyone on *Cocoon*. Had they been out this morning? And would they go out tomorrow?

"I'm sorry about that," he said.

"So am I. So am I," returned the professor. "Won't you sit down?"

They occupied the same armchairs they had sat in on Ed's first visit. None of the lamps was on this time, and the professor's features were dark and obscure against the light

274

from the window. He seemed indifferent to the heat from the fire.

Ed related the story of his early morning trip with the fishermen and outlined some of his thoughts about them and about being at sea. He described the appearance of the island from the sea, including its landmarks. This led to a consideration by both of them as to where the Vikings who raided Lindisfarne had landed. Ed agreed that the Ouse, or the lower end of the Heugh, was a probable place.

It was not until Professor MacDougall had to move the wrapped-up spearhead in order to ferret out a book of reference that Ed was reminded of the night's delirium and his mission.

"Where are we?" the professor was saying. "Ah, yes. They all came to sticky ends. Sicga commits suicide. Athelhard, who fought with him on the River Tyne in winter, dies in the same year. And King Athelred is murdered by his bodyguard two years later. He was avenged however by one of his thanes called—according to Alcuin—Tortmund. That's the man. Revenge was more than sweet—it was a law of life. What have you there?" he inquired of Ed, peering over his glasses at the package in Ed's hand.

"Something for your expert opinion."

"Another mystery? Not more runes? I am curiosity incarnate."

Ed unwrapped the weapon and handed it to the professor, who made several noises of wonder as he examined it in the light from outside and seemed about to speak several times, but changing his mind said nothing.

The window banged again, and Ed with feigned indifference said, "What do you think?"

Professor MacDougall paused further before replying, his head tilted, his eyebrows raised, as he scrutinized the spearhead.

At last he spoke—casually. "Where did you get it?"

"I can't say."

This drew a quick glance at Ed. "Not stolen, I hope? Or borrowed?"

"No."

"Found?"

Ed was silent. The professor spoke again.

"It's genuine, of course. Of some antiquity. A spearhead."

"It is, is it? Old, I mean. How old?"

The professor with his left hand carefully smoothed the tissue paper's shining surface, then spread the newspaper wrapping on it before laying down the weapon.

"It's not for me to say. You must ask an archeologist. But I've seen similar pieces in Oslo and Stockholm—and in the British Museum."

He rooted out a large book and flipped through its illustrated pages. "It's not unlike—this!"

Ed saw a color photograph of a spearhead—similar to his —though his in comparison seemed twice as dark and menacing.

"The circles are in different positions," said the professor. "Apparently they have a ceremonial significance." He read the caption—" 'A spearhead of the Viking age.' "

Ed read on to himself—"The spear was the weapon of the god Odin and a symbol of his cult."

"A fairly reliable book this," commented Professor Mac-Dougall. "And full of pretty pictures. I should say that if your weapon hasn't come from a museum, it should certainly be in one. But where did you get it from?"

The professor's manner was more overtly eager now. Ed smiled. "It was thrown at me last night," he said.

For a moment amazement registered in the older man.

"Thrown!—Ah, now! Now then. Away you go! I really am most curious as to its place of origin."

Ed picked the spearhead up and returned it to its wrapping—to the professor's consternation at its disappearance from view.

"I'm not able to reveal that yet," Ed maintained. "But come to Holy Island tomorrow. Then I'll let you know."

"Surely you didn't find it there! Not on Holy Island!"

"I can't say where it was found."

"That's not, if I may say so, very satisfactory. It's possible there are other weapons where this one was found, and it *may* have some historical or archeological importance. You must certainly have it examined by an expert. Why don't you leave it with me? It'll be perfectly safe, and I'll take it with me to Edinburgh and—"

"I'm sorry. No. Not today. I need it to further my own investigations. I'd like to borrow that book if I may."

"What? Oh, yes. Take what you like. Are you sure—?"

"You've been very helpful." Ed held on to his package firmly.

"How about going out for a drink?" he said cheerfully. "On me this time."

Professor MacDougall gazed at his grinning guest, feeling at several kinds of disadvantage. But at least neither guest nor spearhead were leaving Bamburgh immediately. A drink or two, the professor thought, might ease a way to more information and another look at the other's prize, particularly at the scratches edging the socket which must, he thought, be runes.

"I shan't refuse," he said. "What a bright idea! Where shall we go?"

They decided to drive the few miles down the coast to Seahouses, as Ed had never been there. The spearhead was left beside the fragment—to be watched over by Longbottom—a move that pleased the professor as it meant that Ed would definitely have to return to the castle.

It was not until Ed sat in the driver's seat that he remembered the ring. But that, he thought, would be better left unshown—until later, when he was leaving. Otherwise the professor might get too carried away with speculation and suggestion and ask too many questions. At least the spearhead was, from MacDougall's reaction, a genuine, ancient, find. But *where* had it been found? Ed also wanted to know.

Runa stood on the headland, keeping the winnowing hair off her face with one hand and clutching her coat with the other.

"Erik!" she called—vainly, as the wind at once annihilated her voice and his name was overwhelmed by the ceaseless shattering of waves upon the stony shore. The tide was fast encroaching the island.

"Erik!" she shouted.

There was no sign of him in the wreckage and rubble below the headland, nor on the boulders beyond as they shrank beneath the sea—no sign of life—though everything was alive with movement about her, striving to escape. Even the rigid rocks and white triangle of the pyramid moved when she did, and swayed as she swayed—and the gray sky streamed through her hair.

She thought of the other place where they had been, where she had sat and watched the seal.

She floundered toward it along a path above the shore, hearing no movement she made herself, except the sounds of everything made volatile by the wind and tide, stirring and fleeing about her.

When she reached the place, she steadied herself to look around. "Erik!" she called.

Again there was no sign of him, and no seal in the water. But on the desolate crescent of the bay—exactly as she had drawn it—was a far black figure, facing her, and holding a sword.

In the wide and low saloon bar of a hotel called the Bamburgh Castle, Ed and Professor MacDougall sat holding their respective drinks of draft lager and whisky. Their seats in the window afforded them a partial view of Seahouses' harbor, though there was little movement or activity to divert them. Ed ate compulsively through a packet of nuts as he listened to what the other man was saying.

"Who was Guthorm? You may well ask. You may indeed." Professor MacDougall grimaced at a cheroot he was smoking. "I know no more than you. He was king of Westfold over the sea—his son was Guthrod—and he died before the gates of Bebba's burg. *But*—! There is and was a Westfold and a Bamburgh, and there's said to have been a Guthrod, who was king of Westfold about the year 800."

"Guthorm's son?"

"If you believe our chronicler—and there's no reason not to—Guthorm existed, and so did his son, Guthrod. Do *you* believe that?"

"Yes. I think so."

Professor MacDougall grinned. "The sagas say he was called the Hunter, and also the Magnificent. He was father of two kings who cross the frontiers of legend into history— Olaf, king of Dublin, and Halfdan the Black, who in turn was father of Harald Fairhair, the first king to be called the king of Norway. And our Guthorm was their ancestor. Isn't it splendid? And no one knows but us."

Ed smiled. "Truly splendid," he said. "But what happened to Guthrod?"

"He became king, and married. His son was Olaf, the one who ruled much later in Dublin. The *other* son, Halfdan the Black, was the result of another marriage twenty years later. A forced marriage that brought about Guthrod's death—and gives us another strange link with the past. Oh, it's grand stuff, all this! You see, the woman he wanted to wed was Asa. Her father declined the match, so Guthrod took her by force, killing her father and brother in the process. Asa could not forget or forgive this, and when her son by him was a year old, she got one of her servants to kill the king, her husband. She then very prudently fled back to her father's kingdom with her baby son. Guthrod was never avenged."

"Like his father."

"Like Guthorm."

"Is it true?" asked Ed.

"It depends how much you wish to believe. It's possible. And if you believe a part of it, then you'll think that the rest is true. The people and places are real."

The professor grinned. "I have only to look at your princess from Westfold—Gudrun—to know that legend lives."

It was not until Runa reached the sheltering rock of Lindisfarne Castle that she stopped looking back.

She had run until she ran onto the Wagon Way, blown like a leaf before the wind, by fear of whatever pursued her. Nothing did. Nothing that she could see. But what she had seen on the bay she never doubted—a man with a sword which could only be Erik's sword, the sword he had shown her. As she walked swiftly but unsurely along the Wagon Way, frightening connections formed in her mind between the man and Erik, and the sword and the spear and the ring, and the madness of the night. They were all linked in some way, though she could not understand why, nor what they foreboded.

At last she came to the village and entered the friendly square. But the shock of seeing the man of her own creation on the beach was still with her, and all her suppressed and subconscious fears of the past few days had pierced the surface of her reason.

"Erik!" she called as she shut the cottage door—more to announce her arrival than inquire of his presence. "Erik?"

No answer came from behind any of the closed doors in the hall. With an effort of will she opened the sitting room door, then the bedroom and kitchen doors. Everything was normal within the rooms—yet their very emptiness was disturbing. She opened the door of Erik's bedroom and her heart leaped to see someone there—though that someone was only Erik.

He was sitting on the unmade bed, engrossed by what he was drawing in the sketchbook.

"Erik," she said accusingly. "Why didn't you answer?"

He went on drawing.

"Erik!"

Scowling, without looking up he said, "I *heard* you."

The room was cold. The gas fire was unlit, and she gave herself something to do, some ordinary action, by lighting the fire.

"Where have you been?" she asked.

He paused, before replying—"On the beach."

"What beach was that?"

Erik sighed exasperatedly at her fussing. "Oh!—*I* don't know. A beach."

"On the north side? Near the pyramid?"

"Not *there*. I didn't go *there*. It was somewhere nearer here. Can I have something to eat?"

She remembered it was lunchtime and he must have had nothing to eat since the night before. "I'll see to it," she said.

He was still drawing—with a black pen, and still had not looked at her.

"Are you all right?" she inquired.

"Of course I'm all right," he said indignantly, with a glance at her that was quite in character. "Don't fuss!"

She smiled, reassured a little, and approached the bed to see what he was drawing.

On the large white sheet of paper was an unrelated horde of abstract figures—boats and sundry animals and birds. There were round objects, and squiggly lines, and little rows of runes. And every little matchstick man was armed with a shield and a sword or a spear, and between their little matchstick legs were the grossly exaggerated symbols of their sex.

Later, in the saloon bar of the hotel, while Ed and Professor MacDougall chewed their way through toasted cheese sandwiches, the professor returned to the subject of the spearhead.

By this time, five rounds of whisky and lager had been bought and consumed. To even the score, Ed had just bought a sixth round. He was not used to drinking so quickly—but as he did not have his pipe with him, having forgotten it, the need to have something in his hands had been filled by holding his glass—which being at the ready was speedily emptied. He was moreover listening more than talking and forced into keeping pace with the professor's swiftly drained and undiluted tots of whisky. Dragonish and domestic problems had been pushed into the background as he concentrated on Professor MacDougall's compelling and expressive description of matters historical.

The flow of conversation—from the professor—ran dry when Ed, more brusquely than was necessary, said it was uncivil of the professor to pursue the origin of the spearhead. He said, "I can't say. I won't say. And that's that!"

There was silence for a minute.

For the first time for some time Ed's gaze returned to the

harbor. The sky was heavy with cloud. Exploding waves were now throwing fountains of spray over the breakwater wall, and the turbulent sea outside was sending its outriders into the harbor on the back of the rising tide. The mastheads of the moored boats swayed out of time.

Ed's eyes followed the hovering flight of a large black-backed gull near the hotel. He was wondering how to make amends. Having been reminded of the spearhead, an image of it stayed with him. He recalled the picture of it in the book.

"Why is a spear a symbol of Odin?" he asked.

"Why? Because a spear is a symbol of a warrior's death."

No further comment was forthcoming.

Ed felt annoyed. "We might as well go," he said. "I'd like to go back via Swinhoe, if you don't mind. To look at the pigs."

They'll be better company, he thought, than this surly old goat. Besides, it wouldn't be possible to cross over to Holy Island for a couple of hours because of the tide, and rather than go back to the castle and be closeted with the professor, a tour of the countryside was preferable. There was also a chance he might see Danny, and this, he knew, would cheer him up.

Professor MacDougall had no choice but to accompany Ed, whose happiness at being active again and on the move showed itself in the careless speed at which he drove the car and the praise he lavished on pig farming. The professor made noncommittal noises.

But when they reached the crossroads at Swinhoe and got out of the car, Ed found that the Large White boar had vanished from his enclosure and the sows were sadly indifferent to his endearments. For a while he was at a loss, until he thought of looking for Danny. A laborer who happened to wander by told him where Danny lived, and in pleasant expectation of a meeting Ed carted the professor with him to a farmhouse down the road.

In its garden, full of rose trees, was a small boy steering a toy tractor on the path.

"Hallo," called Ed, getting out of the car. "Is your father in?"

"No," said the boy without stopping his game.

Ed paused at the gate and looked about, at the garden, the house, the buildings behind. A sense of loss, of exile, possessed him. He was unwanted, out of place.

The small boy ran his tractor into a rose tree and looked anxiously up at Ed. He had brown eyes, and fair hair, and could have been Ed's son.

"Tell your father . . ." Ed began. "No. It's nothing. Forget it. . . . Goodbye."

It was high tide. Erik stood by his mother on the jetty, sheltering on her right side from the wind. He was tired. As soon as lunch had been eaten she had said they were both going out for a walk, and though he had protested, the edgy hardness of her voice and manner had meant he was doomed to submit. They had wandered through the churchyard, then onto the beach by St. Cuthbert's Isle and up onto the Heugh before finally reaching the Ouse and walking out onto the jetty. There they had watched a man pull a sailboat in by its mooring rope to the steps. He had loaded the boat with two containers—one of which, as Erik discovered later, was a can of petrol. The other was a tin of bait. The man then messed about with the outboard engine. Erik wanted to go away, to go home. But his mother would not leave. Eventually she spoke to the man. Erik paid no attention to what the adults were saying—he was watching seagulls fighting over something in the water. But all of a sudden his mother was going down the steps. He followed.

"It's not too rough?" she was saying.

"No," said the man. "Not in the lee of the Heugh. You both can swim?" he asked and laughed.

"Oh, yes," she said, and smiled at Erik, with her hair all over her face.

"Come on. We're going for a sail."

"Odin is the greatest and most profound of the Nordic gods," proclaimed the professor. "He is many-faced and terrible, with a ferocious passion for knowledge and wisdom, for which he stops at nothing and sacrifices anything—anyone—even himself."

They had left Seahouses behind them, and the sight of Bamburgh Castle ahead as they drove north along the coast had reminded the professor of the spearhead and its symbolic owner.

Ed was silent, still in a gloom of foreboding. But Professor MacDougall now waxed loquacious on his theme.

"Odin governs the mystic ecstasy," he declared. "He fathoms the soul. He is a sorcerer and master of the runes. He inspires a frenzy in his worshipers and his warriors, so that they face the worst that fate can bring fearlessly and with a kind of rapture. His champions are young men who do a weapon dance in his honor, and his finest warriors are berserks, who howl like beasts when the battle madness comes upon them. He is the god of death and war, and his hall, Valhalla, is at once a symbol of the grave and the field of battle, where his warriors rest, feast and greet their ancestors, and fight again. Mead is his drink, and theirs. The wolf, the eagle and raven are his creatures. He has a mighty spear, a self-renewing gold ring, and a horse with eight legs. For nine days and nine nights he hung on the World Tree, in the manner of his sacrifices, and endured with a spear impaling him. Thus he won the secrets of the runes! But even he is doomed to die, to be devoured by the Wolf. Even the All-Powerful is powerless against Fate! Fate conquers all in the end."

The car swept into the castle, and Professor MacDougall and Ed returned to the tower.

"We have come back!" announced the professor, as they entered the sitting room. "The intrepid traveler has come home! And how's Longbottom?" he went on. "Asleep on the job! Dear me. But nothing has been stolen. All is well."

Ed thought the older man was presenting more of a pathetic figure than the comic one intended. He wished the professor would stop performing and sober up—as he should have done some time ago. Ed felt the tension of a headache beginning to fray his nerves.

One of the windows rattled a warning and he looked out to Holy Island beyond. He would leave as soon as he could. He had been away long enough.

"You're *not* going so soon!" exclaimed the professor as Ed picked up his package off the table. "Not at least before you allow me another glance at your trophy."

"Well . . ." Ed began, then remembered he had something else to show the professor. "All right," he said. "In fact I have another object for your eagle eye."

"Another!"

Ed dug the ring out of his pocket and handed it over for inspection, which was carried out this time in total silence —after Professor MacDougall had donned his glasses.

"Well?" demanded Ed when nothing had been said for a minute.

"You are full of surprises," the professor remarked at last. "And again I suppose you don't— No. You can't say where it came from. . . . A gold ring. A ring of gold. And again,

I would guess, from the Viking age."

"Is it?"

"A swift surmise. But the style—the pattern of the inter-twining snakes. . . ."

"Let me see."

Their heads nearly collided over the ring. Ed's hand was ready to snatch it away in case for some mad reason the other man laid a claim to it.

"Look," murmured Professor MacDougall. "You see how skillfully the bodies intertwine and how the serpents twist and turn about, and bite their neighbors. Exquisite. See. That's a head. And on *this* head, the biggest one—which would have been uppermost on the finger—there's a mark. Look very closely. What does it say?"

"It looks like an X."

"Ah, an X—which is the runic character for our G. This is a signet ring. . . ."

A sudden thought struck the professor. "Just a moment. May I?" he asked, indicating the package.

Ed nodded and took the ring to examine it himself while the professor unwrapped the spearhead. Both of them pondered the significance of what they saw.

"G," repeated Ed.

"G," said the professor, peering closely at the blade.

"G-U-TH . . ." He looked up at Ed with a childish wonderment.

"Guthorm!" he said. "The runes on the blade say 'Guthorm'!"

The two men stared at each other in wild disbelief. The professor's hands and voice shook when he spoke.

"Do you know what this is?" he cried. "Do you know what you have done? *This* is Guthorm's spear. And *that*, if it comes from the same place, is his ring. You have found Guthorm's grave!"

3

Erik was lonely. He trailed through the rooms of the empty cottage in search of something to do. The sitting room was dark and cold, for the fire had not been lit that day, and although the television set was there to switch on if he wished, the thought of watching television on his own was unappealing. He drifted back into the hall, which was even darker, and looked inside his mother's bedroom. It was full of his father's presence and forbidding. The bed was still unmade, he noticed, and he thought of lying there. It would be unlawful, and for this reason a daring thing to do. But he wasn't feeling bold, and didn't have his mother's invitation and welcoming embrace. He quietly closed the door, shutting out the yards of roses winding up the walls, and ambled to the kitchen. But it was not a place for him to play in, and even if there had been anything eatable lying around he would not have been tempted to eat it as he was not hungry. A cut in the tabletop attracted his attention. He ran a finger over it, remembering that *he* had done the damage—but not remembering why. A glance in the bathroom only reminded him of its functional purposes. He thought of playing with his submarine, then abandoned the thought as not being appropriate to the hour or his serious mood. Erik wandered forlornly back to his bedroom.

Like the kitchen the room was lighter than those facing the street. His mother had taken away the sketchbook, so there was no chance of drawing. Not that he wanted to. He was sick of the matchstick men and boats and things he had found himself drawing. They didn't really appeal to him. They weren't his style. They weren't full of action and color and interest—and they weren't *real*. Erik contemplated what he could see of the black tin box under his unmade bed. Even his golden treasures were meaningless. He couldn't put them on, play games with them. They belonged to a man, a grownup, and had the alien, oversized quality of a hostile, adult world. Where were his toys?

Standing at the window, he had vague memories of climbing in and out of the room in the middle of the night. Had he really done that? He wasn't *that* naughty. And had he really fallen on the floor in a fit? That wasn't like him at all.

Outside, a sudden flaring of light from the setting sun illuminated the church and graveyard and shadowed the garden. His loneliness was sharpened by the sight of two pert robins tripping along the garden wall. Despite the boisterous wind they seemed to be happy, enjoying themselves. One of them perched on the stones of his golliwog's grave.

Erik leaned his forehead against the cooling glass, thinking how stupid he had been to bury all his toys, his special collection. They were his. They belonged to him. Why had he thrown them away? How could he have been so unkind?

It was all too much for his understanding. He was only a small boy—eight next year. He saw his pale reflection on the glass brighten with falling tears.

Ed roared around the last bend of the road below Beal before swooping onto the causeway. On the back seat lay the unwrapped spearhead and the ring, on top of the illustrated book of Scandinavian mythology. He had escaped with them despite the professor's entreaties to let him keep them. "Please be careful," cried the professor. "And let me know where you found them. I *must* know!" "Tomorrow!" said Ed, and drove like a demon out of the castle, never looking back at the vast protecting walls of Bebba's fortress reddening in the sunset. He knew that Erik held the secret of the grave—where it was, and what was buried there. And Runa seemed to share the secret. Well, he would wrest it from them. After that, he felt sure, everything else would be resolved one way or another.

When the car tore down to the causeway, head-on into the wind, he saw that its whole length was still under the outgoing tide. But he did not hesitate. Nothing would stop him. His foot trod hard on the accelerator, and racing after the outflung shadow of the car, he plunged into the sea, the wheels making a great bow wave, like a destroyer.

Ten minutes later he abandoned the still-dripping car in the village square, and clutching the book, the ring and the spearhead, advanced on the cottage. But seeing it again diminished the urgent past and recalled the problems of the present that he had left behind. How, and where, were Runa and the boy? Were they at home?

Ed called her name as he entered the cottage—"Runa!"

All the doors in the hall were shut.

"Runa!"

He put his collection of objects on the hall table and began opening the doors and leaving them open. The rooms were all empty and cold. The last room he entered was Erik's.

The boy was lying on the unmade bed, fully dressed, with his face to the wall.

"Where's your mother?" Ed demanded.

There was no answer.

"I'm talking to you! Where is she?"

He had been unnerved by the emptiness of the cottage and the prostration of the figure on the bed. But to have his questions unanswered—to be kept in ignorance and ignored —goaded him into action. Ed seized the boy's shoulder and pulled him onto his back. Erik made no resistance, and his open eyes came to rest, staring above him, at the ceiling. His face, Ed noted with surprise, was wet with tears.

What kind of a game is this? thought Ed, and cuffed Erik's shoulder.

"Come on! I want to know where she is!"

Erik raised his hands to his face more in a token protest at being pummeled than in defense, while Ed continued his treatment, saying—"And that's not all! I want to know where you found the spear, the ring—where you dug them up. Come on. Speak up! I can't hear what you say."

Erik turned his eyes, awash with misery, on his father, and clasped his father's hand in both of his.

"Please," he whispered.

The word transfixed Ed more than the unfeigned wretchedness that shone through Erik's tears.

"What's the matter?" Ed heard himself say—far too loudly. "For God's sake!"

Erik turned his flaxen head and trustfully bowed his face with eyes downcast against his father's hand, pushing his cheek against his father's fingers with a final shiver of grief.

He gave a loud sniff and whispered, "I'm . . . sorry. I really *do* like you, Daddy."

Ed's jaw locked as he controlled the sympathic sorrow that rose in his throat. His eyelids burned despite himself, and he had to swallow before he could speak.

He sat on the bed and said, "Sorry? What for?"

Erik's response was to edge himself toward his father, reaching out with his arms, until his head was awkwardly pressed against his father's chest.

In wonderment Ed realized that his arms were embracing his son.

So Runa found them, when she returned to the cottage from the shops.

Ed turned to look at her over his shoulder.

He gave her an apologetic smile, though his eyes were bright with pleasure.

"Ssh . . ." Ed whispered with wry concern. "He's asleep."

The sun had set when Professor MacDougall walked out onto the windblown beach below Bamburgh Castle, whose high and orgulous outline behind him masked the reddened clouds. When he had perambulated southward for several hundred yards he looked back and saw that the castle was now dwarfed by swirling ascendant streamers of flame in the sky and seemed to be on fire.

The wind had lessened, but still flew gustily over the beach from the sea, and was cold enough to make him regret he had not worn his coat. However, as was his habit, both he and his hamster had gone out for their evening exercise —though they would not be too long about it tonight.

He proceeded briskly on his way, twirling a walking stick, using it to prod the collapsed jellyfish, large and small, that lay scattered along the beach. Longbottom was in his jacket pocket—and more than usually restless despite the mixture of nuts he had with him for his dessert. The professor's brain was as active in darting from postulation to supposition on the subject of Guthorm's grave.

The coincidence of the name on the spear with the name in the chronicle was so extraordinary that it had a ring of truth. In truth the king of Westfold must have been buried nearby—no doubt by his son. But where? Where would the surviving longship have gone after the Viking defeat at Bebba's fortress?—Where else but back to Lindisfarne before returning to Westfold over the sea? Lindisfarne, where the Wardlaws were staying, where Guthorm must have been buried. And Edmund Wardlaw had somehow discovered the grave! Professor MacDougall shuddered to think what damage might be done if the barrow were not excavated properly. His spine chilled with imagining what priceless treasures must be there—which might be destroyed or lost. He resolved to visit the island as soon as he could the following morning. He should have gone back with Ed that evening—He could go there now!

The tide, he saw, was still retreating from the sands. Low tide would be in about three hours' time. A visit might not be welcome, but it must clear away some of the mystery.

Professor MacDougall perched himself on a stranded fishermen's marker buoy to unravel a scheme of action. He narrowed his eyes and huddled himself before the frontal onslaught of the wind. A pink reflection of the sunset glowed in the mass of clouds above the sea, deepening its color. The wall of dunes was behind him.

Longbottom was trying to escape from his owner's pocket, so the professor detached the hamster's hold on the tweed and deposited him on the sand. In fear at finding himself thus exposed to the elements and his enemies, Longbottom flattened himself against the ground, nosing nervously about, while the wind pecked holes in his fur.

"Don't you go too far now," admonished the professor. "And keep away from the dunes. Off you go."

The hamster, assailed by all the exotic scents of the salt sea and seaweed, followed his nose into the wind, and with tentative runs ventured out onto the vast and glooming beach.

"Not too far now," repeated the professor. "And don't get your feet wet!"

With a watchful eye on Longbottom's wary progress, Professor MacDougall distractedly began to draw on the sand with his walking stick. He made lines that turned themselves into the runic characters of Guthorm's name—

ᚷᚢᚦᚷᚱᛗ

"Guth-orm," he mused, meant "Battle-snake," when translated from the Old Norse language. Every name was descrip-
tive then—and was so now, though the nature of words had
altered, making their original form obscure. Something about
the marks at his feet nagged at his memory.

He looked up and was alarmed to see how far Longbottom
had journeyed.

"You better come back to father," he said, more to himself
than to the hamster.

A seagull with a flourish of wings flew over him and
landed gracefully by the hamster. It was a large black-
backed gull. For an instant it stood, eyeing the professor. He
lunged to his feet, and the gull snatched at the hamster with
its beak, and seizing its prey, heavily winged away along the
shore.

Professor MacDougall stumbled after it in desperate pur-
suit, waving the stick and hurling imprecations at the sky,
while the seagull flew further off and steadily higher.

Some fifty yards away it dropped its wriggling catch. The
professor shut his eyes as the hamster hit the beach. When
he opened them the gull was already beside its prey, stabbing
at it, jerking it about, before snatching it up again, and flying away—this time out to sea.

"You devil!" screeched the professor. "You didn't need to
do that! It's cruel! You murderer!"

Trembling, he leaned on the stick, his knuckles white,
and remained so, stricken with sorrow, until the gull had
vanished in the growing darkness.

Brokenly he found his way off the beach, through the
dusky dunes and up to the castle. He could not weep—he
was too old for that—but the pangs of his loss seared his

mind, and a horror at the hamster's senseless, violent death haunted his imagination.

In the sitting room of the tower, the empty tin box was like a tomb, a memorial to its owner's fate. With religious feeling Professor MacDougall lit the candle on the window ledge and put the silver candlestick on the box. He sat in front of it, wondering if the candle's light could be seen on Holy Island, and his eye was drawn by its wavering glow to a scrap of paper reposing on top of the fragment and its cover of tissue. On the paper he had copied the runes from the spearhead—which he had later traced on the beach. The paper had moved. The runes now presented themselves to his sorrowing and unfocused eyes upside down. *"Mrothug"* they said.

Where had he seen that—something like that—before?

He had the answer. In the Wardlaws' cottage on Holy Island! He had thought then that the runes said *"drowun."* Clearly they were misrepresentations of *"mrothug"*—the *"th"* forming one symbol. Ed had copied them wrongly. And the original had been Erik's.

Erik, he recalled with a shock, wrote from right to left.

Erik, then, had written the runes for *"Guthorm."*

But how could he know what he was doing? Or did he know?—Perhaps he did.

In the dark of the tower room, beset outside by the wind, Professor MacDougall began to piece together the words, phrases, objects and actions that had struck a discord in his association with the Wardlaws. The more he plumbed the ominous depths of the week, the more he sank in a mire of inaction and doubt. He told himself not to be daft. But the seagull's attack, and a lifetime of studying the literature of the long-dead past, had made him unduly fatalistic. The more he thought, the more he feared, though *what* he feared was insubstantial, and left him powerless to act.

Yet as time passed, and the tide flowed out, a weaving pattern of evil was revealed—with the hamster's fate only a prelude to tragic ends.

The fire had been lit, the lights put on, the beds made, all the curtains except those in the kitchen had been pulled, and Rose Cottage was warm and trim and bright again. The Wardlaws were having dinner in the sitting room. It had seemed a cheerful idea and a change from eating in the kitchen. But principally it was to give more room for the meal Runa had cooked them—a three-course meal, as no one had had much lunch. It was also to celebrate the reconciliation of father and son. Runa sat between them, with her back to the fire, doling out their portions and encouraging them to eat. To drink they all had a glass of mead, in order to finish the bottle.

Erik was wearing his red dressing gown over his pajamas. On this occasion the rule of "bath before bed" had not been followed. He had had a bath soon after Runa's return.

After pausing at the door of Erik's bedroom, she had entered the room to verify the amazing sight of Erik asleep in his father's arms. It was also something to savor.

"I've just got back," Ed whispered. "Where have you been?"

"Shopping," she answered. "Why is he—?"

Ed forestalled her. "He was crying on his bed when I came in. I don't know why. I just sat down—and—Well. This! He said he really liked me."

"It looks like it!" She smiled.

"It's nice to see you again," Ed whispered.

"I love you too."

They smiled at each other. "Look," he said more normally. "This is, er, more your job."

"You do it very well."

"Thanks. But it's more your line. Why don't you take over?"

At that point Erik stirred and awoke, and Ed relinquished his hold to Runa, who after caressing and comforting Erik decided that a bath would freshen him up. An instinct also told her that their present harmony would continue if Erik was out of Ed's way for a while, until she and Ed had sorted out their own differences—if any now existed.

"Let us have peace, Ed. For once, let us have peace," she said as soon as he joined her in the kitchen after she had settled Erik in his bath. "It's beautiful. All right?"

She went on unpacking her shopping.

"I haven't said a word!" Ed complained.

"Well, don't," she said. "Not to Erik. Not tonight. No. I have been thinking, and I think that all these troubles to do with him are because he is not happy. And they happened because of us."

"You mean because of *me*."

"No." She stopped what she was doing and looked at him. "It is as much my fault as yours. It is *our* fault. We have failed to understand him."

"That's true." Ed was examining what she had bought.

"Pay attention."

"I am. I'm listening. Go on."

"Well," she said, looking out of the window. "You re-member he didn't want to come here. *We* did, so we came. And everything that *we* have done has been done with little thought for him. Most things. We don't consider him, in that way, at all. So naturally he is upset and unhappy. It is because of *us* that he is like this."

"He has a mind of his own," Ed murmured.

"He's only a child—our only child, and we treat him like a guest in the house, like someone from another country."

Ed was silent for a moment. Then he said—"You don't think he's possessed?"

"Possessed! No. But I think you are right. He may have caused those things in the night to happen—to let us know he is unhappy, to get our attention. . . . He cries for help. The trouble is that he is *not* possessed. By *us!*"

"That's very clever. You could be right."

"I am sure of it. And now that we have peace—especially between you both, we must make sure it lasts. So. No questions, Ed. Let Erik rest tonight."

She began to put on her apron, which meant that Ed was supposed to leave her alone to do the cooking.

"There *are* certain matters still unanswered," he said.

"Yes, I know," she said. "I saw the spear in the hall. Did you get an answer about it?"

"It's a Viking spear," Ed announced. "I can show you one like it in a book I brought back with me. And the ring is a Viking ring."

"I thought it was old," she said, getting milk and eggs from the fridge.

"You don't sound very interested. It could be a find of great historical and archeological importance! Did you know, for instance, that the runes for Guthorm are on the spear?"

"Guthorm?"

"You know who Guthorm is."

"Ed," she said, turning to face him. "Why don't you tell me later, after dinner? Can't it wait till then?"

"It's *very* interesting."

"I'm sure it is. But I'm cooking."

"Anyway—what about you? You haven't told me what you've been up to all day."

"I looked for Erik—and found him—"

"Where did he go?"

"To the beach. And in the afternoon we went for a sail."

"A sail! In this weather! Whose boat?"

"You'll find out later."

He groaned. "It's not my night."

She said, "It will be—later."

During dinner Runa told him that she and Erik had been on the jetty when one of the fishermen had asked them if they would like a sail in his boat. The fisherman was Robbie.

"Cheeky devil," said Ed. "And my faithful wife said—Yes?"

"Yes," said Runa—"It was quite safe with him. There was an outboard motor, but we didn't use it and sailed about the harbor, in the lee of the Heugh and St. Cuthbert's island. It was very relaxing—lovely to be on the water again. Wasn't it, Erik?"

"*Ja*," he mumbled, his mouth full.

"You could well have been *in* it," chided Ed. "With that wind."

"Nonsense," she said. "I have been out in worse in Oslo-fjord—and this wasn't even the open sea."

She told him the boat was Robbie's personal possession, which he used for sailing and fishing with rod and line. He preferred this to motorized sailing and mechanical fishing. The boat had been in his family for years, though he was the only one who used it now.

"What did you talk about?" asked Ed.

"We didn't do much talking," Runa said.

"Hmm," muttered Ed with mock suspicion. "Then what were you doing?"

"Nothing," she said. "Sailing. What else can you do in a boat?"

"Quite a lot," he replied. "Don't you remember that after-noon in a boat off Sandefjord?"

They both laughed.

"What are you laughing at?" asked Erik.

"Nothing," said Runa. "You wouldn't understand."

"What else can you do in a boat?" he demanded, but his question went unanswered.

After the meal, they all watched television for an hour, and then it was time for Erik to go to bed. During this time, no mention was made by Ed or Runa of any of the questions and thoughts that had troubled them earlier in the day. The drawing that Erik had made had been hidden away by Runa. The spearhead and the ring had been removed to a drawer in the front bedroom. But the book still lay in the hall.

"Why don't you say goodnight to Erik?" suggested Runa to Ed. She had just left Erik's bedroom after tucking him in bed and kissing him goodnight.

"I'm sure he would like it," she said.

"Should I?" asked Ed. He was on his knees, stoking the fire.

"I think so. Tonight. No questions though."

"Perhaps I should." Ed got up. "What do I do?" he asked.

"Oh, Ed," she protested smilingly. "Do I really have to tell you? Kiss him goodnight."

"Is that what *you* do? Show me."

She went toward him, happy to play his game. She smiled at him. Then, becoming intent on her demonstration she put her hands on Ed's shoulders and kissed him softly on the mouth.

"Goodnight," she said.

"Goodnight," he murmured in reply.

Then his overmastering arms were all about her, folding her into him, crushing her body against him, and she yielded to the passion of his mouth and his embrace. He held her as if she would never be in his arms again.

Loathfully, uncertainly, they drew apart, their eyes still locked on each other.

"I love you," he whispered. "Truly, and forever."

He moved away and left the room. She wanted him to stay, but said nothing and remained where she was, waiting for his return.

Ed knocked on the door of Erik's bedroom after tucking in his shirt. He entered without waiting for a reply. The light from the hall enabled him to make out the bed. A movement told him that Erik was awake—he was curled up on his side, facing the curtained window.

"Hallo," he said. "I've come to say goodnight."

He stood awkwardly in the darkened room, doubtful of the procedure, though with no intention of kissing the boy, waiting for some lead from Erik, who in turn maintained what seemed to be an embarrassed silence.

"Are you awake?" asked Ed.

"Yes."

"I thought so. Well. . . ." What could he say? Goodnight?

Erik spoke in his sing-song treble. "I didn't throw the spear at you," he said.

There was another kind of silence between them.

When Ed asked his question, its two words were like missiles in the dark.

"Who did?"

A long sigh came from the darkness and ended in an answer that chilled his soul.

"Guthorm."

Ed stood stock still, as the name invaded his reason, preventing any further speech while implications, remembered deeds, emerged to haunt him.

Stunned, he backed away from his adversary, retreated from the room and closed the door.

Guthorm! How could Erik have known the name—the name of the king killed long ago at Bebba's burg? The name that was on the spear—which had been thrown at him, at *him*.

By Guthorm?

Ed gazed about the hall for help, and dumbly, dolefully realized he could only, as a man, deal with this danger himself. He went out into the windy night, not knowing where he was going, but sure that even on his own he could, once he was armed with reasons, arrive at a final solution.

Runa heard the front door close and was startled out of her trance. Had Ed gone out? It must have been him. But where had he gone? For a walk? For a drink? He must have gone out to buy some "dumps."

She drifted into the hall, and opened the door of Erik's bedroom.

"Are you asleep?" she whispered.

"No."

"Where's your father?"

"I don't know."

"Are you all right?"

"Yes!"

"Oh. Goodnight."

"Goodnight!"

She shut the door quietly after her and gazed aimlessly about the hall. Her thoughts were confused and undefined. On the table was the book that Ed had brought from Bamburgh. She picked it up, examined the cover, and thought she would look through it until Ed returned.

In the sitting room, Runa settled herself in an armchair by the fire. She felt oddly detached from what she was doing, as if she were afloat without a star to steer by or a helmsman at the stern.

She opened the book and read about the long-ago ways of life and death of her ancestors—some of which she had never known—much of which she had forgotten.

She came to a chapter on "Belief."

On turning a page she saw a large illustration of a carved

wooden post—the hideous face of a man, with his tongue lolling out of his mouth, and his right eye shut as if in a leering wink. It was the face of the one-eyed man she had seen on their first morning.

It was the face of the god who had given his eye for wisdom—One-Eye, Father-of-All, Mimir's Friend, Fenrir's Foe, Evil-Worker, Terror-Maker, *Odin!*

4

For over an hour Ed sat alone in the all but deserted barroom of the Crown and Anchor, with no company other than the Ingram sisters and three of the older fishermen. For a time he had talked to Selby Allison, but with such abstraction that the landlord, sensing his mood was not for conversation, had turned his attention to the fishermen and started polishing glasses. In Ed's state of emotional insecurity, this piece of consideration had seemed like a rebuff. To make it real he had removed himself from the bar and sat in the furthest corner.

His flight from the cottage had taken him as far as the Crown and Anchor—with the conscious intention of sorting out the fantasy from the fact. But he could not make the distinction. His reasoning could not cope with such suppositions that faced him—the reality of Guthorm, his death at Bamburgh and burial on Lindisfarne, the discovery and depredation of his grave by Erik, the source of Erik's knowledge of runes and inhuman strength, the cause of his mental storms, the identity of whoever had thrown the spear. Not since his own childhood had he been faced with believing in what he could not see—that what was dead could live again, that dark forces not only reigned but could rule the living.

Ready as he was to admit a lack of knowledge, to concede some form of existence after death—though in no Christian heaven—he could not surrender his reasoning to irrational belief. That was impossible. Or so he thought. But having ventured into the mists of possibility, leaving behind his hold on matters physical and practical, historical and material, his thinking became less determinate and positive, and with no direction faltered into apathy. Yet he was not without some points of light. He believed that there *was* a grave, probably Guthorm's, and that Erik knew where it was. He also suspected that Runa knew of its whereabouts and perhaps was in some kind of conspiracy with Erik. This thought depressed him. Yet he felt certain that if he demanded that she tell him what she knew out of loyalty and love for him, she would do so. He did not wish to make such a demand. He was not sure now that he wanted to force a confession, by whatever means, from her or from Erik. The possibilities of what he might find out were so appalling that they prevented any further action on his part.

Ed remained in his corner of the Crown and Anchor, building walls of sand against the rising tide of unreason, and keeping the monsters of his own imagination captive and insensible with drink—not thinking that it would madden them in the end.

He passed the time in blankly watching the occupants of the bar and gazing at the furniture and the fire, while images of his life with Runa turned his eyes in on himself. Erik had no part in this life, and eventually, as Ed drowsed and dreamed, neither had Runa. In a swift regression he was himself a child again, playing games, building castles, fighting wars, killing foes, eating, drinking and sleeping. He thought of his father, who had died the year before, and he wondered what his father had lived for and what he had really expected of his son. He had been proud of him—he had treasured his son's achievements. Ed in turn had honored the man for giving him life. Now there was no one to honor—just the name—the family name of Wardlaw.

"Listen!" said Selby Allison loudly.

Ed looked up, and the others looked at the landlord or at the window.

"It's twenty-two minutes past nine," Mr. Allison declared. "The tide is on the turn and the moon is full!"

A guffaw and comments incomprehensible to Ed came from the fishermen. One of the Ingram sisters spoke up— the one who owned Rose Cottage.

"What's so special in that?"

"It's a rare event," said Mr. Allison. "It's not often that the full of the moon and the moment when the tide stands still happen together. It's low tide now, and the moon is full. I noted it would happen this morning. I've a mind to see it now."

He came out from behind the bar, and Ed realized for the first time that the landlord walked with a limp.

"Is your wife not coming in tonight?" asked Mr. Allison, pausing by the door. Ed drained his glass, and banged it clumsily down on the table.

"No," he said.

He got up, remotely stirred by the knowledge that the tide had turned and prompted by the example of the other.

"Are you leaving now?" asked Mr. Allison.

"Yes."

"Ah, well. You'll need to get home."

They went into the hall and then outside, to view the silver moon in the now cloudless southern sky over the Heugh.

"Aye, it's a fine night now," said Mr. Allison.

Ed shivered. Where they stood they were sheltered from the wind, but his shirt gave little protection against the cold.

"There's still that hell of a wind," he said.

"It'll blow itself out tomorrow. That's always the way. It'll blow like this for three days and then die away in an hour. Tomorrow will be a grand day—no doubt of that."

The trees beside the altar end of the priory ruins whispered and shook their tops. They were silhouetted against the luminous sky and seemed to sprout—both trees and ruins —from the blacker mass of the Heugh, outlined beyond.

Another shiver, more than of cold, coursed through Ed.

"You can almost imagine the monks there now, praying for deliverance in the darkness. There's little sense of time on the island."

"Aye. At high tide especially," responded Mr. Allison. "When we *are* an island—at high tide."

"Was Aidan's settlement really there—where the priory is?"

"How do you mean?"

"Well, I can't see—I wondered why it was thought to be over *there*, under the priory. Nobody knows for certain. No trace of it has ever been found—nothing but gravestones where the priory now stands. That may have been where the monks buried their dead, but where was Aidan's church?"

That must have also been, he thought, where they refused to bury Sicga.

"You've wondered, have you?" Mr. Allison's eyes glittered as he looked up at Ed under slanted eyebrows. "They say— they used to say—that Aidan built his church upon the Heugh."

"The Heugh?"

"Aye—somewhere near the coastguard station. That's where it would be."

"Of course," Ed exclaimed. "You're right."

Of course he's right, Ed repeated to himself. They would never have built their church and dwellings in the shelter of the Heugh, but *on* it—the more to mortify their flesh, exposing themselves to the elements, the bitter wind and the biting rain. There they would be nearer God, and in view of Bebba's burg across the water. The craggy Heugh would also serve as some protection against high tides and marauding wolves and bears. It was wide enough and long enough to hold a collection of wooden huts and a timber church surrounded by a stockade, but not large enough for a stone-built priory.

In the moonlight his imagination pictured that pioneering settlement of Irish monks on Lindisfarne, when Oswald was king of Northumbria.

"It's not in the guidebook," said Mr. Allison. "There's no proof, you see. Not many would believe what they cannot see."

"You're right on that," Ed murmured. "And I do believe you're right about the Heugh."

"That's good. I thought you'd like to know. But not a word to anyone in London now," said Mr. Allison jokingly. "No one must know. We want to keep some secrets on the island."

He looked at the moon with satisfaction. "Aye, it's a grand night. . . . I'll away inside now. Remember me to your wife."

Ed switched his eyes off the outline of the Heugh.

"Yes, I have to go. . . . Goodnight."

"Goodnight," said Selby Allison. "Sleep well."

Ed moved away from the Crown and Anchor and into the square, where wind-riven leaves scraped over the road and gathered in shadowy graves. Unbalanced by the chilling force of the wind and the fumes of MacDougall's ruin, he walked unsteadily, his vision punctured by negative images of the moon and the positive daylit line of the Heugh.

He paused to glance into the lane on his left, directed

there by the signpost to Lindisfarne Priory. At the end of the lane, by the churchyard gate, a spear had been cast at him. By Guthorm. Ed laughed to himself. The Battle-snake's aim had not been good. He must be getting old. He *was* old —more than a thousand years old!

Ed laughed aloud, scoffing at the thought of an antique ghost throwing a spear at him. Then he remembered that the spear was as old, and still deadly. He recalled the way it had stuck in the door behind him, thrown with such force that its owner's name on the blade might have been buried within him. He felt angry at such a threat to his life, at such a base and treacherous attack from an unseen foe. His pride and honor had been injured. Such a piece of aggression would have to be requited.

But what could he do?

He saw his answer in the graveyard.

He could find Guthorm's grave and lay the ghost—if there was a ghost—by laying waste his place of rest! Attack was the best method of defense. He would carry the assault into the house of death itself and in so doing would seize whatever treasures were there—weapons and gold. He already had the spearhead and the ring. There must be more to be won, and win he would, for he was invincible—knowing that no other man could vanquish him, and scorning, while he believed in himself, the existence of other powers.

Aroused as he was to martial action, he marched back to the cottage, telling his rational self that the finding of the grave was in itself of great archeological importance, and the sooner accomplished the better.

Ed declared his return to the cottage more loudly than necessary.

"I'm back!" he cried, and banged into the sitting room where Runa was hunched in an armchair by the fire. "Behold, I have returned. And although I have been drinking,

I am not drunk. But I have been thinking. What have *you* been doing?"

He crouched in front of the welcome heat of the glowing coals and looked sideways up at her, noticing that on her lap were some sketches and the book that he had borrowed from the professor. He also observed that she was not looking at him but abstractedly at the fire.

"What have you been doing?" he repeated. "Have you been drawing?"

When she spoke, it was in a monotone.

"I've been reading," she said.

"What?"

"It's no use," she went on, still staring at the fire. "From the first morning. . . . All that I saw and thought I saw, and heard and thought I heard—it was all real. Everything. From the beginning."

"What on earth are you talking about?" he said, vexed at such an indifferent, muddling response to his return. "Aren't you pleased to see me?"

She was silent.

Flushed by the heat and her apathy, he hoisted himself to his feet and was prevented from remonstrance by the realization that the drawings on her lap were not hers but Erik's.

He snatched them up in aggravation. The top one he had seen before—a man on a horse—but the other was much more complex. And on it were rows of runes.

"He's been at it again, I see! Very clever. Very rude—all those phallic fellows running about." Ed paused and shook his head perplexedly. "What gives him such ideas? What does it mean?"

Without looking at him, Runa answered—her voice expressionless and low.

"It tells the tale of how Guthorm, king of Westfold, came

to Lindisfarne with his son, Guthrod. They plundered and killed, and took captives, and then burnt the church and all the buildings. Then they went to Bamburgh. But Guthorm was killed and one of their ships was set on fire, and they could not take the fortress. So Guthrod ravaged everything and vowed revenge and brought his father's body back to Lindisfarne where he buried it with all honor, as best he could—at the center of three trees on a northeast headland. Then he sailed away."

Ed could see what looked like ships, and men, and buildings and beasts and birds—but they were meaningless to him.

"How can you tell?" he demanded. "How do you *know?*"

"It is written in words and pictures."

"The runes? *You* can't read them."

"I can. . . . In the book, this book you brought from Bamburgh, there is an explanation of the symbols. It was difficult—the language is very old—but I understood. Too much. There's nothing we can do."

"Who says so? Who's *this* then?"

He held the other drawing before her eyes. She lowered them and shuddered.

"The horse with eight legs is called Sleipnir, and the rider is the god."

"Who?"

She made no reply.

A wave of anger swept over him—a deep and violent impulse to destroy what had enthralled his wife and hounded and bedeviled his thoughts and actions.

"There is no god!" he exploded. "No god! No Guthorm! Nothing other than you and me. These things don't exist!"

He tore the drawings in half, in quarters, then crushed them together and threw them in the fire.

Runa gasped and held out her hands, first as if to restrain

him, then as if to retrieve the crumpled paper from the fire. But she was still bound and fettered by a fatal inertia and made no other movement—only withdrawing into the arm-chair and staring into the flames with dull foreseeing eyes.

"We are dead," she whispered.

For a moment Ed looked down on her, struck with com-passion by her wan appearance and evident hopelessness. Moved to console her he seized her hands. But her hands were cold, and when she turned her gaze on him, her eyes were lifeless.

"It doesn't matter what you do," she intoned. "We are mocked in everything, and made use of. The web is almost woven."

"Runa . . ." he pleaded. "What is it? You're never like this. What's happened? Is it Erik?"

"No. . . ."

"I'm not going to let you be like this! Do you hear?"

He hauled her to her feet, and the book fell onto the floor. He took her in his arms and spoke words of reassurance as, with her head inclined against his shoulder, she watched the pages of the book flick idly over until they slowed and came to rest at the face of the one-eyed man.

She flinched as if she had been stung, and her fingers dug into his back. When he saw what had so startled her he let her go and picked up the book.

He looked at the picture and read its caption.

For several stupefied seconds his mind refused to make the association that had shattered her will.

"You don't believe—?" he began, and stared at her aghast.

The abject spectacle she presented, inert and so unlike herself, again aroused his anger, filling him with a rage to revenge himself on her persecutors. He ripped the leering page from the book, and mangled it with his left hand. But in the process other pages flew open and revealed themselves, showing symbols, weapons, objects, names that were all anathema to him. He savaged the book with both his hands, tearing the pages from its spine, and rammed the pieces into the fire with the poker, pinning them down on the glowing fragments of Erik's drawings.

"It burns!" he said. "It's paper and it burns! See! You're going to be all right. I'm going to get to the root of this. Sort it out. Make sure that nothing bothers us again."

He stood up. "Where's the grave?"

He grasped her shoulders. "Where did Erik take you? Look at me. Where's the grave?"

She looked at him without seeing him. "At the center of three trees on the—"

"No!" he said. "Where is it *now?*"

Her eyes focused themselves on him. She frowned in the way that Erik did.

"On the headland," she murmured listlessly. "By the pyramid. Over the edge."

"The pyramid. . . ."

He understood. His eyes gleamed. At last he had a direction and an aim. At last he knew where the source of all their ills must be—and under the grave mound would be a hoard, golden gifts and ancient weapons that would be his for the taking.

"I want you to stay here," he commanded. "Make sure that Erik does not leave his room. Sit in his room if necessary. There won't be any manifestations where I'm going if he stays here. Don't let him out of the house. You'll do that, won't you? Just do that. Promise?"

"Yes," she said, frowning again.

Ed seized his polo-neck sweater off a chair.

"What do I need? A torch. Where—? It's in the hall. What else?"

He struggled into the sweater, thinking he should have

something with him to defend himself. But the thought was unworthy of his undoubted courage and strength. Nothing could harm him while he believed in himself, in his own powers of mind and body. No inhuman power would prevail against him.

Controlling his excitement at the prospect of some action, he opened the sitting-room door. Runa moved after him.

"Just keep Erik here," he whispered. "Don't let him out. You'll be quite safe. . . . Do you understand what I'm doing—what I have to do?"

She smiled at him sadly.

He kissed her forehead, and moving away from her, picked up the torch from the hall table. When he opened the front door, a familiar chilling breath of air blew into the cottage. Ed briefly turned and smiled back at her, and was gone.

Though she knew it did not matter whether he stayed or went, she whispered softly, "Don't go. . . ."

Ed restrained himself from breaking into a run. He entered the square at a fast pace and saw a shadowed group of men standing near the Crown and Anchor. He saw that there were eight of them and that some of them carried guns. As he approached them, he identified who they were.

"We were looking for you," said Tam.

Ed glanced at the others, at Jimmy, Farmer, Roger, Charlie, Hector, Malcolm and a tall young fellow with keen blue eyes whom he knew was called Step. They were all thickly dressed in dark protective clothing. Some wore gumboots—some wore capes. Most of them wore woolen headgear. They returned his glance with a watchfulness that belied their murmured greetings and nods of recognition.

He lowered the torch, which he had held in front of him, and eyed them warily.

"What do you want?" he said.

"We were wondering if you would like to come along with us," said Jimmy pleasantly.

"With you?"

"Aye. If you like," said Roger.

"Why? Where are you going?"

Step said, "Here's Robbie."

The group parted to let Robbie through and re-formed themselves in a broken bow facing Ed, with Robbie at their center.

"I was looking for you in the Crown," he explained. "I expected to find you there."

"I was there earlier," Ed replied. "Where were you?"

"In the Rails. We're going over by Fenham Flats. On the mainland. Duck shooting. Would you like to come along?"

"Tonight?"

"Aye. We'll go over now while the tide's low. When the tide's high—soon after three—with the wind where it is, the ducks will be on the move and not settle. They're the best conditions."

"And tonight the moon is full," added Roger, tilting his eyes skyward.

Ed stared at them disconsolately.

"You're leaving the island," he said.

"Would you like to come with us?" asked Robbie.

Ed considered their faces, their clothes, the weapons they bore. Their way of life, of thinking, talking and being, was foreign to him. He could never make contact with them—nor they with him. He was alone in his world.

"I can't," he said. "There's something else I have to do."

"Can it not wait?"

"No." He shook his head. "It can't."

"Another time," said Robbie.

Ed nodded. "Another time."

They began to move away from him.

"Will you be gone all night?" Ed asked.

"All night," said Robbie, turning to face Ed—the wind waving his hair, making it glint in the street light—as his eyes did also. "You'll maybe hear us—if you're awake."

"And tomorrow?"

"What about it?"

"Will you go fishing?"

"We'll be back in good time to put to sea—if the wind has died, as it should. If not, we'll go to bed. Maybe we'll do that anyway." Robbie grinned.

Ed's mouth tightened. The waste and impossibility of his friendship for the other man—their disparate sameness—awakened his sense of isolation and desperate anger.

"I must go," he said, grasping the torch more strongly, as if it were a weapon.

"So you must. So must we," said Robbie.

"Goodbye. . . ."

Ed tore himself defiantly, self-consciously, away from the group, and his sudden action made the nine stop and turn and look for a moment after him.

"So long," said Robbie.

In the cottage Runa sat by the embers of the sitting-room fire, her hands in her lap, her unseeing gaze switching slowly and thoughtlessly from object to object as her mind made pictures of the past. Shadowy people and dim events formed themselves on the edge of her remembrance, and ageless customs, laws and voices informed her thinking. Ed's last instruction went disregarded by her. It did not matter whether Erik remained in his room or in the cottage. Nothing, she knew, would alter the implacable purpose of the one-eyed man and the working out of his grim and secret game. She sat without moving. The room grew colder. But she felt nothing at all.

On the headland it was not long before Ed's darting torch picked out Erik's tracks on the path he had made to the beach. For although he had carefully hidden the grave behind a screen of branches, stones and turves, he had neglected to erase his approach to it. Yet the masking of the burial place was enough in itself to draw Ed's suspicious and nearer inspection. He positioned the torch on a boulder so that its beam illuminated the cliff face, and with both his hands he began to dismantle the mass of flotsam and stones. He pulled it to pieces—more rabidly as the cavernous gash behind was exposed to his fervid stare—until the sectioned rift of the grave was fully revealed. Within it, a shallow arc of stones like teeth grinned back at him. He had found Guthorm's burial place. But the grave was empty.

Cheated of finding its treasures, and more aware now of his sacrilege, he turned his fear and frustration into savage action, and armed with a daggerlike stone attacked the tomb. Before long his furious hacking and rending of the interior unearthed the buried trophy of the sword. He dug it out and seized it fiercely, as if to prevent it being used against him. He claimed it exultantly, as his prize and sign of conquest, and thus rearmed, with its iron strength he set about the utter destruction of the grave—tearing down its walls, its roof, digging up its floor, dragging out the shielding stones that had lined the ship of the king's last voyage. Never would anyone rest there again. Never again would this house of death be a ship and a shield and a fortress for Sicga's foe.

When the wrecking was almost complete, he resurrected

from the earth at the foot of the grave a gleaming band—a ring, which he slipped onto a finger of his left hand. He found nothing else. Erik must have stolen what had been there—the other arms and treasures of the king. Erik knew where they were. But he would not be able to keep them. Ed vowed he would win all the treasures of the grave after laying it waste. Only then would he and his family be safe and victory truly his.

Afire with the fever of battle, he rammed into the ruin of the grave as much as he could of the spars, branches, twigs and wood that had been used to conceal it—the rest he re-built outside. Reluctantly laying aside the sword, he struck a match in his cupped hands. Three times the wind blew it out. But at last the flame flickered long enough for him to light a handful of dried-up grass. He thrust it flaming into the pile and eagerly took up the sword. The unnecessary, unbefitting torch he extinguished and hurled into the sea. Within seconds the wind had fanned the snaking flames into a rampant bonfire, blazing against the headland and bil-lowing up to the moon.

He watched it burn. Then, satisfied with his handiwork, he climbed back up onto the ness. The pyramid glimmered eerily in the glow of the fire, and the grassy rim of the head-land was spiked with flame.

Without looking back at the burning of his enemy's house, he made a moonlit march through the petrified dunes to the Wagon Way—on his left hand the forgotten ring, in his right the avenging sword.

5

He dreamed. The battle before the fortress was being fought once again. The day was bright but dimmed by the thick and billowing smoke from the burning of his ship. He heard the crackle of flames. It terrified him to think of his ship on fire—the ship that had brought him to this shore. It would not take him home now. But his son was with him. His son would care for him. Where was his son? He could not see in the smoke. It shrouded him in darkness, cutting him off from his men. In all his dreaming it had never been so dense —like a cloud about him, making him alone. Then he was alone, with his back to the sea, and the fortress was strangely altered, vaster, with many towers and massive walls of stone. He saw a man appear on one of the dunes before the castle, and he had a sword. The man moved toward him, running, yet seeming to fly, and a new fear filled his stomach, for it had never been this way in his dreaming before. The man was the man who would kill him—but oddly dressed and without a shield. For a moment he took comfort from the voice of his son beside him. But when he looked to his left he saw that it was not his son who stood beside him but a tall man, with a cape and a curious hat, and a hole for one of his eyes. Then he knew that he was doomed, and he could not move. His companion grinned and pointed at the running man. And he saw that the sword that his enemy held was his. He looked down and his own hands were empty. He saw that his feet were bare and like a child's. He knew he had to die, to be killed with the sword again. But he did not want it to be without a fight. Unhappily he faced his foe, who came on toward him, bounding through the air, becoming like a giant in his view. But fettered by fate and helpless as he was, he did not despair. The newness, and his companion, signified much more. Then a huge spear fell out of the sky, fell heavily flat on the ground before him, making it shake. Gungnir, the mighty spear of Odin, lay pointing at his foe. But the running man flew on regardless, heedless of his fate. His voice could be heard now, shouting a name.

With hollow wonder and great weariness the dreamer knew he would dream no more, and that this at last was the hour of his revenge.

"Erik!"

He awoke as his father burst into the bedroom and switched on the light, presenting a terrible picture of war-like fury, his clothes begrimed with earth and sand, his sweating face a tight mask of aggression, his normally narrow eyes dilated, and in his golden fist the upraised sword from the grave.

Erik shrank against the bed-head, appalled by such menace, by such a display of force directed at his defenseless self. The sword had been his, had been buried for his use and touch alone. Now it was lost to him, plundered and defiled. He shuddered at such sacrilege.

"You see!" cried the man. "You see what I have—what I've found! Where have you hidden the rest?"

The woman appeared in the doorway, put her hand on the man's arm. He shook her off and advanced on the bed.

"Did you think I wouldn't find it? Well I have! It's mine now. And the spear. And the ring. And I'm going to take possession of the rest. Then we'll *end* it—all this enmity. Because there won't be any more, from anywhere. Just us three. No grave. No Guthorm. He doesn't exist. Neither does the grave. I've destroyed it. Now it's nothing."

Erik gasped.

"Nothing remains—except what I have and what you've hidden away. Where?"

Erik was silent. No threat of violence, real or imagined, would make him reveal where his treasures were. He clenched his teeth and swallowed his breath in case his voice would betray him.

"Where?"

The man loomed hugely over him and lowered the jagged edge of the sword until it was pointing at his throat.

He was not afraid. For he could not die again. He was dead already.

Then the woman in fear spoke and betrayed them all.

"Under!" she cried. "Under his bed."

"No!" he screamed.

"In his box."

"No! No! No!"

He hurled himself off the bed and scrambled under it—to protect his ancient treasures, to prevent their theft, and to keep within his possession, within his arms, his gleaming, golden hoard.

In a rapture of anticipation Ed paused—as he had before devastating the tomb.

Then, never releasing his grip of the sword, he lifted the bed, heaving it onto its side, so that it crashed against the wall and, like a stone removed from over a nest of vipers, uncovered the frenzy to escape and fear to leave that was trapped beneath. Erik writhed with his body embracing the box, mouthing a mad defiance and hissing his hatred in no language they knew.

For a moment Ed was daunted. Runa again put a vainly controlling hand on his arm. It reminded him of her presence and that he should not harm the small but venomous guardian of the gold.

With a single movement he pulled the blankets from the bed and threw them over the box and its foaming protector. A scream of rage went up and repeated itself in sharp explosions as Ed struggled, still with the sword in his hand, to separate his catch from the box—which jerked and banged upon the floor until by brute force Ed achieved his purpose and overpowered the child.

Erik was dragged from his treasure house, torn from his box, and a rending wail arose from the blankets as Ed pushed and thrust his demeaning conquest into Runa's arms.

"Hold him!"

She did so, more to keep him from hurting himself than from being harmed—more to comfort him now he had lost than to hold him captive. His body shuddered, his breath came in gasps. But he made no other movement or sound as she started to free his head from the snaring blankets.

Ed stared at his prize. He saw the padlock. Not having the time nor desire for further obstruction, he raised the sword. With a single savage blow of the iron blade he shattered the lock.

He knelt and lifted the lid.

Erik began to sing.

His mother released him, backed away with her task incomplete of uncovering him, as the shrill, unearthly summons, last made in the hall the night before, issued from under the blankets.

Enamored, exalted by what was revealed in the box, Ed heard only the echoing song of battle as he gazed on the trappings, arms and ornaments of the king—the iron and glittering remnants of the shield, the arrowheads, the buckle, the brooches, the great gold collar, the golden horn—and the helmet, on whose crest was a fiery dragon that had faced him once before.

A sound of thunder filled the room as something of vast enormity landed on the roof—something so heavy that every timber, tile and brick about them seemed to splinter, crack and grate together, though the walls and ceiling miraculously remained unmarked and did not collapse on top of them. Above these sounds of ruination came the thudding blows of a great bulk shifting its hold and the lengthy reptilian scraping of scales and claws. They heard again the searing breath, the tormented sighs—and after a silence, sniffing.

"There's nothing there!" Ed shouted at Runa, who had sunk to the floor. "Nothing! You mustn't believe it! He's *making* us hear these things. But they're not real! You mustn't believe him!"

Bent on proving his words, on vanquishing the horror on the roof, and believing its cause to be Erik, he sprang to his feet and lunged toward the blankets that draped the immobile, loudly singing figure of his son.

He pulled them off, making Erik, whose body was rigid, rock like a mast in a gale. They saw that his upcast eyes were white and staring orbs.

Seizing him in the savage embrace of the sword and his right arm, Ed clamped his left hand over Erik's open mouth and exerted his will in denial of Erik's illusion.

The singing ceased.

A shocking silence pervaded the room. Runa raised her head.

"Is it over?" she whispered.

Erik's body suddenly sagged, and his eyelids closed. Ed lowered him to the floor and Runa dazedly crawled on her hands and knees toward her son.

"I've beaten him!" Ed exclaimed proudly. "It's the only way. Don't let yourself believe what you *know* isn't there, what *can't* be there. Don't let yourself be persuaded. Are you listening? There's nothing dead that can harm us. How can it? We're alive."

He examined the sword. "We can only be harmed by the living. The dead may touch our minds, but not our bodies. Not even our minds, unless we let them. Do you understand? Believe me."

"Oh look . . ." she whispered.

"What?"

He saw that she was fixedly staring into the hall at something that was visible to her from where she sat on the carpet. Though he could not read the expression of her eyes from where he stood, nor see what she saw, his body caught the chill of terror that possessed her. It froze his movements and his mind, making an eternity of every second he took to force himself to move and stand beside her.

In the hall, directly under the light, was a man—the outline of a man—for everything else, despite the light, was featureless and dark. An upright shadow stood facing them —facelessly—in the hall.

Ed's mind revolted, his reason screaming that this was an illusion. But he saw with his eyes, and so did she, and although he closed his eyes and bent his will to banish the sight, it remained—a thing of darkness shaped like a man, blotting out the light.

In the fractured seconds of time that passed and made no future, Runa's voice made words which spanned into a cataleptic silence.

"You . . . have . . . his . . . sword."

With a superhuman effort of denial Ed slammed the door.

"You have his sword!" she shrieked. "Give it back to him! And this! All this! Then he'll go away!"

She scrambled across the carpet to the box. But Ed forestalled her, thrusting her aside.

As she sprawled on the floor, sobbing hysterically and clutching at his feet, he rammed down the lid of the box and hoisted his prize, the spoils of battle, into his jealous arms.

"No, Ed! No! Don't take them! Oh, please!"

Her desperate hands reached up to him, and they seemed to him to be reaching greedily for his gold.

He knocked her down.

In his madness to escape, to keep what he had won to himself, he smashed the glass of the window with the sword and plunged out into the night.

The wind invaded the room.

When Runa came to her senses, she was ruled only by them, by instinctive responses, and not by reason.

She lay on the carpet, tracing its pattern with her eyes, aware how heavy she seemed and how hard the floor. She registered the occasional flopping motions of the curtains and the sharper, fainter, swirl of the wind outside overrunning the garden. She knew she was alone—that Erik had also vanished. She felt as cold as death.

In time her insensate gaze was drawn to her outflung wrist, to the silent, meticulous progress of the second hand round her watch. The seconds passed, made minutes, and the minute hand moved on. When the three hands met at midnight, Odin's day would end and the battle be won or lost.

He found himself on the beach by St. Cuthbert's Isle. There should have been some boats drawn up on the shore by which he might have been rowed across to Bebba's burg. But in the flooding moonlight he could see that there was none and no huts where there should have been huts, though a hall-like building was not far off to his right. The lay of the land was also somehow different—as was the silhouette of a cross out on the islet where there should have been the shape of a chapel, as he remembered. Then he remembered the monks, and his father, Selward.

It grew darker as the full moon low in the south began to be submerged in a sea of cloud. His loneliness alarmed him. Where were his men? Where were the people and the lighted fires that would keep at bay the terrors of darkness that advanced as the moon sank lower? He felt sure that no dragon nor the undead could harm him—not as long as he denied their existence. He had never looked back at the cottage to see what was on the roof, nor to see if he was pursued by the buried king. But now that his purpose of returning to the fortress with his plunder had been baffled, he was more a prey to shadowy fears and felt threatened and lacking safety.

From far beyond the islet, on the mainland, came the sound of a muted roaring. It seemed to be moving.

He turned his back on it, and seeing the mass of the Heugh, was reminded again of the monks—though the buildings on its crest were at odds with his remembrance. Eagerly he hurried toward it and the sanctuary it offered.

The faraway roaring faded and was replaced by the nearby comforting snorting of pigs. He smiled to himself at this cheerful omen, at the thought of the tamer brothers of his ancestors' emblem, the boar, being on guard at Lindisfarne. Then he cursed, as missing the track he almost fell.

In the failing moonlight he could not see the expected pathway up the rock. Adjusting the weight of the box under his left arm and against his hip, and using the sword as a stave to steady himself, he made his way up the rocky slope. The box was more awkward than heavy. Inside it his captured trophies made a menacing clangor as he climbed.

He reached the summit as the moon disappeared.

A darkness deeper than there should have been invested the Heugh. He stumbled along bemused by the lack of light, by the silence, when there should have been torches and fires, and the sound of chanting. Twice he crashed into walls where there should have been none—into walls of stone, and not wood—and the courtyard was rank with uncut grass. His blindness more completely unnerved him than the error of the place, making his steps so uncertain that he had at last to halt. For he should have reached the door of the church, even be inside it, though his probing sword had touched nothing and his feet still trod on grass.

He squeezed his eyelids shut—to find that his eyes were already closed.

What he saw when he forced his eyes to open made him doubt his sanity, even that he was alive.

For looming against the night sky was none of the shapes he remembered, only some that should not have been there. His only reassurance was a distant point of light in Bebba's burg. But the palisade, the inner buildings, the church itself had gone. There was nothing near him, nothing familiar—only the irreconcilable forms of a high cross behind him, and before him the stark outline of a pyramid on a pole.

As he stared at it, disbelieving what he saw, a swinging beam of light flew over the sea toward him and exploded in his eyes.

He stepped backward and fell.

From somewhere far afield came a rabble of voices—hoarse shouts and bellows, as if beasts declaimed and clamored with the tongues of men. Then a woman screamed. . . .

Where he was, he could neither see nor move. Yet he felt no fear, nor any desire to flee or to fight. Certain of his safety where he was, he lay in utter darkness, feeling only a dull despair at what was happening, at what had happened long ago. For he must be in Lindisfarne, and what he heard at a distance were the war cries he had heard himself one summer morning. But this was the afternoon of the day before—that day when the Northmen landed on Lindisfarne. . . .

Someone near him padded swiftly over a sanded floor,

moving away and pausing, as if to listen to the distant tumult. There were other cries, people shouting, and nearer voices confusedly raised outside in fearful disbelief. Then the urgent tolling of a single bell above him clanged its tidings of alarm. The footsteps ran. A door creaked open and thudded against the wall, admitting the riot of sound outside to the silence within the building. Overhead the iron tongue of the bell dinned loudest of all. People returned, running into the building, their language a gabble of distress, until a strong voice ordered them to shut the door and be quiet. They obeyed and were then instructed to take up the blessed sacrament and the coffin of the Saint, of Father Cuthbert, and remove them at once to safety. Some he told to take with them the altar cross, the ciborium, the chalice, the holy relics—whatever they could. For the raiders, he said, whoever they were, would be after gold. Feet sped hurriedly here and there, garments flapped, men bandied words, wood and stone and metal knocked together as the sacred treasures of the church were taken from their places. Gasps and sighs were forced from those who exerted themselves in carrying out the coffin of the Saint. A tremulous voice began to pray, and a deep voice told him to cease and save his breath. Someone demanded who had the Gospels and the Prayer Book, and was answered that they had already been taken away. Outside, the bell tolled on above the advancing tide of battle cries and dying screams and the shrieks of women. One man within the building exhorted the others by name to be swift, to flee, to hide, to preserve themselves and the ornaments of their faith. *Bear them to Bebba's burg,* he cried. *God save you. God be with you—Go!* Two men declared that they wished to stay behind. The older man, their leader, said they were foolish but could help him to bar the door. This they did, and for a time, though the bell still rang above, there was quiet within and without the church.

Is there nothing else? came a whisper. *Has all been saved?—All that was possible.—So. Then God be praised and give us strength. Let us pray.* The murmur of the paternoster filled the church with accustomed sound, while in the open, men with harsh voices called to each other, asking questions, loudly complaining. Then there was a small cry—the bell's tongue clattered twice, and slowly died away. *Amen*, said a voice within the church—*Amen*. Suddenly the door was struck and the church resounded. An alien voice outside commanded those within to open the door. The older man told the other two to stand by him at the altar. *Fear not*, he said. *They are men, not devils. No son of men can harm us. The Son of Man is with us. Remember that.* But his words of comfort were broken by a thunderous blow of metal against the door. Then another blow redoubled the sound as two axes began to bite their way into the wood. *What will they do?* asked one of the younger men, and was assured that whatever was done to them, suffering would purify their souls and should be gladly offered as a sacrifice for their sins. If they were to die, he was told, they should joyfully embrace their slayers, who gave them life eternal and a place in the kingdom of heaven. Outside, the steady hammer of blows, the splintering of wood continued, and the older man, raising his voice, reminded his companions of their submission to him and the deity. He spoke of their vows, their obligations as servants of God to their fellows, to the church, to their bishop who was absent, to the saints who had gone before them. *Your spiritual grace will support you*, he said. *Trust in me and trust in God. Remember your Redeemer.* The door burst open to howls of triumph and part of it crashed to the floor. Men rushed in, treading heavily, their armor and trappings clinking and clashing, their voices loud in the church. Then one of the raiders quietened his men and spoke. *I am Guthorm, king of Westfold over the sea. Who is the high priest in this place? I will speak with him.* By the altar the oldest man of the three, unafraid, replied. *I am Selward, abbot of Lindisfarne, the servant of God. You profane His house. Go!* The king said it looked more like a hovel, and asked if this was how they treated their gods. The abbot answered that there was only one God, who was everywhere, and had no need of idols. *I have a need,* said the king, *a need for gold,* and he asked how his need might be satisfied. In reply, the abbot upbraided the Northmen for their impious presence in the church and on the island. He condemned their deeds, their godless ways, and urged them again to depart before they were damned beyond redemption. *Old man,* said the king, *be quiet.* He then told his men to seek about the temple for gold, silver, jewels, coins, anything of value and bring it to him. Vociferously they agreed, proclaiming their eagerness for plunder, and began their search. Swords, axes, rang and thudded on stone and wood as ornaments, furnishings, screens were hacked and broken. Banners were ripped. Books were torn. Monuments were defaced. Some raiders tried to lift the slabs of stone on the floor to seek beneath them. But they failed and became angry. Others struck the floor and walls with spear shafts, looking for secret hollows but finding none. What was found was flung in a heap on the altar cloth before the king as he had commanded. His men grumbled and muttered among themselves. Then the king spoke. *It is not good,* said Guthorm. *I see no gold.* He stirred the booty with his sword, saying that he saw silver candlesticks, cups and plates, some boxes of bone and iron stands, but nothing worthy of a descendant of Odin. *Where is the gold, priest?* A silence was filled by the far-off screaming of a seagull. It came again, to mingle with the clank of iron as the king moved over the floor. He paused and said that he had heard good reports of Lindisfarne, how famous it was, how holy, and how rich. He said he was disappointed with what he saw. It angered him a little, for he hated being deceived. But no priest, no temple he had seen had ever been as poor as this. It was like a pigsty. He would not like to go away with this thought. He would not. Some of his men agreed. The king spoke again, saying he noticed a ring on the old man's finger, a ring of gold. He said he would like it. He wished to compare it with his. *Give it to me*, he said. The abbot made no answer. *Hold him, my son*, said Guthorm. *This poor piece of stone, which may be an altar, will serve as a whetstone for my sword. Hold him still.* The sword swished through the air and crunched against the stone. Two gasps of horror and one of pain were lost in the warriors' glee. *I am sorry*, said Guthorm, *I seem to have cut off your hand. But I am grateful for the ring. Take it, my son.* The applause and encouragement of the raiders was interrupted by a cry of outrage, a scuffle, a fall and two uneven thumps. *I am sorry, Father,* said a bright young voice. *I seem to have cut off his head.* Shouts of laughter blotted out the abbot's whispered words of absolution. The king of the Northmen reproved his son for killing the priest but praised him for making the abbot speak. *Perhaps he will speak louder*, said Guthorm, *if we kill this other priest—slowly.* The warriors hailed this sport and called for the blood eagle. The king assented, adding that if the square stone was an altar, it would appreciate sacrifice upon it. He named Guthrod, his son, as the one to perform the task. *Pray with me!* cried the abbot, beginning to chant as clearly as he could the litany of the last rites. His companion loudly declaimed the responses, until he was forced to cry out in his agony. Sometimes he shrieked. But the abbot still called on God to absolve and accept his servant and grant him his heavenly reward. Guthorm raged at the old man's noise. Their voices fought in the church. When the dying man's groans had ceased the abbot was silent. For a while the king ranted alone, until coughing choked his words. Then Guthrod spoke. *Let us also kill this priest*, he said, *and catch some others and make them speak. This place is an island, the tide is flowing—no one will escape. More sport will be had in feasting and tasting the women.* The king agreed. He told his men to take up the plunder, to prepare fire and to fetch a rope. *I am hungry*, said the king. *I thirst for mead.* The movements of men in armor filled the church as they carried out the orders of the king. He spoke again. He told them that the priest would be sacrificed to Odin. *We shall hang him*, said the king. *Hang him from that beam above the altar. But first, to make him level, why not cut off his other hand?* They did so, and the abbot broke his silence. He cried out in great rapture. He thanked God for the torments he had been given, for the grace that had helped him endure them. He gave praise to the Father Almighty for his wonderful goodness and mercy, for opening the gates of heaven to his faithful servant. *I am glad*, he cried, *that my sinful days of struggle on this earth are about to end, that my life is at last to be freed, my sorrow lessened, my soul released from its wretched body. Let my killing, Almighty, atone for my son, Sicga, who killed his king. Accept this payment. Forgive him—as I forgive these men. I am eager now to win my reward, to follow forever the Lamb of God. Soon, glorious angels shall bring me where there is great gladness, joy in heaven, where God's people are placed at the feast, where there is bliss unending among the saints. Soon I shall see my Lord, my Master, the Prince of glory, Creator of men, Savior of souls, Ruler of All, the one true noble King. Soon I shall see my God! Not so*, said Guthorm. *Soon you shall see Odin. I hope he is pleased. Now, my heroes, give this life to the god. To Odin!* They shouted the name. The abbot's voice choked and strangled. The rope and the beam creaked as the men pulled hard. Guthrod spoke. *Did he say his son killed a king?* In answer Guthorm said if it was true, then he would like to meet that man and kill him before he had thoughts of revenge. The king laughed. *How will he ever find us?* he said. *How will he ever know?* Then calling upon his warriors, he encouraged them to burn the church and all the buildings. *Make a fire upon this rock that no one will forget. Make the smoke touch heaven. Make this blaze an immortal offering to Odin. Burn! Burn! Burn!* The Northmen went rampaging from the church. Soon it sang with the many sounds of fire. The building burned. And as it burned, the hanged man's arms dripped blood on the altar below.

He heard the flames, the myriad roar of mad destruction as the church was devoured about him. Close upon him he heard the echoing fall and spatter of blood on stone. It fell like rain before a storm. It fell and splashed above him—its undying echo telling him he lay where the altar was, had been, and would be ever.

He opened his eyes. In the supernatural darkness, made visible as it seemed by the red-gold ring on his hand, he saw beyond his own, a severed hand, reaching out toward him, its surface ebbing and flowing in the fire's light. With a sacred sense of duty and right triumphant he transferred the ring from his pale left hand to the glowing left hand before him. It flared into brilliant, blinding life as the blazing roof of the church collapsed in ruin.

In a dream he heard the wind as it rushed through the withering grass. Silently out of the dark cold night the far-off lighthouse beam flashed over him once again. Under his head was the box, and beside him was the sword. But the golden ring on his splayed left hand was gone.

He got to his feet without knowing that he had moved. Looking about him, he recognized dimly where he was, though the realization made no sense and had no meaning. No time had passed. A moonglow still emerged from the clouded south. A point of light still shone in Bamburgh Castle. On the Heugh, the triangular beacon on its pole, and the tall cross of the war memorial, stood on either side of him. Nothing had changed. Yet everything was wholly different and would never be the same.

In a dream he picked up the box, and armed with the sword staggered insensibly down the overgrown Heugh on the landward side, and at its base climbed over a wall that got in his way. He walked unsteadily over the meadow, intending to return home to his wife and son. But a heaviness of spirit weighted his limbs, and a weariness, as if of life, made his actions, thoughts, his conscious being, purposeless and void. It was as if he were two people—one watching the other who walked across the meadow, one waiting for some final event—while the other moved on, bemused by images of death, by the useless waste and cruelties of the past. A grief at living possessed them both.

Another wall stood in his way, the wall about the priory ruins. On the other side was sanctuary and home.

Still with the box tucked under his arm, still holding the sword, Ed hauled himself onto the wall top with the help of the railings. Below him he saw the indistinct shapes of graves, where monks were buried, where Selward's ashes had been interred, where a stone, sculptured on two sides, had been raised to mark his death and the deathless raid on Lindisfarne.

He heard a voice behind him.

Sicga, it whispered.

333

Part of him wished to ignore the summons, deny its reality. Part of him tensed, grasping the sword more firmly, ready to face his foe.

Sicga.

He could not turn himself about—and he could not let the challenge go unheeded. He had to know.

Sicga.

He turned around on the wall, still astride the railings, to see no dragon, no Battle-snake, no enemy he foresaw.

In the midnight meadow some distance away stood a diminutive ghost, a small white figure, imprinted on its background like a negative image of white on black.

At first the boy seemed to be on his own. Yet a shadow darker than any night stood beside him in the meadow—a shape so huge it had seemed at first to be part of the darkness. But no earthly darkness was ever so deep, so dreadful, of such ineffable blackness that it nullified all light. It stood in the meadow by Erik.

Ed knew at last who his enemy was, who it was he had to kill—and could not succeed in doing.

The shadow of death seemed to move toward him, growing vaster as it advanced, annihilating sight and hearing, overwhelming all his senses with black despair, extinguishing all thought and hope of life.

With a violent final exertion of self, of his strength, his will, and in hopeless defiance of fate, he hurled the sword at his adversary, crying out the name of the god he had always denied and now acknowledged as his destroyer.

Unbalanced by the weight of the box, by the might of his throw, he pitched forward. He could not prevent his fall, though he released the box and clutched at the railings with both hands. But in trying to leap clear he caught his left foot and fell heavily full length on the railings with all the weight of his body. The sharp and narrow railing heads, like spikes, were thrust and thrust themselves into him, tearing and stabbing across and into his body from shoulder to thigh, impaling him on spearlike points, which held him fast, cruelly raised above the ground, as if he were a sacrifice to heaven.

Gudrun's Lament

1

So she found him. On the last stroke of midnight, she left the cottage to look for him, knowing that the battle had been won and lost, and that whoever had the victory was her lord and master evermore. She ran through the sleeping village square, away from the pools of blanching light that gave the buildings substance but no meaning, and finding herself in the meadow before the priory ruins hesitated, being faced with nothing but darkness—until the flaring lighthouse beam illumined a small white bundle on the grass some distance away.

She approached it, knowing that this was Erik, but innocent of why he lay so still. Then she saw the sword—how it stood at an angle in the ground—as if someone held it, with its blade driven through his throat.

She fell on the ground by his fallen body. His eyes were open and fixed. The childish limbs she had washed and cared for—the baby that she had borne and fed, to whom she had given form and life—the loving labor of her marriage lay in a heap in his white pajamas, crumpled, cold, his little hands cupped palm upward on the grass as if asking for her to pick him up and hold him in her arms.

The tears ran down her cheeks, though she made no sound. She only sighed in her pain as she tenderly pulled the rusted blade, the avenging sword, out of the earth and out through the yielding target of his neck. She drew it out with gentleness so as not to hurt him. But its blade, gleaming dark in the lighthouse flare with his life-blood, told her that her loving care was wasted and in vain.

He was dead, and would never need the love of her hands and eyes and voice and being again. Her proudest possession, her own creation, would never astonish his mother by growing into a man.

She tried to close his eyes. Their marbled stare, which would not be hidden, was so unlike him—while his skin was so cold to her touch—that she shuddered and turned away, to be mesmerized by a flicker of gold as the light passed over the prostrate treasures of the king, scattered on the grass below a wall—and above them hung a man.

She crawled toward him, floundering through the fallen armor of the king, expressing the inexpressible emotion of her woe in an insensible moaning.

Dementedly her hands reached out, and could not touch him. The horror of his sacrifice removed him from her help, rendering her as powerless as him.

She bowed before such divine, irrevocable vengeance, and knelt below the wall, still mouthing her grief. In the ever-returning, scything flare of the lighthouse her anguished eyes pieced together his agony, and added it to hers.

He hung head down across the railings—his body transfixed by the spikes. His back was tilted toward her. His long legs trailed uselessly on either side of the wall—his right arm dangled before her. But his left hand still clutched at a spike in front of him, as if even now he might try once more to free himself from his fate. His eyes were closed. The sweat still shone on his face. And every spearlike railing that held him aloft was redly wound with ribbons of blood that spilled down the wall to the grass.

She could look no more. She hid her face in her hands and was silent.

Then a gentle touch caressed her hair. She looked up wildly—to see his strong right hand fall back against the wall. His eye looked sideways down at her. He was trying to speak.

She could hardly see now. So she moved nearer, with her face by his, to see him and to be seen by him, and to hear what he said.

His eye scanned her features, and in it she read his sorrow, his rage, his apology, and then only his love for her.

"I love you," she whispered.

He heard her, and his eye smiled, and she thought she heard him murmur, *"Take me home."*

And so he died.

For a long time she knelt by him until she was as cold as he—as if she were also dead. But she still lived, and heard the sea and the wind that blew over them both. She remembered his words, and knew what she, the wife of a hero, had to do—if she loved him, if she honored him in his death as in his life.

The banging of a window awoke the professor. He had been dreaming, and the sound which had boomed out loudly in his dream turned itself into the thinner rattle and thud of a window loosely closed.

His head ached with imagined fears and his sudden arousal. His face flamed. His arid limbs were stiff and unwilling to move. But the noise would have to be silenced before he could sleep again.

With the dull reluctance of age his body obeyed his mind. Breathing heavily through his nose he hoisted himself out of the bed, pausing unsteadily on his feet to untangle his pajamas and to peer at the luminous dial of his watch. It said half-past three. A shiver ran through his withered frame. The chill of the tower room was almost palpable, and under his feet the carpet was like cold steel as he crossed uncertainly to the window.

In order to shut it securely he had to open it first.

When he did so, the wind flew in with such force that it seemed to penetrate his body, blowing through him into the room and taking possession of everything within. His eyes watered. He blinked several times, and his sight cleared. His mind, made aware by the wind's alarming presence all about him, became alert to unseen dangers and ancient superstitions. With a primitive quickening of the senses he gazed out on the night.

His keen eye caught a point of light far away to the north. It came from Lindisfarne, where Lindisfarne must lie in all the darkness.

Who could be up so late? he wondered. What were they doing? Then he realized that the light could not come from the village, which was masked from him by the Heugh, and that no electric light would shine so evenly, nor so warmly, over such a distance.

A candle! he thought. His signal in the sitting room below was being returned.

For a moment the mystery bewitched him, then spurred him into searching for his binoculars among the articles on the table below the window. But even as he raised them to his eyes, a return of his earlier sick forebodings made him dread what he would see.

At first in his agitation he could not locate the object of his search—nothing but blackness. By controlling his hands he finally found and focused on the light.

In the remote and unreal center of his vision he saw an orb, like a tiny moon, and he saw that it was moving. Someone was carrying it, somewhere near the lower end of the Heugh.

The orb began to descend, and its shattered image appeared below it, reflected on some water.

His hands shook in the gusting wind. A faraway volley of gunshots reached his ears, sounding like the farewell for a soldier.

Then he saw more clearly, though never distinctly at such a distance. And when at last he realized what he saw, he was powerless to prevent the final inevitable act, as the past and present resolved themselves in self-destruction.

She turned to look at the lamp, for its flame seemed in danger of being blown out by the wind. But the wind, which blew her hair off her face and would soon swell the sail of the boat, was no enemy to her resolve, rather an ally. Nothing would bar her purpose, nor alter it. Her fate was decreed, and the mystery of her life had been given a meaning.

She turned and continued down the steps to the boat.

The tide was high, though not yet at its highest. Its movement filled the night with sound. Waves broke on the shore. Beside the steps the boat swayed, bound by its moorings, eager to put to sea.

She had pulled it in as the man had done that afternoon. She had made it fast and filled it with such wood that she could find—making a level platform as best she could before the mast. This she had done in darkness, not needing a light to see what she did, as her hands worked as if by instinct. Then seeking out and finding a wagon by one of the huts she had towed it up the path to the meadow turnstile. There she had left it, and returning to the body on the spikes had lifted it off, limb by limb, making the wounds bleed again, and causing new ones. This did not matter. It had to be done. But she trembled at touching the man she loved. Her strength was great, but she could not carry him once he had fallen onto the grass. So she seized his hands and walking backward dragged him over the meadow, making a dark path with his body through the glistening, gathering dew. Outside the gate the wagon inclined to receive him. She set him upon it and made her way to where the child was lying. She picked him up in her arms, and returning with him placed him by his father. There was more to do. Once more she crossed the meadow, to the other side, and passing through the village reentered the place they had lived in. Here she assembled what she felt was required for the journey, without which the ritual would not be rightly observed, nor her obsession fulfilled. Having lit the lamp she bore it in her right hand out of the cottage, and in her left she carried the bundle of goods and special belongings for the voyage. She paused in the meadow to gather together the scattered gold and armor, putting them in the box, and so brought all her burdens one by one to the wagon, and brought the laden wagon in turn with great labor to the beach.

She had set the lamp on the top stone step of the jetty, while she strove and struggled to load the boat. Her arms and back ached with the toil. Her body cried for rest. And yet no pain could touch or match the torment of her mind, nor stay nor stop her terrible resolve. And when at last her work was done, and everything arranged as best she could after the ancient rites, she fetched the lamp and like a bride descended to the boat.

Far away the sound of gunshots spoke a last farewell.

Fatefully she gazed on the scene of sacred death, seeing the ship that should have been there, richly equipped, to carry her lord, her king, in company with his son, his dearer possessions, dearest of all his wife, across the stormy ocean to eternity with his god.

In the prow were placed the proud and golden arms and treasures he had won. The ring she wore again. The spear-head she had ready. The iron sword, held by his hands, lay straight upon his body, and under him lay, unfinished, the tapestry of roses she had made. His manuscript lay beside him. About him were his pen, his pipe, a small clay pig she had given him long ago. At his feet reclined the rumpled figure of his son, whose open eyes still stared up at the sky.

The tide turned. The wind flew swiftly southward. The boat was urged by both to leave the land, to take the tide and be taken by the wind. Like a sea bird brooding upon the waves the longship waited.

She loosened the lines that held the ship. She entered the boat. The light she set in the stern beside her. Before her the mast stood tall as a sapling—the sail was folded. The back of the ocean stream bore the boat from the shore, show-ing it a sure path to the open sea, and the ship, like a horse going homeward and given its head, shivered with pleasure. It set out strongly needing no rider to guide it.

The prayers on land that should have been spoken, the chant, the dirge, the loud lament, the paean in praise of life and glory, the long seagoing call of the horn—all that should have honored the hero's passing was heard by her in the sounds of the sea and the voice of the wind, and the ship made a song as it moved toward its haven.

Her eyes never left the face of her love. Her hero slept,

and in his sleeping never seemed so fair, so fine, so worthy of her homage. She felt exalted. She smiled with gladness. Soon she would join him. Soon she would sever the thread of life that kept her from his sight. He would come to her and lift her up, lead her into the halls of heaven, where they would live forever.

The seas grew greater. The ship's song soared. The sail-tree yearned for its wings. She also wished to be free.

She took up the lamp in her left hand and made her way to the mast. Embracing it, with her right hand she raised the swelling triumphant sail. The ship flew over the sea.

Then she threw the lamp, the orb of light, upon the golden hoard in the prow. The pyre was lit. The flames, unleashed to eat their fill, leapt out upon the boat. With fierce delight they devoured the wood. The weapons of iron were forged again in the fire-glow. High on the helmet the eyes of the dragon were red with living flame.

She grasped the haft of the spearhead in both her hands and placed its point on her breast. She looked at her lord and spoke his name. She whispered her love and words of welcome. She sought his blessing. Then she thrust the spear within her with all her might.

The sail was split by a sword of flame. It blazed with a brilliant light.

Thankfully she sank by his side. With her arms about him, her face by his, she saw the fire ascend above, and the sparks, the smoke, reach up with her soul to be received by the sky.

A window blew open in Bamburgh Castle, knocking a candlestick off its ledge onto the table below. The guttering candle, all but spent, rolled resistlessly onto some papers. A brown stain spread beneath and burst into flame. The fragment burned.

A fire was lit in the castle that night that answered the fire at sea. In the mind of the man who saw them both, they burned in his madness forever, until he died.

Appendix

Fragment of a Northern Chronicle relating to events A.D. *787–794, transcribed by Richard Douglas, M.A., from a copy of the original, together with some notes and a translation found in the papers of Professor M. MacDougall, late of the University of Edinburgh.*

The ms. consists of two pages which originally formed the innermost leaf in a quire, as the stitching holes and the continuity of the text confirm. The two pages are written in one hand which could be assigned to any date within the period of the late ninth to mid-tenth century. The orthographical forms suggest a more precise date and imply that the annals may have been written about a century after the events they relate.

The text is broadly identical with other versions of the Anglo-Saxon Chronicles but is distinguished by a number of entries not paralleled in any other extant text. In one notable case the annalist actually challenges the conventionally accepted date of the first Viking raid on England.

A northern provenance for the ms. is suggested by the evidence of circumstantial vividness and intimate detail, and this is not necessarily contradicted by the dialect evidence. Such striking features as the annalist's unconcealed partisanship in Northumbrian politics, both ecclesiastical and secular, and his knowledge of facts later used by Simeon of Durham, all surely point to an origin in a northern ecclesiastical center such as Ripon or York. . . .

Translation

[787] . . . at Bamburgh. That was 100 years after St. Cuthbert died. And in this year a synod assembled at *Wincanheale* in Northumbria on September 2nd, and four days later abbot [Ald]bert died in Ripon and his body is buried there, and in his place Sigered was elected. And in the same year there was a contentious synod at Chelsea and Archbishop Janbert gave up a part of his bishopric and at the behest of King Offa, Higbert was elected Archbishop of Lichfield against God's will and the holy Pope, and Egfrith, son of Offa, was consecrated king. In this year the winter was so severe, with snow and frost throughout this kingdom, that the birds fell dead from the trees. Then at this time Bishop George was sent from Rome to England together with messengers from Pope Adrian to renew the faith and peace which St. Gregory sent us through blessed Augustine and through Bishop Paulinus, who converted King Edwin of Northumbria to be baptized, and they were honorably received and sent back in peace. Then the messengers came to York, and there they met first with Archbishop Enbald and then with King Alfwald and all the king's counselors. Then they urged the Northumbrian people in God's name to contemplate the end of the world and hold fast to

the true faith and to elect their kings lawfully according to the advice of the priests and counselors. And they also urged that no man should dare to slay any king, for the king is blessed by God. And they said that it was plain how swiftly they depart from this world who have become the slayer of a king [and how wretchedly they] forego all rights both heavenly and earthly.

788. In this year aldorman Sicga betrayed Alfwald king of Northumbria and shamefully slew him at *Scythlescester* near the wall, and a heavenly light was frequently seen where he was slain, and he was buried at Hexham within the church of the Holy Apostle Andrew. And Osred, son of Alcred, succeeded to the kingdom after him, who was his nephew. And he came there from the fortress on the island which is called *Giudi* (Inchkeith), and his mother and many Picts came with him. Then a synod was assembled at *Aclea*. And Bishop Athelbert journeyed to Rome. And some nobles there were who held no regard for Osred, and they built themselves great strongholds and they ravaged and plundered at will.

789. In this year Bertric, King of Wessex, married Edburg, daughter of Offa, and in his days there came three ships of Northmen from Hordaland, and the reeve of Dorchester rode there and desired to take them to the king's manor because he did not know what they were, and he was killed. And some people incorrectly say that they were the first Danish ships which came to England, but the first arrival took place, correctly calculated, seven years after Bertric came to the throne. And in the same year King Osred's servants fought a great battle in the streets of York and killed the

citizens. And in that summer there was an unusually severe plague in the kingdom so that a great quantity of cattle died and the wretched people starved.

790. In this year, after Easter, King Osred was betrayed and driven from the kingdom by aldorman Athelhard, and his enemies forced him to receive the tonsure and dwell in St. Mary's minster. But he later fled by night to Bamburgh for shelter, just as his father had done before when he [was] driven into Pictland. And Athelred, Moll's son, was restored to the throne. Then [he] drove Osred's mother from the kingdom and everything they owned he gave with many gifts besides to his quarreling thanes. And in the same year Bishop Tilbert of Hexham was stricken by sickness in one side of his body and three days later he died, and his body is buried there within the church. And in the same year Bishop Athelbert returned from Rome and brought with him a portion of the True Cross, and he was consecrated Bishop of Hexham by Archbishop Enbald and by Bishop Higbald. And Sicga seized all the kingdom to the north of the River Tyne as far as Edinburgh.

791. In this year, Baldwulf was consecrated Bishop of Whithorn by Archbishop Enbald and Bishop Athelbert on July 17th at *Hearrahalch*. And the renowned teacher Alcuin went to Aix to help King Charles of the Franks, and King Charles received him with great honor. And in the same year Athelred the king caused Alf and Alfwine, the sons of Alfwald, to be seized from within the church of St. Peter in York and then to be most evilly drowned. Then Saxburg, Alfwald's wife, fled to Lindisfarne and Bishop Higbald took her by sea to Coldingham and there joined her to the com-

munity of the servants of God, and there she served God for
many years. And in the winter aldorman Athelhard led his
forces to the River Tyne and there fought against aldorman
Sicga. But there was a snowstorm, and neither had the
victory.

792.   In this year, after Candlemas, Archbishop Janbert
passed away at Canterbury, and in the same year abbot
Athelhard of the monastery of Louth was elected in his
place. And King Athelred repudiated the vows [made] between him and Edswith his queen [because she] had no
children. God's [curse] was clearly seen to be on Athelred,
for he could not beget any sons, though he was frequently
with concubines. And in this year, when Athelred was journeying in Mercia, the king's hall and all the city of York
were treacherously set on fire, except [the] minster, and that
was spared. And it was only thirty years after the city was
rebuilt. Then Osred came secretly to the kingdom, and
Sicga was unable to go to him since he was sorely wounded.
And Herewulf marched against Osred, and Osred's army
deserted him, and he was captured later at *Aynburg.* And
then Athelred ordered Osred to be cruelly killed and likewise Osgar, Osred's brother, even though he was a harmless
monk at Melrose. And two weeks later King Athelred married Alfled, Offa's daughter, at Catterick.

793.   In this year there were terrible portents over Northumbria and they sorely distressed the people. These were
exceptional windstorms and bolts of lightning, and there
were seen fiery dragons flying in the air. Upon these omens
swiftly followed a severe famine, and shortly after this, in
the same year, on June 8th, there came two ships of North-

men out of Westfold, and they were the first ships of the Northmen to arrive in this land. And they miserably destroyed and plundered God's church on Lindisfarne and slew the servants of God. Some of the brethren they carried off laden with chains; some they slew; many they drove out naked and shamed by insults; some they drowned in the sea. And so they came to Bamburgh. And Sicga rushed out of the fortress with sixty men and they fought in the water against the heathen men and there was great slaughter on both sides. And although they could not prevail against them, nevertheless one of the heathen ships was burnt, and Guthorm, king of the Northmen, was killed. Then Guthrod, Guthorm's son, desired to avenge his father. And he burnt the village and harried in every direction and slew the wretched people wherever he could find them. And then he swore an oath that he would [. . .]

794. And in this year aldorman Sicga died by his own hand, and his body was carried to Lindisfarne. But Bishop Higbald would not allow him to be buried there, and he was put in a boat and burned at sea. And his son . . .